SHUN THE MOON

TERRY CAMPBELL

Published by Water Dragon Publishing
waterdragonpublishing.com

ISBN 978-1-969655-50-0 (Trade Paperback)

FIRST EDITION

10 9 8 7 6 5 4 3 2 1

In some ways, this book is simply the story of a man and his dog. I've had the pleasure of knowing many dogs in my lifetime. From Butch and Wolfie (our time was way too short) as a kid, to Boo-Boo, Babe, Max, and Winston (Dr. Winston O'Boogie) as a young adult, to Festus Magee, Elmo Bodine (forever and always my best friend), Gigante and Raton more recently, and finally to Jynx and Keegan, the two who currently have me properly trained. I've loved each one of them unconditionally, and this book is dedicated to them.

SHUN THE MOON

Prologue

Upstate New York—Autumn, 1761

S ARAH MCGRUDER TURNED AWAY from the path leading up to the Hutchins house and gazed at the length of road that wound steadily through Turner Hills. The night had arrived much more rapidly than she realized. Sarah shivered and pulled the hood of her woolen cloak over her head, ignoring the chaffing the garment caused in favor of the warmth it provided. She took a deep breath and started down the trail, trying not to be frightened, letting her family occupy her thoughts. As she continued towards her tiny farmhouse, the oppressive blackness of the night seemed to creep ever closer, but Sarah ignored her fears. The love of her family and her strong Irish blood combined to dispel her illogical fears of the dark. All would be right. She never even gave a thought to the wolves.

Sarah had been helping a distant neighbor prepare for the upcoming quilting bee, and time had gotten away from her. The cup of tea and innocent gossip with Mrs. Hutchins had delayed her walk home even more. Sarah chastised herself for staying so long, for not minding the approaching darkness and, most of all, for neglecting her children. Her sweet children. She and Jonathan had been so blessed. To have triplets, and all of them survive in these times of smallpox and scarlet fever to their present age of three months, was indeed an act of God. Perhaps the small miracle would even silence the grumbling of the townsfolk upset over the fact that the children were born out of wedlock. Let the town talk, Sarah told herself. She and Jonathan were strong, and the children would also grow to be healthy.

Sarah loathed the idea that she was forced to leave the children in her mother's care, but the simple fact that the family had grown from two to five demanded that she find some sort of work, no matter how meager the earnings. Jonathan's work with the blacksmith paid well but combined with what they managed from trading their crops, it would not be enough. Sarah smiled to herself. She knew in her soul that leaving the children during the day was a necessary evil.

Sarah's feet began to grow weary from the steady climb up the hills. The round autumn moon shone brightly atop the crest of the hills, lighting Sarah's way like a beacon of motherly love. She had made this trek numerous times, but never after sundown. Never in the stifling black of night.

A dense fog was beginning to form in the fields to either side of Sarah, looking like an approaching marauder slithering through the swaying grains of wheat. The crisp autumn breeze whispered through the high maple branches, causing the few remaining leaves to flutter and rattle in unison. These hills were lovely in the autumn months, with colors that matched the flames in the cottage's fireplace. But only in the daylight hours, Sarah thought. The trees were not symbols of beauty in the night. Standing near her, branches leaning and stretching over her head, silhouetted against the gigantic moon like the terrible webbing of some giant spider, the trees looked more like ghastly sentinels of the devil's work.

Sarah turned swiftly about. There had been a noise to her left, a crackling sound of heavy footfalls on the crisp fallen leaves. She thought of calling out to the unseen intruder, but chose to remain still and quiet, hoping to blend in with the rest of the intangible night. Sarah listened keenly, ears tuned to perceive the slightest sound. The chirping of crickets, the *clackity-clack* of fallen leaves bouncing along the dirt road, the distant cry of an owl. Nothing more.

Silly girl, Sarah scolded herself. *You've let your imagination run wild until the shadows have taken shape. You're much too mature to be hearing bumps and scrapes in the night. You've children to watch after now.*

Sarah turned her head to the other side of the road. "La," she said aloud, "'twas only the wind." Then, as if to reassure herself, she repeated, "Only the wind."

The next sound to find Sarah's ears, however, was not the wind. Something was moving beyond the trees. There was no doubt. Again, Sarah strained her hearing. Again, the night fell silent. Sarah's face twisted, her eyes squinted, as if total concentration would force the sound to return to her ears. She didn't want to hear the sound, for it would mean her imagination was not to blame, but she needed to know just what she had heard. Still, there was nothing. The hills were completely silent. The wind had stopped; the crickets had fled.

Sarah listened intently, so determined that she could almost hear the snores from the Smith's house two miles away, hear the earthworms burrowing around the roots of the wheat plants. Suddenly, an old tale that her father told her as a child to frighten her on stormy Irish nights popped into her mind. *When 'tisn't stormin', when the skies and the trees offer no sounds to your ears, and if you listen hard, you can hear the dead turn over in their graves.*

Sarah forced the dark thought from her mind and continued up the hill, quickening her pace.

The crunching of leaves sounded loudly from behind the trees on the road's edge. Not just one, but two, three, more. Footsteps. And not just the steps of one, but many. Sarah froze and peered past the trees into the black fields. She could see nothing but the rise of low clouds in the cold air, as if many lungs full of warm breath released simultaneously. The steps grew closer, and she could hear the breathing of the hidden entities on the roadside.

Then she saw the eyes. Many eyes, emerald-green in color, peering from the stalky weeds that grew at the feet of the maples and pines. The piercing orbs glared at Sarah through the thickening fog, as the sounds of the breaths grew closer.

"Wolves," Sarah whispered, and turned to run.

Grabbing her dress at the knees so she would not trip over the garment, Sarah bolted for the top of the hills. She knew in her mind that it was foolish to run from a pack of wolves, but her feet and her heart knew no such fact. She could hear the snarls of the canines and the hurried thumps of their paws, now striking hard dirt instead of dead grasses and leaves, but she dared not look back. How many were there? Sarah had counted at least a dozen eyes before the panic had gripped her and forced her to flee. The wolves' yips and growls seemed to be only inches away. Sarah's legs began to ache with the effort of her uphill sprint, but she forced herself onward. Was it her imagination, or could she feel their collective hot breath on her ankles? She expected to feel the strong jaws encircle her tiny feet, the sharp, brutal teeth sink into her soft flesh at any moment.

Sarah gasped for breath; the cold night air seemed to wrench the very air from her aching lungs. She thought she might collapse face-down on the dusty road when she remembered the children. Sarah had just brought three incredible babies into the world, and she had no business leaving them for Jonathan to care for alone. The very thought gave her renewed vigor, and she forced herself along through sheer determination.

Suddenly, the wolves stopped. Sarah could not comprehend what had happened for a moment. She then realized that the animals had abandoned their chase. Sarah stopped, almost at the crest of the steep hill. Confused by the wolves' actions, she turned to face the animals. There was at least a score of the large canines. They hung farther back down the road, whimpering, moving along the road with their snouts to the ground and their tails between their legs, like farm dogs scolded for getting into the chicken coop. The placid display of the wolves compared to their earlier vicious attack seemed almost comical.

Suddenly Sarah heard her name shouted from the hilltop. She turned to find the large frame of a man silhouetted against the backdrop of the moon. For a moment, she thought it was Jonathan coming to her rescue, but the figure was much too large to be Jonathan. This massive frame could belong to only one man.

"Booth," Sarah whispered.

"Sarah," answered the faceless man in a deep, rumbling voice.

"There are wolves," Sarah said, as if to warn the man.

"The wolves will harm no one. They are merely your guides."

"My ... guides?"

"You shun the moon, Sarah McGruder," said the dark figure. The voice was a low, dull monotone. "Never shun the moon."

"I've told you before, William ..." Sarah started.

The dark figure suddenly spread its arms wide and threw its head back and screamed into the night air. It was then that Sarah noticed the man was nude. His organ swayed gently between his legs, its girth evident against the bright light from the moon. The wolves behind Sarah began to move closer, boldly as they had initially. Sarah jumped as she felt the cold wetness of a canine nose against her bare ankle. The wolves circled behind her, deep rumbles emanating from their throats.

Suddenly, a terrifying, piercing cry split the night air. Sarah looked back at the man on the hill. Her eyes widened in disbelief. He seemed to be growing larger in front of her very eyes. His arms widened, his legs lengthened, the muscles in his thighs expanded. Sarah watched in fascinated terror, unable to tear her eyes from the spectacle. The man's fingers elongated; nails sprouted outward from his fingertips. She stared at the man's head, still tilted back in a gripping howl to the skies, and a large protrusion sprouted forth from the center of his face.

Sarah dropped to her knees, no longer able to gaze upon the unearthly scene. "Dear Lord," she pleaded softly. "Send Jonathan to help me, Lord. Please."

Sarah heard the heavy steps of the abomination moving closer to her. The wolves were moving in slow circles around her, their snarls rumbling in her ears, their hot breath tickling her cheeks.

The footsteps ceased, and Sarah could see the man's feet mere inches from her face. His feet were black and hairy and clawed, like the paws of a wolf. She looked up to his face as his glowing red eyes locked onto her teary orbs. A huge, clawed hand reached slowly to her head, the sharp nails glistening in the moonlight like blades of grass on a dewy morning.

Sarah's tear-stained eyes fluttered rapidly; her flushed cheeks twitched uncontrollably. The claws were only inches from her eyes.

"I warned of what would happen if you chose to shun the moon," the black beast said.

Sarah screamed as the massive hand wrapped around her face, blocking out what precious little light the moon allowed.

•   •   •

Jonathan Lucas awoke with a start, tumbling forward from his crude, pine chair. He peered about at the encroaching darkness, momentarily unsure of his surroundings. He squinted and rubbed the crust from his sleep-heavy eyes until the second piercing howl reminded him of what had stirred him from his slumber.

Hurriedly, Jonathan stumbled forward in the darkness, grabbing a whale oil lamp and lighting it with a dwindling candle. His newly acquired fatherly instinct directed him to take a quick glance at the three tiny infants sleeping soundly in their crib atop a straw-filled mattress.

The third howl split the foggy November night, making the hairs on Jonathan's neck stand on end and beads of sweat form on his heated brow. A chorus of howls shriller in pitch drifted through the rustic countryside. Jonathan knew they were wolves, but the first cry, the howl that had bolted him awake and sent him into a fit of panic, was not made by a wolf. He knew the source of the guttural, rumbling shriek that split the night. Jonathan grabbed his musket and streaked for the back door.

"Momma McGruder!" Jonathan shouted. "Tend the babies! I must go!"

Jonathan did not wait to hear the mumbled reply from the elderly woman. His Sarah was in trouble.

The door swung shut behind him, and Jonathan ran through the yard and across the fields behind their farmhouse. The neighbor's hound dog bayed at his heels, giving close pursuit.

Jonathan sprinted through the back field, his thighs aching from the high steps necessary to negotiate the tall weeds. He could not see where his feet would land; the fields were covered in a layer of thick fog. Jonathan prayed that the chosen shortcut to the road winding through Turner Hills would provide him ample time to reach Sarah.

He could hear the savage snarls of the wolves—*his wolves*— ahead, as well as the devilish shouts of his adversary. Then suddenly, without warning, he heard the scream. Jonathan instinctively stopped. It was the scream of a woman.

"Sarah!" he shouted, jolting his legs awake. "Oh, Lord! Please let me not be too late!"

Jonathan ran hard, tripping and stumbling through unseen depressions in the land. The sound of the wolves grew louder as he approached, growing in its intensity. Jonathan could see the break in the trees ahead, and he fired his musket into the air. The din of the wolves' snarls did not diminish with the crack of the firearm.

The canine shapes were now visible through the brush. Jonathan willed his legs to pump faster, straining with every muscle in his being. He crashed through the underbrush and paused.

The wolves turned their attention to the sudden intrusion. Some moved away from the form lying still in the road, only to return seconds later. Jonathan could not see what the wolves were gathered around, but he feared the worst. The beasts were within the musket's range now. Jonathan dropped another ball into the barrel of the musket, raised the weapon to the canines, and fired. The wolves scattered immediately, bolting for the bushes on the opposite side of the road. One leapt backwards and fell to its side, kicking up dust from the dirt road.

"Go on!" he shouted. "Away, you filthy varmints!"

Only then did Jonathan look down. The pile of clothes lay in shreds at his feet. He recognized the woolen cloak he had given Sarah on her last birthday. Jonathan's eyes woefully followed the blood-drenched dirt to the crumpled nude form in the road.

Jonathan moved forward and dropped to his knees, his musket falling to the side. "Oh, Lord. Oh, dear Lord. Why? How could you allow this to happen?"

Jonathan nestled his sweet love's head in his strong arms. He tried not to look upon Sarah's ravaged remains, but something inside of him forced him to take a long, hard study. Her body had been mangled by the sharp teeth of the canines. Steam rose into the cold air around the still warm wounds.

"Oh, my dear Sarah," Jonathan cried. "I'm so sorry I couldn't save you. I'm so, so sorry. I was too slow."

The wounded wolf whimpered where it had fallen. Jonathan glanced over at it. He saw the eyes of the others still watching from the brush. They moved farther up the hills, breaking through the bushes and trotting up to the foot of the hill. Jonathan hugged Sarah's head and prayed for her soul. He watched the wolves as they crested the hill. The wounded wolf heaved and lay still beside Sarah. Jonathan wanted to mourn for the animal, to forgive the wolves for what they had done to Sarah. They were not responsible for this travesty.

Jonathan's vision blurred around the wolves, when a larger wolf, darker than the others, appeared through their ranks.

"Booth," whispered Jonathan through clenched teeth.

Jonathan could see the immense wolf's eyes, felt the animal's intense vision lock onto his. Unspoken words passed between the two. Grieving man and defiant animal.

The wolf began to change. Its torso stretched; the hind legs lengthened. Its head widened and its ears sprouted, stretching further to the moon. The beast stood gigantically on two legs, its chest heaving in a slow, hypnotic rhythm. The beast began to laugh, quietly at first. Its small rumbling chuckles grew, gradually building to a roaring crescendo of uncontrollable hysterical laughter.

Jonathan rose to his feet and leveled his musket at the blasphemous beast. The black creature threw its head back, spread its arms wide, and released a terrifying, heart-twisting howl into the frigid air. Then, it was gone.

"Booth!" Jonathan Lucas shouted into the still air. "I'll get you, Booth! I'll not rest until I've avenged sweet Sarah's murder! This I promise you!"

Jonathan dropped to his knees and wept. The events of his long life began to flood into his conscience—the good times, the happy times ... the sad times. He thought of the day he met Sarah. He thought of the love that had developed between them. He thought of the night they conceived the triplets. But most of all, he thought of the void that now filled his heart.

"Do not worry, my sweet Sarah," he cried. "The children will be reared by capable hands, this I promise. I'll do my best to bring them up with a firm hand and an understanding heart, just as you would have, my love. And I'll have them not forget their dear, sweet mother." Jonathan wiped a smear of blood from the woman's cooling lips as he bent to kiss them. "Goodnight, my dear. Sleep well. The cursed moon shall torment you no longer. You are free of its heinous grip. Sleep well, my precious Sarah."

Jonathan held Sarah in his arms, stroking her soft hair and singing a soothing lullaby. Slowly, inevitably, the vile moon was replaced by the sun rising in the eastern sky, but the golden, warm light cast over the dusty, country road by the shimmering globe did little to brighten the darkness that was growing rapidly in Jonathan Lucas' heart.

PART ONE

UPSTATE MAINE 1994

1

N ATASHA LIFTED HER MUZZLE to the heavens and inhaled deeply. An exhilarating blend of scents drifted through the cool night air, enticing her natural animal instincts, driving her to explore every opportunity available in her new-found freedom. She absorbed the smells wholly: the sweet petrichor of the rain-soaked earth, the decaying pine needles scattered along the forest floor, smoke from a chimney atop one of the many farmhouses that dotted the countryside. But these smells were lesser, weaker than the others, only remote diversions that served as little more than background clutter to the one scent that was now driving Natasha forward. This scent was much greater, overpowering all the others, leaving little doubt as to its origin. This was the musky, undeniable odor of a male.

Natasha's ears pricked, and she threw her head back, releasing a shrill, splitting howl into the foggy air. He was out there, in the deep woods, somewhere. He would answer her call, of that she was certain. Her breath hung around her, and she strained her acute hearing for his reply. There was none.

Natasha whimpered. He had been here, and not long ago. She was sure of that; the scent was just too powerful. Puzzled, Natasha dropped her snout to the ground and began shuffling through the leaves, trying desperately to pick up a stronger dose of the driving scent. She found it difficult to locate an exact source of the odor; it seemed as if his smell was everywhere, drifting through the pine branches, rising from the moist soil, surrounding her, following her every step. This confused Natasha's senses, for it betrayed everything known to her natural instincts. She should be able to follow a direct scent but couldn't.

Natasha squatted close to the ground and urinated. Perhaps if she marked his territory, he would pick up Natasha's own scent and come to her. She lowered her head and sniffed the musky odor of her own glands. The aching in her loins was becoming almost unbearable. Never before, even in her most intense cycles of heat, had Natasha felt such an urge. She turned and sent another long, lonely cry into the darkness, but still, he did not answer.

Natasha began to move on. Her anxieties would not allow her to stay in one place for too long. She had to keep trying, following the scent that was all around her, hoping to pick up a trail of the elusive object of her desire.

Natasha turned toward a sudden noise, and when the breeze met her nostrils, she almost swooned from the sudden, overpowering odor. It was the same, unattached smell she had encountered all evening, but its strength was unmistakable now. He had arrived. She uttered a low warning growl out of pure instinct. She could hear his heavy breathing, but he made no other sounds. Natasha snarled aggressively, hoping to draw him into the open, but he did not appear. Why did he not answer her? Why was he hiding? Determined to find the unseen intruder, Natasha moved forward. His scent grew stronger, making her head spin faster. The aching in her body intensified, and she growled again. Each breeze brought his musk deeper into her nose, and she moved closer to him.

Suddenly, Natasha stopped. The intense odor had abruptly vanished; now only the discorporate, floating scent remained. The sound of his breathing was gone as well, the forest quiet but for the chirping of crickets, and the distant hoot of an owl. She growled softly, more a defensive maneuver than anything, for she was suddenly frightened. All signs of the mysterious intruder were gone. He had simply vanished.

Natasha inhaled deeply one more time and suddenly bristled in fear. He was behind her. How had he moved so swiftly, so silently? She could hear his breathing once again, and the sound of his heavy feet crunching the leaves as he moved toward her. Still anxious, but tingling with anticipation, Natasha turned to face him.

He was large—much larger than her. His coat was as black as the night, glistening in the light from the moon, and his eyes glowed a deep blood red. Natasha's eyes met his, and for the first time, he spoke—a low guttural snarl that seemed to shake the very earth on which she stood. His hot breath blew steam high into the crisp air, and a long string of saliva dripped from his yellowed teeth, and dropped, sizzling in the moist dirt.

Natasha growled as he bared his teeth in a wide, sadistic grin. Her heart beat rapidly with the anticipation of mating. The wolf began to circle her in an attempt to move up behind her. Natasha crept backwards teasingly, trying to keep the beast away from her. She growled at him to stay away, but his growl was fiercer, clearly announcing his intentions. He moved his snout to her backside and sniffed ravenously. Natasha snarled again, and the wolf snapped at her hind leg. Natasha yelped and turned her head back to him, snapping in return, but he continued to explore her backside. Slowly, the desire she had felt earlier began to grow inside her, building in her lower extremities a fire she had never felt so intensely. Natasha moaned at the wolf's incessant advances, and she backed into him. She could feel his body stiffen as he mounted her from behind.

Natasha quivered and her legs buckled under as the great beast entered her. She cried out at the unexpected power of the black creature. Each thrust of his powerful hindquarters threatened to knock her to the ground, and he shouted his disapproval each time she stumbled. She tried to hold herself up, but the great beast pushed harder, and she found it more difficult to stand under his oppressive weight. His savage growls began to frighten Natasha; her natural instincts for survival began to override the urge to mate. He grabbed the nape of her neck in his strong jaws and bit down. Natasha could feel a warm trickle of blood as it oozed from her neck and matted her fur. Natasha cried out in terror; this animal frightened her. His unnatural appearance and overtly powerful mating were beyond what she could comprehend as normal animal functions.

The wolf's body was rock-hard as he continued his incisive advances. He was so muscular, so large. Natasha's knees began to weaken further, and she spilled to the ground. Angered by the interruption, the wolf backed away momentarily. Natasha, sensing an opportunity, tried to scramble to her feet, but he was so large and quick that he was on her again. She squirmed beneath him, trying to keep him from reentering her. Once again, he sank his fierce jaws into her, and Natasha howled in pain. She writhed and twisted beneath him, but she could not budge the terrifying animal. He shook her neck in anger, sending tufts of fur flying in either direction. Natasha snapped and snarled at air, trying hopelessly to spoil his attempts, but the beast would not be denied.

•   •   •

The Potters Sheriff's Department cruiser glided down the lonely, hilly stretch of Highway 92, its tires singing along the asphalt road. It was one of the few asphalt roads in Potters, Maine, a small farming community whose secondary roads were combinations of gravel and clay at best. A peach morning glow peeked between the branches of the coniferous trees that lined either side of the highway. The sky was cloudless after the previous night's rains.

Inside the squad car, deputies Blane "Smitty" Smith and Oliver Mason said little. The silence was broken only by occasional blips from the radio. That was normal fare for the small town of Potters, Maine. Normal, that is, until recently.

"What do you think we'll find?" Mason asked.

Smitty shrugged. "We probably won't find anything out on this side of town." He glanced out the driver's window at the rustic countryside. "Not many farms out this way."

The missing livestock issue was becoming big news among the townspeople. The reports were widely scattered and usually occurred no more than once or twice a month, but the farmers were getting restless. The losses weren't great, but to a small town like Potters, in which almost every resident had a vested interest, the loss of even one cow was intolerable. Everyone had a theory; everyone had an answer. Sheriff Barnes suspected rustlers. Fred Hackles, a local farmer, believed it was wolves. Others thought it was teenaged pranksters coming down from one of the larger towns such as Franklin. Everyone had an answer, but the simple fact remained: farmers were still losing animals.

Until last night, no physical evidence had been found. Trevor Blaylock had called early that morning. He had a mutilated heifer in his back pasture.

"What do you think it is?"

Smitty sighed. The younger Mason annoyed him at times by asking so many questions. Just like a damn kid, he thought. Why is the sky blue? Why is water wet? Why do dogs bark and cats meow? Smitty glanced over at Mason but said nothing.

"I would've kept going with Sheriff Barnes' theory if this cow hadn't been found. Now, I just don't know. Maybe it *is* wolves."

Smitty snorted. "Except, there haven't been any wolves in Maine in years."

"That's true," Mason admitted. Then, his eyes seemed to light up. "Hey! What about dogs? Just a pack of wild dogs? You know, people get German shepherds and Rottweilers for their kids, never even thinking about how big they'll get. And when they grow up, they just dump 'em out in the country somewhere."

Smitty stared ahead at the road. "Mason, there aren't enough people in this whole county to buy enough dogs to dump somewhere to form a pack of wild, vicious dogs."

Mason twisted his lips and shrugged. "Well, they could've—"

His words were cut off as deputy Smith slammed on the brakes, bringing the squad car to a screeching, skidding halt.

"Jesus, what are you doing? Tryin' to get us killed?"

Mason readjusted his hat atop his head and looked at Smitty. Smitty was pointing to the side of the road. Deputy Mason followed the path of Smitty's finger.

And then he saw it. There was something on the side of the road, and it was moving. It was not a large object. Uniform brown in color, it seemed to be some sort of animal.

"What do you think it is?" Mason asked.

Smitty didn't mind this question. It seemed highly appropriate, but he didn't have an answer.

The two deputies continued to stare at the unidentified object. It kept moving only slightly, as if slowly exploring the ground at its feet, shuffling from left to right. Suddenly, it stood upright on two legs. It turned to face the squad car, a single pinecone in one hand.

"Oh, shit," said Smitty, embarrassed.

He and Mason looked at one another. "Coogan."

Jackie Coogan was easily one of the most discussed characters in Potters. The village idiot, the town drunk, the local legend. The entire population knew him as the peculiar old man who lived on the outskirts of town in a tiny aluminum trailer, and who supplemented his income by collecting aluminum cans and pinecones, though what he did with the pinecones was anyone's guess. He could always be seen in the early mornings, rain or shine, toting his bags up and down highway 92.

The little old man stood staring at the cruiser. His cracked and weather-beaten face, heavy with stubble, peered from the confines of a blue winter hat. His dirty brown overcoat covered him from shoulders to feet. He held a filthy burlap sack in each hand. One seemed to be more stuffed than the other. The old guy looked away from the deputies and placed the pinecone into the fuller bag.

Smitty and Mason got out of the car and walked down the small incline to where Coogan stood.

"Morning, Mr. Coogan."

The old man glared at the two deputies with a scornful eye. "Deputies," he said, in a cracked, whiny voice.

"Whatcha got in the sacks?"

"You know what I got in the sacks, son. You stop me nearly every blamed morning."

"Now, now. You didn't answer my question." Smitty prodded Mason in the arm and shook his head, silently reprimanding the younger officer.

"I know. I know. Cans and pinecones," Mason said.

Coogan turned away from the officers, kicking at a bright object on the ground that turned out to be just a gum wrapper.

"What is it exactly that you do with these pinecones, old timer?"

Without turning around, Coogan said, "I make crafts with 'em, you know that."

"Well, how come I've never seen any of these crafts?"

"Maybe you've never bought any," replied the old man.

"We haven't been drinking already this morning, have we?" Deputy Mason enjoyed pestering the elderly man.

"I haven't, Deputy. Have you?"

Smitty turned away and snickered. Mason looked at him and back at Coogan.

"Am I being arrested?" Coogan asked Smitty.

Deputy Smith chuckled and slapped Mason across the back. "No, Coogan. You're free to go about your business. Just be careful. Don't get too close to the road."

Smitty motioned for Mason to return to the squad car. Mason frowned at the old man before turning up the slope. "Crazy old bastard."

Smitty closed the car door and fastened his seat belt. He smiled to himself. He enjoyed seeing Coogan throw one of Mason's annoying questions back in his face.

"Sells those cans to buy liquor, I'll bet. What do you think?"

"I don't know."

Smitty started the engine and pulled the car back onto the highway, spewing gravel behind them.

"Crafts," mumbled Mason, disgusted. "What do you suppose he does with those pinecones?"

"I don't know, Mason. Maybe he wipes his ass with them."

The cruiser passed the old man. He was at the edge of the trees, bending over, picking up a pinecone.

•   •   •

Jackie Coogan stood at the base of the ditch, watching the deputies speed away, the squad car throwing dust and small bits of asphalt gravel over the two-lane road. He watched until the black-and-white cruiser disappeared over the crest of the hill, then added his latest pinecone to the rest of his morning collection. He held the bags up evenly, testing the weight of each. The pinecone bag was much heavier; it always was. Cans were scarce in the small town, but each one counted. It was a little more money to add to his monthly pension checks from Boyd Cannery, the factory where he had worked for twenty-two years. And the pinecones? They were just a hobby really; Coogan thought they were pretty. He didn't make crafts from them. He would never blatantly commercialize something of nature. He just said that to the annoying looky-loos to shut them up.

Coogan began to move on down the highway toward his trailer. It was still early, but he wanted to be closer to home before the sun got too bright. It wouldn't be hot in the late September afternoon, but he was an old man, and any bit of humidity tended to wear him out.

Coogan stole a glance down the highway and thought of the Potters police force. He disliked that damned Deputy Mason. He was a smart-ass kid, still wet behind the ears, full of himself and his so-called power. He took every opportunity he could to harass Coogan. Smitty was okay; Coogan never really had any trouble with him. And Sheriff Barnes was all right as well. Then there was Stoner. Stoner was made from a different mold altogether.

Coogan shuddered. He didn't like to think of Deputy Stoner at all. Stoner didn't bother Coogan much, but Coogan hated their occasional run-ins all the same. Stoner had a quiet, confident air about him that somehow chilled Coogan.

The rest of the town pretty much dismissed Coogan as harmless, and that's just the way he wanted it. They could call him a drunk, a bum, a drifter (even though he'd lived in Potters longer than many of its denizens), whatever they liked. He heard them in town as he walked down the cracked sidewalks on the main stretch of town, inside the general store where the locals sat around playing dominoes. It didn't matter to Coogan. As long as they stayed away from him, minded their own business and let him tend to his, they could call him Satan for all he cared.

The trouble was, if anything went wrong in town, and the sheriff's office didn't have an explanation for the good citizens of Potters, Coogan's name was the first to come up. There was the incident back in summer when the kids were driving down from Johnson County, breaking windows and knocking down mailboxes, and who did the townsfolk blame? Old Coogan, that's who. Damn fools. Coogan couldn't even swing a baseball bat or throw a rock without his arthritis killing him. But such was the duty of the town scapegoat. Take the blame for what the inept city officials couldn't figure out.

Coogan had been reading about the missing livestock. Every now and then, about once or twice a month, some farmer would call the sheriff's office complaining that he was missing a few head of cattle. The police would investigate, but no one ever found the missing animals. Coogan figured it was only a matter of time before he got the blame for that, too.

Coogan bent over, spying a mud-encrusted can, and pulled it from the ground. The beer can had been there for a while. Must've missed that one before, he thought. Coogan dropped the can into his sack and turned to head home.

The missing cattle and his impending bout with the sheriff's office were still on Coogan's mind, which frightened him even more when he saw the wolf break from the trees along the side of the road.

•　　　•　　　•

"Oh, shit," David Wagner mumbled.

He bent down and inspected the broken link in the chain and sighed. He had had every intention of having a chain link fence installed around his backyard for some time now, but it was one of those things that he just kept putting off. This was bound to have happened sooner or later. Disgusted with himself, David tossed the chain aside and peered off into the hills that led to the forest behind his house.

"Shit," he whispered again.

The sun was just beginning to peek over the distant tree line, and that had David worried. In the last few months, there were several instances of missing livestock among the farmers and ranchers of Potters. Many people had offered opinions and suggestions as to who or what was responsible and how to deal with it. Among the ideas were the existence of wolves. Natasha was 98% MacKenzie Valley timber wolf, 2% Alaska malamute. She looked exactly like a wolf, and for all intents and purposes, she was a wolf. David knew the backwoods mentality of some of the town's farmers. If it walks like a duck and talks like a duck ... David had to find Natasha, and quickly.

David scrambled to his Jeep, determined to locate her before the sun rose much higher in the sky. As he wheeled the vehicle out of his yard, he caught the end of a farm report on KRLY-AM. A cow had been found mutilated in local farmer Trevor Blaylock's back field. David knew Trevor Blaylock; they were neighbors, and Blaylock was high on the list of those who suspected wolves. He had given David some wary glances several times during David's morning walk with Natasha. It was only a matter of time before he started crying "wolf".

The fact that an actual carcass had apparently been discovered worried David as well. He had hoped that the culprit would turn out to be human: rival farmers, wayward kids, whatever. Now, it was apparent that the problem was indeed an animal of some sort.

David smashed his hand against the steering wheel and cursed. "Dammit, Natasha! Where are you?"

David glanced toward Blaylock's house as he passed along highway 92. There was a police car parked in front. David caught just a quick glance, but he thought it was Deputy Stoner. He didn't like Stoner. He had that "I'm a badass cop and I carry a gun and there ain't shit you can do about it" kind of attitude. But Stoner was the least of his problems.

David ran his fingers through his hair and sighed. The thought of losing Natasha was something he hoped he wouldn't have to face, not for a long time anyway. He had purchased Natasha from a breeder near Flagstaff, Arizona just a few weeks before he moved to Maine. She was six weeks old at the time and the most adorable puppy—*pup*, he corrected himself—David had ever seen. He hadn't really planned on buying a dog at the time, but he had needed something to help take his mind off his divorce from Mindy. The $400 dollar price tag and all the special training and care required to properly raise a wolf-hybrid were well worth it. Natasha had turned out to be the most loyal and loving thing—animal or human—that David had ever known. Her companionship was undying.

David, a freelance writer of magazine articles, lived alone. His article on wolf-hybrids in Dog Fancy was well received. His career, and his current location, didn't offer much in the way of social activities. Add to that the stress and paperwork of a divorce. Natasha was his only companion. She was his pet, sure, but sometimes, he thought it might go deeper than that. Sometimes, in that lonely old farmhouse in the middle of a forested mountain, where a more superstitious man might start hearing noises and seeing ghosts in the solitude, David thought he might crack if it weren't for Natasha's ever-present company. And now, he thought, she was alone and in an environment that didn't match up well with her.

David crept the Jeep along the sides of the road, keeping far over on the shoulder, and glanced from left to right for any clue to Natasha's whereabouts. He glanced at the radio clock. It was 8:30. David could see that the sun had now risen completely above the tips of the coniferous trees alongside the road. The sky had grown much lighter.

•   •   •

Jackie Coogan stood perfectly still and tried to stay calm. The big wolf had just stepped from the trees and into the clearing along the roadside. He didn't think it had seen him yet. Maybe if he stood still, it wouldn't.

The wolf lifted its muzzle higher and sniffed. Coogan realized what a beautiful animal it was. That was stupid. Like admiring a speeding, bright red sports car seconds before it smears you all over the highway. The wolf's fur was matted and muddy, but the thick silver/gray coat was still evident. The animal had a sort of regal manner to it as it stood tall, sniffing the early morning air. Coogan was about to relax when the wolf peered directly at him.

"Oh lordy," he whispered.

The animal's unblinking brown eyes stared into Coogan's. He tried to get a reading through the wolf's eyes, its body language, anything, but the wolf was not telegraphing its next move. It simply stood perfectly still, as if it were waiting for Coogan to move. Coogan did not break his eye contact with the animal. He tried to show no fear, though he was scared witless. Why couldn't those damn deputies drive by now?

The wolf tilted its head slightly, as if studying the little man in front of it. Its tail moved up over its back. Coogan relaxed his stance slightly. Something in the animal's deep brown eyes calmed him. It didn't seem like it was going to attack.

That's when Coogan noticed the collar, and a short moment later, the piece of chain trailing from the collar to the ground.

"Jiminy," he scoffed. "It's just a dog. It's a husky or something like that." He started to take a step toward the dog.

The animal stepped back, its ears pointing skyward. *You damn fool,* Coogan thought. *A tame dog can chew your stupid throat out just as easily as a wolf if it takes a notion to.* Coogan dropped to one knee and showed his hands to the dog.

"C'mere, boy," he called quietly. "Come to old Coogan. He ain't gonna hurt you."

The dog's ears laid back, and for a millisecond, Coogan wondered if it was a show of friendship or aggression. Then, its tail wagged, and the dog approached Coogan.

"There," he said. "I'm not gonna hurt you, boy."

He began to inspect the animal. What Coogan thought was mud turned out to be dried blood. There was a deep cut along the nape of the dog's neck. He felt along the belly of the animal for more wounds.

"Oh," he said. "Seems I owe you an apology. You're a girl, not a boy."

Other than the cut on the neck and the dirty coat, the animal seemed to be fine. Coogan rubbed the top of her head briskly, and the dog seemed to enjoy the attention. He ran his hand along the thick fur under her chin, hoping to find an identification tag. He did.

"'Natasha'," he read. "'David Wagner. Box 32. Highway 92.' You're not too far from home, are you girl?"

Coogan stood up and looked down the road. "Let's see now. Thirty-two should be north from here, I think." He rubbed the whiskers on his chin for a moment before deciding. "Yeah, I think so." He turned to Natasha. "You want to go back home to your owner? You're probably getting pretty hungry, aren't you?"

Natasha jumped up and barked once. She certainly is a friendly dog, Coogan thought. And there I was thinking she was a wolf.

"C'mon, let's get you home."

•   •   •

"You're the old farm hand, Trevor. You tell me what it is," said Deputy Devin Stoner.

He stared down at the half-eaten carcass of the Holstein heifer at his feet. From the back, one might think the cow was just lying down. It wasn't until one walked around to the other side, saw the huge open cavity in the animal's belly, the ravaged pile of purple entrails, that the obvious became apparent. The poor animal's eyes were locked open in a dying squeal of terror. The early morning sun had already drawn the flies in scores.

"I just don't think it could be a pack of wild dogs," Trevor Blaylock said. "The grass around the body isn't smashed flat enough to indicate more than one animal." He looked back at Deputy Stoner.

Stoner was a large, imposing figure. He stood about 6' 4", all of it solid muscle. His blonde, longish hair—long for a deputy—framed his ruddy face and his piercing blue eyes.

Stoner sighed and looked at Blaylock. He found it amusing that he was standing here discussing the possible cause of this cow's demise when the remnants of the animal's innards lay comfortably digesting in Stoner's stomach even as they spoke. He had slain the animal the previous night in another nocturnal tirade, slit open the animal's fat belly, and feasted on its stinking guts. Devin Stoner was a lycanthrope of the most vicious type. He was responsible for all the lost cattle of the previous weeks. The early autumn air had invigorated him, driving his moon-powered thirst for blood to new levels, as it so often did as the day of the Festering, the annual gathering of evil lycanthropes, grew nearer.

"Well, you've got no tracks here, what with all the grass. Nothing I can do there."

"Yeah, well it damn sure ain't no kids. Never did believe that story anyway. Devil-worshippers and what not."

"Well, you never know."

"C'mon, Deputy. You've been watching too much Oprah."

Stoner rested his hand on his Browning 1910 9mm and turned from the dead cow. "Well, that's about all I can do this time. We'll make more rounds down the highway at night. Check on each farm. That sort of thing." He turned to face Blaylock. "But if you want my opinion, I think this thing will pass before too long. Give it some time."

"I don't have time, Deputy," Blaylock said angrily. "I've lost ten head of cattle so far. I can't afford that. This has got to stop."

"Well, until we have more to go on, there's not a lot we can do."

"Wait a minute," said Blaylock, holding up a hand. "I've got something you can check out."

Stoner raised his eyebrows, expecting another of the many crazy suggestions the farmers had been offering. Blaylock pointed past his barn.

"What?" Stoner said, annoyed. He wasn't a damned retriever.

"Next door. Wagner."

"What? You think Wagner did it? That's ridiculous."

"Not Wagner. That goddamn wolf of his."

Stoner shrugged his broad shoulders. He knew about Blaylock's neighbor's unusual pet. It was half-wolf half-husky, or something like that.

"Yeah, you see I'm right, don't you?" boasted Blaylock, sensing a feeling of agreement from Stoner.

"It's possible," Stoner admitted. "But why would his dog do this? It shouldn't need to feed on anything but its own dog food."

"It doesn't kill to eat. It's a fuckin' wolf, for God's sake. It enjoys killing!"

"Isn't it fenced in?"

"Nope. Keeps it chained to a tree out back. Go see for yourself."

"Well, if nothing else, he shouldn't keep it restrained only by a chain. That could be dangerous."

Blaylock held his hands out toward the house down the way as if to show directions. Stoner peered at him for a moment.

"Well, I'll check into it if it'll make you happy. That's what the Potters Sheriff's Department is here for. To make you people happy," he said, winking at Blaylock.

"Just do your damned job, Deputy."

Deputy Stoner turned and headed back through the field to his squad car. He didn't care much for Trevor Blaylock. He didn't care much for anyone. But as long as Blaylock kept coming up with new explanations for the disappearance of the livestock, as long as all the stupid locals continued to offer their opinions, he would have something else on which to blame the disappearances. Maybe it would keep the townspeople off his back for a while, make life easier for Devin Stoner the law enforcer as well as for Devin Stoner the blood-thirsty killer.

•   •   •

David had driven up and down highway 92 several times, as well as a few back roads, but there was still no trace of Natasha. He began to realize that the hope of finding her in this secluded country was very remote. He would have to hope she made it back home on her own, and that none of the farmers found—

The sight ahead of him filled David with mixed feelings of joy and worry. It was Natasha, being led on her broken chain by Jackie Coogan.

David had never actually met Jackie Coogan. He saw Coogan pass in front of his house several times a week dragging those two burlap sacks and often wondered what was in them before realizing it might be best if he didn't know. He would see Coogan in town now and then, but their only communication might be a passing nod at best. He had heard all the local opinions of the little old man who lived on the outskirts of town. All those myths combined with the strange visage the man presented led David to be believe that Jackie Coogan was a man best left alone.

The only trouble now was that he had David's dog.

David suddenly realized that the man was walking away from the far end of town, away from Coogan's trailer. He must be bringing Natasha home to me, David thought. Thank God for that ID tag.

David pulled the Jeep over to the side of the road, threw it into Park, and jumped from the vehicle. Coogan had turned around to face the new arrival.

"Mr. Coogan?" David called out with caution.

The man stared apprehensively at David. Recognition swept across Natasha's face, but she did not leave Coogan's side. "Can I help you, son?" asked Coogan.

"Yes, sir. That's my dog," David said, trying to sound polite as possible.

"Oh, yeah?" Coogan eyed David suspiciously. "What's your name?"

"David Wagner."

Coogan knelt and felt for the tags again. David watched the old man, amused. Coogan stood back up and smiled. "So, you are."

"Where did you find her?"

Coogan pointed back to the south. "About two miles up the highway. She came out of the bushes. 'Bout scared the piss outta me. I thought she was a wolf."

"She's part wolf," explained David. "A wolf-hybrid."

"'Zat a fact?"

"Look, Mr. Coogan. It is Coogan, isn't it?" The man nodded. "I appreciate you finding her, but I'll take her from here, if you don't mind."

"No, not at all. She's your dog, Mr. Wagner."

David reached for the chain, but Natasha held her ground. "Let's go home, girl," David coaxed. Natasha whimpered. "It's amazing how she's taken up with you. Hybrids just don't do that."

"Animals take to me real easy, son. 'Specially dogs."

"Yeah, but she's not a dog," said David. It's probably the odor, he thought rudely. "Well, I can't thank you enough, Mr. Coogan."

"Just Coogan would be fine. No need for fancy formalities."

David nodded. "Thanks again."

Coogan nodded and turned back to the north, slinging one of the bags over his shoulder. David heard the faint clink of metal.

"Coogan?" he called. "What's in the bags?" Coogan gave David a strange look. David sensed the insult in Coogan's eyes. "If … if you don't mind my asking." He suddenly felt very foolish.

Coogan nodded. "Aluminum cans in one, pinecones in the other."

Before David could stop his mouth, he heard himself ask, "Pinecones? Why do you hunt pinecones?"

Coogan smiled. "I make crafts out of 'em."

2

D AVID GLANCED WARILY at the group of men gathered around the small card table in the back of Flander's Mercantile. He noticed the way their voices had fallen silent when he stepped into the store. Trevor Blaylock was there, as well as some of the other townspeople that he knew not by name but by face. The men glanced up from their game of dominoes and stared in David's direction. They leaned toward each other, their voices inaudible whispers.

David moved away from the front door, shaking the rainwater from his jacket. The scent of freshly cut hay wafted to his nostrils. David kept most of his attention on the table as he grabbed a 50-pound sack of Pedigree Mealtime and slung it over his shoulder. Random discernable words made their way to his ears now and then; he thought he heard his name mentioned more than once.

"Trump!" a voice shouted from the table, followed by coarse chuckles and a mix of profanities thrown in for good measure.

David set the bag on top of the counter. A short, cheerful woman of about forty years appeared behind the counter. David had seen her working the front desk at the feed store before; her name was Wanda.

"That gonna do it for you?"

David smiled and nodded, reaching for his wallet.

"Hey, Wagner," a voice called from the table. David recognized the strain of semi-intelligent words attempting to exit vocal cords and maneuver their way around a wad of chewing tobacco. Blaylock.

David turned to face him. Wanda seemed nervous.

"What do you do, Wagner? Feed the bitch dry dog food for a few weeks in a row, then let her out one night a month for fresh meat?"

A frown crossed David's brow. "What?"

The other men snickered. Blaylock said nothing.

"Don't pay him no mind," the woman said. "He's just upset about the missing cattle."

"Is that what this is about?"

"Something's killing my cattle."

David moved closer to the table. A few of the faces seemed surprised.

"Oh, I see," David said sarcastically. "And you think that my dog is responsible."

"I don't know about yer dog, but I know goddamn good and well yer wolf did it." Blaylock stood, scooting his chair to the side with a loud scrape.

"And what makes you think Natasha is responsible?"

"Well, what else could it be? There ain't no wolves around here anymore. Nothing human did that to my cow."

"Natasha isn't the only dog in the county either. Every one of you has at least ten old hound dogs running around your farms."

"Ayuh, you're right about that. We all got hound dogs, but you're the only one's got a wolf."

"She's not a wolf." Blaylock's partners in the fine art of slacking off turned their attention to him. "She's a wolf hybrid. If you weren't so stupid, you'd know the difference."

A chorus of rumbles emanated from the men gathered at the table. A domino fell bouncing to the floor, clinking in the sudden silence.

Blaylock moved closer to David; the men's gazes locked. "Stoner come to see you yet, Wagner?"

Stoner? David thought. What the hell does he have to do with this? He surely didn't want Stoner messing around his house. "What about Stoner?"

Blaylock grinned. "Oh, I expect he'll be paying you a visit before long. You'll find out then."

"Natasha did not kill your cow. She hasn't killed any of the livestock."

"Let the law decide, boy," Blaylock said grimly.

Ignorant damned hicks! David thought and stomped back to the counter. He paid the smiling woman, grabbed the dog food, and headed back out into the rain.

•   •   •

The rain had lessened considerably by the time David pulled back into his muddy driveway. He was thankful that his Jeep was four-wheel drive; many of the roads in Potters (not to mention his driveway) became prime mudding spots during a driving rain. The vehicle bounced along the driveway, past the side of the house and into the back where David always parked. He expected to find Natasha in her doghouse, hiding from the earlier rains, but instead she was standing in front of her shelter. And Jackie Coogan was standing right beside her.

"What the hell?" David mumbled aloud. "What's he doing in my back yard?"

David parked the vehicle and stepped out into the wet grass. Natasha leapt eagerly upon noticing David's arrival, standing on her hind legs, restrained by the length of the chain.

"Morning, Mr. Wagner," Coogan said. He had a natural brightness to his old green eyes.

"Mr. Coogan. Little late in the morning for you, isn't it?"

"Oh, I've already finished my morning walk. I just came by to see Natasha here." The old man studied David with apprehension. "You don't mind, do you?"

"No, no," David lied. He didn't even like the idea of the strange Mr. Coogan being on his property.

"She didn't get out last night?" David shook his head. "You know, you really oughtta consider having a fence put in."

"Yeah, I know. I've been thinking about that."

"She needs to run. She needs exercise. A dog needs to feel free."

"I know, I know." David tried not to sound annoyed. He looked at Natasha. Her legs were muddy all the way up to her knees. The grassless path she had worn in front of her doghouse had turned to soupy muck. Despite her obvious happiness, David knew Natasha must be miserable in the cold rain. "I know."

"It's just a suggestion." The old man ruffled the top of Natasha's head.

"Oh, I know. I'm sorry if I sounded rude, Mr. Coogan—"

"Coogan," the elder man interrupted. "Just Coogan."

David smiled. "All right. Coogan. It's just that … things are getting kind of crazy around here, and …"

"And you think all these dumbshit farmers are gonna start blaming your baby for the killin's," Coogan finished. David looked at Coogan, amazed by his apparent mind-reading abilities. "Am I right?"

David reached for the sack of dog food. "Yeah, you're right."

"Well, she's not alone in that." Natasha studied the two men, whimpering and wagging her bushy tail. "I 'spect it's only a matter of time before they blame me."

David took a long perusal of the comical old man standing before him. He seemed so in place, so natural, like something from a Norman Rockwell painting. He was just a tired old man who could never harm a soul, and David felt sorry for ever secretly fearing the man. *Could I be just like all these backwards townspeople that I loathe so much? Just another one of the assholes quick to take the easy way out by blaming everything on the town misfit?*

David threw the dog food over his shoulder and headed for the back door of the house. He considered inviting Coogan in for coffee.

"Well, I'll be shovin' off now, Mr. Wagner," said Coogan. He knelt in front of Natasha, the knees of his dirty trousers sinking in the soft mud, but he didn't seem to mind. Natasha whimpered and licked at the old man's face.

"David. Please call me David."

Coogan stood up and turned to Natasha's owner. "All right, David. We'll talk to you later."

"Goodbye, Coogan."

David fumbled with the back door key, finally finding it and setting the dog food just inside the door. He turned to the back patio and searched for Coogan. He could see the small frame of the man in the distance, heading back across the hills of highway 92. Natasha sat in the mud at the end of the chain, tail gently wagging, staring in the direction of Coogan, whimpering.

•   •   •

David stood in front of the microwave, waiting for the blessed invention to announce that his Cheez Whiz tortilla melts were hot and ready. He had been thinking a lot about Jackie Coogan. The citizens of Potters, including himself, had always thought the little old man who collected pinecones was a menace to the small community. But after just a few minutes of talking with the man, David didn't believe his reputation did him justice. He just seemed like a gentle, caring, maybe even nature-loving old man who should be someone's grandfather, not a town's most wanted criminal.

The microwave beeped, breaking David from his thoughts on Coogan. He glanced at the clock as he retrieved his gooey, steaming creations. It was six-thirty. Almost dark.

David went to the refrigerator, grabbed a Diet Coke, and sat down at the kitchen table. The day's mail lay in a small heap in front of him. David took a bite of one of the tortillas, cursing as the scalding cheese dribbled down his chin. He opened the soft drink and reached for the mail. A bill from the insurance company, a piece of junk mail, a letter from Mindy's lawyer. What does she want now? he mused.

"You're not getting the microwave," he said aloud.

Suddenly, there was a loud rapping at the door, so forceful that it made David jump. Damn, David thought. Just when I made my tortillas. They taste like crap cold. David wiped his hands on a napkin and went to answer the door.

"Evening, Wagner," the big, blond, uniformed man at the door said.

David swallowed. "Deputy Stoner."

Jesus, what does he want? David thought. The very thought of Stoner standing at his door, of coming into his house, terrified him. Cops had always made David nervous as hell, but Stoner scared the piss out of him. Was it just the uniform? The authority? Maybe it was the deep blue of his eyes.

"Mind if I ask you a few questions?" the deputy asked. His voice hinted at no single emotion.

"Sure." David pulled the door open and motioned Stoner in.

Stoner's imposing frame temporarily blocked the light from the sixty-watt bulb lighting the front porch. David could hear the carpet being smashed by his heavy steps, heard the crunching of his leather patrol jacket. David was reminded of the cop in Police Academy who rescued cats by shooting them out of trees. The thought brought a brief smile to David's face despite his nervousness.

"Would you care for some coffee?"

"No, thanks. This won't take long."

"What's the problem?" asked David, trying to sound more confident.

"Do you own a dog, Wagner?"

"I have a wolf-hybrid. A female. She's 98% MacKenzie Valley timber wolf and 2% Alaska malamute."

Deputy Stoner scribbled David's responses into a black notebook. David had been expecting a visit from the local authorities even before Trevor Blaylock's earlier comments. He thought of his previous encounter with Jackie Coogan and suddenly wished, for some strange reason, that Coogan was there with him.

"What name does the dog answer to?"

"Natasha. Her name is Natasha." David wondered what other information Stoner might ask for. "She's just over three years old. I bought her in Arizona in 1990. She's registered with the UKC. All her vaccinations are up to date, of course."

"I understand the animal is confined only by a length of chain."

"That's correct," David said, cursing himself again for putting off the fence.

"Not the wisest way to keep a dog, especially such a large dog, is it?" For the first time since scribbling in the pad, he looked up into David's eyes.

"It's kind of the only choice I have right now," David answered.

Stoner nodded. "Did your dog escape her leash two nights ago? Tuesday night, early Wednesday morning?"

David sighed. "Yes, yes, she did. I didn't notice it until around seven Wednesday morning. Jackie Coogan found her and brought her back to me."

"Coogan, huh?" Stoner wrote that down as well. "You're aware, I'm sure, of the missing livestock over the past few months. And you've probably heard that your neighbor Trevor Blaylock had a Holstein heifer mutilated."

"Yeah. I might've heard something like that."

"Can we take a look at the animal?" asked Stoner. Even when he was polite, it made David cringe.

"Sure. Right this way."

David opened the back door and pushed the screen door open. He stepped out onto the covered back patio, Stoner close behind. The sun was just beginning to sink below the tree line in the distance, casting long shadows across the huge back yard. David yanked the string on the overhead light, illuminating the porch area.

"She's just out here," David said, pushing a second screen door.

Natasha's head protruded from the doghouse. Her ears lay back happily when she saw David, and she pounced from the house. The screen door slammed shut behind David, and Stoner walked up beside him. Natasha stopped. Her ears dropped again, but this time, she did not wag her tail. David stopped. Natasha's teeth were bared and a low growl rumbled deep within her throat.

"She's a beautiful animal."

David started to thank the deputy, when Natasha began barking furiously, backing up at the same time. Her silver-black hair bristled, the hackles on her neck stood on end.

"She's a little wary of strangers," explained David. He suddenly remembered how quickly Natasha had taken to Coogan.

"As well she should be."

David tried to position himself between Natasha and Stoner. She had never bitten anyone before, but considering the way she was reacting to Stoner's presence, he didn't want to take a chance. All he needed was for word to leak around town that the wolf at Wagner's house had attacked a Potters deputy.

Stoner knelt to the ground. He removed a tape measure from his jacket and began taking measurements of one of Natasha's paw prints in the mud.

"This is purely for our records, Wagner. I suppose I should explain. Some of the farmers in town believe that Natasha may be responsible for the lost cattle."

"She's not," David interrupted. His pet's implied involvement in the incident made him bolder.

"I doubt that myself," Stoner complied. "But, just in case we ever find any tracks in the future, we'll have her measurements on file. That's all."

Natasha had calmed somewhat. She hung back at the far length of her chain, pacing back and forth, still growling.

"You know the whole notion of a domesticated pet killing livestock is totally ludicrous. Granted, she did escape the other night, but that's the only time she's ever been off her leash, except when she's inside with me."

Stoner's gaze drifted from Natasha back to David. God, his stare is unnerving, David thought. "Like I said, I don't really think she's responsible."

"Well, all the same, I hope you find the culprit soon. It really is a shame that some of the farmers are losing money. Even that hard-ass Blaylock."

Stoner smiled, but there was little humor in the gesture. "I thank you for your cooperation in the matter, Wagner. I'll just go around the side of the house."

David thanked the deputy, though he didn't know why. Natasha began to settle down when Stoner disappeared around the corner of the house. She slowly moved back to where David stood, though her attention was still focused on the area where she had last seen the intruder.

David knelt beside Natasha and rubbed her back. "It's all right, girl. I don't care much for that man, either."

3

NATASHA SNIFFED THE AIR and whimpered. She disliked the rain. It dulled her senses, affected her ability to smell the aromas of the distant world. She trotted through the mud to the extent of her chain and scanned the horizon, letting her gaze travel where her feet could not.

She wondered if the old man would come to visit her today. Natasha liked the man who had found her that morning when she was lost. He was a nice, friendly sort and his scent was pleasing to her.

Natasha turned and paced back and forth from the tree to her house. She was growing restless. The morning hours were pleasant for Natasha. Her owner took her for long morning walks, and sometimes when they returned, the old man would visit her.

But Natasha was not happy at night. The darkness had frightened Natasha ever since the night when the giant wolf attacked her. The big, uniformed man with the frightening scent had visited at night. Now, the night had begun to bring pain with it as well.

Natasha could sense it coming as soon as the sun began to sink in the western sky. The anxieties would grip her; the fearful anticipation would cloud her mind. And when the sun dropped from the sky and the darkness enveloped her world, the sharp jabs of pain would rack her body once again.

•   •   •

"What do I do if I get a call tonight?" the young dispatcher asked.

Sheriff Barnes seemed puzzled. "What do you mean 'if you get a call'? Do the same thing you always do."

"That's not what I mean. I mean calls from farmers."

Sheriff Barnes glanced at Deputy Stoner. "Oh."

"I mean, if the pattern continues like it has, it could happen tonight."

"Well, if it does, it likely won't be discovered until morning anyway. I wouldn't worry about it."

"But what if they do call?" The rookie was not satisfied with the answer.

"Then call one of us. Just like any other complaint. Call me or Deputy Stoner, or Mason or Smitty. I don't care."

"Excuse me, sheriff," said Stoner. "If you don't mind, I'd rather not be disturbed tonight. I haven't been getting much sleep lately, and … well, I could use a night of uninterrupted sleep."

"Sure," the sheriff said. "Getting ready for your big hunting trip, huh?"

"Yeah. Getting ready for the trip. Although it still won't be for a while."

"Well, I know how you like to get everything prepared ahead of time."

"Sheriff?"

"Call me, Johnson," Sheriff Barnes snapped. "Just call me at home."

Johnson slid down in his chair and reached for a copy of *Field & Stream*. The two officers moved to the front door and headed for their cars.

"Where you going this year, Devin?"

Stoner paused, as if in thought. "Oh, we're heading to Minnesota. I hear there are some big whitetails there."

"Yeah, there are. Elk, too."

Sheriff Barnes fumbled for his truck keys, found them, and unlocked the door. "God, I hope that kid doesn't call and wake me up tonight."

"I wouldn't worry about it, Sheriff. I doubt if anything happens tonight and, like you said, if it does, we probably won't hear about it until the farmers wake up."

"Yeah, that's probably true. Anyway, we'll see you in the morning."

Stoner waved and slid into his Explorer. Dusk was settling across Potters, and the evening sun was bright in his eyes. He pulled the visor down and glanced back at the office building. Johnson was still leaning back in the chair, sipping a Pepsi and reading his magazine. What if something happened tonight? the kid wanted to know. Something would happen tonight, as it did every full moon. When the great round orb rose high in the sky, the hunger would call, the lust would be appeased. Stoner chuckled. He wondered what would happen if the kid had to answer something really big in the middle of the night.

•   •   •

David sat in front of the computer monitor, his notes scattered haphazardly to his side. He had started working on the article earlier, but the words were not coming easily. He leaned back in the rolling chair, stretched, and yawned.

David was worried about Natasha. She had been acting strangely the past few days, especially at night. She would start whimpering just before sundown and continued crying and yelping as if in great pain the rest of the night. He had even heard her howling a few times. The sound was unnerving. Even though her blood was thick with wolf genes, she never really howled that often. Only at the sound of distant sirens, and never like the piercing cry David had heard the night before. He sighed and reached for the slip of paper the vet had given him earlier. The doctor had run tests on everything from parvo to rabies, even though she had been vaccinated for all the typical canine diseases. David even had her checked for heartworms again. All the tests had come back negative. David was very worried that Natasha may have picked up something from her unauthorized romp through the woods weeks ago. If the wound he had found on her neck was any indication, she may have even been in a fight.

David peeked out the den window from his desk. The rain had started earlier in the afternoon, and it hadn't let up since. He could see the sheets of rainwater pouring from the roof even against the black night.

David stood and moved over to the window. He was frustrated with himself for his unsuccessful writing attempt. He was worried about Natasha, but that wasn't the entire story. It's funny, he thought. One of the reasons he had moved to Maine was that he thought the mountains and the rural lifestyle would enhance his creativity. But he'd been wrong. Oh sure, he'd managed to sell enough articles to make a living. But this small town and its belligerent natives were not to his liking. They were just too quick to pass judgement without gathering all the facts. And he was ashamed to admit that he had started to become just like them with his opinion of Jackie Coogan. David had simply adopted the town's pre-established opinion of the man without bothering to conduct his own investigation into the man's personality.

Now, David decided that Jackie Coogan was just like any elderly retired person with no family and no friends. He had seen Coogan playing with Natasha several more times in the last month, and David had even gone out to speak with the older man on several occasions.

David stared out the window at the rain, bracing for the boom when a great flash of lightning lit up the outside world. At least Blaylock hadn't lost any more cattle since Deputy Stoner had visited David. That was always welcome news. David sighed and rubbed his eyes briskly, as if doing so would drive the sleepiness from his body. The steady sound of the rain dripping from the roof didn't help his attempt at staying awake.

David wondered if Natasha was managing to stay dry. From his vantage point in the den, the covered patio blocked any view of the doghouse, but David could see the tree on which he had the chain tied. When lightning lit the backyard, David could see that her chain lay in the direction of the doghouse. He usually let Natasha in when it started raining, but this storm had come so suddenly, and he hadn't felt like drying her off to let her inside. She could handle rain anyway.

Another flash of lightning flickered across the walls, and David thought he heard a sharp cry under the following crack of thunder. Natasha had been quiet for most of the evening. David assumed that the long trip to the vet had tired her out enough to make her want to sleep. David pressed his ear to the window and listened. He could hear low moans outside, coming from the back yard. Natasha had made a number of strange noises in the last few days, but these sounded altogether different. Puzzled, David left the den and went into the covered patio. Turning on the overhead light, he opened the door that led into the yard. The steady curtain of rainwater falling from the eaves obscured the vision of his surroundings. The light from the patio did not penetrate far. David stuck his head farther out and listened. He could still hear the moans over the din of the storm. A flash of lightning illuminated the backyard, but still David could see nothing.

"Natasha?" David called out.

Normally, especially during a driving rain, Natasha would bound from her doghouse and nearly knock him over to get into the house when he called her name, but not this time. There was no answer, and no sign of Natasha.

David felt a slight twinge of uneasiness begin to rise in his belly, and he reached for the umbrella hanging on the coat rack. Grabbing a flashlight, he stepped out into the yard, letting the screen door slam shut behind him. That would ordinarily bring Natasha running as well, but there was still no sign of her.

"Natasha?" David called out again, opening the umbrella.

David stepped into the rain from the narrow sidewalk that ran in front of the patio. He could still hear the muffled cries, and they appeared to be coming from Natasha's doghouse. David peered into the black night at the house. It was dark, the light from the full moon blocked completely by the stifling swirl of the swollen rain clouds.

"Natasha? Girl, you in there?" There was no answer, save for the sobs.

David looked down at his feet. Shining the flashlight downward, he could see the chain that had held Natasha lying on the ground, with the collar still attached. Cursing under his breath, David knelt to inspect it.

"How the hell did that happen?"

David turned back to the doghouse. The cries had decreased to an almost inaudible snivel, like a child crying itself to sleep. David's heart began to beat rapidly as he approached the house. Something was not right. The noises coming from the doghouse didn't sound like Natasha. They were more human than canine. David crept slowly toward the house and knelt at the opening.

"Natasha?" The cries stopped.

David shined the flashlight into the house and stumbled back in shock at what he saw.

There was a naked woman in Natasha's doghouse.

She was crouched on her feet at the back of the house, cowering and whimpering. Her pale, smooth skin was smeared with mud, and her long dark hair was dripping wet. Her eyes squinted in the glare of the flashlight.

David peered into the house in astonishment. The woman began to sob harder as she held up a muddied hand to block the glare of the flashlight. David was at a loss for words. Many thoughts raced through his mind, but they were having great difficulty reaching his lips.

"Where's my dog?" David blurted above the din of the rain.

The woman did not answer him; she only sobbed louder. "Who are you? What are you doing in my doghouse?" David asked, realizing, but not caring, that he wasn't giving her enough time to answer.

The woman buried her face in her hands and released a long, slow wail that unnerved David. David realized that whatever was going on, however bizarre the situation, this was one terrified young woman.

•   •   •

Natasha cowered fitfully in the corner of her house, holding up a pink, hairless "paw" to shield her eyes from the penetrating light. She was terrified. Her body had been racked by searing pain only moments earlier, pangs of agony much more excruciating than those she had experienced in the last few days. Her body had moved and changed in a way inconceivable to her animal brain. Her legs had stretched, elongated, and her feet had changed into something altogether different from the padded paws that normally served her so well. Her fur had disappeared completely, except for the long dark locks on her head, leaving only soft, pale skin. The driving rain muddied the ground around her and clung to her naked skin, chilling her to the bone.

It was then that Natasha realized the man shining the light and shouting at her was her owner. She recognized him only by sight, for she could no longer discern that pleasing, familiar scent that marked her master. He was acting strangely as well. He was shouting and scolding her, and she didn't know why. She had done nothing wrong. She didn't understand his sudden angry outburst, and that frightened her even more.

Natasha cried out, but her voice was much higher in pitch now. Her incessant fear must've finally been noticed by her owner, for his face suddenly softened, returning to its normal, pleasant demeanor.

"I'm sorry," he said gently. "I'm sorry I frightened you. Can I help you?" He extended his hand to her.

"Oh, David!" she blurted suddenly. "I'm so scared!"

She bolted forward and grasped David's hand tightly, throwing her other arm around his neck. David helped her out of the house and pulled her to her feet.

"How did you know my name was David?" he asked. "I don't believe I know you."

Natasha hugged David fiercely and buried her head in his shoulders. "But you do know me," she cried. "I'm Natasha!"

David gasped in shock as she pulled her head away and gazed into his eyes. "Oh David, I'm so very scared and confused. Please hold me. Please," she sobbed.

Her beloved owner said nothing. Natasha knew that her normal senses had been dulled, but she was aware of the heightening of other senses. Her mind was thinking in ways never before accessible to her, and she sensed that her master was as confused and frightened as she was. Natasha buried her head in David's arms and cried. If anyone could help her with this strange occurrence, it was her master.

•   •   •

The black beast peered through the bushes along the edge of the tree line. It snorted angrily, blowing away the rainwater that had collected on its snout. The house, still several miles away, was visible through the raging storm. The scent weighed heavily in its nostrils, drawing it closer, arousing its desires.

The source of the scent was there; it could see her clearly now. But there was another smell, and the beast recognized this smell also. It was an angry smell, a foreign smell, an odor that did not belong.

It could see the man, standing beside the female.

The beast snarled furiously and turned back into the woods.

4

NATASHA'S OWNER STARED at her with an expression she had never seen on his face before. It was a frightening countenance, a stare he might give a stranger. It was not the face he wore when he brought out her leash for their morning walk. It was not the look he showed when he rubbed her fur and scratched her ears. She pulled the bathrobe tightly to her new, hairless body, for David's cold stare chilled her.

Bathrobe, she thought. *Terry cloth. Velour. Satin.* Her eyes glanced at the items on the kitchen table. *Salt. Fork. Bread. Table.* These were all things she should not know but did. The words formed in her head as swiftly as her eyes focused on the objects. She knew these items, knew their functions. The thoughts came as naturally as blinking her eyes, but they couldn't be more unnatural.

"Look, lady," her master began.

Lady. Woman. Girl.

Natasha looked up from the table into David's eyes. *Confusion. Anger. Concern. Emotions.*

"I've felt these feelings before, but I didn't know what they were called," Natasha said.

"What?"

"I know what these things are," she said. "Clock. Time. Hours. Minutes. It's 11:15."

"Good," David said. "That's just great. I'm really happy for you. Now, suppose you tell me who you are and what you were doing in my backyard."

"I told you already," she said. "My name is Natasha. I was in the doghouse because that's where I live. I don't know how this happened, or how to explain it, but I am Natasha. I am your dog."

David grinned and took a sip of his coffee, suddenly wishing he had some real hard Kahlua to go into it. "No. No, you're not. Natasha is running around in the woods right now, probably because you let her loose, and I really should be out there searching for her."

"David, I've felt this happening for several days now. You know how I was acting. Whining and howling at night. I was hurting. I could feel things moving around inside of me. You even took me to the vet the other day, David."

"How did you know about that?" he asked. "And how do you know my name is David?"

Natasha's gaze dropped to her coffee, still untouched. "I don't know. I'm sure I've heard someone call you by your name before. I just picked it up, is all."

David laughed. "You sure have this down pat, whatever the hell it is. How can you speak to me if you're my dog? How do you know how to converse with me?"

She frowned. "I don't know. I can't explain that any easier than I can explain the rest of this. It feels as if I'm going to speak as I normally would, but words are coming out. Words that I don't even know, that I shouldn't know, yet I do. David, I've suddenly been tossed into a world in which I have no business being. You can't know how frightening that is."

David nodded. "Did you see a dog outside earlier? Big, kind of silvery hair?"

Natasha let her head drop to the table, exasperated. "No, I didn't. I told you I'm your dog. I am Natasha."

David stood up and laughed. "I'm sorry, Natasha, or whatever your name is. I'm not calling you a liar, but you've got to see this from my point of view. It's pretty hard for me to accept the notion that my dog has suddenly turned into this beautiful woman I see before me now."

"Where is Natasha then? How do you explain her collar being removed? How do you account for me?" Natasha argued.

"I don't. I'm not even going to try to account for you. As for Natasha, it's time I look for her. So, if you'll excuse me."

Natasha shook her head angrily. "You seemed so much nicer before."

"Yeah, well, you haven't exactly caught me on my best night. There's a lot of crazy shit going on in this town, and I don't need some insane, naked hitchhiker to make my life any crazier. Now, please, if you'll excuse me, I have a dog I need to find." David opened the closet door and began digging through some old clothes.

Dog. Chain. Jeep. Rain. Mud. Old man. Pinecones ... Deputy.

"What about the deputy?" Natasha asked suddenly.

David turned abruptly to face the woman, his heart suddenly racing. "What about him?"

"You don't like him," she said, feeling as if she'd hit a nerve. "And I don't like him. You saw how I responded to him the other day."

"What about him?" David repeated. How the hell did she know all this?

"What if he's out there?"

"He works days." David pulled a sweatshirt, jacket, and a pair of jeans from the closet and tossed the clothes onto the woman's lap.

"There's a bathroom down the hall to the right. You can get changed there."

"Where are we going?"

"I'm going to look for my dog," David answered. "I don't give a damn where you go."

Natasha stood up and peered at David fearfully. "You're making me leave?" she said, her voice quivering.

"You'll be all right."

"But you can't throw me out, David. Where will I go? What will happen to me? I'm scared and confused, David. How will I live outside like this?"

"Anyone who came up with the story you told can take care of herself, I'm sure. I'm tired of discussing this with you. Now, please. Just get dressed and leave." David pointed to the door.

Natasha stood up and walked past her owner, pausing to let him see the tears in her eyes. She stepped into the bathroom. *Towel. Soap. Toilet. Sink.* More words, more things she shouldn't know, but did. Everything she had known, everything she had experienced was different. The smells were different; her vision was different. She couldn't smell anything, but she could somehow see better. Natasha untied the bathrobe, letting it fall to the floor, and reached for the jeans. Natasha began to cry, not a whimper, but real tears. She wasn't even cognizant of the fact she was pulling the jeans over her legs without even thinking about the process. She pulled the gray sweatshirt over her head and stared into the mirror. A pale, sad human face stared back at her. Natasha could remember seeing her canine reflection in this same, full-length mirror before at some point in time, but the memory was murky and seemed to be fading even as she stood there. She pulled her dark hair from the sweatshirt and let it fall across her back. The human stared back at Natasha with large, brown eyes, and she could see tears rolling down the person's cheeks. Natasha knew that this human, this stranger, was frightened. She wiped the tears from her face.

Shoes, Natasha thought. He didn't give me any shoes. I'll need shoes in the cold.

Natasha's attention returned to her face in the mirror. Her dark eyebrows moved toward her nose, forming an angry grimace, and Natasha screamed. She smashed her soft hand into the mirror, cracking it, and she fell back onto the commode and wept.

David pushed the door inward and his head peeked around the corner. "Are you all right?"

"I shouldn't even know what shoes are," he heard the woman mumble.

"What did you say?"

Natasha looked up at her owner and tried to smile. "Shoes," she said. "You didn't give me any shoes."

•   •   •

Damn, she was attractive, David thought.

David hit the brights on the Jeep and scanned the two-lane highway from left to right. This is ridiculous, he thought. I'll never find Natasha in the dark, especially in this rain.

David thought again of the strange woman. She was beautiful. Big brown doe-eyes, dark, almost black hair, gorgeous body. Thinking back, David realized that he had been resisting the attraction during their entire conversation. The woman had literally turned him on. He hadn't had sex since Mindy left, hadn't even thought about being with a woman for about six months. Was it any wonder the first woman that he was around for any extended amount of time turned him on? Especially when she's absolutely beautiful, naked, and dripping wet.

"Who the hell was she?" David said aloud.

Why had she been hiding in Natasha's doghouse? Why was she so disoriented? Had she released Natasha so she could use the doghouse as shelter from the rain?

David made a U-turn in front of his house and began another trek up highway 92 for about the twentieth time. He hadn't seen a clue as to Natasha's whereabouts. Come to think of it, David hadn't seen the woman again, either.

●　　　●　　　●

Natasha hid under a bridge near her home to avoid the rain. She was still very cold, very scared, and very alone. Her dear master, the only soul she had ever trusted, had betrayed her. But she couldn't blame him for it. He had no way of comprehending what had happened, had no viable reason to believe her story. He really felt his dog was loose in the woods again, and his determination to find her only proved that he did care for her. Natasha buried her nose in the sleeve of her shirt—his shirt—hoping to find comfort in her owner's scent. But her sense of smell had changed with the rest of her. Natasha peered out from under the bridge into the pitch-black woods beyond, and thought of the huge, black wolf she had encountered during her last journey into the forest. She pulled her legs tighter to her body, bracing herself from the elements outside and the fears inside. Her master did still love her, she repeated to herself. But that evening, hiding under the bridge listening to the frightful, eerie sounds of the dark woods, and fearing the return of the great beast, that thought held little comfort for her.

●　　　●　　　●

David Wagner was still thinking of the pretty woman with the dark eyes the next morning when he stepped into his back yard. To his joy and surprise, Natasha had returned sometime during the night. She bounded from her doghouse, barking and apparently famished. It wasn't until David knelt to pet her that he saw the blue fabric inside the doghouse.

David crawled forward and reached into the house. His hand closed around the material and pulled it from the house. Natasha sat at his side, eagerly awaiting her morning meal.

"I don't believe this," David mumbled.

He reached again into the house and pulled out the remaining garments: a gray sweatshirt, an old fleece-lined ski jacket, and a pair of running shoes.

The same clothes he had given the woman to wear the night before.

David thought again of the woman he had last seen walking north on highway 92. She was indeed very beautiful, a little mysterious, somewhat sad. Now, David thought, he might have to add dangerous to that list.

·　　　·　　　·

Sheriff Barnes sat the phone back on its hook and looked at his deputies. His face was grim.

"Another one?" asked Smitty.

"Afraid so."

"Where this time? Blaylock again?"

The sheriff shook his head. "Farther up north. Zeke's place. Two head this time."

"Jesus," Deputy Mason muttered. "He find remains of both?"

"Ayuh. Both of 'em half-eaten. Smitty, you and Mason go check it out."

"What do we tell him?"

"We won't tell him anything," Smitty told his partner.

"Sheriff?" Mason tapped his knuckle on the Sheriff's desk.

"I don't know, Mason," Barnes said, agitated. "Tell him we're callin' in an expert. Tell him you'll take pictures, measurements of any tracks. Tell him anything, I don't care."

Smitty grabbed Mason's elbow and pushed the younger deputy to the front door. Sheriff Barnes watched the deputies through the window as they hopped into the squad car. He sighed and glanced at the half-eaten jelly roll lying on his desk.

"Jesus, I'm getting tired of this shit," he mumbled.

This morning's news represented the third piece of hard evidence that something was killing and eating livestock in Potters. Sixteen animals had disappeared in the last four months. The farmers were demanding an answer, and Sheriff Barnes didn't have one. He supposed he would have to start setting traps, develop some type of grid system mapping the attack sites in hopes of discovering a pattern, or maybe even stake out some of the more recent crime scenes. But that would be difficult to do, at least during the upcoming weeks. Deputy Stoner was going on vacation in less than two months. Stoner was the best deputy the sheriff had, and Barnes wanted this mess resolved before he left. Smitty was dependable, but Mason was still wet behind the ears. Johnson, the night dispatcher, was good for just that: answering the phones at night.

Sheriff Barnes picked up the file that lay under the pastry and thought of David Wagner. He had only met Wagner a few times in town, mostly at the feed store where he bought food for his dog. Barnes opened the file and reviewed the report Stoner had filled out.

Like it or not, Sheriff Barnes was going to have to pay David Wagner a visit.

•   •   •

David was not surprised to find Natasha gone when he went to feed her Thursday evening. The bulb from the covered patio offered little light, but David could see that the collar had been slipped from her neck again. David knelt to inspect the collar and chain. The rain had stopped early Wednesday morning, but the ground was still muddy around Natasha's house. David studied the many paw prints his dog had made throughout the day, not knowing exactly what he was searching for.

But he knew when he saw it. Human footprints. Bare. Small. Like those of a woman.

David leapt from his crouching position and ran back inside the covered porch. He had placed the clothes he had found in Natasha's doghouse on a folding chair near the patio table. They were gone.

"That does it," David said under his breath. "I'm going to the police."

•　　　•　　　•

Natasha could see the single light burning in the window of the small trailer, and she knew someone must be there. She pulled the ski jacket tighter to her body. The night was clear, but very cold. The highway behind her was silent and deserted.

Natasha made up her mind and started for the trailer. It was set back into the sparse woods several hundred feet. The yard was littered with junk. *Tire. Bicycle. Box spring.* The words did not bother her much anymore.

Natasha approached the trailer. She could see movement inside. A set of unstable wooden stairs led to a small metal door.

Natasha scanned her surroundings again. *Wash tub. Clothesline. Lawnmower.*

The door swung open, banging against the side of the trailer. "Who's out there?" a voice shouted.

A small, elderly man stood in the doorway, dressed in an undershirt and gray trousers with suspenders. The man seemed familiar to Natasha, but it was not her master. David's face was the only one she could truly remember well.

The man finally saw Natasha standing in the yard past the remnants of a rusted table saw. He squinted his eyes, trying to see in the scant light.

"Who are you? What do you want?"

Many thoughts, many responses sped through Natasha's mind. "I'm lost," she finally said. "My car broke down about a mile up the road." She stepped forward into the light. "My name is Natasha."

The old man eyed her suspiciously. Was he going to be friendly? Natasha wondered. Was he ogling her as if he liked her, like he thought she was pretty? She had no idea.

"Natasha, huh?" said the old man. "You need to use the phone?"

Phone, Natasha thought. I know what that is.

"I ... don't have anyone to call," she said.

The man nodded. "Well, garage'll be closed now, anyway. C'mon in. My name's Coogan."

Coogan. She knew that name. She had heard David say it before. Just like she had heard the deputy's name. This Coogan was familiar to her.

"Well, c'mon girl. It's cold out there. Get yerself on in here."

Natasha stepped onto the rickety stairs, balancing herself, and stepped into the cramped trailer. The air was smoky and smelled of mildew. The inside of the trailer appeared pretty much as the yard did. Piles and piles of useless stuff. And pinecones.

"Pinecone," Natasha said as she sat at the kitchen table.

"Pretty, isn't it?" Coogan said. "I collect them. Not for any reason, just 'cause they're pretty. I shouldn't pick up so many, but it just seems like each one I find is a little better than the last one. I 'spect I have a few thousand laying around here. Inside and out in the yard."

"I know you," said Natasha, her eyes bright. "I know who you are."

Coogan frowned slightly. "I suppose you've heard all kinds of things about me in town."

"No, I know you from the other day," she said. "When you found ..." Natasha stopped mid-sentence.

"When I found what?" Natasha said nothing. "I haven't seen you before. Are you new in town?"

"Yes," she said. "No ... I'm not sure anymore."

"Pardon me?"

Natasha shook her head. She remembered Coogan now. Something from her animal side had finally clawed its way to the surface and into her human rationale and identified the man. Was it the smell? she wondered. She didn't think so. The only thing she could smell was cigar smoke and mildew. *Cigar smoke and mildew.* But the man was Coogan. He had found her last month; he had started to take her home when David showed up. He had visited her. She enjoyed his scent. Natasha smiled. Coogan was a human she could trust. She knew that.

"Would you like something to drink?" he asked.

"Water, please," Natasha answered.

Coogan stood and moved over to the kitchen sink. He rinsed a small glass and filled it with water. "You never really answered my question," he said, reaching into the freezer for ice. "Are you from around here?"

"Will you believe me if I tell you?" she asked.

"'Course I would. Why wouldn't I? Did you believe my story about the pinecones?"

Natasha nodded, though she didn't know what the pinecones had to do with anything.

"Then I'll believe you," said Coogan. "Got no reason not to."

"We've already met. I'm Natasha."

The old man appeared puzzled. He handed Natasha the water and looked into her eyes. "I know that. You already told me your name."

"No," she said, taking the water. Coogan noticed her fingers shaking as she gripped the glass; the ice cubes clinked against the sides. "Before tonight. We met before tonight."

Natasha could sense Coogan's confusion, and she was aware of how foolish she was sounding. And she hadn't even gotten to the good part yet.

"I was a little ... different the last time we met," she explained.

"You were a child," Coogan guessed. "I knew you when you were a kid. Is that it?"

Natasha took Coogan's weathered hands in hers and patted them. Coogan's words were of confusion and ignorance, but Natasha read in his eyes an air of understanding. His blue eyes sparkled.

"I was a dog the last time you saw me," she said.

"'Zat a fact?" Again, his eyes exuded a sense of understanding.

Undaunted, Natasha continued. "You found me on the highway, and you started to take me home. My owner came along and took me home." Natasha waited for Coogan to start laughing, but he didn't. "Last night and tonight, I changed from a dog into a human. David didn't believe me last night. He gave me these clothes and told me to leave. I stayed under a bridge last night. Tonight, I changed again. I found the same clothes. I left before my owner came out to feed me. And I came here. I don't know why, and I don't know how I found you. I wasn't looking for you, but I wound up here."

Natasha stopped and peered into Coogan's azure eyes, so bright and clear for a man so old. There was a long space of silence between them. Finally, Coogan smiled and squeezed Natasha's hands.

"I'll sleep on the couch here, and you can sleep down the hall in my bed. It's small, and it probably smells like cigars, but it's comfortable."

"Do you believe me?" asked Natasha.

"Of course I do," Coogan said. "Why would you lie about this?"

"You're just humoring me."

"Well, you can think what you want," Coogan said.

A tear formed in Natasha's eye. "You do believe me. Then why doesn't David believe me?"

"He just doesn't know," said Coogan. His voice was soft and soothing. "You can't blame him, Natasha. He has no way of knowing."

"Neither do you. But you believe me."

Coogan stood up and reached for a small pot of warm milk on the stove. "I believe you, Natasha." He poured Natasha a cup. "Why don't you take a small sip of this. It's not too warm, but it'll calm your nerves. Help you sleep."

Natasha took a sip of the sweet milk. It tasted good.

"It'll do you good. Trust me."

Natasha stood up. "I do trust you, Coogan. You're the only one I can trust, I think."

•   •   •

Jackie Coogan awoke the next morning as the bright rays of the sun began to filter though the ancient venetian blinds in the trailer's front window. He rolled over, coughed, and rubbed his sleepy eyes.

Coogan swallowed and grimaced. The events of the previous night seemed almost dreamlike, but he knew they were real. Coogan got up and slipped on his shoes. He paused to turn a burner on under a pot of water, then shuffled past the round kitchen table and into his bedroom.

He was not the least bit surprised to see the wolf sitting on his bed.

5

J ACKIE COOGAN HAD LIVED a hard, tough life. He'd lost loves, seen loved ones die, watched friends come and go, won battles and lost wars. He'd lived a lifetime, probably more than his rightful lot of one, during his many years. The years had come and gone with no hurrahs, no parades, no birthday parties and celebrations for so long, he'd stopped counting them long ago. He really didn't know how old he was, couldn't remember what year he was born. He'd traveled a lot but always managed to stay close to his home in the rural Northeast.

As a younger man, he believed in a lot of things, love being not the weakest belief on the list. He had believed in ghosts, in Bigfoot, in UFOs, all at some point in his life; he remembered that much. No one had ever proven that such things didn't exist, so why assume they don't? But that was the thinking of a clearer, crisper mind not cluttered by years of disappointment and tragedy.

Jackie Coogan stopped believing in lycanthropes and werewolves a long time ago. But that foolishness ended the night a dark-haired, brown-eyed woman came knocking on his trailer door.

Coogan leaned forward and ruffled the soft, bushy hair along the dog's back. She peered up from the bowl of milk he had poured for her and wagged her tail.

"Glory be, child," Coogan muttered. "Where did you come from?"

Natasha sat on her haunches in front of Coogan and laid her ears down happily. Coogan scratched her ears for a moment, then leaned back on the sofa. He would have to tell David Wagner what he had seen, and that would not be easy. It was obvious Wagner didn't believe Natasha's story, and why should he? He was just an innocent person, now caught up in the dangerous game of lycanthropy. An innocent, but more than likely stubborn person. Coogan knew he couldn't just tell David Wagner the truth: he would have to show him.

Coogan got up and went into his bedroom. He found the clothes Natasha had worn lying on the floor. Natasha followed at his heels. Coogan picked up one of his sacks and stuffed the clothes inside. On top of the clothes, he poured a small bucket of pinecones.

"Are you ready to go home, girl?"

Natasha barked eagerly, and she and Coogan headed out the door.

•   •   •

About halfway to David Wagner's house, Coogan began to wonder if the clothes would be enough evidence to convince Wagner of Natasha's predicament. The man had already ignored a lot of evidence, and he would probably create a logical explanation for the clothes as well. This Wagner was a scientific thinker, and that type was prone to ignoring proof.

Coogan glanced over his shoulder at Natasha. She followed closely behind, her nose to the ground. Coogan looked back up in time to see the deputy cruiser coming over the hill toward them.

Coogan squinted to see through the driver's window. Only one person, and it wasn't Sheriff Barnes.

Stoner.

Coogan tensed as the car began to pull over to the side of the road, and Natasha seemed to sense something was wrong as well. She lifted her head, ears pointed skyward and began to pace and whine. The car door opened, and the large deputy stepped out.

"Morning, Coogan," he said, adjusting his sunglasses.

Coogan stood still. "Deputy."

Stoner pointed at Natasha. "Wagner's dog?"

Coogan nodded. Natasha moved behind Coogan's legs and started to snarl uneasily.

"I understand you found her the last time. I wonder why it is that you always seem to happen across her?"

"She ... she likes me," said Coogan. "She sees me out here, she comes to me. We're usually out at the same time o' day."

"Wonder why she's always running off?" Stoner pondered. His words seemed more like a cross-examination than a question. "Why is she always so anxious to get away?"

Coogan shrugged his scrawny shoulders. "Dogs run off for lots of reasons. Maybe she's in heat."

"There's been more cattle lost the last two nights. One last night, two the night before out at old man Zeke's."

"She didn't do it, Deputy," Coogan said.

"I used to believe that, old timer. But the facts are starting to stack up against her. She just happens to be running loose every night some cattle come up missing."

"The dog didn't do it."

"I'm running out of ideas." Stoner folded his arms across his broad chest.

"Maybe you ain't checked out everybody," said Coogan.

Stoner's expression shifted. "What do you mean by that?"

Just shut your smart mouth, Jackie, Coogan scolded himself. *Just shut up and maybe he'll go on about his business.* "Rival farmers."

Stoner laughed. "That's about the stupidest idea I've heard yet, Coogan. I'll have to add that to the list. Step aside."

Stoner squatted to the ground and held his hand out to Natasha. She moved back behind the old man's legs, still growling softly. "You want to go home and see your master, Natasha?"

"I'll take her home," offered Coogan.

"Shut up, Coogan."

"She won't go with you."

Stoner snapped his fingers repeatedly and called Natasha soothingly. He tapped the ground with his other hand. Coogan watched as Natasha stood staring at the deputy. The hackles on her neck began to lay back down, and her growls slowly diminished.

Stoner sat still, close to the ground, his right hand held steadily in front of him.

I can't let him take her, Coogan thought. I can't.

Finally, Stoner stood up and walked back to the squad car. He opened the back door and whistled once, sharply. Natasha moved gingerly to the car and stepped in.

"Damn it," Coogan said under his breath.

"I'll take it from here, Mr. Coogan," said the deputy, a wide grin crossing his face. "Oh, before I leave. Anything in the bags I should know about?"

Coogan thought of the clothes Natasha had worn, the clothes he had planned on using to convince David. Coogan shook his head. "No, just the usual."

Stoner nodded and shut the door. The car roared to life, did a screeching U-turn in the road, and headed back down the highway.

Coogan didn't know where Stoner was taking the dog. He hoped it was back to Wagner's house.

•   •   •

David glanced at the speedometer as he sped toward the sheriff's office. Seventy-five. He could easily get a ticket if Deputy Mason was out patrolling, or worse, one bump would send the top-heavy Jeep flying. But David really didn't care.

Natasha had not come back. The missing clothes and human footprints in his backyard could mean only one thing. For some reason, that crazy naked lady was sneaking into his yard at night and stealing Natasha. She had apparently brought Natasha back the night before, and for some reason, stripped naked again and left the clothes there for the next night. The woman obviously had a thing for nudity. Under different circumstances, that might be an appealing trait, but now, it just made the lady seem that much weirder.

But she hadn't returned Natasha this morning, not that it would've made any difference. David had made up his mind to talk to Sheriff Barnes about the mysterious newcomer to Potters. Hell, she might even have something to do with the disappearing livestock. That would make the cops happy. Maybe her gang was killing cattle, and they wanted Natasha as a scapegoat. Maybe she was from a flying saucer that swoops down and mutilates cattle. Maybe she was a part of some strange race of vampires that thrived on cattle blood. Haitian voodoo vampires from hell.

Stop it! David shouted to himself. He reached down and turned on the radio. A news report announced that three cattle had been killed over the last two nights.

"Great," David sighed.

David pulled the Jeep into the Potters Sheriff's Office parking lot and hopped out. The morning air was chilly, and he hadn't bothered to throw on a jacket. David took two more steps before breaking into a full sprint to escape the cold.

David stepped inside, his breathing slightly labored. Johnson, the night dispatcher, was just leaving.

"Cold out this morning," Johnson said.

David smiled but otherwise ignored the remark. He scanned the building quickly. He could see Deputy Smitty down the hall that led to the four cells, apparently doing some type of routine morning inspections. David doubted any of the cells were occupied. Deputy Mason was at a small table behind the counter, pouring himself a cup of black coffee.

"Mr. Wagner," a voice called. "I was just about to give you a call."

David looked up to see the hefty Sheriff Barnes stepping out of his office. The sheriff had a personable visage that always seemed to set a person at ease. He reminded David of Sheriff Taylor in Mayberry, though the real and fictional sheriff had no similar characteristics other than personality. Sheriff Barnes was the only Potters law enforcement officer that David would feel comfortable with discussing his female visitor.

"Sheriff Barnes," David started. "I need to speak with you."

David moved to the end of the counter and lifted the partition. He started to move toward the sheriff when he saw the dog sitting on the floor next to one of the desks.

"Natasha!" David exclaimed. "There you are! I was so worried about you."

"She got loose again last night, apparently," said the sheriff.

"I'm afraid so," answered David, dropping to his knees. He started to inspect Natasha. He ran his hands along her sides and belly, checking for any wounds she might have incurred during the night. There were none, but something struck David as peculiar. There was no mud on

Natasha, not even on her feet. It had rained as hard the first night she escaped as it had earlier in the week, and Natasha had been extremely dirty when David had found her walking with Coogan. He could only assume that the woman had cleaned Natasha before releasing her. "I have plans to build a fence soon. That should solve the problem."

"Uh, Mr. Wagner," Sheriff Barnes began. "I hate to bring this up right now, but we had some more cattle destroyed the last few nights."

"Yeah, I heard it on the radio on the way in."

"I've been delaying this, not wanting to jump to conclusions, but I'm getting a lot of pressure from the community." Sheriff Barnes put his hands on his hips. "I'm not saying anything is certain, but it is a fact that your dog was loose every night we've had livestock come up missing."

"Actually," David began, "that's not true. Yes, for the last two months, there have been some coincidences, but we had cattle disappearing for several months before Natasha ever got loose."

The sheriff raised his eyebrows. "You have a point there. Uh, you're sure she hadn't been loose before?"

"Yes," David said. "September 23rd, that's the first time she got loose."

Sheriff Barnes rubbed his cheeks and sighed. "Well, we're going to have to figure out something. She needs to be restrained by more than just a chain."

David started to mention the woman but decided it wasn't the right time. "Sheriff Barnes, where did you find Natasha?"

"He didn't," a booming voice said from behind David. "I did."

David recognized the voice before he turned around. It was Deputy Stoner. The big man strode slowly over to where David and the sheriff stood, his heavy boots clicking on the linoleum floor.

"You ... found her?" asked David. His voice squeaked.

Stoner nodded and took a sip of his coffee. "She was asleep on my front porch when I left for work this morning."

David laughed weakly. "You're kidding."

"He brought the dog in with him this morning," the sheriff confirmed.

"And in view of what happened the last two nights, I figured it best to bring her here for observation. Or at least until you could tell us where she was last night," added Stoner.

"I told you, I don't know where she was last night. She got loose from her chain." David had no intention of mentioning the woman in Stoner's presence.

"And how are you able to keep her in here with strang—" David started. He suddenly looked down at Natasha. She sat there quietly, panting weakly. Natasha stared ahead in one direction, her eyes fixed in a blank stare. David remembered how she had initially reacted to Stoner, how she acted around everyone she didn't know, except for Coogan.

"What did you do to her?" David said to Stoner.

"What are you saying?" Stoner stepped closer to David.

"You know damn good and well what I'm saying, Stoner. She damn near ripped your head off that night at my house, and now look at her. Did you tranquilize her or something?"

Sheriff Barnes looked at his deputy. Stoner turned his attention from the sheriff back to David. "No, I didn't tranquilize her. I didn't do anything to her. This is how she was behaving when she woke up."

For a moment, David thought of what the strange woman might have done. She could've drugged Natasha, maybe slipped something in a piece of meat and fed it to her. How else could she have approached Natasha?

"Listen, Mr. Wagner, if my deputy says he didn't do anything to your animal, I believe him. Maybe she's just exhausted from romping around all night. Maybe she's even a little sick. She could've picked up something in the woods. You might even consider a trip to the vet."

David rubbed the top of Natasha's head. She peered up at him, finally showing some recognition, but her eyes were listless. "We just went to the vet a few days ago. Everything was fine. Well, she seems to be alright. Just a little groggy." David extended his hand to Stoner, wincing when the deputy squeezed. "Thanks for taking care of her. I'll get her home now."

"Not so fast," Stoner said.

"Deputy Stoner has an idea you may want to hear," Barnes said. "It may help to clear Natasha as a suspect in the cattle thing."

"I have a fenced-in backyard—"

"Absolutely not," David said immediately.

"We could put her there for a while. Keep her closed in. Then, if any more cattle are lost, we'll know she didn't do it."

"I said no."

"Mr. Wagner," the sheriff said. "I think that's a pretty good idea, and it will help us a lot to know that we can scratch her off the list of suspects. Good for your piece of mind, too."

"Sheriff Barnes, I appreciate the offer, but you don't understand. Natasha isn't like a normal dog. Wolf-hybrids need special care. They're raised to believe their owner is the head of their pack. They simply won't respond to other keepers and, quite frankly, they can be dangerous."

"She won't be in contact with anyone but Deputy Stoner."

"No, thank you. I'll keep her in the house from now on if I have to."

Sheriff Barnes shrugged. "Well, we can't make you do it. All right, you can take her home now if you want."

"Thank you," said David.

David gripped the homemade rope leash around Natasha's neck and pulled her forward. She responded slowly but followed David.

Stoner stopped in front of David. "You're going to have a lot of explaining to do if she gets out again." The big deputy strolled out of the building; the door slammed shut behind him. David waited until he heard the squad car leaving the parking lot.

"Sheriff Barnes, I don't want to sound uncooperative, but I really do think it's a bad idea."

Barnes patted David on the shoulder. "It's okay, son. I understand. I don't have a lot of experience with hybrids."

"Oh, one other thing, sheriff. I almost forgot the reason I came here." David fidgeted in front of the officer. "This is going to come from nowhere. But the night before last when I noticed Natasha was gone, I found a woman in her doghouse."

"A woman?" asked the sheriff, surprised.

"Yeah. Natasha's collar was still attached to the chain. I was thinking that this woman must've let Natasha go so she could get in the house. You remember, it was raining pretty hard that night."

"Ayuh. Did this woman say anything?"

"Well, I let her come in out of the rain, and I gave her some clothes, and then—"

"Gave her some clothes?" said the sheriff. Deputy Mason glanced up from his paperwork. "You mean this woman was nude?"

"Yeah, I know it sounds crazy, but it happened. She tried to tell me that she was Natasha." Sheriff Barnes rolled his eyes. "I know, I know, but that's what she said. She said that she was my dog and that she turned human."

"What?" asked Mason. "Like a werewolf?"

Barnes raised his hand for the deputy to be quiet. "So, what did you say to that?"

"I told her to leave, and then I went out searching for Natasha. But the strange thing is, the next morning, Natasha was back in her house—"

"Natasha the dog."

"Of course. Anyway, Natasha had come back, but the clothes that I gave to this lady to wear were in the doghouse, too. You see what I mean?"

Sheriff Barnes rubbed his chin. "Hmmmm. Had you ever seen this woman before?"

"No."

"Can you give me a description?"

"Dark hair. Brown Eyes. About 5'8". Slim, very attractive. But I still haven't told you everything. I laid those clothes inside my covered porch, and the next night when I went to feed Natasha, she was gone and so were the clothes."

Sheriff Barnes said nothing. He glanced momentarily at Deputy Smitty. "So, what do you want us to do?"

"What do I want you to do?" David asked, shocked. "I want you to find this woman. She's obviously the one that's been letting Natasha loose, and I'm afraid she might be dangerous."

"Dangerous to you or to the dog?"

"I don't know ... just dangerous."

"Mr. Wagner, don't you think if there was a naked woman walking up and down highway 92 leading your dog around, we'd have heard about it by now?"

"What are you griping about anyway?" said Mason. "I wish I could find naked women in my backyard. What's your secret?"

"Mason!" the sheriff snapped.

Mason quickly returned his attention to some okay paperwork on his desk. Sheriff Barnes met David's gaze. "Uh, look, Mr. Wagner. I'll write down the description you gave, and we'll ... we'll keep our eyes open, okay?"

"I don't trust this woman, Sheriff. She's obviously snooping around my house at night, and I don't like that."

"Well, we'll drive by your house several times a day. We'll be watching for her."

"Thanks, Sheriff. I know it's crazy. I felt really stupid telling you."

"There's some crazy things going on around here, Mr. Wagner. Maybe crazy answers are what we need."

David led Natasha out of the sheriff's office. She looked around once they had stepped outside, a sign that her normal demeanor was returning. By the time David had pulled the Jeep back out onto highway 92, Natasha was bouncing happily around in the back seat.

•   •   •

David untied the homemade rope from Natasha's neck and tossed it into the garbage can. He didn't want anything of Stoner's in his possession. David couldn't believe Stoner's nerve, wanting to keep his dog at his house. Natasha would rip his throat out if he even tried it.

But something was bothering David. Why had Natasha been so passive inside the sheriff's office? Why had she not reacted to Stoner's presence the way she did when he came over that night to question David? It was obvious that Natasha didn't like him for some reason. Maybe he was afraid of dogs, and Natasha sensed that.

David found himself wishing that he had mentioned the woman in Stoner's presence. This woman was taking Natasha from his yard, and now, Stoner apparently had the same thing in mind. Could it be that this woman knew Stoner? Could it be that they were part of some plan? Maybe Stoner was responsible somehow for the disappearing cattle.

No, David thought. That's stupid. Stoner may be a rough SOB, but I'm sure even he likes his meat cooked somewhat.

David looked down at Natasha. She jumped up and rested her feet on David's shoulders and licked his face.

"Are you hungry?" David asked. "Is that what you're trying to tell me?"

Natasha barked her answer and dropped down to all-fours. David opened the cupboard and grabbed a can of Pedigree.

"Your bowl's still outside," he said, more to himself than to Natasha.

David opened the back door and stepped into the covered patio. The early morning sun shone through the hardware cloth that surrounded the porch. David had almost made it to the screen door when he stopped.

The clothes were lying on the chair.

6

D AVID SAT IN THE EARLY MORNING darkness of the family
room, lost in deep thought as the four walls around him
gradually grew brighter with the rising sun. Life was slowly beginning
to regain some semblance of normalcy. He had finished and
submitted several articles in the last month and sold another. The
locals hadn't lost any more cattle. Natasha hadn't managed to escape
in three weeks. The mystery woman hadn't shown up anymore, and
the clothes were still lying on the chair out back. Sheriff Barnes hadn't
pursued his theory of Natasha's possible involvement in the livestock
affair, and Deputy Stoner hadn't pushed any further on his idea of
keeping Natasha in his own yard.

David yawned and pushed the plush recliner back. He did some
of his best thinking here. Most of his ideas were written in his head,
leaning back in the recliner listening to Crosby, Stills, Nash & Young
long before he sat down in front of the computer monitor. Something
about relaxing in the chair got his creative juices flowing, but it also
got his sometimes overactive imagination started.

David thought of the woman he had found naked and shivering in
Natasha's doghouse that night. Time had slowly begun to distort or

push away all illogical explanations for that strange incident. He had only seen the woman that one night and, apparently, according to the sheriff's office, no one else in town had ever reported seeing her. David had convinced himself that the woman had let Natasha go in order to use her home as a shelter. That made sense, but what about the other time? Those small footprints had to belong to her. If she was coming back, and if she was releasing Natasha for whatever reasons, why did she take or leave the clothing each time? David didn't know why he had left the clothes on the back porch where he had found them the morning he brought Natasha back from the police station. Did something inside of him hope for the woman to return? Was that it?

A day hadn't passed since the incident that the woman hadn't crossed David's mind in some capacity. Sometimes it was the attraction; most of the time, it was the anger over her transgressions, but her face would always form in his mind as vividly as if she were standing in front of him. David normally forgot a woman's face soon after seeing her last, but now, this woman's face was easier for him to visualize than that of his own ex-wife.

The woman's physical beauty was evident enough, but David had sensed so much in her eyes, a deep feeling of recognition, as if he knew her from somewhere. He supposed something in her eyes reminded him of Mindy, although she had blue eyes, and this woman brown. David found himself wishing he knew the woman's name. *You do*, he told himself. She said her name was Natasha. Obviously, she had read the name on Natasha's tags.

David rubbed his eyes and sighed. "You need to get out and start dating again," he said aloud. "No, better yet, you need to forget about women all together."

Just then, David heard the only female in his life barking in the back yard. It wasn't a frightened bark; it was her happy bark. Must've seen a squirrel, David thought.

He pushed the recliner forward and wandered into the kitchen. David could now hear another voice, a human voice, over Natasha's joyous antics. It sounded like Coogan.

David opened the back door and stepped out under the covered patio. It was Coogan. David could see him and Natasha through the screen material. Coogan must've heard the door closing; he turned and peered into the patio.

"Morning, Mr. Wagner," he called before David had even stepped out into the yard.

"Coogan," David said, glancing at the woman's clothing in the chair. "How are you?"

"Oh, fine. Fine." He knocked Natasha's front legs back to the ground.

Natasha looked at David and barked once in his direction before turning her attention back to the elderly man. David stood silently and watched Natasha leap about, happily playing with Coogan. It struck David with wonder the way Natasha had taken to the man so readily. Her display of affection made David smile, but it also made him a little jealous to see Natasha accept someone else.

"I'm going to have some coffee, Coogan. Care to join me?"

Coogan grabbed Natasha by the neck and pushed her backward. She caught herself and immediately bolted back to Coogan. "Sure."

• • •

David and Coogan sat at the wrought-iron table under the covered porch. The two men sipped hot coffee, as Natasha lay dozing at Coogan's feet.

"So," David said, breaking the silence, "what's your life story, Coogan?"

Coogan sat his cup down on the table and leaned back in the chair. "It's a long story, so long that I don't remember a lot of it."

"You lived in Potters long?"

"Twenty-seven years," said the older man.

"Wow. You must've seen a lot."

Coogan snickered. "Town hasn't changed a bit."

"Did you fight in WWII?" David asked.

"Yeah. I spent two years in Germany. Survived the Battle of the Bulge." He looked away toward the distant tree line. "That wasn't a fun time in my life."

"Sorry. My natural instinct as a writer." Coogan shrugged. "Where were you born? Where'd you grow up?"

"Born in New York. My parents moved here and there along the Northeastern coast. My father was a salesman. We moved a lot."

David spied the clothes still lying in the vacant chair. "Coogan, you're up and down the highway a lot."

"Yeah."

"You ever seen a woman? Dark hair, pretty?"

Coogan glanced up from his coffee and said, "Nope."

David scratched his head and grinned. "Craziest thing. I found this woman in Natasha's doghouse a few weeks back, and she claimed that she was some kind of monster. A werewolf, to be exact."

"A werewolf? She told you that?"

"Well, not in so many words. But she did say that she was Natasha and that she had turned into a person."

"And you didn't believe her?"

"Of course I didn't believe her. She scared me. That was one strange lady. And you haven't seen her?"

Coogan lifted the cup to his lips. "Can't say that I have."

"What worries me is that I think she keeps coming back to my house and taking Natasha." David reached into the chair and picked up the clothes. "You see these clothes? I gave these to her that night, and now, they keep showing up and disappearing every time Natasha comes up missing."

"What would she want with your dog?"

"Hell, I don't know. I went to the police one morning to file a complaint against her. They acted like I was insane. But I did find Natasha there."

"You found your dog?"

"Yeah, Natasha," said David. "Deputy Stoner brought her in. Said he found her sleeping on his porch."

Coogan sat up, knocking the coffee cup over and spilling the liquid to the floor. "Stoner? Stoner had her at the station?"

David scooted his chair back to avoid the dripping beverage and dropped a dishrag over the spill. "Yeah, he brought her in that morning."

"Stoner didn't find your dog at his house. He took her from me that morning."

"From you?"

"Yeah, I ... I found her in ... my yard that morning, you know, snooping around. I started to bring her back to you, when he drove up. I didn't want to let him have her, but ... there wasn't much I could do about it."

"I didn't buy his story about finding her on his porch. Natasha hates him; she's frightened of that man. I couldn't understand why she was so relaxed around him. And then he had this foolish idea about keeping her—"

"You listen to me, boy," Coogan interrupted, speaking sternly. "Whatever Stoner wants to do, do not let him do it. You don't let him near your dog."

"Well, I wasn't planning on it. I told him no."

"And you keep on tellin' him no, David. That Stoner is a bad seed. I've known him for a long time, and he's nothing but trouble."

David fidgeted in the chair. The idea of someone else having a bad opinion of Deputy Stoner made him nervous. "Why, what's he done? I mean, I don't like the guy either, but is he ... dangerous?"

Coogan glanced down at Natasha. "Oh ... I wouldn't call him dangerous exactly. Unpredictable may be a better word. But rest assured, if he decides he wants something, he'll stop at nothing to get it."

"And he wants Natasha," David said. "But why? Why would he suddenly want my dog?"

"She's a remarkable animal, Mr. Wagner. Maybe more so than you realize."

"Well, she's highly intelligent. That's her wolfen instinct. Say, you don't suppose Stoner knows this woman? Do you think they're partners or something?"

"Apparently, you're the only one who's ever seen her."

"Hmmmm. It would seem that way, wouldn't it?"

"Just take care of your pet, David," Coogan said. "Take extra care of her. I'm gonna be going now, but you do what I say. Don't let her outta your sight. Sorry about the coffee."

"Don't worry about that. I'll clean it up."

Natasha had stirred from her sleep. She stood up and began circling Coogan's legs, whimpering.

"I've never seen her take to anyone like she has you."

"Animals like me," Coogan said with a smile.

•   •   •

Deputy Stoner grabbed the file marked "Wagner, David" and sat down at his desk. Deputies Smith and Mason busied themselves with last-minute preparations for their morning patrols. Stoner reached for his steaming black coffee and opened the file.

"Whose turn was it to get donuts this morning?" Mason asked.

"Yours," came a chorus of replies.

"Oh ... I guess I forgot," said the deputy.

Stoner thumbed through the sheets inside the manilla file. There weren't many. He passed over the copy of the report he had made the night he questioned Wagner and his report pertaining to the morning he brought Natasha to the station. But those papers were not what he was seeking. Something Mason had said earlier ...

Stoner pulled the sheet from the rest of the file. It was an informal report written on a sheet from a loose-leaf notebook in Sheriff Barnes' writing.

"Mason," Stoner said, without looking up, "were you here the morning Wagner came and got his dog?"

"Yeah," Mason answered. He was checking his weapon.

"What happened after I left?"

"What do you mean, 'after you left'? When did you leave?"

"About the woman in this report." Stoner said angrily.

"Oh, that," the deputy said, laughing. "I wouldn't pay much attention to that."

"Tell me!"

Deputy Mason seemed surprised by Stoner's attitude, and Smitty peered around the corner. "He just said there was some woman snooping around his house, maybe letting the dog loose. It should all be in the file."

"I have the file," Stoner growled. "What was her name?"

"Natasha. Same as the dog."

"Natasha." Stoner nodded almost imperceptibly.

"Why? Do you think there's something to it?"

"Could be. It could be a lead anyway."

"Things have been pretty quiet," Mason said.

Deputy Smitty added, "It's about time for them to start up again. Happens about once a month. Last killings were three weeks ago."

Stoner continued to scan the report. There was not much information. A brief physical description, the woman's name, Wagner's complaint.

"Sheriff Barnes didn't think there was anything to it. He just scribbled the shit down on a piece of paper. Didn't even bother with a report. Maybe we ought to look for her. Wagner said she was a real babe. And she apparently likes to get 'nekkid'."

Stoner stood up and returned the file to the cabinet. The part concerning the clothes was of particular interest to Stoner. The appearance and disappearance of the clothing always coincided with the animal's escapes. Stoner turned from the cabinet and headed to the front door.

"Wouldn't mind getting 'nekkid' with her myself," Mason joked.

Deputy Stoner wheeled about suddenly and grabbed Mason, slamming him against the county map. His vice-like grip closed around Mason's neck, as the younger deputy wheezed and gasped for air. Smitty bolted to the other officers to break up the scuffle.

"I don't like the way you talk about women, Junior," Stoner said, his blue eyes cutting into Mason. "Better clean up your act."

"Devin," said Smitty, placing his hand tentatively on the large man's shoulder.

Stoner shoved Mason once more and stomped out the front door into the crisp morning. The two men stood silent as the door slammed shut behind Stoner.

"I'm glad Sheriff Barnes wasn't here to see that," Smitty said with a grimace.

"Jesus, what's got into him?" Mason rubbed his neck.

"You pissed him off, I guess." He didn't turn his eyes from the front window until he saw Deputy Stoner's cruiser merge onto the highway.

•　　•　　•

David pushed open the screen door, making one final check on Natasha before going to bed. She lay sleeping just outside of her house, and she raised her head at the sound of the opening door momentarily before letting it fall sleepily back to the earth. David stood quietly for a moment, still struggling with the idea of bringing Natasha inside. He didn't want her getting loose again. But she was an outdoor dog and often grew restless rather quickly when cooped up inside the house. He thought of letting her stay inside the patio, but she could easily burst through the screen door if she wanted.

Finally, David gently closed the screen and went back into the house. He would check on her through the night.

David headed back to his bedroom, still thinking of Coogan. Coogan didn't like Stoner any more than David did, and from the tone of his voice, he had run-ins with the burly deputy himself. David wanted to believe that Coogan's hostilities stemmed from various unpleasant, albeit normal, encounters with Stoner, possibly over vagrancy or loitering.

There you go again, Wagner. Thinking of Coogan the way the rest of the town does. David knew now that there was a side of Coogan that the locals did not know. No one had ever bothered to discover the man behind the sacks. Coogan was very old and very wise, and he knew something about Stoner. Something that he wasn't saying. Coogan's words kept haunting David.

Whatever Stoner wants to do, do not let him do it. Pretty stern stuff. Coogan's warning was more than a simple "don't speed around Deputy Stoner, he's a tough cop" kind of warning.

It sounded to David as if Coogan really did believe Deputy Stoner to be dangerous.

•   •   •

David had heard nothing during the night. Natasha usually woke him up at least once every night barking at squirrels, rabbits, raccoons, anything that might wander into the yard from the miles of forest surrounding the house. But she hadn't made a sound; not that he could hear anyway. But still, when he went out to check on her the next morning, she was gone.

David stood next to the dog collar, staring at the ground dumbfounded. Why hadn't he kept her inside last night? David's rational mind began to determine the cause of Natasha's latest disappearing act, when he thought of the woman. For a quick moment, David's thoughts brightened with the thought of the beautiful woman. But those happy thoughts dissipated when he spied the chain.

David bent over to inspect the ground around Natasha's doghouse. It had not rained in several days, but he thought the ground was still soft enough to show the prints of anyone who had been there during the night. There were many dog tracks, so compacted that he couldn't discern any one print. But one thing was certain; there were no human prints.

This puzzled David. She must've pulled free from the collar herself, he thought.

The clothes.

David turned and ran back onto the covered porch. The clothes were still lying on the chair in the same position that they had assumed for the last few weeks.

"Shit." He didn't like to curse, and it made him angry when he did so. "Shit," he said again.

David returned to Natasha's house and dropped to his knees. Perhaps the woman's prints were here, and they had just been tromped over by Natasha's constant wandering. David inspected the ground closely. Lots of dog tracks, but then, what did he expect? Nothing indicated anything other than Natasha's normal back-and-forth pacing from her house to the tree and back again. One solid print in a particularly soft area of earth. Many more spots where the earth had been trampled by—

Holy shit!

David stared down at the damp earth, his eyes not believing what they were seeing. How had he missed it before? He could see one track—a dog's print—at the edge of Natasha's house. There may have been others, but they must've been spoiled by the other tracks. David studied the track closer. It was huge, and obviously not Natasha's. A part of David's conversation with Stoner came back to him. He remembered the deputy measuring Natasha's prints. David couldn't remember the exact size, but it didn't take a genius to tell that this print was much larger than all the others.

"There must've been another dog here last night," David mumbled. "And what a dog."

But it didn't make sense. Natasha would've surely gone crazy barking if any animal had shown up during the night, especially another dog. David wasn't sure if Natasha had been in heat; she hadn't acted like it. But apparently, she had pulled free of her collar and followed this other animal.

Even though his pet was gone again, David felt a little relieved by this escape. At least the weirdo lady hadn't taken her this time. It was obvious that Natasha had just chased after another dog this time.

Considering all the other times, this was a jail break with which David could cope.

•   •   •

"Hello?" David said into the receiver.

He had just stepped in from the back yard, grabbed a leash and his coat, and was about to go searching for Natasha when the phone rang.

"Mr. Wagner," the voice said.

David's heart jumped. It was Stoner.

"Yes, Deputy," said David weakly. He hated the way he always sounded like such a wimp when he spoke with Stoner.

"I have your dog again."

Shit, David shouted in his head. "I … don't know what to say, deputy. I … thought about leaving her inside last night. I found other tracks around her house. Big tracks. Must've been one helluva dog."

"Uh-huh."

"Is she at the station or your house?"

"She's here with me. At my house."

Great, David thought. "I guess she was in heat. She just broke loose and followed that dog."

"I'm going to keep her here," Stoner said abruptly.

Don't let him do it, Coogan said in David's head.

"She is definitely in heat. She was whining and acting very restless."

"No," David said.

"Beg your pardon?"

"No, you're not keeping her there. I'm coming to get her. Where do you live?" David didn't relish the idea of going to Stoner's house, but he would have to.

There was a long pause at the other end. "Where do you live?"

"Pick her up at the station." Then the line went dead.

•　　•　　•

He's drugging her somehow, David thought. That's the only explanation.

David knelt in front of Natasha, looking into his dog's eyes. They were glazed and dopey, almost lifeless. She hadn't even responded to David when he walked into the sheriff's office. It was almost like looking at a mount in a taxidermist's shop.

"We're going to give it one more chance," Sheriff Barnes said.

"You son-of-a-bitch! What did you do to my dog?" David said angrily.

78

Stoner crossed his arms and peered at the sheriff before returning his stare to David. "Not very grateful, are you?"

"Now, gentlemen," said Barnes.

"C'mon, Sheriff Barnes!" David shouted. "This is not how Natasha acts! This is not how wolf-hybrids act! I could show you tapes, articles! She should be jumping at every one of your throats right now, for God's sake!"

"All the more reason why she should be restrained!" Stoner countered. "It's obvious that you don't know how to control this animal, and I do! She's come to my house twice now. She responds to me! I should keep her in my yard!"

"I've told you once and for all you're not keeping my dog at your house!" David did not let his stance waver.

"He's not taking your dog this time, Mr. Wagner," Barnes said. "But if she gets out one more time, then I'll have no choice but to take her into custody. We have children in this town, Mr. Wagner. We can't have a dangerous animal—"

"Dangerous, Sheriff? Really now. Look at her. She's so doped up she doesn't even recognize me."

"I have done nothing to that animal. I ought to slap you so hard—"

"Do it." David approached him. "Do it, and I'll throw a police brutality suit at you so fast—"

"Gentlemen, gentlemen," Sheriff Barnes said. He put a hand onto each man's shoulder and pushed them away from each other. "Mr. Wagner, just take your dog and go. Don't let her get out again, or Deputy Stoner will have my permission to take her into his own legal custody."

David grabbed the new homemade leash around Natasha's neck and pulled. She did not move. David placed his hand on her back and gently pushed. Natasha held her ground at first, but then she stood up. She still showed little sign of awareness.

David led Natasha slowly to the front door. He wished to be away from this place, away from Stoner, as quickly as possible.

"Wagner." Stoner called to him. "What did you pay for the animal? When you first got her, how much did she cost?"

"Four-hundred dollars." David was emotionless, worrying more about Natasha than anything Stoner would throw at him.

"I'll buy her from you," said the deputy.

David stared into Stoner's cold blue eyes, then to the sheriff and back to Stoner. "Go to hell."

7

NATASHA LAY UNDER THE BED in her owner's guest bedroom, watching the walls slowly grow darker and darker as the sun sank outside. She was afraid of the night, terrified of the pain that it brought. She had felt the movement in her body the two previous nights, when the moon shone almost to its fullest. Now, as the moon began to break free from the invisible barrier that held it under the distant hills, Natasha began to feel the odd sensations stirring deep within her body once again.

Natasha whimpered quietly, afraid to attract her master's attention. She could feel the bones in her legs, in her head and along her back, popping and stretching. But more frightening to Natasha than the physical sensations were the thoughts developing in her mind. She thought of her doghouse, of its warmth and comfort. She pictured in her mind the chain attached to her tree, the chain which, even though it restrained her, still said "home." Natasha dreamed of the woods, of the quiet distant sounds, the subtle aromas of all things unexplored. And then she thought of things unknown and foreign to her. Pictures formed in her animal mind: an old man, a trailer, piles of cast-away junk. Her owner, a man named David. A man who loved her but did not understand the changes that had befallen her. A building, white linoleum, men in uniform. A tall man with cruel blue eyes.

Natasha cried out as the pain gripped her every nerve. The air grew black and unforgiving around her, and Natasha succumbed to the night.

•   •   •

David awoke from a deep nap to the opening theme from Letterman. He knew it must be eleven-thirty, and he was upset with himself for dozing off for so long. He had every intention of finishing his article on the baseball and hockey strikes of 1994, until the sleep gremlins took him as theirs.

He yawned and thought of Natasha. She had slipped into the guest bedroom and scooted under the bed, and she seemed to have no intention of coming out.

He had decided to leave her inside the house until he could think of a more secure method of keeping her locked up. Sheriff Barnes' warning was stern and perfectly fair. He was a good man, and he had given David every opportunity to keep Stoner from taking Natasha. David would not let that happen.

He had called a local remodeler earlier to inquire about the installation of a fence, but the man said it would be three weeks before he could get to David. All the farmers were having additional fences installed for fear of losing more livestock, and he was backed up with work. David supposed he could do it himself, but he was never much of a handyman, and he wanted the fence done right. He would call one of the larger towns nearby in the morning.

David found himself wishing Coogan was there. He wanted to tell the older man about his most recent confrontation with Deputy Stoner. David couldn't believe the man had actually offered to purchase Natasha. She wasn't a used car or a head of cattle to be bartered. She was a pet, for God's sake. Why was the deputy so intent on owning Natasha? If he wanted a dog, he could get one easily enough. There were plenty of reputable wolf-hybrid breeders just across the Canadian border.

David pictured Stoner in his mind. Did Stoner really want Natasha, or did he just like to stir things up? Did he enjoy arguing or irritating the townspeople? An intimidation factor to keep the citizens in line? Maybe that was the only thing about the man that made him so unappealing to David. After all, how bad could Stoner be? He was a deputy in a small northeastern town. Where was the harm in that?

But there was something about Stoner. David knew it, and Coogan knew it as well. Hell, even Natasha knew it when she wasn't drugged. Maybe Coogan had some idea as to how Stoner was able to approach Natasha the way he did. Coogan himself was able to handle Natasha, but not like Stoner.

Then David heard a sharp cry coming from the back hallway of the house. It was Natasha.

She had begun acting strangely again the night he had last brought her home from the sheriff's office. David wished he'd had the vet check for drugs or poisons; perhaps whatever Stoner had given her was making Natasha ill.

David jumped up from his recliner and moved swiftly down the hall to the spare bedroom. He opened the door and turned on the light, illuminating the dark room. "Natasha? Are you okay? Ready to come out from under there now?"

David heard a weak snivel coming from under the bed, but Natasha did not answer. David frowned. He called out to her again, but the only response was another muted sob. It sounded almost like what he heard—

"No," whispered David. "No." He shook his head to clear his thoughts. "C'mon, Natasha. Come out from under that bed."

There was another cry, louder and sharper, and David felt his knees weaken. "N-N-Natasha ... please."

David could hear sobs choking back. It sounded like a kid trying to stop crying for fear of getting a spanking.

"Oh God," David said as he knelt to lift the bedspread.

It was her. David cried out and scrambled backward, his legs still kicking involuntarily in an attempt to flee the situation even when his progress was impeded by the closet doors. "No," he pleaded. "No, oh my God, no. This can't be."

David stared ahead, his eyes large. The edge of the blanket began to move, and David saw an arm—a human arm—push through. A shock of dark hair, a smooth bare back, and the woman rolled from under the bed. She sat on her knees in front of David.

"It's happening again," she said.

David cried out and turned his face to the door. This couldn't be happening, his mind cried out. This is just a dream. A very intense dream.

"David," said the woman, sniffling.

David forced himself to look at the woman. Her dark brown eyes, reddened by the sobs, stared into his soul; tears ran down her soft cheeks. Her tussled hair, as dark as the night sky, cascaded over her shoulders and over her breasts. David began to feel captivated by her beauty and, despite the perverse feeling, his gaze continued down across her body, momentarily studying the carpet dimples pressed into her stomach, to the dark, triangular patch of hair slightly visible between her closed legs, every bit as dark as the hair on her head. Her pale, smooth skin, shining in a bath of warm incandescent light, offered a striking contrast to the ebony depth of her hair. She was the most beautiful woman David had ever seen.

The most beautiful woman in the world, David realized, was not human. She was an animal, a household pet.

A dog.

"This can't be," he finally spat.

"Now do you believe me?" she asked.

David wanted desperately to believe that this strange woman had been hiding in his house, that she had shoved his dog out the window and waited for David's arrival to culminate this great hoax, but he knew that wasn't so. This woman was Natasha.

"I believe you," whispered David. "I believe you, ... but I don't understand."

Tears began to form once again in Natasha's eyes. "Neither do I."

David struggled to his feet and extended his hand to Natasha, helping her from the floor. Natasha wrapped her arms around David and began to cry uncontrollably. David hugged her fiercely.

She must've been going through hell, David thought. She's just a dog, plain and simple. Now she's been thrown into a man's world, suddenly capable of feelings and thoughts totally alien to her. And on top of that, the one individual she thought she could trust turned against her when she needed him the most. How could he have been so cruel to his beloved Natasha? How could he have tossed her out in the cold rain that first night? Even though she was now human, she was still his companion, his dear pet.

"I'm so sorry for not believing you the first time," he said.

Natasha looked at him with her big, brown eyes. Puppy dog eyes, David thought. How many times have men used that expression to describe a pouty woman? "How were you to know?"

"How did this happen?"

"I don't know," Natasha sobbed. "Please hold me, David. Just hold me. I'm so confused."

David held Natasha tightly. He was confused, too. She needed him to provide some type of answer to her unthinkable dilemma but, for the moment, holding her was all he could do.

•   •   •

David and Natasha held one another, for how long they didn't know, absorbing and relieving the others' mounting anxieties. David retrieved the clothes from the back porch before building a roaring fire in the den. Sharing a relaxing cup of hot coffee while sitting in front of the fireplace had done wonders for them.

"This is so strange," said Natasha, taking a sip of coffee. She made a face at the taste of the bitter liquid. "Being here with you like this, talking to you, being able to speak and have you understand me. This is the first time we've ever actually communicated."

"Do you speak to me when you're a dog?" David asked, wincing when he realized how absurd the question sounded.

"Of course, I do. I speak to you all the time; you just can't understand me." She smiled sheepishly.

Natasha pulled her legs up under her and snuggled comfortably into the plush couch. She glanced around the small den, noticing all the items, the names popping into her brain with no effort.

"I think I actually learned a few human words before any of this happened," she said, as if speaking to the air. "Of course, I knew Natasha. But ... it seems like I understood words, certain words and what they meant. Like walk and food. Things like that."

"I imagine you were just responding in a Pavlovian way to words," David suggested.

"Pavlovian?"

"You learned to associate the sound of a certain word with a particular act through the continuous action."

"I wonder why I know all the words now. How do they come to me so easily?"

David shrugged. "Well, if you consider the legend and lore of lycanthropy, it's not all that surprising. Whenever a man becomes a wolf, he takes on the savagery, the instinct, the total mind of the animal. Why wouldn't the same happen if the situation was reversed? Why wouldn't the animal totally assume the human mind?"

"I don't know what any of that means," said Natasha, "but it sounds logical."

"Do you remember Coogan?" David asked.

"Of course, I do."

"I think he might be able to help us figure this out. I think he knows quite a bit that he hasn't told me."

Natasha nodded. "He believed me."

"What?"

"Yeah, he believed me. On the second night that I changed, I went to his house. I don't know how I found him, but when I saw him, something in my mind remembered him."

"You went to Coogan's house?" David asked, surprised.

"Well, I had to go somewhere." She smiled. "You would've just thrown me out again."

David shied away in sorrow.

"Anyway, he talked to me that night. And he believed me."

"And he brought you back the next day or started to. He's the one that brought the clothes back, too. So, you'd have clothes to wear when you changed the next time. That explains a lot. But I still can't figure out how this happened. I'm stretching my imagination to believe in the concept of werewolves." David chuckled. "I don't have to stretch too far anymore. Anyway, something must've happened to cause you to change. Any ideas?"

"The only thing that comes to mind is that wolf."

David leaned forward, suddenly very interested. "Wolf? What wolf?"

"The wolf that mated with me."

David felt the coffee cup almost slip from his hand. "A wolf mated with you?"

Natasha pulled her knees up to her chin. Her hair fell across her arms with an intriguing glimmering effect. "Yeah." She shivered. "That first night I got loose. You remember? I was—what do you call it, 'in heat?'—that night. I broke the chain, and I just ran. I can remember all the trees flying past me, all the smells in the air, and it was so exhilarating. I guess I was looking for a mate.

"I could smell him. I could smell his scent everywhere, but I couldn't find him. I don't know how far I traveled that night, but I kept searching for him. Finally, I think ... he found me. He was so large, bigger than any of the dogs around here." A small sob escaped Natasha's throat. "He attacked me, and I couldn't get away. He was so powerful; I couldn't move him. He bit me, and he kept hurting me. It hurt so bad. Then, it was over. He just stood over me, panting and baring his teeth, almost ... almost like he was smiling about what he had done."

"Jesus," David whispered. "A werewolf. That's what's been killing the livestock, and it almost got you."

"It did get me."

David scooted over on the couch and Natasha reached for his comforting warmth, letting her tears dampen his shoulder. David believed her at last, and it helped. She loved her master, and now, she believed he would always be there for her. But Natasha's thoughts kept drifting to the old man in the trailer. Coogan knew things her master did not; Coogan was the one who could help.

And still somewhere in the back of Natasha's mind crept a single dark figure, draped in shadows, framed in black.

•　　　•　　　•

David sat in the darkness of the den, the dying embers in the fireplace casting a warm glow across the couch. Natasha lay sleeping in his arms, the steady rise and fall of her breathing a soothing symphony.

The evidence of a werewolf running loose in Potters weighed heavily on David's mind. All accounts of livestock deaths had been reported the morning after a full moon. Natasha disappeared that first night, the night of her fateful encounter, under a full moon. That strange woman showed up during a full moon. Natasha's subsequent disappearances also occurred on full moon nights. And last night, when Natasha turned into a woman, the moon had reached its full phase once again.

David tried to present everything he knew as fact in a logical order to determine his next move. All signs pointed to Coogan, and that frightened David a little. Could Coogan be the werewolf? It was possible. One thing was certain, David needed to find Coogan, werewolf or not. If he believed Natasha's story from the beginning, then Coogan obviously would be the best source of information. Their mutual dislike for Deputy Stoner made Coogan another viable ally.

Shit, David thought. Could Stoner be the werewolf?

Hell, anyone in the whole town could be the werewolf.

Natasha stirred in David's arms and relaxed again. Her breathing pattern did not falter. David leaned forward and kissed the top of Natasha's head. The fragrance of her hair was undeniably feminine. David closed his eyes and absorbed the aroma, concentrated on the heat from Natasha's body, the pleasant feel of her breasts pushing against his body. It had been a long time since David had held a woman, and even though his entire consciousness screamed out against his thoughts, he could not deny his arousal.

David let his head fall back against the back of the couch, and he stared up at the ceiling, hypnotized by the shimmering effect of the waning fire.

"God help us," he said as he fell asleep.

8

"**Y**OU KNOW?" the voice said over the phone.

David knew it was Coogan's voice when he picked up the receiver. He cleared his throat. "Know what?"

"The dog was inside the whole night. You must know."

David ran his hands through his hair. It was too early in the morning for this to start. "Yeah," he sighed. "Yeah ... I know."

"A bit surprising, I'm sure."

"You could say that. Look , uh ... Mr. Coogan. I really need to talk to you."

"I'll come over tonight, after the sun goes down," Coogan said. "I want to talk to you and Natasha." The line grew silent, then he added, "It's about Stoner."

David felt his breath quicken. "Okay."

"One other thing," said Coogan. "Is Natasha still in the house?"

"Yeah. "

"Good. Leave her inside. Don't let her out of your sight, understand? I'll see you tonight."

David hung up the phone and looked at Natasha. She lay on the floor of the den in the guise of his precious pet, peering up at

David as if she sensed his concerns. David gazed into her eyes and tried to picture the eyes he had stared into the night before. They were the same eyes, but they weren't.

David fell backward on the couch and wondered how this mess had all started.

•   •   •

When David saw the squad car pulling into his driveway, he thought about hiding Natasha in the spare bedroom. But it was only Sheriff Barnes.

What's he doing here? David wondered. Better him than Stoner anyway.

David pushed open the front door and walked out onto the wooden porch to greet the officer. The chilly morning air bit deeply into David's flesh, and he shuddered.

"Sheriff, what brings you out here this morning?"

"Morning, Mr. Wagner. Just wanted to ask a few questions, if you don't mind."

"No, of course not. What's up?"

"Have you heard any news reports yet this morning?" asked the sheriff.

"No, I haven't. Haven't been up very long."

"Four head of cattle found mutilated. Three different sites."

"Jesus," David muttered. "Four?"

Sheriff Barnes nodded grimly. "Your dog get out last night?"

"No," said David, bewildered. "No, she was inside the house all night long. I made sure she didn't get out."

"Well, I'm glad to hear that."

"Four head," David said. "This is getting out of hand."

"Yes, it is. And I'm at a loss to explain it. Do you mind if I take a look at the area where you keep the dog?"

"No," David said. "Just follow me."

David turned and headed around the side of the house. He was happy. Now, he had evidence that Natasha had nothing to do with the disappearing livestock; he had a solid alibi.

"You seen any more of that woman you talked to me about?"

David turned his head away from the sheriff, hoping to hide the surprise on his face. "No. I thought you didn't think anything of it anyway."

"Well, hell. I'm gettin' desperate. I'm ready to settle for any kind of clue I can. All these damn farmers are gonna chase me out of the county if I don't give 'em some answers soon."

David stopped at Natasha's doghouse. All the mud had nearly dried since the last rains. The remaining prints—Natasha's, a few of David's, and the one large dog track—were so congregated that little could be observed from them.

Sheriff Barnes leaned over to inspect the dried ground. "These tracks are old, probably a few days. No new tracks here."

"Sheriff, I told you Natasha was inside with me last night."

"Oh, I believe you, son. I'm just doing everything by the book here. The more of this info I get down, the better the chance that we can scratch Natasha off the list of suspects."

"Do you have any more suspects?"

"Shit, no," Barnes said with an angry shake of his head. "I used to think it was just kids, but it's gone on way too long for it to be a bunch of bored teenagers. I'm beginning to think it's something really big."

"Like what?"

"Well, this sounds kind of silly, but I'm starting to think maybe something escaped from a zoo somewhere. I've put in calls to all the larger zoos in the surrounding states, but I haven't heard anything yet."

"That sounds logical," David said.

"Just as logical as anything else I've heard." Sheriff Barnes scratched his head and peered into the distant woods. "Well, I won't take up any more of your time, Mr. Wagner. I'll just show myself back to the car. Much obliged."

David watched the sheriff disappear around the corner of the house and sighed. Maybe one of his more major concerns had been alleviated. At least he wouldn't have to worry about the police anymore. And as long as he kept Natasha inside, Stoner could do nothing about trying to take her.

David looked around for Natasha's food bowl. He had not brought it into the house the previous night because Natasha had been hiding under the bed. Then, of course, the craziness started. Come to think of it, Natasha hadn't eaten since yesterday morning. She was probably about ready to chew David's head off.

David spied the bowl resting against the side of the house. Natasha liked to use the bowl as a toy when it was not serving its normal purpose, and she had apparently knocked it out of the chain's reach. David walked around the patio to retrieve the bowl.

It lay in the shadow of the eave, and David felt his feet sinking in the soft mud. This part of the house received little sunlight. Moss grew at the bottom of the slab, and the ground stayed moist except during long dry spells.

"Awww." David lifted his foot up and inspected the bottom. He was still wearing his slippers.

David knelt and reached for the bowl. It was partially buried in mud, and David yanked hard to pull the bowl up. A chunk of mud spiraled briefly in the air, amusing David, and he watched it sail and land back in the …

… footprint.

David dropped the bowl. His gaze followed the moist earth that ran along the side of the house, just under the windows to his bedroom, bathroom, and den. And there were footprints all along the entire back side of the house. Big footprints. Animal footprints. Wolf footprints. Everything came to David at once. The track was similar to the print he found earlier near Natasha's doghouse, the one he had passed off as belonging to a large dog. Now, the same prints were lined across his house like the tracks of a pacing, caged animal, and they were concentrated heavily under the den window. The window to the room he and Natasha had stayed in last night. It had been here during the night, and it had watched them.

David absentmindedly reached again for Natasha's bowl and went inside the covered patio. He stopped just before entering the back door and stared again at the heavy tracks. David dreaded the coming night. He dreaded Natasha's imminent change, Coogan's approaching revelation, and the possible return of whatever had made those tracks.

•　　　•　　　•

Natasha pulled herself from under the bed and reached for her clothes. The bed seemed to represent a sense of security to her canine form. Natasha could hear the voices coming from the front of her master's house. The transformation occurred only moments ago. They seemed to be coming easier for her. She found herself calmer before the actual process, and the pain of the transformations seemed to be lessening in intensity.

Natasha opened the bedroom door and followed the main hall into the front room. The voices belonged to David and Coogan; she already knew that.

Natasha was glad that Coogan had come. She felt a special sense of calmness and safety in his presence, a feeling that her owner could not quite match. She supposed that the feeling was due in part to Coogan believing her story, when David had rejected her. But the old man had a definite knack for curbing her anxieties. Natasha wished desperately to stop these changes. She had no desire to be human. Even though the language and the actions of human nature came easily for her, she was not human. She was a canine, and she wished to stay that way.

"Oh, here she is now," David said upon seeing Natasha turn the corner.

Natasha moved close to Coogan and embraced him. "Coogan, I'm so glad you're here."

"Everything's going to be all right," Coogan said. "This I promise."

Natasha pulled back from Coogan's arms and looked at her master. He had that same conveyance of hurt and jealousy that still lingered in her canine memory from the times Coogan had played with her. Natasha reached for David's hand and grasped it firmly.

"Let's go into the den," David said.

The trio stepped into the den, and Natasha and Coogan sat down on the couch. David walked over to the windows and drew the curtains tightly. He turned to the others.

"It was here last night," he said. "I saw the tracks right under this window."

Natasha looked frightened. Coogan nodded. "I assume you believe everything now."

"I don't have much choice."

"What do we do now?" Natasha picked up a throw pillow and pulled it tightly to her chest for comfort.

"I tell you what I know, and what I think I know," Coogan began. "You both know now that there is a lycanthrope living in our area. It's been killin' all the livestock, and a few months ago, it attacked and raped a dog. Namely you, Natasha."

"How did you know that?" David asked.

"It wasn't that difficult to figure out. Now, let me continue. Stoner is the werewolf. Deputy Stoner is a lycanthrope."

"I had a hunch," David said. "But how do you know?"

"Trust me. I know. Stoner is an evil lycanthrope. He's the foulest, blackest, darkest type of beast known, and he stops at nothing, absolutely nothing, to get what he wants."

"Why is he here?" David asked. "Why does he stay in such a small town? What does he have to gain?"

"He has nothing to gain in this small community. But he pretty much has absolute control of the town. He can make Sheriff Barnes do anything he wants."

"Does he control the sheriff somehow?"

"Not supernaturally. He has no mind control over him if that's what you mean. But Stoner is a very imposing, extremely intimidating character. He can win people over, either by charm or by force.

"Anyway, back to what I was saying. Stoner usually does nothing conspicuous around here; all his real activity will always take place elsewhere, and I'll get to that later. This town, this life he leads here is merely a front, and the more innocent it appears for him, the better.

"But recently, Stoner has found a reason to become active in this community, at least until he gets what he wants. He has found something he wants."

David glanced at Natasha and back to Coogan. "What?"

"He wants Natasha."

"But why?" David asked, running his fingers through his hair and pacing across the room. "Why does he want Natasha?"

Natasha's eyes peered straight ahead in thought. "Because," she said meekly, "wolves mate for life."

"I'm afraid she's right."

"What, you mean, he wants to marry Natasha?"

"I wouldn't say marry, but you can bet yer sweet ass he wants to possess her, he wants Natasha to be his one hundred percent."

"Oh, David. What are we going to do?"

"Do you think he'll try to take her?" David asked, sitting next to Natasha.

"I think he's already trying," Coogan stated. "He took her from me that morning and then made up that cock and bull story about finding her on his porch."

"I don't remember that!" Natasha cried.

"And he found her again on his porch—or so he claimed—the next time she escaped."

"I don't think she escaped that time," said Coogan. "I think he nabbed her."

"But I don't remember Stoner coming here.I don't remember anything like that. I don't remember being at his house or at the sheriff's office."

"I'm pretty sure you were drugged somehow when Stoner had you. Besides, I would've heard him that night if he had tried to take her. Natasha would've barked her head off."

"She wasn't drugged, David," Coogan said. "He hypnotized her. That's why she never barked."

"I thought only vampires could hypnotize their victims," David said.

"You're going to have to throw out everything that fiction and folklore have told you about lycanthropy, David. They just won't get you very far here."

"So, he hypnotized her. He didn't drug her, he hypnotized her." He looked at Natasha. "Well, that does explain the way you were acting at the police station."

"What was I doing?"

"It was like you weren't even there mentally," David said. "Like you were stuffed, or asleep." David turned back to Coogan. "That still doesn't explain one thing: I didn't see any tracks, no human footprints," David argued. "The only other print I saw was—" David stopped in mid-sentence. He thought of the huge wolf print he had found that morning.

"Big dog tracks?" asked Coogan. "Just like the ones you found under the window this morning?"

"Holy Jesus," David whispered. "How did he do that?"

"He only changed his feet that morning. Yeah, he can do that," Coogan said, noticing the puzzled looks on David's and Natasha's face. "He only changed his feet so he could lead Natasha away without leaving any evidence that could link anything to him. Stoner is a very powerful lycanthrope. He can change whenever he wants to. He doesn't have to wait for a full moon. He can change anytime; he can change whatever parts of his body he wants. He can take either of two forms: full wolf or man-beast, a kind of half-wolf, half-man monster."

"Oh, come on," said David with an exasperated movement of his hands. "That's just insane. This is getting pretty damned hard to believe."

"No," Natasha interrupted. "No, it's not." She grabbed David's shoulders, spinning him around to face her. "Look at me, David. Just look into my eyes. I'm a human. I'm sitting on a couch. I'm speaking to you. All you have to do is accept that, and you have no choice but to believe. You must believe everything."

Natasha could read the fear and pain in her master's eyes, and she wanted to cry, as much for him as for herself. She looked back at Coogan. "What are we going to do? I don't want to go with him."

"We have to stop him. We have to tell the sheriff."

"And what do you think he'll say?" asked Coogan.

"We'll prove it to him."

"How? What evidence do you have? Do you have even an inkling of evidence?"

"I have all the evidence in the world right here," David said, taking Natasha's hands.

"What do you mean?"

"We can just take her to the station during the next full moon. What more evidence would he need?"

"That won't work, David." Coogan almost snarled out the words.

"Why not?"

"Listen to him, David."

"Well, what are we going to do then?" asked David.

"Just listen," Coogan said. "Both of you, just relax and listen." Coogan held out his hands in front of David and Natasha. They leaned back on the couch, holding their silence. "Good. Good. Now listen, we're going to have to come up with something. We're going to have to get both of you away from here. It's true that wolves mate for life, but you gotta remember, Stoner isn't a wolf. He does have wolfen instincts, but he also has human instincts. Given time, he'll stop worrying about Natasha, especially if he finds another mate.

"Now, Stoner is going to be leaving town soon," he continued.

"How do you know that?" Natasha asked.

"He leaves town for a week the last full moon of October every year. He takes a week's vacation under the pretense of going hunting."

"'Under the pretense'? What's that supposed to mean?"

"Each year at that time the evil lycanthropes gather for 'the Festering'. I don't know where he's going this year—I don't know any year, but it will be happening soon. The Festering is a huge, bloody week of decadence and orgies between the evil werewolves, and they always meet in a large, crime-ridden city. They work themselves up for several months, a slow rise to a climax. That's why we've had all these killings. Stoner has been killing the livestock to drink their blood and eat their raw flesh."

"It's kind of like a witch's sabbat," David said.

"Exactly. This is the first year he's attacked domesticated animals, and that has me worried. He usually kills deer, rabbits, you know, small, inconspicuous things. He's drawn a lot of attention this year. Not to himself necessarily, not yet. But he's definitely taking a chance." Coogan paused for a moment. "He's either getting stupid ... or he's beginning to feel invincible."

"What is this 'Festering?'" David asked. "I mean, other than the obvious. What purpose does it serve, and how do you know Stoner will go?"

"Oh, he'll go. The lycanthropes become more powerful with each Festering. He won't miss it."

"Coogan," said Natasha. "You said bloodletting. What do the werewolves kill?"

Coogan sighed and looked away as if he didn't want to answer the question. He finally turned and met Natasha's eyes. "Humans," he said flatly.

"Jesus," David mumbled.

"Will he kill people here?"

"Used to, I would've said no. But I'm not sure what he's capable of anymore."

"Coogan, how do you know so much about werewolves, and about Stoner?"

Coogan smiled. "That's a good question, and one I might answer in due time. For the time being, let's just say that I used to study up on everything supernatural, paranormal, ghostly, whatever you want to call it."

"Does Stoner know you know what he is?" Natasha asked. It was a question she had been wanting to ask the entire evening, and she was sure David was pondering the answer as well.

"No. That's one good thing about my reputation. Stoner would never suspect me of knowing anything."

Natasha stood and took Coogan's hand, pulling him up. She held both his hands and stared into his eyes. "What was it that made you believe me that first night when I came to your trailer? You had no reason at all to believe me any more than David did, yet you didn't turn me away. Why not?"

Coogan smiled and gazed into her brown eyes. "I saw the truth in your eyes. You can always read a person's thoughts if you know what to look for in their eyes."

Natasha gave Coogan a warm smile. "What do you see in my eyes now?"

Coogan gently squeezed Natasha's hands."On the surface, I see fear. I see the animal, the frightened animal that lives inside you. But, when I dig deeper, when I see past the obvious and into your soul, I see strength. And that's not just the strength of the wolf. It's the strength of the human side of you, too. It's the strength of your will."

"You think I'm strong?"

"I know you are, child," he said. "You've already proven that."

David grasped their interlocked hands with his own. "We're all strong."

"It's getting late," Coogan said. The clock above the mantle read past one o'clock. "I'd better be going."

"You can't leave," Natasha said with a cry. "What if he's out there?"

"He is out there." Coogan pulled away from Natasha.

"But I thought you said he didn't have to change during the full moon." David walked over to the window and parted the slats with two fingers, peering outside.

"He doesn't. But that's when a lycanthrope is at its strongest. When the moon is at its fullest, so are the powers that it harnesses."

"What about Natasha? Can she control her transformations?"

Coogan shook his head. "She's too inexperienced. She hasn't even begun to realize the scope of what she's become." He smiled at Natasha. "In due time."

"You can't go," Natasha begged. "It's not safe."

"It's perfectly safe," Coogan said. "He's not going to bother any humans."

"How can you be sure?" asked David.

Natasha detected the change in Coogan's eyes. Just as he had explained to her, the truth was in the eyes. The comfort in the old man's eyes was replaced by a twinge of fear.

"I'm sure," Coogan said. He held a finger up to David. "Don't let her out of your sight."

•   •   •

Jackie Coogan stepped off the gravelly shoulder of highway 92, and onto the more level surface of the asphalt road. The bright, round moon more than adequately lit the way before him. The cloudless sky, which had so much warmed the skies earlier in the day, now brought a frigid chill to the air.

Coogan pulled his flannel jacket tighter to his scrawny body and forced his feet to move despite the cold that seeped into his old shoes. He glanced repeatedly to either side of the road, watching warily for any movement in the black bushes beyond the ditches.

He had told David and Natasha that he would be completely safe on his journey home, turning down politely the offer of a ride, much to the protests of his two hosts. And he really did believe that he would be.

But now, in the light of the full moon, which somehow proved both comforting and menacing, he was forced to begin convincing himself of his own thoughts.

"Git your old feet a'moving," Coogan mumbled under his breath, and he trotted up the asphalt road.

9

DEPUTY DEVIN STONER PULLED his cruiser onto the highway and pointed the wheels south, toward the far end of the county. Quincy Deacon lost two head of cattle and a yearling colt the previous night. Deacon lived just north of the county line, out farther than even old man Coogan's ramshackle trailer. The latest activity of the cattle slayer had brought the total number of lost livestock to twenty cattle and one horse. Sheriff Barnes was furious. He wanted his best man to work full-time on solving this dilemma, and that was Devin Stoner. Stoner smiled and glanced at himself in the rear-view mirror. How convenient.

Now, Stoner could manipulate the investigation however he saw fit, and that would give him all the leverage he needed. This knowledge relieved Stoner. He had begun to screw up. His bloodlust had grown stronger with each passing month. The urge to kill and drink the blood was all-consuming. His monthly excursions were reaching a point of no control. He could scarcely believe he had killed three animals the last two nights. That was far too many, and he knew it.

Stoner shifted in his seat and pressed the accelerator harder. The draw of the Festering, still a month away, was devouring him inside, and he couldn't understand why. He had never acted so blatantly over-confident prior to any previous gatherings. Why was this year so different? Was this to be an extra special Festering? Would there be someone there? A woman, perhaps? Or an exceptionally violent gathering? He didn't know.

But he did know that things were changing in his town. He knew his own mistakes were partially to blame, but he also believed there was a reason for his irrational thoughts lately.

Stoner pulled the squad car to the side of the road and let the vehicle idle in neutral. He peered out the passenger side window at the small farmhouse set back from the road. The deeply rutted dirt driveway wound toward the back of the house, and Stoner could see the rear bumper of the Jeep parked in the back yard.

The bitch was inside the house; he could feel that much. Wagner probably would not leave her outside again. Perhaps he shouldn't have tried to force the man's hand. Wagner had more reserve than Stoner had anticipated. He was determined to keep the animal from escaping again.

Stoner didn't know how another lycanthrope had managed to take up residence in Potters. Natasha was a lycanthrope, just as he was. He had known when he first heard about Wagner's complaint of the woman in his back yard.

She was the reason his brain was not functioning normally. Natasha was his female, and he would have her. He longed to know her again as he had that first night, and he ached to have her as a man has a woman, in the forms of their human selves.

Stoner detected a slight movement in one of the front windows. He could see Wagner's face through the small gap in the blinds, could even see his eyes, almost read his thoughts.

He knows, Stoner thought. *He knows what I am.* Wagner is a smart man, and I've made too many mistakes for him not to figure it out.

Stoner stared into the window a moment longer. Wagner had not moved from his spot. The deputy extended his right hand toward the house, lifted his thumb straight into the air and extended his first finger forward. He held that position for a long moment.

He brought his thumb down slowly. "Bang," Stoner whispered. "You're dead."

Wagner closed the blinds.

Stoner laughed and moved the cruiser back out onto highway 92 toward the Deacon farm, where he would listen to the farmer's complaints as they stood over the remains of the previous night's bloody meal.

•   •   •

David sat on the sofa in the den, rubbing the top of Natasha's head as she snoozed soundly at his feet. She responded with a light thumping of her tail. The sounds of a soap opera—*Days of Our Lives*, it sounded like—played quietly in the background, but David had no interest in it. His mind was a swarming myriad of insane thoughts.

The shock of Stoner's actions that morning had slowly diminished, but it was still very much on David's mind. Stoner had pretended to shoot David with his hand, much as children do when playing cops and robbers. The act was very juvenile, almost comical, but it could mean only one thing. Stoner knew. Why else would he see David as something to be exterminated? Or had he always viewed David as an opponent simply because he was Natasha's owner?

Coogan also played a large part in David's unsettling thoughts. Like it or not, David's thoughts kept drifting back to how the locals viewed the old man. David was forced to accept the facts as they were. Here was an old man, a loner that no one seemed to know anything about, a man who collects pinecones, of all things (David suddenly had a vision of opening a closet door in Coogan's trailer and being buried by pinecones, ala Rob Petry and the walnuts nightmare on *The Dick Van Dyke Show*).

Let's face it, David thought. This man doesn't have the finest reputation in the world, you know absolutely nothing about him, and you're listening to him tell stories about monsters and werewolves and orgies. It was true, obviously, that something unnatural had happened. Of course, David had to admit that. The proof was lying at his feet.

And that was the predominant thought occupying David's muddled brain. David looked down at his dog, and he had a hard time thinking of his pet and the gorgeous woman as one and the same, even though he knew it to be true.

David suddenly remembered a crush he had on his Aunt Kelli when he was fifteen. He was old enough to experience a desire for members of the opposite sex, and he certainly had a desire for her. He could remember seeing her at the annual summer family reunions in her cut-off shorts and bikini top. But the thing that David remembered most about the experience was that, no matter how badly he wanted to sleep with Aunt Kelli, no matter how desirable he found her, it was something he could never do. It was morally wrong, and it was just out of the question. Aunt Kelli had gotten married a few years later and now had a couple of kids. And that was the end of that.

But David felt the same way toward Natasha as he had for Aunt Kelli. Was it because it had been so long since he had even seen a woman? Was that the attraction? Was it because of her exceptional beauty? He had always had an attraction for dark-haired women; there seemed to be such an air of mystery about them. Could that be it? Was he attracted to the mystery that Natasha's situation warranted? Or was it her vulnerability, a machismo desire to hold and protect her?

David leaned back on the sofa. Natasha stirred slightly at the movement. David could see the tips of her ears rise above his knees; then they dropped back down.

Or was it because he already loved Natasha so much? David winced and dismissed the thought. He attempted to force all weird thoughts from his mind, but this one remained.

Why not? the inner voice persisted. You've had this animal for three years now. She's helped you through lonely times, through a hard divorce, a cross-country move. You've been through a lot together. Owners and their pets often grow very fond of one another. David had read stories in which animals laid their lives on the line for their owners, and vice versa.

Which brought up the old moral question: Can a person really love a pet? Really *love*, in the purest sense of the word? What the hell is love anyway? David thought. I loved the shit out of Mindy and look where that got me. Six years of arguments, of fighting over the stupidest things, of the most forced and plastic love two people ever had to endure.

David suddenly remembered a poster he had seen on a wall at a pet store back in Arizona. It read simply: *The love of a pet is the truest form of the emotion.* It sounded incredibly contrived and commercial when he had read it, but now he wondered.

David tried to force the thoughts from his mind, shutting his eyes tightly as if that would help. He thought of the looks of affection that he had always received from Natasha, and how that look never wavered when he met eyes with Natasha the woman. He remembered the other night when he held her as she cried herself to sleep. The smell of her hair, undeniably human, still seemed to linger in his nostrils. The warmth of her body against his still soothed his soul.

But is that love or lust? David thought of last night, of how he held Natasha after Coogan had left. He had tried to deny it, to convince himself that it was nothing, but he knew he had come very close to kissing her. David's mind formed a mental picture; he had almost kissed a dog. And it wouldn't have been a little "peck your dog on the top of its head" kiss. It would've been a real, intense, romantic, down and dirty kiss. David knew that much.

Shouldn't such a thought disgust and embarrass him? No, because it wasn't a dog that I was holding. It was a woman. A real life, flesh and blood, warm, breathing female of the Homo Sapiens variety.

And what was wrong with that? What's wrong with kissing a woman whom you have spent an entire night getting to know, with kissing a lady that you feel extremely attracted to, and who you think feels the same toward you? He wasn't some pimply-faced teenaged goofball, standing on the front porch of his prom date's parents' house, wondering if her father is peeking through the curtains to make sure he doesn't try to grab a tit, pondering if he should attempt to sneak a quick good-night kiss before the porch light comes on. He was a grown man, struggling with his emotions, wondering if he should make a move on a grown woman or not. What the hell was wrong with that?

Everything, when that woman is really a 98% MacKenzie Valley timber wolf, 2% Alaska malamute wolf-hybrid.

Damn, David thought. It sounds awful when I word it that way.

Was it awful? Was it right? Was it wrong? Was it bestiality? Hell, no, he thought. Do people call it bestiality when an owner kisses his or her pet?

They do if this kissing involves deep breathing, tongues, and perhaps a bit of fondling.

David grinned. Wouldn't this entire episode make a hell of an article? *Article?* he thought. No, this is pure fiction; it would have to be. Send this one to *Amazing Stories.*

David knew he should be working on something, but there were just too many things occupying his mind. Stoner's capacity for violence and Coogan's unstable reputation should have been the most important of David's mental perusing, but they weren't.

•   •   •

Natasha lay at the foot of her master's couch, her head resting across her front legs, her eyes closed. Sleep was not coming easily; in fact, it did not come at all. Things had changed in her for the last few months, and not just when the pains came. Thoughts raced through her mind, inhibiting her attempts at rest, thoughts that normally did not enter her canine brain. She couldn't really remember how her life was before.

She vaguely remembered dreaming of running through the woods, of chasing rabbits and squirrels, of fetching tennis balls with her owner. Now, her thoughts were plagued by things she could not quite fathom. Dark shapes lurked in the recesses of her mind, black movements that seemed to threaten her. Figures and objects appeared in her mind, forms that she did not know, shapes that frightened her. Her name was in there as well, but so were others. David, Coogan, Stoner, as well as other words. They formed in her mind, yet they were unclear to her. She didn't know why the thoughts had come to her. She didn't know what they even meant.

And the strongest thought, the one that should've held the least importance to her, was of mating. She remembered the time when she had encountered the wolf in the woods, the wolf she had mated with. She remembered that she had eagerly anticipated the act, until the attack had begun.

Now, she was feeling that anticipation again, and she was not in heat. It didn't feel the same. For some reason, Natasha believed that it wasn't her instincts that were the basis of her thoughts. The feeling was coming from her mind, not from her instincts. It was not the relentless drive to continue the species. It was very different. Natasha felt the same way she did when she saw her master coming from the patio to play with her. She was experiencing that eagerness, that fondness that she felt only for her owner.

But Natasha was feeling it in a manner she had never felt for him before.

•   •   •

David picked up the phone call on the first ring. He was afraid that it would be Stoner, possibly claiming he had Natasha again. But David could see Natasha from where he stood in the kitchen.

It was Coogan.

"I'm glad you made it home all right," David said.

"I told you I'd be okay.How's Natasha doing?"

"She's fine. She's just laid around most of the day."

"Good."

"So, what's up? Anything new?"

"David," Coogan started. David did not like the tone of his voice. "I'm pretty sure we'll have another full moon tonight. Natasha will change again."

"Yeah, I think I'm finally getting a little used to it. As much as can be expected."

"Well, I'm not goin' to be there with you tonight."

"Is this leading somewhere?"

"David, I'm an old man, but I remember what it was like to be young. And I remember what it was like to be in love. Barely."

David sighed. This was beginning to sound like some kind of father-son chat. The birds and the bees.

"Natasha is very beautiful; even I can see that. And last night ... I kinda noticed some things." Coogan sounded unsure of himself.

"What are you saying?"

"I'm just sayin' you need to be careful. Just watch yerself and don't get caught up in a moment."

David couldn't believe what Coogan was saying. It offended him deeply, yet he was amazed at the old man's accuracy in his summation of the facts. "Are you saying what I think you're saying?"

"David, you're going to need to be on your toes tonight. At least until Stoner leaves. You need to have all your wits about you, and if one thing can strip a man of his wits, it's a woman."

"Mr. Coogan, really." David felt his cheeks flush.

"Just remember what I said."

"Okay, I got it." David hung up the phone.

Jesus, he thought. Was it that obvious? He thought he had hidden it pretty well. If Coogan had noticed, then Natasha probably had as well. What did she think? That he was just like all other guys.

Don't be stupid, Wagner. She doesn't know all other guys. She's just a dog.

Holy God, did that sound stupid, David groaned. Natasha had her head down, but her brown eyes were open, watching his every move. David wondered what was going on inside her head at that moment, before deciding he didn't want to know.

10

THE LONG, SLOW WAIL reverberated through the cold night air, traveling through the thin walls of the old farmhouse and finding its way into Natasha's ears. The sound slithered down her spine and grabbed her heart.

She looked nervously at David. "Is it him?"

David paused and peered out the kitchen window where he was standing. "There are lots of dogs in this area. It sounded more like a dog." Neither his voice nor his face portrayed much confidence.

"I wish he would just go away," she said, her voice almost childlike.

David went to her and placed his hands on her shoulders. "It's going to be all right."

Natasha nodded and stared at the floor. David touched a finger to her chin and tilted her face to meet his.

"How was dinner?"

Natasha smiled. "Dinner was fine."

"I do make a mean grilled cheese sandwich, if I do say so myself."

Natasha wasn't looking at him. Her focus had switched to the back door, her thoughts on the black woods beyond.

"That was a joke," David said. "I'm afraid I'm not much of a cook."

"Dinner was fine," repeated Natasha.

Again, David touched her cheek and turned her to face him. "Natasha, you're distracted."

"I'm sorry."

"Why don't we go into the den and relax."

"The den must be a retreat for you. You spend a lot of time there."

"My den is my sanctuary from the outside world. That's why I keep my computer in another room. When my writing frustrates me, whenever my mind isn't working the way I want it to, I can just lock myself in the den, turn on the TV, and throw myself on the couch."

"I like it, too," Natasha said. "I feel safe in there."

David grasped Natasha's hand and led her from the kitchen into the comfort of the den. Natasha pulled her long hair up and let it cascade over her shoulders and sighed. "The sandwiches really were great."

"Better than dog food?"

"I don't know," Natasha said. She knew David was trying to make her feel better, but his efforts were fruitless. "I don't know, David."

"Hey, it was a lame comment. I'm sorry if it bothered you."

"It's not that. It's just that I'm finding it harder and harder to distinguish events between my two lives."

"What do you mean?"

"I'm having trouble realizing what happened when, and remembering things that happened earlier, things that occurred during my canine form."

"Well, Coogan said you were hypnotized."

"It's not just that," she said, her voice cracking. "It's everything. Everything is getting twisted around, mixed together until I don't know what's what anymore."

"You're just having trouble adapting. You'll get used to it."

"I don't want to get used to it. I just want it to go away. I want all of this to go away."

"This will be the last full moon of the month. Maybe we'll figure something out before the next one."

Natasha dropped onto the couch and folded her arms across her breasts. "I doubt it."

"What about the things Coogan said? Maybe you can learn to control it."

"I don't want to control it. I don't want it at all, can't you understand? If I could control it, I'd be outside asleep in my doghouse." She detected a faint look of pain in David's eyes. "Don't get me wrong, David. Please don't take it badly, but this is wrong. It's wrong for me to be in here. It's wrong for me to be speaking to you. This whole crazy thing is totally unnatural."

Natasha shut up and stared ahead. She expected a reply from David, perhaps even an argument. But there was none.

Natasha sniffed back a sob, trying to contain the emotions. "I'm feeling things that I've never felt before. Feelings that I shouldn't have, that I shouldn't understand, and yet, I do. I feel like I'm being pulled in two directions."

"What kind of feelings? What do you mean?"

Natasha wiped a tear from her eye. "Sometimes ... sometimes I think I would like to be human, if things were different, if it weren't for ... Stoner. I think of certain things, pleasant things, and I think they're things I could get used to. Not that I could learn to like them, because I already do. They're things that I could learn to love, and ... maybe ... I love them already.

"I just don't know what I would do if I could control this ... this lycanthropy. I can't place human thought and canine thought side by side and compare them, evaluate the pros and cons of both lives. God, this sounds so confusing."

"No," said David with a strong sense of calm that he was surprised he held. "No, it doesn't."

"I think that being human has so much more to offer, but then again, there's so much more responsibility. There are more feelings, there's more capacity for bad things to happen, there's more chance for heartbreak."

She turned to David. "There's the possibility for love."

"Is that one of the feelings you mentioned earlier?"

Natasha turned away. "I don't know."

She sat in silence, watching tiny tongues of flame dance across the logs in the fireplace. The warmth of the fire seemed to reach out from the hearth, embracing her in a soothing hug of comfort. Natasha closed her eyes momentarily. The tangled emotions that had been pulling her apart swarmed and seethed inside her body. She felt deep in her belly a seething boil of confusion, and suddenly her clothes were heavy and clumsy on her body. The warmth of the fire seemed almost oppressive now, and tiny beads of sweat formed across her forehead. She breathed deeply, opened her eyes, and gazed at David.

He was so handsome, framed in the glowing light of the fire, and Natasha realized at once the culmination of her thoughts. David stared into her eyes for a long time, and Natasha recalled the words Coogan had spoken the night before. *Reading the truth in the eyes.* And she remembered what David had said about the possibility of her taking over the emotions and instincts of a human, and the truth became evident.

She loved her owner. She loved the man. She loved David Wagner.

David reached for Natasha, and she let her eyes close slowly. She felt his tender lips touch her forehead. Natasha moved forward on the sofa and reached her arms around David's back, as she felt his hands on her waist. David's mouth moved to hers, and she felt her lips part involuntarily, felt her tongue touch his. Natasha tilted her head and concentrated on the soothing sensation of David's hands moving slowly up her back, his fingers weaving in and out of her silky hair.

Instinctively, Natasha gently raked her nails along David's back. Natasha felt a small gasp escape her throat as his warm lips moved along the nape of her neck. She inhaled deeply the pleasing musky aroma of his masculinity, and she realized some instincts were shared by humans and animals alike. Natasha shuddered as she felt David's hands move down and under her sweatshirt, sliding up her soft belly until they reached the warm cups of her breasts. Natasha let her head drop back, and she uttered a whispered moan.

She felt her fingers curl, her nails claw into David's back as her passion mounted. She felt the sweatshirt being lifted over her head, the pleasant sensations peaking as her falling hair dropped across her breasts, tickling her nipples. David gently lowered Natasha onto the couch, and again, their lips met, and Natasha could see the flames in the hearth, their warmth paling in comparison to the heat inside of her. David's head moved over, blocking the view of the fire, and Natasha closed her eyes, succumbing to the tingling in her body.

The only thing she saw was blackness, an ebony depth of ecstasy. The only aroma in the air was the strengthening scent of their rising passion. The only sounds she heard were the pounding of her heart and the heavy gasps of their pleasure.

Natasha hardly noticed when, far from her world and muffled by the distance, a wolf howled.

•   •   •

Jackie Coogan stood outside of Apple Jack's Liquor Emporium, peering in the window at the rows and rows of liquid courage. The clock above the cold storage read 11:45. Still fifteen minutes before closing time. Fifteen minutes. *An eternity.* Fifteen minutes to make the biggest mistake of his life. Correction. The biggest mistake to date. He'd made many big mistakes in his life. And Jackie Coogan knew that liquor had been involved in every one of them.

Coogan let his eyes roam the nearest shelf from left to right. All his old friends were there: Wild Turkey, Jack Daniels, Smirnoff, the whole family. It's good to see old friends now and then. Old friends are good for the soul. Old friends make you feel young again.

Old friends take you down.

It would be so easy to walk in there, buy a buddy, go back to the trailer, and say good-bye to his troubles, say good-bye to werewolves, say good-bye to responsibilities. That would be the easiest thing to do.

He could throw it all away, all those years of being clean. There weren't very many, not in comparison to the years of drunkenness. He would have to stay sober a long, long time to even the score. But he had been sober for many years in a row, and that record was something to be proud of. So, what if the townsfolk in Potters called him a drunk. Coogan often found it amusing that he was never called a drunk during all the years he actually was one, and now that he was straight, he had a reputation as the town slosh. Then again, there'd been no one around him during his life-long bout with alcohol. No one that would've known, anyway.

But his current streak was something to be proud of, he supposed. He couldn't remember now how many years he had avoided the bottle, but it was a lot. Forty, fifty? He just couldn't remember anymore. He'd spent all that time in his little trailer at the far end of Potters, Maine, taking walks every morning collecting beer cans to supplement his income and pinecones for the hell of it. Fifty some-odd carefree years away from the juice.

Maybe that's just it, Coogan thought.

The years were carefree. They were trouble-free. They were hassle-free. *You lived on your pension, you sat on your decrepit ol' ass, you did nothing. You had no troubles; you had no damn reason to run to the bottle.*

Now, the first problem that comes your way in fifty or so years, and here you are, standing in front of a liquor store with your head up your goddamn ass! You haven't changed a bit, have you Jackie ol' boy? Oh, sure, you can talk all the shit in the world when you're high on the hog, and you got nothing to worry about. But the slightest inkling of trouble, and you're ready to throw it all out the window. All those years of kicking the habit were a joke, just a big damned lie!

Where will it leave Wagner if you go in there and dive into a fifth? And Natasha, what will she do? What will become of her? She needs you now. You're the only one who knows what they're up against. You must be strong for her. You have to walk away, Jackie. Don't do it again.

Deep in the distant woods, almost inaudible but still very much evident to his ears, a wolf howled.

Jackie Coogan stood in front of Apple Jack's Liquor Emporium, peering in the window at the rows and rows of liquid courage. Finally, he pushed the door inward and walked inside the brightly lit store. Cowbells jangled overhead, taunting him. He paused and stared.

Don't do it.

The bottles were so pretty, so inviting. He reached out and wrapped his hand around an amber liquid filled fifth.

"Can I help you?"

The voice startled Coogan from his thoughts. A young girl with dark hair lingered behind the counter. For a moment, he thought it was Natasha.

Coogan gently pushed the bottle back onto the shelf and exited the store.

•   •   •

The great beast paused at the entrance to the doghouse and sniffed. Her scent was there, but it was old, weak. The bitch was inside again. The man was keeping her there. The wolf snorted angrily and moved slowly along the perimeter of the covered patio. Her scent was inside the porch as well, but again, it was faint.

His large, splayed feet sank deeply into the soft earth under the eaves of the house, obliterating his earlier tracks. He moved slowly, methodically, past a bathroom window. He moved onward, quiet in his motion, and stopped in front of a large window. He turned to face the glass.

Her scent was heavy, the same intoxicating aroma he had followed on that night so long ago. The smell of the bitch in heat. But there was another smell, stronger and more intense. A womanly smell.

Devin Stoner smiled and rested his hirsute hands on the brick sill under the window. Wagner was in there also, and Stoner could smell his odor as well. It was strong, and it mingled with the invigorating smell of the woman. It was the aroma of spent passion.

Wagner had had his bitch.

•　　•　　•

Natasha lay awake on the plush oriental rug spread in front of the fireplace, with David asleep next to her. She gazed down at her nude body, momentarily enthralled by the wavy pattern cast by the hearth's dying embers. She marveled at the way her human body looked, compared it to her canine form. Lean, sleek, graceful. She glanced over at David and comically imagined him as an animal. She laughed silently and turned to stare at the ceiling. She sighed at the mixed jumble of emotions dancing through her head.

The many problems that had plagued her thoughts had culminated in the act of lovemaking. Natasha thought that her head would be clearer now, but it was not. If anything, she was more confused than ever. What she and David had done was wrong. She was still an animal, and David a man. People have loved pets for eons, but she had loved her owner in a way no dog had ever experienced. It had been wonderful, but Natasha's newly acquired human emotions screamed that the act was wrong.

But how could something so lovely, so special, be wrong? Natasha reached out and stroked the hair on David's head. Her master was a wonderful man, a special man. Something in her psyche told her that men like David Wagner were not easy to come by. She truly loved him—she knew that now—and he loved her.

Natasha thought of what Coogan had said about learning to control her lycanthropy. Deep inside her soul, Natasha longed for the outdoors. And not just the doghouse and the life she had learned to live. But she longed for the great outdoors, for an expanse of wilderness where she could run wild and free and never answer to anyone and never have any problems and never experience the tangle of stress and emotion that she now felt. She understood that she was almost a full-blooded wolf, and that part of her soul would never die. But now, she thought of what a life with David might be like.

She thought of taking care of him, of learning to cook for him, of making love to him every night. Natasha knew that David had known another woman, although David had not mentioned it in their brief times together. She had seen the pictures that, for whatever reason, David had not managed to throw out, and she also saw the hurt in his eyes. Natasha wondered if she could alleviate that hurt, to make David forget that woman ever existed, and she realized that these were the thoughts of a genuine female human. The thoughts of a woman pondering the concept of love and eternity.

Could she grow to forget her former self if she did learn to control her abilities? She wished dearly that she could compare the two sides of her existence in a rational, logical way, but so far, she hadn't been able to. If she was to continue to be with David, wouldn't it be more enjoyable to be with him as a human? She could learn things, study, adapt herself completely to the life of David's mate. She could be his wife or be his pet. Possibly even raise a family with David. The thought made Natasha smile.

It took her mind a moment to realize what was happening even after her eyes saw the dark figure looming high above her head. Natasha started to scream, when a powerful, hairy hand shot forth and locked around her throat. She hadn't even managed to make a sound while she felt herself being pulled upward. Her legs flailed madly about as she was lifted from the floor. She felt her foot hit David's sleeping body, and as she looked down, she saw David stirring from his sleep before her head was turned around to face the intruder.

The face was hideous. It was a horrid cross between an animal and a man, a snarling, salivating visage with bestial features. But even at that, Natasha knew it was Stoner. She could smell him, and a hint of his blue eyes lingered somewhere beneath their seething red glow. His nose was wide and flat, protruding slightly from his face in a smashed, canine snout. His mouth was large and dripping, and his teeth were not human at all. The beast was nude, and its muscular, hairy body was supported by two legs. Stoner pulled Natasha to his face and snarled. She could smell the horrendous odor of rancid flesh on his breath.

Natasha could hear David shouting and moving about, but Stoner's snarls overpowered his words. Out of the corner of her eye, she saw David move toward them. Stoner shifted to his right, apparently anticipating David's actions. Natasha felt Stoner release her neck and immediately grab her arm. He lifted her up again with his left arm, while he shoved David with his free arm. Natasha watched David fly over the couch and smash into a bookcase. The shelves toppled over onto him, spilling books across the den.

Stoner stood over David's motionless form for a moment, then he snarled wildly and headed for the door. Natasha screamed and flailed about in his grip.

"Stop it!" Stoner snarled.

Natasha stared at him in amazement. His head had changed completely to its normal human visage. Natasha tried to listen for David to come after them, but she heard nothing. Stoner dragged her into the kitchen, and with one swift kick, the back door exploded into splinters. Natasha felt the cold rush of air embrace her nude body, driving the breath from her lungs. They stepped out under the covered patio, though the screen door, and out into the night.

•   •   •

David slowly regained consciousness, his mind groggy and his head aching. He felt the shelves of the oaken bookcase resting across his shoulders, and he squirmed to crawl from beneath the weight. Everything happened so swiftly that he had no time to react. His head was still reeling from the blow but he knew he had to act quickly.

David got dressed and rushed into the kitchen. The cool air hit him seconds before he saw the shattered remains of the back door. He thought about phoning Coogan but decided he didn't have time. David grabbed a flashlight from his front closet and cursed himself for his strong political views of gun control. Finding no other weapons, he hefted a baseball bat over his shoulder and ran out the back door.

•   •   •

"Where are you taking me?" shouted Natasha. "Where are we going?"

"Shut up, bitch!"

Natasha squirmed and tried to break free, but Stoner's grip was undaunting. She tried to turn her head to get a bearing as to their whereabouts, but the trees and bushes flew by at too great a speed. Natasha screamed and called out into the air, yelling Coogan's name as well as David's.

Stoner laughed. "Coogan? What's that old fool going to do for you?"

Natasha ignored his remark and continued shouting into the black night. She was sure David would come after her, so she had to keep yelling.

"Where are we going?"

"We're going back to my house where we belong."

"But I don't belong at your house! I don't even know you."

Suddenly, Stoner stopped and shoved Natasha to the ground. Natasha's head slammed into a tree, causing her to swoon. She grasped the back of her head and shut her eyes tightly to drive the pain away.

"You do belong with me, woman! I had you first! I was the one you mated with!"

"You didn't mate with me!" she snapped back. "You mated with a stupid dog, a young naive dog in heat that ran away from her safe home and got into trouble! You raped me!"

"I mated with you, and that's all that matters! Our kind mates for life, and now you've mated with another! I should kill you for that!"

"Oh, you talk as though I'm the unfaithful one. Are you always faithful in your human form, or do you live a double life? Saying one thing and doing another?" She hoped to keep Stoner shouting to allow David to catch up. Or maybe, she would get him so angry he would make a mistake. That could backfire, though, she thought. He could get mad enough to hurt her.

"I chose you carefully—"

"You didn't choose me; you ran across me. I was convenient. I was no more chosen than a whore you pick up in a bar!"

"That's not true!" screamed Stoner. "And even if it was, we still mate for life! I have a right to you now. I own you! And your sweet master can't understand that he has no rights to you any longer."

The bat caught Stoner on the right side of his head, just above his temple. The loud pop sounded through the countryside, and the wooden bat shattered in David's hands. Natasha watched as Stoner staggered backward and fell to the ground. She jumped to her feet.

Natasha hugged David fiercely. His breath was coming in ragged gasps, but he had saved her.

"I think I broke my arm when the bat snapped ," he laughed, and let the shattered end of the bat drop to the ground.

"Let's go before he gets up," said Natasha.

"Oh, I don't think he'll—"

The low, guttural snarl invaded the night air, and Natasha peered around David's shoulder. The huge wolf stood where Stoner had fallen. His red eyes glowed in a sea of ebony darkness, his huge, bushy tail swayed slowly behind him. The wolf stood about five feet at the shoulder and was three feet wide. Natasha's mind flashed back to the night when she had first experienced this horrible visage.

"Oh ... my ... God," David muttered.

The two humans were rooted, unable to tear their frightened eyes from the savage, unnatural beast. Natasha wanted to run, but the bones and muscles seemed to have escaped her body.

"Natasha, run," David whispered.

"I'm not leaving," she said.

"Natasha, RUN!"

She met David's gaze quickly, but he shoved her back before she could speak. She stumbled backward when she saw the wolf move.

She thought for a moment that it was lunging forward, but it was still standing in the same spot. It wasn't moving; it was elongating. Its body slid forward like a hairy piece of rubber stretched at both ends. Then, the back of the wolf seemed to quiver, and its hair began to stretch skyward as its back grew in height. Its front legs began to shorten as its torso molded into an upright position. Its hind legs widened and lengthened.

The wolf now stood on two legs, stretching some ten feet into the air. Its front legs were long, spindly arms with huge, sharp claws, and its torso was long and gangly. The monster lurched forward, its slavering, rotten mouth snapping toward them. It seemed as though the beast had barely moved, and it was on them. Its hands grasped David firmly by the shoulder.

"Natasha!" he screamed. "Run!"

Natasha stepped backward and tripped over an exposed tree root. She fell hard on her bottom. Stoner slammed David's body into the base of a tree, repeatedly pulling him back and smashing him into the trunk again. The creature swiped back and forth across David's face, slashing deep gashes into his skin.

Natasha knew that she had to do something, or David would die. She scanned the ground for a branch, anything that would help. But she had seen Stoner take a blow from a baseball bat to his head and shrug it off. A stick wasn't going to faze him. Natasha thought of Coogan; he would know what to do.

Suddenly, a thought hit Natasha. If she could learn to control her changes, she wouldn't have to become human. It stood to reason that she could make herself change back into a wolf. It was her only chance.

She didn't know what to do, but she closed her eyes tightly and concentrated. She pictured Coogan, his wisdom and strength, in her mind. She thought of wolves, of her earlier vision of running wild and free in unspoiled wilderness. She thought of chasing a mighty elk across vast plains, through shallow streams, the muddy water splashing across her face as she closed in on the large animal's hairy flanks. She could hear David's cries and the snarling of Stoner, and she tried to block out the sounds. She lowered her head to the ground and inhaled the pleasant earthy smell. Her heart beat madly in her ears while the sounds of the battle diminished. She saw Coogan in her mind's eye. She squeezed her eyes tighter, and then she could smell Coogan. She could almost hear him in her head, and she could hear the running waters of a brook, the call of an owl, the distant bay of wolves. The smells of the wilderness wafted into her senses, and the taste of raw meat, of fresh blood, and the exhilaration of the kill invaded her thoughts. And lying beneath these sensations, she saw the moon. The round yellow orb floated in and out of her mind's eye, and she felt movement deep inside of her.

Then, she heard nothing. The sound of silence disturbed the mental picture in her head, and she looked up. To her horror, Stoner held David's battered and bloodied body in his arms. Natasha felt hot tears slashing their way through her eyes, stinging them madly. Stoner locked eyes on Natasha, fixing his gaze to hers. He lifted the lifeless corpse to his jaws and buried his massive snout into David's throat, ripping and shredding the flesh. He pulled away and, blood dripping from his savage teeth, Stoner dropped David at his feet. Natasha stared at his crumpled body, and instinctively, she grabbed a branch and charged the wolf. Natasha wept loudly, and she swung the branch at Stoner with all her might. The stick shattered against his steely arm, and he did not waver. Instead, his facial features shifted and distorted until they were human again. Stoner smiled and placed a wolfen foot across David's unmoving chest. Natasha watched, stunned, as he threw his head back. In a terrifying instant, she saw his nose and mouth shift and extend into a snout, and he released a terrifying, gut-wrenching howl into the cold night air. As he dropped his head down to face her, the snout withdrew, and his face returned to normal.

Natasha stared into Stoner's cold blue eyes, momentarily hazed by the steam rising around his face. Natasha's human eyes locked onto Stoner's human eyes, but deep in her soul, she felt a fierce clash of pure, animal instinct in its basest form.

"He'll have you no more," Stoner said though gritted bloody teeth. "You are mine now. All mine."

Natasha dropped to her knees and buried her face in her hands. She heard Stoner's guttural laughter, and she looked back up at him. His body shifted and wavered as he dropped to all fours. Natasha stared into the black soul of the wicked, evil beast, and he smiled again. Then, as swiftly as he had come, the wolf stepped over David's lifeless body and disappeared into the woods.

Natasha sat on her knees, almost emotionless, staring into the woods where she had last seen Stoner. Slowly, inevitably, the tears returned. She crawled toward David, fell across his limp body, and patted his matted, bloody hair. Her mind flooded with thoughts of the wonderful moments they had shared only hours earlier, and the sudden realization that they would never experience them again. She thought of Coogan, the sweet, wonderful man who had accepted her for what she had become, and she couldn't keep from cursing him. When she and David had needed him the most, he was not there. Where was Coogan, and why had he deserted them? She thought of Stoner, the one who had robbed her of her true love. Why had he left? Why had he spared her?

But most of all, she thought of her owner. His life had been normal until Stoner had invaded it. She couldn't help but wonder if she could have made things different. Perhaps she should have gone to Stoner. Maybe this entire situation could've been avoided. They should've just let Stoner win. After all, he had anyway.

"I'm so sorry, David. I love you so much, and I always have. Sleep well, David. Sleep well tonight."

Natasha lifted David's ravaged body higher to hers. She held him, rocking back and forth, and cried until she could cry no more.

•   •   •

Natasha awoke to the sounds of humans and their machines. For a moment, she forgot where she was, but the reality slapped her hard when she saw David's body lying next to her. She lowered her head and licked his face, kissing him tenderly, ignoring the sour taste of dried blood.

She remembered everything, though her canine mind had difficulty comprehending some of it. She remembered mating with David. And then Stoner had kidnapped her, and he had killed David. Her mind remembered the human events much easier now, but she wished that it couldn't.

Natasha saw the men getting out of their vehicles. There were two vehicles and three men. Natasha heard them speaking. Some of the words were clear, but she didn't understand many of them. Natasha watched as the men stopped ahead of her.

•   •   •

"Holy Jesus," Sheriff Barnes said. "Will you look at that?"

"I told you, sheriff," another man said. "I told you I heard something out here last night."

"Okay, Blaylock. I believe you. I believe you."

Sheriff Barnes peered through his binoculars at Wagner and the dog. "Jesus Christ, I would've never believed this. Not in a million years would I believe this was gonna happen."

"Look at that damn wolf. I knew that thing was a goddamned wolf. Just standing over its kill like it's so damn proud," said Blaylock.

Sheriff Barnes looked at Deputy Stoner "What should we do? Any suggestions?"

"Shoot the damned thing," Blaylock offered.

"Blaylock, do you mind?"

"It's dangerous," the farmer persisted. "It seems pretty obvious to me. I've read about these so-called wolf-hybrids. They're damn near one-hundred percent wolf. Unpredictable as hell. Only one thing to do if you ask me."

"Yeah, well no one asked you." The sheriff shooed Blaylock back. "Jesus, I can't believe this happened to the kid. I would've never thought that animal would turn on him like that." He looked down at the ground and kicked at a rock. "You'd better get the tranquilizer, Devin."

"Right." Stoner headed back to the patrol car.

"You're not gonna shoot it?"

"I might shoot you if you don't knock it off."

Deputy Stoner returned with the tranquilizer gun. He opened a case and retrieved a cartridge of liquid and inserted it into the dart.

"Well, maybe animal control can tell what went wrong. What made her do that," the sheriff said. "You still want the dog now, Stoner?"

The deputy raised the rifle and leveled it. "I don't know. We'll see what they say."

11

J
ACKIE COOGAN DIDN'T SUCCUMB to his cravings for alcohol
that night, but he did spend half the night struggling with the
demon inside the bottle. And he realized that during that time
when he was fighting with his inner self, David Wagner had died.

Coogan reached across the table and slapped the power button
of the clock radio on his kitchen counter, turning off the morning
report that had given him the news. He drew a deep breath, held it
for a long while, and let it out with a sigh.

So that's it, Coogan thought. Stoner had done it. He had killed
David Wagner.

Even though the news reported that the unidentified individual
had been apparently mauled to death by his pet wolf-hybrid, Coogan
knew better. Stoner had done it. No doubt in his mind.

Coogan rubbed his eyes, fighting back the tears that were forcing
their way forward. He had won the battle over the struggle for the
booze, but the alcohol had defeated him anyway. David was dead now,
and Natasha would soon be put to sleep or placed in Stoner's custody.

"It's not fair, dammit,' Coogan cried. "I won. I won. I didn't drink
anything."

But you weren't there, old boy. You weren't there when the big bad wolf came to blow the house down. You talked big, and you told them everything would be all right, but when the shit went down, you weren't there for them. You left them to face the final conflict alone, two naive individuals who had no idea what they were up against. You let them down, Jackie. You let David down, and you let Natasha down. Just like you've done everyone else that ever mattered in your life. Just like you did—

"No," Coogan muttered. "No. Not this time. I won't let her down this time, so help me God."

Coogan jumped up from the table and grabbed his jacket. He stormed out of the tiny trailer and walked south toward town.

•   •   •

Sheriff Barnes stared at the bruised, pale body of David Wagner lying in a drawer of the Barnhardt County Morgue. The massive wound on Wagner's throat did not seem any less horrible than it had when the sheriff had first witnessed it, even though it had been cleaned. He shivered. Sheriff Barnes hated morgues. Other than their obvious connection with death, the overbearing whiteness of morgues seemed inappropriate, almost blasphemous.

Sheriff Barnes rubbed his chin and sighed. This time yesterday morning, he had been standing in Wagner's back yard carrying on a normal conversation with the man. And now, he was staring at him on ice. "What do you think?" Barnes asked the coroner.

"Well," Dr. Drake said. He touched the wounds on Wagner's throat. Barnes shivered again. "The wounds on the victim match the bite radius numbers on the animal in question. Close enough, anyway."

"What do you mean 'close enough'?"

"Well, some of the injuries show some variance, but that could be caused by any number of things."

"Such as?"

"It's a very jagged wound, made by a very large mouth. You have to allow for the struggle of the victim, slippage of the attacking animal's teeth once it's established a grip. Either of these things could show a larger wound than the animal could account for."

Sheriff Barnes nodded his head.

"What happened exactly?" Drake asked.

"We've had a lot of livestock killing in the last few months down our way. A lot of people blamed Wagner's dog. Big wolf-hybrid. It kept getting loose, so we suggested he keep it inside for a while in order to prove its innocence." Sheriff Barnes shrugged. "I guess she didn't like being cooped up all day. Best that we can tell, she busted through two doors, he chased her down, and she attacked." Barnes looked again at Wagner's body.

"Stir crazy, sounds like."

"I guess so. Any other injuries?"

Dr. Drake nodded and pointed along Wagner's upper torso. "He has some pretty severe bruises along the upper torso, right along in here. I assume the animal landed on him at some point during the attack. The dog weighed, what, sixty, seventy pounds?"

"Probably more than that," said Barnes. "Closer to ninety." He stood a moment longer, still staring at David's remains. "So, it's your professional opinion that the animal we have at our animal control is responsible for these injuries?"

Drake nodded. "Yes, I'd say so."

"Yeah, I thought so too." The sheriff headed toward the door. "I was just hoping it wasn't so."

•   •   •

"How has she been since we brought her in?" Stoner shouted over the din of the barking dogs.

Natasha threw her front legs against the cage door, growling and barking savagely. She bared her teeth viciously and saliva flew from her rapidly snapping jaws.

The attendant stepped back from Natasha's cage. "She was fine until now."

"She's just a little cagey from being locked up so long." The deputy approached the cage. Natasha's snarls intensified. "Hello, girl."

"Uh," the attendant said. "I wouldn't get too close."

Stoner held his hand up to the man, pushing him back. "It's good to see all the effects of the tranquilizer have worn off. Have you sedated her any?"

"Ayuh, so we could take the tests."

"Have you finished with the tests?" Stoner knelt before Natasha's cage until he was eye level with her.

"We finished taking them, but we don't have the results yet."

Natasha had dropped to all-fours. She stood rooted at the door, her teeth still bared. Stoner extended his hand to Natasha and held it steady. She growled and snapped, but she did not back away. Slowly, Stoner moved his hand closer to the wire cage.

"Uh, d-d-deputy, be … be careful."

Natasha's ears rose, and her head cocked to one side. The growling in her throat softened, and she whimpered. Stoner's hand glided slowly to the cage's edge, and his fingers slipped between the wires and rubbed Natasha's nose.

"Damn, how'd you do that? I ain't never seen nothing like that."

"You just have to show them who's in control. Never show them any fear." Stoner stood and turned away from Natasha's cage. "How long before the tests are back?"

"A day or two. Why?"

"Well, if she's not sick or diseased, I may take her off your hands."

"You will?" the man said in disbelief. "Deputy, you do know this dog ripped a man's throat out."

"He didn't know how to handle her. I'd met the guy, and he knew nothing about raising hybrids."

"Is that a fact? "Well, if you're planning on claiming this dog, there's something else you might want to know."

"Oh," Stoner said, turning back to the attendant, "what's that?"

"She's pregnant."

Stoner raised an eyebrow. "You said the tests weren't back yet."

"Don't need a test to tell you that," the man said. "Her teats are swelling. Yeah, she's about six weeks along."

Deputy Stoner smiled. "Six weeks, huh?"

"At least."

"Call the sheriff's office and let me know the minute you get the test results."

"Will do."

•　　•　　•

Sheriff Barnes stapled the last of a new batch of "wanted" posters to the bulletin board hanging near the station's front doors. "Devin, are you sure that's such a good idea?" Sheriff Barnes asked.

"Well, why not?"

"Oh, Devin, I don't know. That animal is dangerous. She should probably be put down, regardless of what the tests show."

"Sheriff Barnes, she's much too magnificent an animal to be put down. Besides, Wagner didn't know how to handle her."

"And you do?"

"I think I do. Wagner was spineless; he didn't know how to control her. You saw how she behaved when I was around. She was like a puppy. Believe me, I can handle her."

Barnes shrugged. "She did seem to do whatever you told her. Well, if she's healthy, and you want to, I don't see anything wrong with it. But you just make sure she never—I mean never—gets out. She does, and I'll have her ass and yours."

Deputy Stoner saluted the sheriff. "Yes, sir."

Sheriff Barnes shook his head. "I still think it's crazy."

"Something else that's kind of crazy. I just heard it over at animal control."

The sheriff dropped into his chair and leaned back. "What's that?"

"The dog is pregnant."

"Jesus, how did that happen?"

"Maybe Wagner did it," Deputy Mason chimed in.

Sheriff Barnes leaned forward in his chair and jumped to his feet. "Mason! Go out on your patrol!"

"I've already done my afternoon patrol."

"Do it again!"

Mason fumbled for his clipboard and slipped away like a scolded child caught with his hand in the cookie jar.

"Dumbass kid," Sheriff Barnes mumbled.

Stoner sat on the edge of the sheriff's desk. "Anyway, back to what we were discussing. My guess is, she met up with another dog during one of her midnight runs."

"Makes sense, but do you mind?" The sheriff grabbed a handful of thumbtacks and threw them at his deputy's backside. "What are you going to do with the puppies?"

"Sorry, boss," Stoner removed himself from the sheriff's desk and retrieved the thumbtacks. "As far as the puppies? I don't know. Might keep one. Sell the rest."

"They'll more than likely be mutts," Deputy Smitty called out from his desk.

Stoner turned to face him. "Oh, I don't know. I have a feeling they'll be pretty special."

"Why this sudden interest in animals anyway?" Barnes asked.

Stoner picked up a photograph of Natasha from Wagner's file that lay on Sheriff Barnes' desk. He gave the photo a long study. "I don't know. I've always liked Wagner's dog. She's a gorgeous animal. Too bad what happened to him, though."

"Just make sure it doesn't happen to you," Smitty said.

Barnes added, "And watch those damn puppies. They can be mean, too."

"I will, Sheriff. Oh, by the way—I guess I'll be taking off on the hunting trip once I find out about the dog, if that's okay with you."

Sheriff Barnes shrugged. "Sure, I don't know why you've waited this long. All the good bucks are probably gone by now."

"Well," said Stoner. "I didn't want to leave while all this business with the missing livestock was going on."

"Oh, you're so dedicated," Smitty chimed in.

Stoner laughed. "I am. More than you'll ever know."

"So, I take it you think the killings are over now," noted the sheriff.

"Yeah, why wouldn't you think so? I thought all along Wagner's dog was doing it, and what happened last night only confirmed it. And now that she's locked up, and with the possibility of my owning her ... yeah, I think we've heard the last of our irate farmers."

"God, I hope so," Sheriff Barnes said. "But what about all those other times?"

"What other times?"

"Well, according to Wagner, we had a few killings happen before this dog of his ever got out."

"He probably said that to cover his own ass," Stoner offered.

"Or maybe some of our other theories were responsible for those first few killings," said Smitty. "You know, delinquent teenagers ..."

"Mutant slime-monsters."

"Toxic aliens from another world," Sheriff Barnes added.

They all laughed. "Now we're right back where we started with all the cornball ideas," Smitty said.

"Yeah, yeah," said Sheriff Barnes. "Case closed, let's assume."

•　　•　　•

"Hello?" Coogan called out, his head poking through the wide-open double doors of the animal control center.

A chorus of baying canines followed, but he heard no human sounds. Coogan took a few steps into the building. Directly in front of him, a large German shepherd barked hoarsely. Coogan peered around the corner and studied the long hall of cages. He couldn't see anyone.

"Hello?" There was still no answer.

Coogan started down the hall, glancing into each cage as he passed. A black lab, a mutt, a chow mix. He stopped.

Coogan knelt in front of the cage, and peered in at the silvery, sleeping canine inside.

"Natasha."

The dog immediately lifted its head, ears pointing alertly. Natasha seemed to recognize Coogan. She barked twice, her tail wagging happily, and she threw her heavy body against the cage door.

"Can I help you, Mister?" a voice said from behind Coogan.

Coogan stood and turned to face the man.

"Oh," said the man, annoyed. "Coogan."

"Bobby."

"What do you want, old timer?"

"Oh, nothin'. Just came to check out some dogs. Thought I might take one home with me."

"You? What do you want with a dog? You can barely take care of yourself."

"Well, I tend to get lonely out at my trailer all by myself. A dog makes good company."

"Well, you better give up on that one. She ain't going nowhere."

"Oh?" Coogan feigned ignorance. "Why is that?"

"She mauled her owner to death is all."

"That's right," Coogan rubbed his chin. "I heard something about that on the radio. Such a shame."

"Yeah, it is." Bobby didn't sound very sincere. "Coogan, I don't care if you take a dog, but look at the others. Not this one."

"Okay, okay. Say, what's gonna happen to this one, anyway?"

"What do you think's gonna happen to her?"

Coogan nodded in understanding. "Even though she's pregnant?"

"How did you know that?"

"I've been around animals long enough to know."

Bobby studied Coogan for a moment. "Like I said, if you want a dog." He extended his arms to the cages on either side of Natasha's.

Coogan nodded and walked slowly along the rows of cages. The attendant turned away from Coogan to the back of the building. Coogan watched him until he was out of sight, and then he moved over to the desk, piled high with unorganized stacks of papers. Coogan thumbed through the papers, occasionally glancing up to check on Bobby's possible return.

Finally, he found a copy of Natasha's admittance paper. Coogan moved closer to the open doors and held the paper in the sunlight. He moved his fingers across the slip of paper, searching for the information.

Name: Natasha. Owner: David Wagner. Breed: wolf-hybrid. Percentage: 98, MacKenzie Valley. Coogan stopped, his finger resting on the paper. He read the line again. Breeder: William Forrester, Flagstaff, Arizona.

Coogan ran his fingers through his scraggly hair. Hearing the attendant's footsteps down the hall, Coogan shoved the paper under the rest of the stack and left.

He found the information he was searching for.

●   ●   ●

The good thing about small, rural towns? Coogan thought. There's never much in the way of security. It had been easier to sneak into the morgue than it had to sneak into Animal Control.

Coogan took a deep breath and held it a moment. The closet was dark. Coogan pressed his ear to the closed door and listened. He heard a door shut, and the clicking of hard-soled shoes moving back down the hall. He waited until the sounds of the steps had diminished, then opened the door a crack. Coogan peered up the hallway. There was no one in sight. He stepped out into the bright, white hallway.

Coogan drew a deep breath. The sign over the next door read "Refrigeration Room." Coogan said a quick prayer and pushed the latch. There was a loud click. Coogan pulled back; the latch gave freely. Unlocked. Glancing back over his shoulder, Coogan pushed the door open and stepped inside.

The room was cold, not only in temperature, but in atmosphere. Coogan pulled his old khaki jacket closer to his body and walked over to the rows and rows of drawers. *You're a goddamn fool for doing this*, his inner voice warned. But he had to see David Wagner one last time. Coogan stopped at the label bearing David's name. He closed his eyes briefly, took a deep breath, and slid the drawer open. It pulled open smoothly and effortlessly.

"Dear God," Coogan whispered.

David's nude body lay flat on the cold, steel drawer base. He was pale, so pale, and his face had a faint tinge of blue to it. The wound on his throat had been cleaned, but the ferocity with which it had been inflicted was still horribly evident.

"Dear, dear God."

Coogan stepped slowly down the length of the drawer and stopped at David's head. He hesitantly reached out and touched David's face. It was cold, colder than he expected it to be. But that's death.

"Boy," Coogan started, speaking in barely a whisper. "I'm so, so sorry you got dragged into all this craziness. I can't begin to tell you how sorry I really am. You didn't deserve to get caught up in this, and you certainly didn't deserve this."

Coogan felt tears slowly rolling down his cheeks, their warmth temporarily soothing his face before the chill of the inhumane room chased the sensation away. "But listen to this, David. I promise, by everything that I've ever held dear in my miserable life, I am going to make sure that Natasha and the children are safe.

"Yeah, I know about the children. I can't blame you for what you did. It made Natasha happy, I'm sure. And whatever makes her happy is fine by me. But I swear to you, if I have to lay down my own life, Stoner will not have her again. Rest easy knowing that, son. I let you and Natasha down once. I've let a lot of people down in my life, but not this time." Coogan let his head drop to David's cold chest and began to weep.

"Not this time! You have my word on that."

12

E VERYTHING HAD TURNED OUT better than Devin Stoner could've imagined. Wagner was out of the way, and Stoner had managed to make Natasha the scapegoat in his death. He had eliminated the enemy without drawing attention to himself. Natasha would soon be his property. The tests for diseases would prove negative, and he would acquire legal custody of the animal. The Festering would soon begin, and Stoner had managed to prepare and strengthen himself for the occasion, again using the bitch as a crutch.

And now, to top it all off, Natasha would bring his offspring into the world. He was sure that Natasha was pregnant with his children. The animal control attendant said she was at least six weeks pregnant, but that was the guess of a man who wasn't exactly overflowing with knowledge; she was probably further along. Too far along for the children to be Wagner's.

This pleased Stoner most of all. His prime bloodline would continue. The children would be strong and savage full-blooded lycanthropes. He would raise the children under his proper guidance, prepare them for their tasks ahead, and make them ready to attend The Festering with him one day.

And they would just be the first. Natasha would bear him many strong sons and daughters. His blood would flow through hundreds of lycanthrope veins, making his name the strongest in the annals of their society. He would be the most powerful of them all; he would rule The Festering for many, many years to come. Indeed, for eternity.

The female would learn to love him; he would make sure of that. He would not allow her to mourn the death of the weak and inferior Wagner for long. She had not yet begun to realize the magnificence of what she was. She had no idea the control, the power she could have standing at his side. She would come to accept the ways of the lycanthrope, and she would take part in the proper rearing of their children. Stoner envisioned the day of future Festerings, his entire family at his side, reveling in their undeniable power. She would get caught up in the celebrations, the bloodletting, the savagery. It was, after all, a part of her. She was a lycanthrope.

•   •   •

David was dead; Natasha realized that now. She knew it in her heart and her head. She understood the concept, knew what it meant, and comprehended the finality of it. The word "dead" floated in and out of her mind, and the image of David's crumpled body and the memory of holding him in her arms lingered in her consciousness. Natasha began to remember it all now. Her abduction by Stoner, the final conflict with the evil lycanthrope, and most painfully, the night she spent with David. The memories and the words that helped her understand what she was recalling flooded back vividly.

And Natasha cried. The sound was no more intense than canine whimpering, and it certainly got the attention of the hound dog next to her, but the pain inside of her was too intense. She was alone now since David was gone. It didn't seem fair that he was taken from her so soon after they had just begun to get to know each other.

She had not asked for this disease, this lycanthropy. She had not wished to transform into a human female in order to experience human pleasures with her master. But it had happened. She and David only followed their natural instincts of love and survival. And now, it seemed they were being punished for it.

The hound next to her released a single piercing yelp in her ear, and Natasha wanted it to shut up. The chihuahua to her other side continued its incessant yapping , and Natasha longed to bite its head off. These were emotions and thoughts that were not coming to her when she had first arrived at this place, the Potters Animal Control Center. She had heard the man answer the phone with those words.

And with the heightened intelligence and capacity for logic came plans. Natasha had been searching for ways to escape her prison, but it was futile considering the tools with which she had to work. She had tried loosening the latch with her paws when the attendant was away, but they were just too clumsy.

Natasha remembered what Coogan said about controlling her abilities, but try as she might, she had not been able to do it. She felt that she had almost managed to change into her animal form when David was battling Stoner, but she just couldn't recall the key element that had caused it. It was probably just as well anyway. She would be in even more trouble if she did change to her human form. She would have to stay the way she was. For now.

•   •   •

"You'd better put this leash on her, deputy," Bobby said as the two men stood outside of Natasha's cage.

"We won't need the leash," Stoner said.

"Devin, I think you'd better put her on a leash, just to be safe. I know you think you can control her, but don't get cocky," said Sheriff Barnes.

Stoner looked at the sheriff. "I don't need a leash."

Bobby glanced at the sheriff, as if to ask permission. Sheriff Barnes nodded, and Bobby opened Natasha's cage.

"Now, you're sure this animal is totally healthy?" Barnes asked.

The attendant nodded. "Rabies, distemper, parvo. It all checks out. Plus, we've had her under observation for three days, and she shows no sign of aggression. Except the first time you showed up," he said, nodding to Stoner.

"Oh?" Sheriff Barnes said.

"And didn't I get her settled down right after that? Besides, does she seem ferocious to you now?"

The men looked at Natasha. She sat still in the cage, watching them, trying to understand what was being said. She managed to pick up on a word here and there, and she came to the conclusion Stoner was taking her with him.

"She seems pretty docile."

Stoner knelt and snapped his fingers at Natasha. Natasha stepped out of the cage and sat down between the men. There would be no need for Stoner to hypnotize her this time. Natasha wanted to be in control of her own mind. She would cooperate with Stoner, pretending to obey his commands.

"Let's go, girl." He and Sheriff Barnes turned toward the exit.

Natasha followed her "new master" like a good little puppy should. She paused to take one last glance at the stinky place that had been her home since David's death. She was out of the cage now, and that was part of the plan. Once in Stoner's custody, the opportunities for escape would be much greater.

•   •   •

Coogan stood beneath a window that opened into one of the back storage rooms of the Animal Control Center. Even though the afternoon sun burned bright in the sky, the air was chilly. Coogan rested against a gas meter, tilting his ear toward the window. Sooner or later, Bobby would have to go to the bathroom. As soon as Coogan heard the rustling of newspapers and the click of the door, he would act.

His only hope was to break Natasha out of the control center. If Coogan couldn't get her out of there, one of two things would happen, neither of which represented a favorable scenario. If Natasha was found to be healthy and non-violent, then Stoner would surely take her. If the vets thought she was too aggressive, she would be euthanized.

Coogan could allow neither of those to occur. It would be much easier to take Natasha from the control center with the dim-witted Bobby on duty than it would be to attempt to pry her away from Stoner. Coogan hoped Stoner didn't know Natasha was pregnant. That would only make matters worse; Stoner would surely take her then, especially if he thought the children were his. Coogan shuddered. If Stoner thought they were David's, he might even kill Natasha, certainly kill the children if he still had Natasha when they were born.

Soon enough, Coogan heard the unoiled hinges of the bathroom door creak open and shut. Time to act.

Coogan moved swiftly around the side of the building and to the open double doors. He had to act quickly, before Bobby finished his business. Coogan stepped cautiously through the doors, trying to move as quietly as possible. Hopefully, most of the dogs would be asleep. Coogan looked to the first row of cages. The little terrier mix in the second cage was snoozing away, but the big German shepherd in the first cage wasn't. It sounded its warning to the others, and the center came alive with the sounds of angry dogs.

"Hell with it," Coogan sputtered, and he headed swiftly for Natasha's cage.

It was empty.

Coogan stood solemnly, his tired old hands resting on his tired old hips, the hound dog to his right howling away. Dammitall! Coogan shouted at himself. I'm too late. The entire community of the Potters Animal Control Center barked and growled; the din began to hurt Coogan's ears.

"Shut up, you damned old mutt!" Coogan yelled at the hound dog.

It jumped slightly, then threw itself against its door, yelping when its snout smashed into the wires. Then Coogan heard the creaking of the bathroom door.

"What the hell you bastards barking at now?"

He stepped out of the bathroom, newspaper in hand, stains covering a good percentage of his coveralls.

"Oh, Coogan, what do you want now?"

"What happened to the dog that was in this cage? The wolf-hybrid?"

"I told you not to worry about that one, didn't I?" Bobby approached Coogan.

"She wasn't put to sleep?"

Bobby stood tall over Coogan's smaller frame, glaring down at the older man. "Why don't you just get out of here, old man."

Coogan moved swiftly and deftly, before the slower man could even react. He grabbed the lapels of Bobby's filth-smeared coveralls and slammed him hard against Natasha's empty cage. "Don't mess with me, shit-for-brains! Now, what happened to the dog?"

The attendant struggled against Coogan's surprising strength. "Awright, awright!" Bobby howled, not unlike the hound dog in the next cage. "Stoner took her!"

Coogan relaxed his hold. "Stoner."

"Yeah, she was healthy and all, so he took her."

Coogan let go of the man and stepped back. Bobby rubbed the back of his neck and adjusted his coveralls. "Damn crazy old fool."

"You don't tell anyone I was here, you got that?" said Coogan.

"Get fucked."

With lightning quickness, the attendant got shoved against the cage again, sending the center's inhabitants into another display of territorial squawking.

"Okay, okay! You weren't here."

Coogan turned from the attendant and exited the building. Stoner had Natasha under his legal ownership, but that didn't change things. It only complicated them a bit.

13

THE LAST FULL MOON OF AUTUMN was little more than a week away. The time of the Festering drew near. Stoner felt it in his black soul. The anticipation of the annual event had nearly reached its pinnacle. The craving for blood and sex gnawed at his being, and Stoner reveled in it. The risks he had taken these previous months, the taste of human blood, the acquisition of a permanent mate all swarmed and seethed to bring him to a frenzy.

Stoner peered out the back window at his beautiful new mate. He watched as she pushed her snout along the ground, attempting to get closer to the fence, only to be restricted by the chain. He could take no chances. The chain would restrain her and prevent any attempts at digging under the fence. And she would be kept inside while he was away.

It had been difficult for Stoner to control his desire for Natasha. He longed to see Natasha as a woman, to drink in what he was sure would be a glorious vision, to have her as Wagner had. The thought of his bitch mating with another angered Stoner, but it had been against her will. She had not fully understood her new situation, and Wagner had taken advantage of her. Natasha would never sin against her mate.

But Stoner forced himself to battle the urge. To indulge in pleasures of the flesh so near the Festering would only weaken his strength and virility for the blessed event. He would have plenty of opportunities for that during the week-long activities, and when he returned, Natasha would be all his.

Stoner turned back to the activities at hand. His hunting gear was laid out on the living room floor. Either Sheriff Barnes or one of Stoner's fellow deputies always dropped by, and he had to perfect the hunting facade. Every year before the Festering, Stoner would load his Explorer with sleeping bags, shotguns, Coleman lanterns, and other camping equipment and depart through the main stretch of downtown. Deputy Stoner off on his yearly hunting trip. No one ever knew any different.

Stoner went back into the kitchen and out the rear door. Natasha twisted about upon the sound of the slamming screen door. Her expression did not change. *She'll learn to respect her real master,* Stoner thought. *She's already behaving much better.* He had no need to hypnotize her anymore.

"Good morning, Natasha."

Stoner knelt before her and unfastened the chain. He stepped back a few feet. Natasha sat still, staring up at him. Stoner walked back to the door. He returned his gaze to Natasha, snapped his fingers once, and pointed to the door. Without hesitation, Natasha trotted toward him and into the house. *She fears me.*

Deputy Stoner downed the last of his morning coffee and strolled confidently to his squad car.

•　　　•　　　•

The abrupt sound of the engine starting snapped Coogan awake. He jerked forward, gasping. His shoulder slid off the trunk of the tree that he was dozing against. Coogan fell onto his belly and peered through the bushes.

The squad car backed out of the driveway and careened down highway 92 toward the sheriff's office. Coogan glanced at the yard. Natasha wasn't there, at least that he could see as the sun had not quite risen yet. Coogan saw one light still burning in the house. *That's probably where he's keeping her.*

Coogan made another check down the highway, making sure Stoner's car was completely out of sight. He scrambled to his feet, grabbing the crowbar he had brought with him. He sprinted for the house and struggled over the chain link fence. Coogan positioned himself under a window. Saying a quick prayer, he rapped on the window and shouted for Natasha. She answered with a sharp cry.

She's in there.

Coogan had to act quickly. Raising the crowbar high over his head, he shattered the window with one swipe, raking the bar across the edges to remove the jagged shards. He didn't care if his point of entry was obvious. If everything worked out the way he planned, he and Natasha would be out of the county before Stoner even knew he'd been there.

Coogan reached up and grasped the inside windowsill and pulled himself up. Kicking his skinny legs for leverage, Coogan found his upper body inside Stoner's bathroom. He shifted himself to the right, thrust his legs forward, and swung into the bathroom, dropping to the bathtub.

With Natasha barking madly, Coogan stepped out of the tub and into the hall.

•　　•　　•

Deputies Mason and Smitty couldn't believe their eyes at first. They saw the legs of an unknown individual extending from the bathroom window of Deputy Stoner's house, kicking and flailing wildly. Even from a distance, they could tell that the window had been shattered.

"Who do you think it is?" Mason asked.

"I don't know. But we'd better call the office and let Devin know."

Mason looked away from Smitty and back toward the illegal entry in progress. He squinted, trying to sharpen his vision to identify the intruder.

Smitty soon had Deputy Stoner on the radio. "Devin, I hate to tell you this, but we've got someone breaking into your house."

"Do what?" the voice over the radio cried.

Just then, Mason saw the man's head as he swung his legs into the house. "Holy shit, Smitty. You're not gonna believe this. It's Coogan."

"Are you sure?" Smitty asked, holding the mouthpiece away from him.

"I said come again," Stoner's voice boomed.

"I saw him. It was Coogan."

Smitty called into the radio, "Uh, Devin. We may have a positive ID on the suspect. It's Jackie Coogan."

"Coogan?"

"Roger," Smitty said. "What do you want us to do?"

"Arrest his ass! And hold him. I'll be there in a minute!"

"Ten-four," Smitty said, and returned the mouthpiece to its holder. He exchanged amused glances with Mason, and they both burst into laughter.

•　　　•　　　•

Natasha greeted Coogan happily, jumping up on her hind legs and licking his face. He rubbed Natasha's fur enthusiastically and dropped to his knees. She barked at Coogan, and her tongue shot forward a few more times, happily licking at air. Coogan gently rubbed the soft hair on her head and scratched her ears. Natasha's brown eyes stared intently into his, and Coogan realized there was a lot more thought and intelligence in those eyes than he might've expected. This soon anyway.

"Had you given up on me, girl?"

Natasha's ears dropped happily, and she whimpered once. Coogan moved his hand under her chin and scratched.

"I told you I'd make everything okay, didn't I? I'm just a little late, honey, is all. Much too late for David, I'm afraid. But never too late for you."

Natasha stepped forward and licked Coogan again. He laughed and hugged her. Then, Coogan placed a hand under each of Natasha's ears, and gazed deep into her eyes. There was understanding in those eyes. She knew who he was, and why he had come for her.

"Natasha, I don't know how much of this you can understand, if you can understand any of it. I didn't find out for sure until yesterday, but I think ... I think I knew it, somewhere in my heart all along."

Natasha's brown eyes seemed to sharpen in concentration, as if listening intently to every word, and somehow, Coogan knew that she was.

"Natasha," he said. "I think I'm your father."

Coogan grabbed Natasha's neck and hugged her tightly as tears filled his eyes. He didn't feel the least bit apprehensive about telling an animal what he had just told this one. After all, she wasn't an animal, and neither was he.

"What the hell is this?"

Coogan scrambled to his feet. Natasha crouched to the floor, barking and growling protectively. Coogan's heart pounded in his throat. He had been so worried about making sure Stoner was gone that he had forgotten about the other peacekeepers of Potters.

"D-d-deputies."

"What the hell are you doing here, Coogan?" demanded Mason.

"You want to answer that, Mr. Coogan?"

"It ... it ain't right. It ain't right that Stoner takes Wagner's dog. It ain't right."

Smitty shined a flashlight into Coogan's eyes. "Is that what you're here for? To take the dog?"

"Oh, man," Mason said. "This is too much." He grabbed his portable radio from his belt and called for Stoner. "This is a wild one, Devin. He was trying to steal your new baby."

"Natasha?" Stoner's voice sounded incredulous.

"Whatever its name is." Mason felt along the dog's neck for a nametag.

"Why did you do it?" Smitty ignored the radio conversation.

"She's not happy here," Coogan had to keep his true reasons away from them, away from Stoner, praying the deputies had not heard his paternal admission.

"Coogan, she might've been put to sleep if Stoner hadn't been willing to take her in. Do you realize that?" Smitty had always tried to give the old gentleman the benefit of the doubt, but this pushed his understanding.

"What were you going to do with her?" Mason concluded his conversation with Stoner and set the portable microphone aside on his vest.

"I don't know," said Coogan defiantly. "I was just going to take her is all."

"Well, Stoner's on his way now, and he's probably pissed."

Coogan let his hand rest on Natasha's head, trying to calm and comfort her. He had blown it again.

•   •   •

The air was tense inside the Potters Sheriff's Department. The pleasant aroma of a freshly-brewing pot of coffee did little to settle the atmosphere. "He worked at a canning factory in New York for twenty-two years. Lives on his pension. Other than the various police reports in our files, that's all we have on him," Smitty said.

"No date of birth?" Sheriff Barnes asked.

"Nope. No date of birth, no birthplace, no proof that he even exists."

"How old are you, Coogan?" the sheriff asked.

Coogan sat in front of Deputy Smitty's desk, his eyes focused on an imperfection in the linoleum floor. He could feel Deputy Stoner's eyes boring into his back, but he did not look up. "I forget."

Sheriff Barnes gave Smitty an exaggerated shrug. Smitty rolled his eyes.

"Give me a guess," said Smitty to Coogan.

"Seventy-two?" Coogan seemed to actually guess, still not removing his gaze from the floor.

Smitty glanced at the sheriff questioningly. Barnes waved his hands as if to say 'go with it.' Smitty scribbled the number on the report.

"Any idea where you were born?"

"New York."

"Where in New York?"

Coogan glanced furtively at Stoner, caught the deputy's fierce gaze, and quickly returned his attention to the floor. "Just New York."

"New York, New York?" Sheriff Barnes asked. "Is that it, Coogan? The city New York?"

"I don't remember," he said, picking at a loose thread on his trousers.

"Write it down," Sheriff Barnes told Smitty.

Smitty finished the last piece of writing and laid the pen down. "Well, that's it. Such as it were. Devin, anything you want to add?"

Coogan shifted his eyes so he could see Stoner out of the corner of his eye. He could see the big deputy move from the desk on which he had been leaning. His heavy boots clicked on the smooth floor. Coogan could see Stoner's feet coming into view. They moved in front of him and stopped. Stoner towered over him.

"One more time," said Stoner. "Why were you trying to take my dog? The truth."

"Already told you," Coogan replied defiantly.

"Tell me again."

Coogan wanted to scream. He wanted to shout, "You shouldn't have Natasha because you're the one who killed her owner!" He wanted to yell, "You're the one responsible for all of the missing livestock that you blamed on the dog!" Coogan wanted to stand up and tell the world everything for which Stoner was responsible, everything he had ever done wrong in his miserable, unholy life.

But he didn't. "I wanted her," is all Coogan said.

Smitty said, "He was seen walking with the dog on several occasions."

Sheriff Barnes nodded his agreement. Stoner stared at his colleagues. The room fell silent under Stoner's oppressive gaze.

"See that the judge makes his bail astronomical," Stoner finally said. "I don't want him getting out."

Coogan tilted his head back in the chair and closed his eyes. It was obvious Stoner was never going to let him go.

14

"**D**AMN, DEVIN. DO YOU THINK you have enough stuff to last you?" Smitty asked, as he looked inside his fellow deputy's packed SUV.

"I like to be prepared. I never know what kind of situation I'll find out there while I'm roughing it."

Smitty reached into the vehicle's rear storage area, rummaging through the pile of equipment. "Look at all this. Rifles, shotguns, lanterns, stoves, coolers. Two sleeping bags? Why the hell two sleeping bags?"

Stoner chuckled. "Well, it's kind of an embarrassing story."

" I'm listening."

"Okay, it's like this. Once I was camped on the bank of a river. Connecticut, I think it was. Anyway, I had left camp to go hunting, and this huge rainstorm came along suddenly. I swear, that river must've risen five feet before I got back to camp. Needless to say, my sleeping bag was long gone. So now, I take a backup."

"Devin, if I didn't know you any better, I'd swear you made that story up."

Stoner grinned. "You know me pretty good, huh? C'mon, let's go back in. I want to say good-bye to the bossman."

Smitty turned and followed Deputy Stoner into the office. Sheriff Barnes stood at the coffee pot, cup in hand.

"I guess you'll miss Mason. He's out on patrol," said Smitty.

"You gone, Devin?" Barnes asked.

"Yeah, pretty soon. It'll take at least a day to get there. Want to get an early start."

"Well, be careful out there. Lord knows those woods will be full of drunks."

"Yes, sir.".

"Bring me back some more of that good wild boar sausage, will you?"

"Sure thing." Stoner laughed. But he was laughing harder on the inside. These humans were so easy to fool, so willing to accept anything he told them, so eager to be his buddy. The so-called "sausage" he had brought back a few years ago was actually smoked and dried flesh from some prostitute's thigh. His colleagues never knew otherwise.

"Well, I'd better be on my way." Stoner gripped the doorknob and paused. "Oh, one other thing. Can someone drive by my house every so often, just to check on things?"

"Of course," Sheriff Barnes said.

"Devin, I don't mind stopping in and feeding the dog every day," Smitty offered.

"No, that's okay. There are two full feeders, food and water, and a heater in the garage. She'll be fine. Just check the house for me, okay?"

"Will do."

"Oh, and another thing. Have Johnson check on the old man's cell, maybe once an hour or so. I don't want that crazy bastard getting out."

"Sure, Devin. Done deal." Smitty clapped Stoner on the back.

Stoner opened the door and turned back to the others. "See you in a week."

"Have a safe trip, Devin. Don't you go speeding trying to make up time."

"Wouldn't dream of it."

•　　　•　　　•

Natasha paced in front of the garage door, sniffing the ground. She could feel the cold draft seeping into the room from the bottom, and she knew freedom was just beyond the door. She reached one corner of the door, and rose to her hind legs, using her front paws to scratch at the door trying to locate an opening. Her efforts were futile.

Natasha dropped back down and turned toward the back of the garage. The concrete floor was cold and damp; the entire room was chilled. It was warm near the small box in the corner, but it burned her if she got too close to it. She had food and water, but the rank odor of the room chased her appetite away. She had made a conscious effort to relieve herself in the opposite corner from the feeders and heater, but the cramped dimensions of the room, combined with the draft from the bottom of the garage door spread the foul smell around generously.

Natasha sat down a few feet from the heater. Although the small bulb over her head burned brightly, she could feel the darkness gathering on the outside world. She felt the sharp pangs in her body, feelings that were beginning to lessen in intensity if only through their growing repetition.

Natasha remembered the time when she had tried to turn herself into the wolf. It had almost worked, but she had been in her human form then, controlled by her superior human brain. Although the concept of the attempt to control herself surfaced in her canine memory, somehow Natasha didn't think she had the mental capability to succeed.

And now, it didn't matter. Natasha felt the black night creeping in on her, felt the movements deep within her body. Soon, the change would come, regardless of whether she chose it or not.

• • •

Coogan sat on the hardwood bench in his tiny cell, staring at the bars in front of him. The low-watt bulb hanging precariously over his head cast a gloomy, dim glow over his surroundings, but Coogan knew that outside, darkness had fallen across the countryside. He had nothing to occupy his mind except his own thoughts.

The full moon graced the Maine skies even as Coogan sat there. Natasha was somewhere inside Stoner's house, Coogan was sure of that. And she would have changed. Coogan prayed that she would be able to find a way to escape, but he doubted it. Stoner was highly intelligent. Coogan was sure he had made Natasha's prison escape-proof for humans and canines alike.

The moon was full, and Stoner was gone. He would be miles away by now. If only Coogan had planned his actions better. He should've waited until Stoner had departed for the Festering. Coogan didn't think Stoner knew what he really was, but one thing was certain: His actions had alarmed Stoner. The deputy made sure he stayed right where he was—in this cramped, dismal cell. It would be more difficult than ever for Coogan to save Natasha, if not impossible.

Coogan looked around his quarters, surveying all possible routes of escape. There weren't many. Solid cinder block construction on three sides, no window, and two-inch thick bars in front of him. Solid, solid, solid. There was only one person on duty at nights in the Potters sheriff's office—the kid, Johnson—and he wasn't really an officer. He just answered emergency calls at night and contacted Sheriff Barnes if anything drastic happened. But Johnson was not what was holding Coogan in. It was the cell.

Coogan moved to the front of the cell and rattled the door as quietly as possible. Johnson didn't seem to notice. The door was latched completely. Coogan moved along the concrete walls, feeling for any weak links or cracks, loose blocks, whatever. He looked under the bed for any possible access, air ducts, anything. Acts that he had already gone through countless times since his initial incarceration.

Coogan dropped onto his cot and fell back onto the pillow. He had failed again. He thought of Natasha, sitting cold and alone in Stoner's house. She would be frightened. She would feel betrayed, abandoned. He thought of David, probably lying in the cold ground somewhere, maybe Arizona. He thought of his long-dead wife, his lovely Sarah. It had been so long since he had seen her face that the memory of it had almost dissolved away. Until he had seen Natasha on that first fateful night, the familiarity he felt hadn't struck him at first.

Something about the woman who showed up at his trailer that night lulled Coogan into a sense of trust and security, but he couldn't remember any overwhelming sense of recognition. Perhaps it was the eyes, or the personality—the feel of innocence

Natasha had conveyed. Perhaps it was a sense of parental instinct, a feeling of long-forgotten fatherly pride. Perhaps, he had really known all along. But reading the paperwork on Natasha at the Animal Control Center had convinced Coogan. David Wagner had purchased her in Arizona.

Coogan rubbed his head and wished that he had a drink. Not of water, but of something much stronger. What would it hurt now, Coogan pondered. This is it, the end of the road. You've let Natasha down; there's nothing you can do for her now, old man. She's done for. She'll be Stoner's personal love slave from here to eternity. Does that surprise you any, Jackie? Is it surprising to know that you let someone down when they really needed you? Hell, no. You've made a life-long career out of letting loved ones down. Jackie Coogan's Disappointments Unlimited. No situation too grand to foul up. Special rates for loved ones. Fateful mistakes at crucial times, no extra charge. After all, it wouldn't be the first time you'd let Natasha down.

Although she doesn't know it, you've done it before. You could even say three times in all actuality. Hell, Natasha's pretty lucky, really. At least she's still alive. Look at everyone else you've let down. Sarah, David Wagner. Both dead. And what about Natasha's brothers and sisters? For all he knew, they could be dead too. Yeah, Natasha's a pretty lucky one at that.

You've been failing people you love for a long time, Jackie Coogan. Even before you were Jackie Coogan—back when it all started, before you even had the alcohol to blame everything on— you were failing people. Isn't that how you failed Sarah? That wasn't alcohol was it, Johnny ... Jackie? Can't blame that one on the snoot, can you, Lucas ... Coogan? That's not why Sarah died, is it? She died because you weren't quick enough, because he was quicker, because he chose ...

... the moon.

The moon, Coogan thought. He leapt from the cot and shuffled to the back wall of the cell. He placed his hands against the cinder blocks, feeling their rough texture on his wrinkled old hands. He pressed his face to the blocks, felt their uneven surface against his cheeks. Just beyond this wall was the outside world. The trees, the ground, the earth, nature ... and the moon.

The moon was full tonight. Natasha would change. Stoner, wherever he may be, would change. *He* could change.

Coogan breathed deeply, the musty odor of the dust-laden cinder blocks permeating his nostrils. It had been so long since he had accepted the moon's glory. Coogan pressed himself harder against the bricks, turned his eyes to the stained, yellowed plaster ceiling where, just beyond several feet of dried texture, concrete, insulation, hovered the moon. Particles of dust floated in front of his vision. Coogan closed his eyes. It had been so long, so very, very long; could he even remember how? He pictured the moon in his mind. He smelled the brisk night air, heard the crunching of brittle leaves under his feet. But underneath his concentrated visions was the outlined form of a prison cell, and the acrid smell of porous, odor-filled brick. Coogan squeezed his eyes shut tighter, grimaced, gnashed his teeth, but the only smell was mildew, dust, seldom-changed bed sheets. Concentrate, dammit. Think. Natasha needs you. Coogan pressed himself further against the blocks, until it felt as if their coarse surface cut into his skin. He tried to see himself outside the brick walls, standing on the outside of the sheriff's office. He would feel the dirt at his feet, the chilled breeze on his face, would see the tall evergreen trees before him. But still, there was nothing.

No, Coogan's mind raced. I can't let her down again. This is my last chance, her last chance, Sarah's last chance. I must redeem myself. For once in my long, long, sorry excuse for a life, I must do the right thing. I must save Natasha from Stoner. Only then can I redeem myself. Only then will my promise to Sarah be kept.

Coogan remembered the solemn promise he had made to Sarah's rapidly cooling body so long ago. He remembered the loyal oath, the ridiculous simplicity of it, and the absolute shambles he had made of it, of the utter failure he had made of the one thing he could've done for his precious Sarah. It was such a simple task, and he had failed miserably at it.

Oh, Sarah my precious, Coogan cried in his thoughts. I'm so sorry for what I've done with all these years. I made a promise to you, and I didn't keep it. I know I told you that I would look after the children, that I would raise them properly so that you could look down from the heavens and be proud of the wonderful children you brought into the world. I'm so sorry for what I did. I failed you. I couldn't even give you that. I failed to raise the children at all. But it was so hard for me after you were gone. I didn't know what to do with them. They were so young, so tiny, so helpless, so totally dependent on me. I guess I couldn't handle the pressure. Your mother died shortly after your death, and I was left alone with them. I know I should've been stronger; please know that I tried. I tried harder than any man ever tried at anything, but I turned to the bottle. I turned to the bottle, and I turned to the moon, so that I wouldn't have to accept the responsibilities of raising the children.

Coogan inhaled deeply to fight back the tears that were already streaming down his face. He pressed his mouth to the cinder blocks to stifle the sobs. He tasted the chalky residue of the concrete, the bitter taste of the dust, and the dirt ...

The dirt?

The dirt from the earth, the earth that lay just outside this wall. This wall of only two feet of concrete, this wall that stands between me and the moon. Coogan inhaled again deeply, and the scent of the moist earthen forest floor came faintly to his senses.

A tiny chip of mortar fell bouncing to the concrete floor; a wisp of dust floated into the stale air. Coogan's fingers pressed harder against the unyielding bricks. *Remember the moon, Jackie. Remember its strengths, its powers. Remember the outside world. Remember the trees and the mountains and the animals.*

I'm so sorry, Sarah. I never meant to forget you or the children, but by the time I beat the liquor, my mind and body were so old that I couldn't do it. I couldn't keep the children. You see, I had to do what I did. It was best for them, or I thought it was the best thing at the time. I see now that it wasn't, that it was probably the worst thing I could've done. But I can make it right now. I can save Natasha, I can know her, and she can know you. And you won't have died in vain. Natasha needs me now, and for once, I can't let her down, and I can't let you down, Sarah my darling.

Coogan breathed in again, his voice low and gravelly. He opened his eyes, and saw his fingers dug into the softening mortar that held the blocks firmly in place, the dust mixing with the blood from his raw fingers.

Coogan gasped and felt the searing pain rip through his body, through his ancient limbs. He tilted his head back and screamed from the agony, the glorious agony of the moon.

Yes, yes! his mind shrieked.

The pain was excruciating, yet it was the most wonderful feeling in his life. Coogan heard the stretching of age-tightened tendons and ligaments, the popping and altering of his arthritic bones. Coogan threw his head back and shouted defiantly into the air, the sound echoing maddeningly in the confines of the cell. His fingers pressed deeper into the blocks, his claws raking deep cracks into the mortar, his rippling sinews forcing the blocks loose.

The smell of the earth was intoxicating; the glow of the moon filled his eyes. His clawed feet scraped and clacked on the concrete floor, fighting for leverage against the crumbling wall.

•　　•　　•

Johnson fell forward in his chair, his feet propped on the desk falling hard to the floor. He grabbed the desk for balance and turned his head from left to right in an attempt to orient himself.

"What the hell?"

He strained to hear, trying to determine the direction from which the sound had come. He was about to decide that he had dreamed the noise, when the deafening roar filled the office again.

"Jesus Christ!"

He started to reach for the phone to dial the sheriff's house when the sound filled the air again. Instinctively, the young dispatcher leapt to his feet, stumbling over the phone cord. He hated to think about what was happening.

The sound came from the old man's cell. He's probably having a heart attack or a stroke or something! *Oh man, I've never had a prisoner die while I was on duty! Sheriff Barnes is gonna be pissed!*

Johnson sprinted down the small row of cells and slid to a stop on the tiled floor. He peered into Coogan's cell, expecting to see the old man writhing on the floor. Instead, he saw smoke. He thought it was smoke until the musty odor hit him, and he realized it was dust.

"What the hell?"

He stared into the cell, trying to peer through the thick cloud. The dust was beginning to dissipate, and he could make out a form close to the floor. *Oh man, the guy's gonna be dead.*

The animal glared at Johnson and growled deep within its throat. Johnson gulped and slowly reached for the gun that was not on his hip.

Sheriff Barnes didn't let him carry a gun. The animal snarled savagely, and Johnson felt a warm gush between his legs.

"H-h-holy shit."

Only then did Johnson notice the crumbled bricks lying on the floor amid a layer of mortar dust. He felt a sudden chill in the building, and then he saw the huge hole in the back wall. The animal snarled one last time, and then it disappeared out the hole and into the night.

The young attendant suddenly forgot all about Coogan's health.

•   •   •

Natasha donned the pair of jeans and flannel shirt that Stoner had apparently left for her and pulled the old tennis shoes over her bare feet. She scooted closer to the heater and wrinkled her nose. The smell in the garage was awful. Natasha grinned a humorless grin at the irony of her situation.

She rubbed her arms to warm herself. The garage was quite chilly, and the small heater provided little warmth. She was hungry. Stoner had left only dog food. An oversight, or had he done that purposefully? The thought of eating dog food disgusted Natasha. More irony.

Natasha scanned the ceiling for any possible exits. She had already checked the door leading into the house. It was locked and deadbolted. The garage door was also locked. Stoner had made sure that the room would be escape-proof.

Natasha tried to occupy her thoughts with methods of escape, but soon, other thoughts crept into her mind. This was her first night of human experience since David's death, and his passing was clearly on her mind. That was a full month ago.

David must be buried and gone by now. She hadn't even got to tell him goodbye, didn't even know where he was now. The thought saddened her.

She knew that she loved David, and she knew that it would take a long time for her to get over his death. And to make matters worse, she would belong to Stoner now. She would have to answer his every command.

She tried to think of more pleasant things. She remembered taking walks with David and chasing tennis balls in the backyard of his house. But the most pleasant memories of David were from her human moments shared with him, as few as they were. She pleasantly recalled the nights they had spent talking, of expressing their fears and hopes, and especially the one and only time that they had made love.

Natasha smiled and placed her hands on her belly. She could feel the slight roundness of her abdomen, the first indications of the children growing inside of her. The thought filled her with mixed emotions. They would always remind her of David. How would she react to that? Would she see David's face each time she looked into their eyes? Would the thought make her happy or sad? What would she tell the children about their father? They would never know him, not even what he looked like. How would she raise the children alone? It would be so difficult, she knew, but she made a silent promise to David's memory. She would raise the children to be young and strong and free, just as their father was. David would be proud of his children someday.

15

C OOGAN BROKE THROUGH the tree line that started just beyond the back fence of Stoner's house. He sat down on his haunches, panting heavily. He was old, and the distance travelled from the sheriff's office to Stoner's house had left him exhausted. Saliva dripped in streams from his lolling tongue, and his sides ached. Arthritis had attacked his human joints long ago, while the affliction remained in his rediscovered wolfen form.

Coogan paused to survey the yard, concentrating on the area around the doghouse. He could not see Natasha, nor did he expect to. She would be locked inside the house somewhere. He prayed that he picked the right area, for the sirens wailing in the distance indicated that time was of the utmost importance. Sheriff Barnes was more than likely on his way to the station now, and once it was discovered that he had escaped, Stoner's house would likely be the first place checked.

After regaining his breath, Coogan moved out of the bushes. He reached the chain-link fence, but the gate had been padlocked. He didn't like the idea of entering from the front of the house. If one of the cruisers did arrive, a rear entrance would give him more time.

Coogan observed the moon shining down upon him and illuminating the yard. He lowered his head, closed his eyes, and tightened every muscle in his body. He forced himself to concentrate, willed his body to become rock hard. A slow, patient transformation would be less painful, but he didn't have the time. It had to be now.

The wolf snarled and snapped at the air, his front paw sliding in the dirt, trying to gain a foothold in the soft soil. Coogan threw his head back and howled into the night. His muscles stretched and strained, his bones popped and creaked, and he suddenly felt very cold. Coogan remained still, close to the ground. His head pounded, and his eyes were blurry and sore. He opened them slowly. He was human, and he was naked.

Ignoring the sudden biting wind, Coogan grasped the top of the fence and gingerly hoisted himself over. He made his way over to the bathroom window he had entered once before. Stoner had not bothered to replace the broken pane; a square piece of plywood covered the window. Coogan slipped his skinny fingers behind the board and pried it from the window. Without looking back, Coogan hoisted himself into the opening, and dropped deftly to the tub. Conveniently, a robe hung from a hook on the door. Coogan slipped it on and went out into the hallway.

He turned toward the bedroom where he had found Natasha the first time, but a familiar scent beckoned him in the other direction, toward the kitchen.

·   ·   ·

Natasha awoke abruptly from a light doze. She rubbed the crust from her eyes. The smell of urine and feces drifted to her nostrils, and she coughed.

Confused by whatever had awakened her, Natasha listened intently. She could hear nothing either inside or outside of the house. Then the scent hit her nose. It was faint under the overpowering odors in the small room. She could not identify the smell, though it was familiar. Could it be Stoner returning? She didn't think so; the odor did not frighten her. Instead, it put her at ease.

Just then, Natasha heard a noise beyond the door leading into the house. Natasha moved to the door to listen. She jumped back at the sound of the voice.

"Who's there?" she called nervously.

"Natasha?"

"Coogan!"

"Natasha, stand back from the door. I'm smashing it in."

Natasha stepped back to the heater. She heard muffled footsteps on the other side of the door. There was a pause of silence, then a loud bang. The tip of an axe appeared through the wood above the deadbolt, then disappeared with a loud creak. The axe came through again just above the gash from the first blow, breaking a small hole through the door and dislodging the deadbolt. Natasha watched as a small, wrinkled hand appeared through the hole and fumbled for the doorknob. The door swung open.

"Coogan," Natasha embraced him.

"Had you given up on me?" he asked.

"Never!" She pulled away to look in his eyes. "But I was beginning to wonder."

"C'mon. We can't stay here."

"Where are we going?"

"You'll see. Let's go."

•　　•　　•

"And the only thing in the cell was a dog?" Sheriff Barnes asked, his voice dripping with sarcasm.

"A big fuckin' dog," Johnson corrected.

The sheriff looked at Deputy Smitty, and back at the frightened dispatcher. "You never saw the old guy?"

"No," said Johnson. "I heard the scream, and I ran in here. It was dusty at first, but when it cleared away, there was a big dog standing by the hole. It barked once, and then it ran."

"I don't get it, sheriff," Smitty said. "How the hell did that hole get in the wall? And where's Coogan?"

"I don't know." Sheriff Barnes squatted and sifted through the chunks of cinder blocks.

Smitty continued the interrogation. "What kind of dog was it?"

Johnson gave an exaggerated shrug. "I don't know. Big. It was dark. You see the bulb is busted."

"Was Coogan with—"

"Smitty, you're beginning to sound like Mason!" Barnes knew he was losing control of the situation.

"Sorry. I'm just confused."

"You and me both."

"We gonna call Stoner?"

"How? I don't know where the hell he is. Somewhere in Minnesota. Probably ain't a lot of phones where he's at, anyway."

"We'll just tell him when he gets back?" Smitty did not wish to offend the sheriff.

"I guess that's all we can do, except go get Coogan."

"Stoner's not going to like this," Johnson said.

"I don't like it," mumbled Sheriff Barnes.

●　　　　●　　　　●

Standing in the room brought a lot of painful, bittersweet memories flooding back into Natasha's mind. She stared longingly at the fireplace. Once filled with the fiery colors of a warm autumn fire, it now sat black and cold and lifeless in the corner of the den. The couch on which she had David now seemed hard and foreign. The den offered little more comfort than the cold garage from which she had just escaped.

Coogan must've read the thoughts swimming through Natasha's mind. "I know it's painful coming back here, but I think this is the safest place for us right now. I don't think they'll look here."

Natasha nodded. The air seemed stale and thick.

Coogan scooted closer to her and took her hands. "I have a lot to tell you, Natasha. And not much time to do it in."

"I'm listening."

"Did you understand what I told you the other day, before the deputies took me away?"

"I heard it. But I'm not sure I understand."

"I told you I think I'm your father."

"Yes, I remember that."

"You can understand in your canine form." Coogan stroked her hands. "That's good. Better than I would've expected so soon. You're a bright girl."

"You believed me when I first came to you. You knew then?"

Coogan shook his head. "I don't think I did, not really. There was something familiar, but thinking back, I think I just accepted you because I knew you were a lycanthrope."

"What is a lycanthrope, Coogan? I mean, Father. What am I?"

"It may be easier to explain all of this if I just started at the beginning. I let you and David think that you became a lycanthrope due to the attack. There was no sense in confusing you with all the details at that time. Plus, you were probably better off knowing as little as possible.

"Anyway, at the beginning." He sighed and rubbed his forehead. "Geez, where is the beginning? It was so long ago.

"Natasha, you're going to find this very hard to believe, but just hear me out. I was born in the year 1622. I'm 371 years old. Hell, I've held up pretty good for an old man. Now, I know you're wondering how I've lived that long, and I'll get to that later. But first, let me tell you about yourself.

"You, Natasha, were born in 1761."

"1761?" Natasha gasped. "How can that be?"

Coogan patted her hands. "Now, just listen. You were born to me and a wonderful woman named Sarah McGruder. We lived in what is now New York."

"What was she like?"

Coogan eyes beamed with the question. "Oh, she was lovely. A blue-eyed, red-haired, stubborn Irish lass. That's your mother. Your mother was a normal human. She wasn't a lycanthrope.

"You see, lycanthropes, werewolves, whatever you want to call us, we're not unearthly monsters. We're just people. We're not different than anyone else really. We just have ... certain abilities. You're half-human, half-lycanthrope. That's why I'm so surprised by your abilities. You show powers that some half-breeds just don't have.

"The only difference in lycanthropes and humans, other than the obvious, is that we don't age. We're immortal; we'll never die of old age." Coogan seemed to be looking at something else only he could see. "Some say it's a blessing. Some say it's a curse."

"You've aged," Natasha surmised. "You're not young, like I am, like Stoner is."

"You're very bright. You see, Natasha, our power centers around the powers of the moon. We don't have to change during a full moon; we can control it, we can change any time of the day or night once we've mastered it. To maintain our youth, to alter the aging process, we absolutely must worship the moon. By worship we must respect it, we must change during the full moon, for that is when we are at our most powerful. If we become our fullest once a month, we never grow old. If we shun the moon, if we reject our blood, our ancestry, we grow old. We die, just like the mortals."

"And you have refused the moon," said Natasha.

"Yes, that I have, until this very night. I hadn't transformed in over fifty years, until tonight."

"Why did you do it tonight?"

"Silly girl, I did it for you. I did it for your mother."

"Father, what happened to my mother. Is she alive?"

Coogan bowed his head. "No, your mother was killed shortly after you were born. I'm sorry, Natasha."

"What happened?"

Coogan closed his eyes. "Stoner killed her."

"Stoner?"

"I'm afraid so. Only he didn't go by the name Stoner then. It was Booth. William Booth."

"He killed my mother, as well as David." Natasha shivered. "And now, he expects me to be his mate for life." David's old house was empty; the utilities turned off. The cold night air was invading the usually warm farmhouse. Why did he kill her?"

"Because she chose me instead of him. Sarah—your mother— knew what we were. She knew about lycanthropy. We were in love before Booth even came into the picture. She was pregnant, and I promised her that we would move away, that I would shun the life of the lycanthrope, and we would raise all of you children in a normal style and grow old with each other."

"Children? I have brothers and sisters?"

"Somewhere," Coogan looked defeated. "Two brothers. After your mother's death, I swore that I would take care of you and your brothers, that I would raise you as she and I had planned.

"But things didn't go the way I had planned. Your grandmother took care of you while you were very young; she carried most of the burden. I was so grief-stricken and riddled with guilt. I blamed myself for Sarah's death, because I had shunned the moon. If I had only continued in the ways of lycanthropy, I could've beaten Booth.

"But I was no match for him. Soon after, your grandmother died, and I was left alone to raise three small children. I was alone and frightened; I didn't know what to do. So ... I turned to the bottle. I started drinking heavily, and I turned back to the ways of the moon. I can't really recall my exact logic, but it seemed right at the time. I wished to stay young, to stay the same age that I was when your mother died.

"So, I continued the ways of the lycanthrope, and I helped you and your brothers to change with me. I don't know, I guess in my grief-stricken mind, I thought I would get over Sarah's death eventually, and we could start where we left off, not a day older, none the worse for wear.

"But it didn't happen that way. The bottle took control of me. I worked in the fields or wherever a few hours each day, then I would come home, feed you, then start my drinking. The days melted into weeks, the weeks into months into years." Coogan had a faraway look in his eyes. "Many, many years. I didn't know where I was any more. You and your brothers never aged. You were month-old babies during that entire crazed time. You were all so easy to care for at that age.

"I never kept my promise to your mother; I never raised you to be the children she would be proud of," Coogan said. "I failed to save her life, and I couldn't even keep that one simple promise."

"I turned out alright." Natasha squeezed her father's hand, hoping to comfort him.

"David Wagner raised you, Natasha," Coogan said shamefully. "I had nothing to do with it."

"What happened to me and my brothers? How did I come to be here?"

Coogan sighed, and Natasha could tell that the relating of this tale was difficult for him. "My ... drinking continued for a long, long time, Natasha. I was a drunk for over two-hundred years. I had my last drink in 1952. Anyway, I finally sobered up for good. I gave up the moon then, too. But I kept helping you and your brothers to change once a month. I still didn't know what to do with you.

"Then, three years ago, I took a long hard look at myself, and I didn't like what I saw one damn bit. I had three tiny babies that were over two-hundred years old. They didn't know who they were, what they were, where they were from. I was ashamed. I spent more time with my kids than anyone ever had. It made me feel very selfish, very shameful. I had all those years to keep my promise to your mother, and I wasted them.

"I finally decided that I wanted to raise you guys, but I knew that I was too old. I had totally blown everything. I had no business raising you; it would've been blasphemy, and self-righteous of myself if I tried to bring you up when my mind was finally right. I couldn't do it.

"But I did want you and your brothers to know what it was like to live. I couldn't just continue to keep you like I had for so long. But I was still worried about Booth, who had become Stoner at this point. If he ever found any of you. I don't know what he might do. So, for safety purposes, I set out across the country with you and your brothers.

"I took you in your canine forms, and I left each of you with a wolf-hybrid breeder at different places. I left one of your brothers in North Dakota, one in Oregon, and you, I left in Arizona. That's how I figured that you were my daughter, when I found out that David had purchased you in Arizona.

"You were too young to remember your situation, to know that you were lycanthropes, so you would never change again. You would've grown up normal, happy household pets. I had to leave you as animals; it was much more logical that way. You have no birth certificate. I couldn't have put you up for adoption as a human baby. Do you understand, Natasha?"

Natasha nodded.

"I suppose that when the wolf—Stoner—attacked you that night, the shock, the stress of the situation brought on the transformation at the onset of the next full moon, and it continued after that. That's the only thing that I can guess." He paused. "Well, what do you think?"

"I think you made some mistakes, Father," Natasha was straightforward. "But I think you were very confused and alone, and frightened. You did what you could do."

"I'm so glad you feel that way." Coogan hugged her.

Natasha hugged her father back. She found it easy to forgive him for whatever mistakes he had made, because she understood how confusing their special situation could be. "What do we do now?"

Coogan did not immediately pull away from Natasha's hug. He held the embrace a moment longer, then finally released her.

Natasha peered into her father's sad, green eyes, and she knew that she was not going to like his answer.

"I'm going to have to send you away," he said.

"But, Father. Why?"

"Now, listen to me, Natasha. This must be done. I know that you're pregnant, and we have to think of your children as well. I'm not going to make the same mistake twice."

"But what about you?"

"I know a man who lives in Canada. His name is Jeremiah Reed, and he's one of us. He's a lycanthrope, a good man. He owns a feed store, and he breeds wolf-hybrids. That's where you're going."

"But why don't you go with me?"

"I have to stay behind, Natasha. I must sew up all the loose ends here. I've already spoken to Jeremiah. He's expecting you. I'm putting you on a bus tonight."

"But Coogan ..."

"Natasha, you're going to have to think of the children. You're in a situation a lot like I was years ago. You're facing the obstacle of raising a family alone. Jeremiah's will be the best place for you. It's quiet, it's in the wilderness. You can have the children, and you'll have a peaceful environment, far away from Stoner, to decide how you want to raise the children."

"Will you come back?"

"I'm going to try, Natasha," said Coogan. "For years, I wandered around this little town, and for the longest, I had no idea why. I suppose I used to think I would try to exact some kind of foolish revenge on Stoner, but now ... I think I know why I stayed here so long."

"And why is that?"

"I had a promise to keep." Coogan smiled.

"I'll miss you."

"You'll be in good company. We don't have much time; the cops are probably searching for me right now. But I want to show you something first. I want to teach you how to control it, how to control the transformations." Coogan stood up and helped Natasha from the couch. She stood in front of her father. She was shocked when he began removing his clothing, until she realized why he was doing so. Natasha reached for the buttons on her shirt and began to disrobe.

"Let's squat down on the floor. The key to forcing the change is to think about whatever you love the most about the form that you're trying to take. If you were trying to change into your human form, you would think about your unborn babies, or David ... or even me." Natasha smiled at her father. "If you're human and going for the wolf, then the moon is the most important thing. The moon, the earth, the trees, anything of nature.

"Take my hands. That'll help. It's how I helped you and your brothers to change. The power will flow through the both of us."

Natasha grasped Coogan's wrinkled old hands and closed her eyes. The empty farmhouse was silent except for their breathing. Painfully silent. Natasha could feel her heart beating, and could think only of David. David, and the moments of bliss she had shared with him in this very room.

Natasha could hear her father's breath become ragged, as a low, guttural roar rumbled in his throat. She opened her eyes but her focus was past him to the couch, the dark fireplace.

"Natasha, you're not with me," Coogan said softly. "Close your eyes; picture the moon."

Natasha closed her eyes again, and she saw in her mind's eye her doghouse, sitting empty and alone in the backyard. She could see her muddy and scratched bowl, her naked tennis ball, ripped nearly in half, lying in a puddle of rainwater.

The smell of the mud found her nostrils, and the far away scent of the forest beckoned to her. She saw the busted ends of her chain lying in the dirt, and beyond that, the beginning line of trees. And she was free, free from the chain that held her, free to explore the vast wilderness. And she ran. In her mind, Natasha ran and ran, and when she opened her eyes, she saw the wolf.

Natasha leapt back in fright, snarling and snapping at the beast before her. She stumbled backward, her rump bumping into the foot of the recliner. She turned to run, to dart through the trees and bushes, across the streams to freedom.

Then she realized that the wolf in front of her was not Stoner. It was her father.

Natasha whimpered and moved slowly over to Coogan. Their snouts nuzzled against one another, and Natasha licked the side of her father's face. He turned his head sideways momentarily, accepting the affection, and then scooted beside her, letting his chin rest across the back of her neck. Natasha understood the soft grunt he gave.

She felt Coogan's body begin to quiver and shake, and then she felt her own body moving. The movements were soft and gentle, almost lulling, loving hands caressing every inch of her body. It was a pleasurable experience, and when Natasha opened her eyes, she was human again. She realized that, for the first time, the transformations had not been painful at all.

"I want you to be able to transform to the wolf in case there's any trouble on the way to Jeremiah's," Coogan told her.

Natasha reached for her clothes and slipped them back on. "I'll ride the bus as a human?" she asked.

"Yes, I think it would be best that way. I thought of boxing you up and sending you to Jeremiah, but that's too risky. Stoner could trace you if we did it that way." He held Natasha's hand. "Now, let's get away from here. We have to stop by my trailer before we leave for the station."

Coogan opened the door and he and Natasha left the den behind in its darkness. Natasha caught a final glimpse of the couch just before the door closed shut.

"There's something in here you might like to take with you," said Coogan. "I saw it one day when I was having coffee with David." He opened a drawer of a table next to the phone. "He said they were some proofs of a publicity shot he had done for a magazine." He handed it to Natasha.

It was a picture of David.

"Something you can show the kids someday," he said, pressing the small photo into her hand. Natasha stared at the photo for a moment, then clutched it to her bosom. She didn't have time to shed tears.

•   •   •

Coogan pushed open the door of his trailer. He peeked out the crack of the door before closing it behind him. He turned and headed for a metal box sitting atop the kitchen countertop.

"I have Jeremiah's address and phone number for you. Dammit, I forgot to grab it earlier. Didn't want to have to come back here tonight. We're going to have to travel by the woods and backroads. Want to avoid the highway."

Natasha was only vaguely aware that her father spoke to her. Her eyes wandered about the room, picking up on all the eccentric, unusual items that Coogan had collected. They brought back warm memories of the first time she had set foot inside this trailer. Coogan had accepted her; she had found someone she could trust.

"Okay, you take this." He shoved a paper into Natasha's jacket pocket. "Don't lose it. I'm going to burn the rest of these papers. I don't want Stoner finding anything that might lead him to Jeremiah's place."

Coogan took the box and led Natasha outside. He dropped the papers, cardboard box and all, into a small fire pit. He then squirted a generous amount of lighter fluid over them before setting them ablaze. Together, he and Natasha watched them burn. Satisfied, Coogan dumped a bucket of sand over what remained and used a poker to mix it into the rest of the ashes.

"Let's get movin', girl," he finally said, reaching for her hand.

Natasha turned to follow him, a pinecone clutched tightly in her hands. "Can ... can I take this with me?"

Coogan stopped, and Natasha thought she saw a tear on his cheek. "Of course, you can. Now, let's git."

If the tear had been there, it was gone now.

16

NATASHA TOOK A SEAT near the back of the bus, the small handbag resting neatly on her lap. Inside the bag were her only possessions: the picture of David, Coogan's pinecone, a sandwich, and a $20 bill. She stared out the window at her father, his frail figure appearing even smaller in the wet now that had begun to fall. The flakes melted on contact with the warm panes and a bead of water trickled down the glass, cutting Coogan into two distorted halves. Natasha continued to watch her father even as the window fogged over.

She didn't know where she was going; she didn't know what the future held in store for her. So much had happened in her life in a few short months, and she'd never been given time to catch her breath, to process any of it. Other than the obvious turning point in her life, several more major occurrences had befallen her, events that would drive even the strongest will insane. She was about to travel west into the deep wilderness of Canada, with children growing inside of her, to face a new unknown predicament.

Who was this Jeremiah Reed? Could she trust him? He was obviously a friend of Coogan's. But would she be accepted in her new home? Her entire world consisted of the earth she could travel within the confines of a 20-foot chain. The only other living creature she knew was David, her owner. Now, she was headed to an unknown place, where she would meet unfamiliar faces.

And what of the children growing inside her? When would she bring them into the world? How would she raise them, teach them, allow them to grow? Should they be raised as animals, as her father had elected to do with his children, or should she raise them as humans, allow them to go forth into the world, to learn the ways of man? And when the day came to explain their heritage, to tell them of the moon and the powers it would hold for them, how would she handle it? They would want to know everything, and she knew so very little herself. And what of their father? Her children would know no father.

And what about the man, the beast, who had robbed her of mother and lover? What would Stoner do when he discovered she was missing? Would he come for her? Stoner was very clear in his belief of mating for life, and he was sure to remain adamant in his thoughts.

Natasha closed her eyes to combat the sudden rush of tears. She leaned her head on the thinly padded backrest. The snow started falling harder, the white flakes swirling in the cold wind. Natasha opened her eyes at the sound of the bus engine roaring to life. She glanced out the window at the small crowd of bundled-up people standing at the bus stop. The bus began slowly rolling forward. Natasha craned her neck, looking back at the people, trying to see her father for one last wave goodbye. She spotted him momentarily, standing alone, bracing himself from the cold wind, but the bus lurched forward, and she lost sight of him.

Natasha couldn't find him again.

17

“SHERIFF, MY HOUSE was broken into again,” Deputy Stoner stood defiantly before the entrance to the Potters Sheriff's Department. His face was reddened, either by anger or the cold wind. “My dog is gone. Where the hell is my dog?”

Sheriff Barnes and Deputy Smitty appeared surprised by the newly arrived deputy. Smitty cast a wary glance at the sheriff. The law officers pushed the doors of the squad car closed, bags of burgers and fries from the burger joint in downtown Potters in hand.

“Devin,” Sheriff Barnes began, “we didn't expect you back 'til later in the day.” He held the greasy bag up higher. “We didn't get you anything.”

“I don't want anything. What happened? My dog was taken.”

“Devin, why don't we go inside and sit down. Pour yourself a cup of coffee.”

“I don't want any coffee, either. I want to know what happened.” Stoner placed his hands on his hips and shifted, blocking the entrance. “Where's the old man? Where's Coogan?”

“Devin, do you mind?” the sheriff said, pushing through the big deputy. Reluctantly, Stoner stepped aside. “Coogan escaped.”

"Escaped?" Stoner followed Barnes and Smitty inside. "How the hell did he escape? Can't you people keep a 70-year-old man behind bars?"

"This is a little strange ..."

"I leave for one week and the whole damned department goes to shit?"

"Devin, please. Just calm down," Smitty pleaded.

"You calm down, Deputy!" Stoner stepped forward and came face to face with Smitty. The smaller officers stood his ground, meeting Stoner's steely gaze.

Sheriff Barnes slammed the bag of burgers on his desk. He didn't like the way his best deputy was acting. In fact, Devin Stoner's personality had been slowly changing ever since the ordeals with David Wagner's dog began. "Come here, Devin. I want to show you something."

Sheriff Barnes motioned Stoner to follow him, and the two men headed down the hallway to the cells. The sheriff unlocked the first unit, and he and Stoner stepped inside.

"It's cold in here," Stoner said.

Sheriff Barnes nodded and reached for the 4X8 sheet of plywood leaning against the cell wall. The board creaked loudly, then slid to the floor, revealing the huge hole in the brick wall.

Stoner stared at the hole in the wall. "Holy ..."

"That's how Coogan got out," said Sheriff Barnes. "Now, if you have any ideas as to how this happened, I'd be glad to listen, but until you can explain it, then just shut your damned mouth.

"I know you're upset. I know your dog's gone, and I realize that the old man more than likely has her. But Devin, there's some crazy shit going on around here, and I'm pissing in the wind when it comes to finding answers. We've gone all over this county in the last few days searching for Coogan, but he ain't out there. He's not in his trailer, he's not anywhere."

Stoner sighed and ran his fingers through his blond hair. "I'm sorry, sheriff; I blew my top. What happened?"

Sheriff Barnes shook his head. "It happened at night. Johnson was here. He heard a noise, came back here, and found the hole. He never saw Coogan, just a big dog."

"A dog? Was it my dog?"

"Hell, I don't know. I doubt it. Coogan obviously went for your dog after he busted out of here. Why do you think he wants her so much, Devin?"

"I don't know," Devin said.

He hadn't known before, but now, Stoner thought that he might.

•　　•　　•

Stoner closed the smashed door of the old trailer, propping it shut with a tree branch. The lock had been easy to break. Stoner stepped from the shaky wooden platform, clutching an old shirt in one hand. He raised the shirt to his nose and inhaled deeply. It stank of perspiration and cigar smoke, but the scent was Coogan's. Stoner tossed the shirt to the ground and broke for the woods.

When Sheriff Barnes had first mentioned the dog in Coogan's cell, Stoner assumed it was Natasha. Before his mind could comprehend and put things into a logical order, he had figured Natasha had escaped from his house and helped Coogan to escape. After all, she could've turned human during the full moon, she could've thought rationally and went for the old man. But the door to the garage where he had put Natasha—axed from the inside—was evidence that someone had freed her.

No, the old man must have taken Natasha. And that left only one explanation. The gaping hole in the cell wall. A large dog in the cell.

Coogan was a lycanthrope.

Stoner smiled to himself as he continued to cut a path into the woods. Imagine that. Three lycanthropes in one small area in Maine. What were the odds?

But who was Coogan, and why hadn't Stoner figured out sooner that he was a lycanthrope? He assumed it was because Coogan had always maintained such a low profile, keeping as far away from the public eye as possible. The only town gossip concerning Coogan revolved around his reputation as the town drunk. Now, Stoner began to wonder—was that just an act? Was Coogan hiding his secret for a reason?

And why did he want Natasha so badly? Surely, he didn't want her for himself. And even if he did, Coogan should respect the fact that Stoner and Natasha were mates. Was he trying to take her because of what happened to Wagner? As far as he knew, Wagner and Coogan never had any kind of connection with each other.

Whatever the questions, Stoner would have his answers soon enough.

·   ·   ·

Jackie Coogan heard the muffled sound of footsteps on snow, caught a whiff of the smell in the air long before Stoner emerged from the underbrush and into the old man's makeshift campsite. An old military tarp stretched between two logs, forming a lean-to. A sleeping bag and a foam cooler sat beneath it. Coogan reached his hand into the cooler and retrieved a couple of Mountain Dews, then looked up at the new arrival.

"I've been expecting you, Deputy," Coogan said. "Thirsty?" He held one of the drinks to Stoner.

"Where is she, old man? What did you do with my dog?"

"Dog?" Coogan held his hand to his eyes in a mocking manner and moved his head from left to right. "No dogs here."

"Wise up, Coogan. You're in a lot of trouble as it is. Tell me where she is, and maybe I'll go easy on you."

Coogan popped the top on his soda and took a slow sip. "Natasha is gone, Stoner. She's far away from here now, in a place where you'll never find her. You won't ever hurt her again."

Stoner's lips curled into a snarl. "Where is she, Coogan? You're trying my patience."

"Oh, sit down, Stoner. Have a drink with me. Sorry I don't have anything stronger. We've got all day. Like I said, I've been waiting for you to show up so we could have a little talk. I figured the sheriff would never find me out here, but I knew you'd be along soon enough."

Coogan paused. "Yeah, that's right. I know what you are, Stoner. Let's skip the bullshit, shall we? I know what you are, and I'm betting you know what I am."

"Who are you?"

"Oh, c'mon, Stoner. Think. It'll come to you."

Stoner clenched his fists and gnashed his teeth in anger. "I said, who are you?"

"Or should I just call you 'Booth'?"

Stoner's eyes widened. Coogan reveled in the shocked recognition that swiftly spread across the deputy's face.

"Now do you know who I am?"

"Lucas."

"Smart boy. And that should give you a clue as to who Natasha is," said Coogan.

Stoner laughed. The hearty, merciless laughter disturbed Coogan to his soul. "Well, Lucas, Coogan or whoever you are. It seems as if you're going to lose another woman in your life to me!"

"And how do you figure that, Booth? Like I said, you'll never see Natasha again."

"Oh, don't underestimate me, old man. Have you forgotten the ways of the moon?"

Stoner's hulking figure continued to laugh. Then he threw his head back and snarled. Stoner's nose lengthened, his ears sprang forth, and when Coogan looked into his eyes, he found himself staring into the eyes of a beast.

"You've shunned the moon again, Lucas," the beast snarled, the light from the waning campfire reflecting in his angry eyes. "You've grown old and weak. It cost you the life of your beloved Sarah the first time, and now, it will cost you your daughter."

"I'm afraid you're wrong this time, Booth," Coogan replied. "The moon is what robbed you of Natasha."

"Maybe, but only temporarily. What a fool you are, Lucas. You were a fool then, and you're an even bigger fool now. You should've let the sheriff find you after you hid Natasha; you would've been safe. He thinks you've flown the coop now. No one will ever know the difference if you're never heard from again" Stoner reached down and wrapped his hirsute fingers around Coogan's scrawny neck and lifted the old man to his feet.

"Now," Stoner said. "Tell me where she is, and maybe I'll let you live."

Coogan smiled. "For a long time, I had to live with what you did. It haunted me for more than two-hundred years. I followed you, Booth. I don't know why, and maybe, I didn't even realize I was doing it, but I always knew where you were. I always knew we'd meet again."

"Where is Natasha?" Stoner's grip tightened.

"Like I said, she's gone. Face it, Booth. You failed."

"NO!" Stoner pulled the smaller man closer. "Tell me where she is or you die!" Coogan's gaze was unwavering. The smell of foulness in the area was overpowering. "Change. I want to see you change. I want you to see how goddamned foolish you were for shunning the moon all these years."

"I don't need to change any more," Coogan said defiantly. "Isn't it ironic, Booth? All these years you worshipped the moon, bathed in its glory, shed blood in its honor, while I shunned it all. But when I needed it one last time, it came through for me. And it's not going to help you one damned bit. Face it. I defeated you, Booth."

Stoner's brow furrowed into an angry grimace. "NOOOOOOO!"

Coogan closed his eyes. Stoner snarled savagely, and Coogan felt the vice-like grip of his ancient adversary's fingers squeezing tighter into his neck, cutting off his oxygen. He shut his eyes tighter, and a vision of his long-dead love appeared in his mind's eye. "Rest easy tonight, Sarah. I'll see you soon."

At last, Jonathan Lucas had kept his promise.

PART TWO

THREE AND A HALF YEARS LATER

18

THE WOMAN STEERED the four-wheeled ATV down the narrow, graveled lane, sending clouds of white dust into the warm, mid-summer air. She listened to the sounds of the morning: the birds flitting though the nearby woods; the road crunching and popping under the tires; and the constant baying of the dogs. She inhaled the cool morning air, taking in the glorious aromas of rain-soaked earth, decaying pine needles, and smoke from a distant trash fire. She glanced back once, making sure the trailer she towed behind her was still straight.

Natasha smiled and parked the vehicle.

The dogs around her barked excitedly, anticipating their morning feeding. Hurricane-fence pens to either side of the road caged scores of registered wolf-hybrids. They went crazy around her as they always did, even the ones she had already fed, who now wanted play in favor of nourishment.

Natasha walked to the nearest gate, unlatched it, and turned back to the trailer. She gripped the 50-lb. sack of Iams Eukanuba—the third one she had gone through this morning—and hefted it over her shoulder. She was getting used to the lifting, and so were her muscles.

Sargent, the occupant of the pen, stood at attention, awaiting his breakfast. Sargent rarely barked but was always diligent.

"Morning, Sargent," Natasha called cheerfully.

Sargent was a thirteen-year-old male, and a full-blooded timber wolf. He was Jeremiah's favorite. Only she and Jeremiah could approach Sargent, for reasons known only to Natasha and Jeremiah.

Natasha pulled on the white string woven into the top of the bag and zipped it open. Sargent waited patiently as Natasha poured the bowl half-full. He knew the routine. Natasha returned from the trailer with some chunks of raw beef and mixed it in with the dry pellets.

"Eat," said Natasha, and ruffled Sargent's fur along the nape of his neck.

She stepped back out onto the road and closed the gate behind her. The dogs went into a renewed frenzy. Natasha busied herself with the rest of her feedings, then parked the ATV in front of the last two pens.

Natasha enjoyed feeding the dogs in the crisp, morning air. It gave her a chance to relax and clear her mind. Time seemed to have flown by since she had taken up residence at Jeremiah Reed's place of business. Three years had managed to dull the pain, to alleviate the fears somewhat, but both the pain and the fear were still there, and they always would be. Jeremiah welcomed and accepted her, given her a room, and even paid her a small salary for helping with the chores. He was very kind and always spoke of Coogan with great affection. That made Natasha happy.

She stepped off the vehicle and approached the pens. The one on the right held a trio of three-year old males, while the pen directly opposite held a single three-year old female. Natasha lifted the latch on the pen holding the males and entered, as the female watched inquisitively.

The three dogs bounded toward Natasha, leaping happily in front of her. She slapped playfully at their heads, grabbing their necks and pushing them back, only to have them pounce back at her immediately.

"Hello, my babies!"

Natasha sat down on the ground in the center of the pen. The three dogs lay wallowing in the dirt around her, and she caressed each one's fur, switching from dog to dog. She needed three hands, for when she left one to pet another, the abandoned dog would leap toward Natasha to regain her attention. They were so spoiled and jealous. Natasha happened to glance across the way where the female watched them. Natasha gazed at her for a long moment, absentmindedly petting the same dog continuously, until the remaining two brought her unintentional favoritism to her attention.

Natasha stood up, pushing the dogs away, and exited their pen. The female's eyes followed Natasha's moves as Natasha entered her pen.

"Good morning, Tiara."

She squatted down to the ground as the female slowly approached. Natasha scratched the dog's ears, and the female lowered her head.

"I'm sorry you have to stay in a pen by yourself," Natasha said. "I know you'd rather be with your brothers, and I hated to take you out. I don't want you getting pregnant by your brothers, and well, they just don't know any better right now."

Natasha peered into the dog's clear blue eyes. Tiara had not been the same since she was placed in the cage next to the males. She had become distant, aloof, and unhappy somehow. She missed her brothers' companionship. Natasha leaned forward and kissed the dog on the head.

"Get them all fed?"

Jeremiah approached her, pulling his leather work gloves from his meaty hands. He was a large, burly man with dark, disheveled shoulder length hair tinged with a dash of gray. His bushy eyebrows met above his nose, and he had large mutton chops that barely wavered even when he smiled.

"Of course," Natasha said. "All in a day's work."

Jeremiah clapped a hand on her shoulder and squeezed gently. "You are like a hurricane."

He turned and scanned the pens and their occupants. "How are they?"

Natasha stood up. "Fine, I guess. Tiara's still acting strange."

"She still doesn't understand why she was taken away from her brothers. They're very social. But she'll get used to it."

Natasha watched her daughter. "I know, but I hate seeing her look so lonely."

Jeremiah patted the top of Natasha's head. "C'mon, I'll make you some coffee."

•   •   •

"Have you decided yet what you're going to do?" Jeremiah asked as they sat atop bales of hay stacked inside the feed storage room.

From where she sat, she could see most of the pens, and beyond that, the wilderness of the Caribou Mountains in northern Alberta. Her children—Tiara, Luke, Simon, and David—were at the end of the lane; she could barely see them through the other pens and animals.

Jeremiah reached across and playfully nudged her shoulder.. "Natasha? Earth to Natasha. Come in, Natasha."

"Sorry. Lost in thought." She turned back to Jeremiah and gave him a half-smile.

"Natasha, they're three years old now. Young adults."

"I know," she nodded, sipping the black coffee, recalling for a moment the first time she tasted it in David's kitchen.

"It's just that ... they're not getting any younger. Then again, they're not getting any older, I suppose."

Natasha's gaze met Jeremiah's dark brown eyes. "I don't know what to do. I'm nervous. I'm scared I'll make the wrong decision."

"You've already made the decision, sweetie. Right or wrong, you made that decision three years ago, but it's just now coming to a head."

"Do you think it's time?"

"Are you asking me as a friend or as an old pro?"

Natasha stretched and yawned. "Both, maybe?"

Jeremiah smiled. "You made the decision when they were first born to let them grow to young adulthood before you told them what they are. Now, as I see it, you have either of two choices to make. One: you can just let them continue to grow, to age, maybe set them free, maybe let them grow old and die in their pens." He could tell Natasha didn't like that option. "Or, two: you can go on with your original plan. And, if you decide to do that, then yes, I would say it's time."

Natasha returned her attention to the pens. "What do I tell them? How do I explain it? I wouldn't even know where to start."

"Your father didn't know what to do either, and he was in a lot tougher a situation than you are."

Natasha turned back to Jeremiah. "I miss him, you know."

Jeremiah reached for Natasha's hand. "I know you do, baby. I miss him, too."

"Sometimes," Natasha began, "I wonder where he is, and I hope and pray that he's still alive, and that he'll visit us sometimes, just turn up at the front door with a bagful of pinecones, but ..." She snickered, but the mirth quickly fled from her face. "But I know that probably won't ever happen."

Jeremiah remained silent, giving Natasha a moment to work through the emotions.

"Jeremiah," she finally said. "Did you ever have any children?"

He didn't answer right away, as if he was struggling with what to say. "Yeah, I did."

"Were they like us?"

"You mean, lycanthropes? Of course they were."

"Where are they now?"

He only shrugged.

"How did you tell them?"

"I can't really remember how I told them."

"You don't know where any of them are now?" Natasha asked.

"Not really. Oh, I know the towns. I know where some of them live, but most of them chose to ignore their 'other lives'. They're living human lives. I would only remind them of what they're trying to forget."

"That's unfortunate." She returned her gaze to Jeremiah. "Do you think my children will do the same?"

"I can't answer that, Natasha."

Natasha rubbed her eyes, already beginning to grow weary even though it was still early.

"Now is the time to do it, Natasha. They need to know. They need to see the other side of their lives, even if they eventually reject it. It's only fair to them."

"I know. You're right."

"It's what Lucas—I mean, Coogan—it's what Coogan would've wanted. And David."

Natasha smiled, her eyes moist at the memories. "Yes, it is. And I did make a promise."

•   •   •

Natasha lay on her side in bed, her head propped up by a pillow. From her room on the second floor, she could see most of the kennels. The nearly full moon lit up the grounds, and Natasha could see her children in the pale light. The boys lay curled up in sleep or rest; Tiara sat on her haunches at the far end of her pen, staring past the grounds to the woods beyond.

Natasha rolled out of bed to sit by herself in the gloom. Tomorrow, the moon would be full, and she would take the children into the woods and show them the change. It was something she certainly did not relish, but she had to do it.

Natasha wasn't even sure if showing the children the ways of lycanthropy was the right thing to do. They were safe in their pens, safe from the outside world, safe from things that might harm them. They were in a place where she could always watch over them; she would always know where they were. But that wasn't fair to them. They were living, breathing free spirits, and they needed to run wherever they wished. Their pen was the chain that had once held Natasha to the tree in David Wagner's backyard. Natasha could remember, even as a canine, her deep desire to break free, to go beyond the barriers, to explore the sights and smells that beckoned her to the dark woods beyond. And she was sure that the kids wanted the same things.

Natasha sighed and thought of Jeremiah. He had become her will to continue, her pillar of strength to grab hold of when she felt as if she might collapse. She found herself thinking of him as she had once thought of her father—a man she could trust, a person who would always be there for her.

But Coogan wasn't there for her anymore. Natasha knew in her heart that her father was no longer alive. Something in his voice, in his eyes—*reading the truth in the eyes*—had told her the night he put her on the bus for Canada. Everything about him that night held such a tone of finality; she somehow knew that she would never see him again.

And then, of course, she thought of Stoner. Three and a half years had passed since she last saw him. Three and a half years with no sign of him. But he was out there. Somewhere.

And approximately three and a half years earlier, in the late summer, this madness had all started.

Natasha scooted over on the bed and opened a drawer on the nightstand. She reached in and pulled out the framed picture of David her father had given her.

Natasha studied the picture for what seemed like hours, until the image blurred and softened at the edges. Every so often, one of the dogs would bark in the yards below.

A tear splashed onto the glass that protected the framed photo. Natasha wiped it away.

"So, David," she whispered. "Are you ready to see what your children look like?"

Natasha returned the photo to the drawer and laid her head down, but she did not sleep.

19

NATASHA STEPPED QUIETLY through the dark undergrowth, a laundry bag in one hand, the powerful light from the full moon guiding her way. It was well after midnight, and the late summer night was a little on the cool side. Her steamy breath drifted around her. She was glad she brought the extra clothes. Natasha glanced quickly over her shoulder. The four wolves followed obediently in single-file procession behind her, never deviating from Natasha's trail.

Natasha stopped at the banks of a large stream. The stream widened at one point to collect in a small pond. Reflections from the moon danced off the rippling water like a sea of fireflies on a summer night. Natasha dropped the bag and began to remove her clothing. The wolves gathered around her, reacting now and then to night sounds in the nearby woods.

Natasha sat naked at the edge of the stream, letting her feet dangle in the cool water, and changed. The transformation was little more than an afterthought for her now; she had grown so accustomed to it. There was no pain at all anymore.

The large silvery wolf-hybrid trained its eyes on the others. The children did not seem to notice the arrival of a new wolf, and that was good. That meant that they still accepted her as their mother, regardless of her form.

Natasha barked a command at the children, and they sat down before her. Natasha raised her snout to the moon and howled once. The children did the same. Somewhere in the distance, probably from the kennels, possibly from the wild, other wolves answered.

Natasha nudged each child with her snout, and they lay flat on the ground. Natasha positioned herself above them and then lay across her children. She growled softly for them to be still.

Natasha closed her eyes, and thought of the kennels, of her room, of the picture of David.

Her body began to move from within.

The children started to whimper, to fidget restlessly. They cried out at the pain inside their bodies. Natasha knew that the first transformation would be painful to them, and it hurt her to cause them pain.

As Natasha lay across the children, she felt their bodies moving and changing against hers, felt the fur on their bodies give way to soft skin.

After a moment, Natasha scooted back and rested on her knees.

David, Luke, Simon and Tiara lay nude on their bellies before her.

Natasha could see her children clearly in the light from the moon. They were all attractively formed, lean and toned. The children rolled over and lay on their backs, staring up at the night sky, silent. Natasha continued to watch them, giving them a chance to catch their breath and regain their composure.

"Children," she finally said.

They all turned their heads toward her. She could see the color of their eyes. The three boys had brown eyes; Tiara's were icy blue. Her children were beautiful.

"M-m-m-mother," one of the boys stuttered.

The children sat up to face Natasha. They marveled at their outstretched hands, expressions of sheer wonder etched on their bright faces. They touched their hands to their feet, let them slide up their long legs. The kids studied one another with smiles of wonder. They reached out and touched each other's faces, letting fingers trace the outlines of their features.

Natasha watched them. Warm tears streamed down her face.

"Mother," one of the boys said. It was David. Natasha recognized him by scent. "What has happened to us?"

"Stand up, children," said Natasha. She handed each of them a sweatsuit from the laundry bag. "I have a lot of explaining to do."

•　　•　　•

The children listened quietly and intently as Natasha told them the story of their origins. She told them about lycanthropy and the abilities it provided them; she never mentioned their father, and the children didn't ask. Natasha would tell them about David at some point, but she didn't feel that now was the time. She had already thrown enough at them.

"So, we can become one or the other at any time?" asked Simon. Natasha noticed that he and Luke were about the same height in their human forms and considerably smaller than David. All three of the boys had dark hair.

Natasha nodded. "When you learn to control it, you can change any time you wish."

The three boys sat in front of her along the banks; Tiara stood at the water's edge. Her three boys were handsome, but Natasha was especially awed by David's beauty. Not that he was more handsome than the others.

He bore an uncanny resemblance to his father.

It was incredible, Natasha thought. In every way, he mirrored David Wagner. His eyes, his build, his voice, even the way he carried himself.

"Mother, can we go swimming?" Tiara called out.

Natasha turned her attention to her daughter, standing barefoot in the water.

"I suppose so. Though it is a bit chilly."

Tiara shouted and removed her sweatsuit. She called out to her brothers to join her, and she splashed away into the stream. The boys jumped up and disrobed in a flash. The displacement of water from the combined splashes almost doused Natasha as the boys joined their sister.

Natasha moved over to the water's edge and watched the children play.

Luke swam on his back toward Tiara, while the other two boys disappeared under the water. They soon surfaced behind Tiara, and David leapt quickly for his sister, pushing her head under water. She resurfaced quickly, her hair wet, the moon shining across her face.

Natasha listened to the children's happy banter, glad that Tiara was able to rejoin her brothers. Tonight was the first night the four of them had played together since Natasha had separated them. Tiara was different physically from her brothers. They had dark hair and dark eyes; Tiara had blue eyes and blonde hair. But all her children were beautiful, both as wolves and as humans. David would be so proud of them.

Tiara leapt toward David, landing in his arms. He lifted her up into the air and dropped her with a splash back into the water. She emerged laughing and splashing water back at David. She was happy again, Natasha thought, now that she was reunited with her brothers. But Natasha had to make other decisions that would be life-changing for her children.

"Mother?"

Natasha was pulled from her thoughts. David stood in the shallow water. The moon glistened off his wet body. He did resemble his father so much.

"Mother, why don't you join us?"

"Yeah, come on," Tiara shouted from the water.

"All right." Natasha stood up and pulled her shirt over her head. David dove back into the stream, and Natasha joined him. She swam fast and grabbed at David's feet. He kicked away and disappeared under the water. Simon swam toward Natasha, laughing.

Natasha splashed and frolicked with her boys. Luke pulled Simon's feet from below, and Simon retaliated, chasing his brother into the deeper parts of the stream, with David close behind.

Natasha noticed that she couldn't see Tiara. She scanned her surroundings. With the excitement of the romping diminishing, the water suddenly grew quite cold.

Then, Natasha spotted Tiara. She was sitting on a large boulder near the water's edge. She was paying no mind to the carefree frolicking of her brothers; she seemed to be more involved in herself. The moon bathed the rock and Natasha's daughter in a cool, blue light. Tiara's hands moved up to her small breasts and cradled them. Her body was still covered with drops of cool water, and her nipples were erect. Natasha watched as Tiara let her hands slide down, across her belly to her inner thighs, and back up to the downy hair between her legs. Natasha assumed she was fascinated with her new body, but her daughter's behavior struck her as odd. Then, as if suddenly becoming aware of her mother observing her, Tiara splashed back into the water and sped toward the boys, still carousing in the shallow pool.

After a while, the children grew tired of the water. Natasha and the children dressed and ambled back toward the house.

Natasha felt better at having finally cleared one major obstacle, but her worried mind did not allow her to rest easily.

20

"WELL, IT'S BEEN A WEEK," Jeremiah said. "How do you think they're handling it?"

Natasha did not hear Jeremiah enter the room. She had been intently studying David, moving from pen to pen, busy with the daily task of cleaning the kennels. Natasha thought it a good idea to divide some of the chores up among the children, and Jeremiah agreed.

"I don't know. It may be too early to tell. Luke and Simon seem to be indifferent at best to the whole idea. David's handling it well. He seems to enjoy working the pens."

"And Tiara?"

Natasha sighed deeply. "I don't know. It's hard to get a read on her sometimes."

"Well, she is a woman."

Natasha chuckled. "You know what I mean."

"I'm afraid I do." Jeremiah pulled a chair from beneath the table and plopped down beside her. "I wouldn't worry about her. It may take her a little longer to adjust. The boys stayed in the same pens. Now they room together as humans. They always have each other."

"Yeah, and that bothers me a little. I can't help but feel we're alienating her. Always keeping her away from her brothers."

"No, I don't think so. We kept them in separate pens for obvious reasons. You offered to let her share your room, but she chose to have a room of her own." Jeremiah reached for a slice of toast left over from breakfast and munched on it. "She's a teenager, Natasha. She's a lycanthrope, sure; but she's still just a young woman when you get right down to it. She wants her privacy, that's all."

Natasha stood up and patted Jeremiah on the shoulder. "You're right, as usual."

"You'd think you'd be getting used to that by now.".

Natasha pushed the back door open. "Don't let it go to your head."

"Oh, Natasha," Jeremiah called out. "Don't forget there's some folks coming to check out some pups."

The late morning sun was warm and soothing as Natasha strolled down the lane toward David. She found herself instinctively checking the pens that he had already cleaned. They looked good. David always did a fine job at whatever chores he was given. He was a responsible young man.

Natasha peered down the line of kennels. David was already at the end of the row. As she scanned the pens between her and David, Natasha caught a glimpse of something along the outside of the pens along the left, toward the two-lane blacktop highway.

It was Tiara. She sat in the grass wearing her faded jeans and oversized sweatshirt, her knees pulled up to her chin. Her long blonde hair was whipping in the wind, and she seemed to be staring toward the road, watching any cars that happened to venture this far into the mountains.

Natasha remembered that Tiara was supposed to be helping David with the cleaning. From the looks of things, David had done most, if not all, of the pens alone.

"Hi, honey," Natasha called to David. "Almost done?"

David dumped a shovel full of solid waste into a plastic garbage bag. He smiled at his mother. A chill ran up Natasha's spine.

God, he looks so much like David when he smiles like that.

"Just finishing up."

"Can I give you a hand?"

"Mom, Tiara wasn't much help today." This was the first time he had voiced a concern.

"I know. I'm going to talk to her."

"I don't want to get her in trouble, but she should do her share."

"However, in all fairness, she's had a lot on her mind lately."

"Mom, we've all had a lot on our minds lately," David noted.

"Well, it may take a little longer with Tiara. She's a little different."

"Just because she's a girl?"

"That has a lot to do with it."

"Women sure do get away with a lot of stuff." David gave her another disarming grin.

Natasha left David with the final clean-up details. The wolves in the last few kennels leapt and barked for her attention, but Natasha ignored them.

From the back, Tiara resembled a little girl in the middle of a summer free from school, gently idling the hours without a care in the world. The thought saddened Natasha somehow, probably because she knew that wasn't true.

Natasha moved up beside Tiara, following her vacant gaze to the roadway.

"Hi, Mom," Tiara said without a glance at her mother.

Natasha sat down next to her and pulled a wildflower from the grass. "Whatcha doing?"

Tiara shook her head.

"Do you know where your brothers are?"

"Jeremiah helped Luke and Simon wolf out a little earlier. They went into the woods." "Wolfing out" was a phrase the kids had coined to describe their transformations.

"Luke and Simon spend a lot of time in the woods," Natasha said, staring out into the trees as if she could catch a glimpse of her sons. "Your brother was expecting you to help him with the pens."

"I know," said Tiara. "And I'm sorry. I started, but then ..."

"What's wrong?"

"It's just that ... it gets so boring out here sometimes. There's nothing to do but take care of the dogs."

A little red sports car zipped past the buildings and disappeared over the horizon. Natasha noted that Tiara had followed the car the length of the road.

"You could take off through the woods, too. Try to catch Luke and Simon."

Tiara turned her head momentarily to the woods before directing her attention back to the highway. Somewhere in the distance, the red sports car screeched around a corner. "No, that gets old, too."

"You're watching the road a lot."

Tiara smiled, briefly, then it was gone. "I like watching the cars."

"You do, huh? What if I taught you how to drive Jeremiah's truck?"

Tiara looked up, and for the first time since Natasha sat down with her, made eye contact with her mother. Her eyes were like the Canadian sky. "Really?"

"Sure, it would be fun. Just a mother/daughter thing." Natasha leaned into her daughter. "No boys allowed."

"I'd like that."

"Under one condition. You don't neglect your chores."

Tiara uttered a little sigh. "Okay. I'll behave."

"Great," Natasha said, and hugged her daughter.

Their embrace was interrupted by Jeremiah shouting for Natasha. She craned her neck around to look.

"The people are probably here to see the pups."

Jeremiah stood at the house with a family of four. The children—a boy and a girl—appeared to be about sixteen and ten. Natasha hurried along to greet the family.

Jeremiah was in the middle of his "raising a wolf hybrid is a lot different than raising a regular dog" speech. The man and woman listened intently, while the little girl stood next to the pen that held the puppies. Natasha opened the gate and entered the kennel. The puppies immediately rushed toward her. Natasha searched for Tiara's help.

Tiara was talking to the boy. They both stepped back down the lane a bit, away from the others. As far as Natasha knew, this would be the first contact Tiara—or any of the children—had with anyone outside the family.

"Bring one of the males," Jeremiah called to Natasha.

Natasha picked up the largest male pup and brought it to the man and woman, placing the furry ball at their feet. The little girl squatted immediately to play with the pup. The puppy looked around nervously for a moment, trying to find its mother, but eventually warmed to the little girl's affections.

Natasha returned her attention to Tiara. She and the boy were still talking quietly in the distance, and Natasha could hear an outbreak of laughter every now and then. It seemed innocent enough, but something about the two of them together disturbed Natasha. She supposed it was the motherly instinct to protect her children.

"Well, we'd like to take a few days and think it over," said the man.

"No, Daddy! I want him now!" the little girl cried.

Jeremiah laughed and rubbed the girl's hair. "Let me get you one of our videos," he said to her father. "It'll show you a little of what's involved. Give you something to think about."

Jeremiah placed a big hand on the man's shoulder, leading him back to the office. Natasha started to put the puppy back in the pen when she heard the man call for his son.

The boy turned and yelled something back that Natasha could not understand. Natasha knelt at the gate and pushed the pup back into the pen as the boy trotted past her. He seemed like a nice enough kid. Kind of tall, short dark hair, slight build.

Natasha watched him disappear through the door leading to Jeremiah's office before glancing back at Tiara. Natasha's daughter stood there a moment longer, staring toward the building where she had last seen the boy. She then went back down the lane where she sat in the grass and resumed her lonely vigil over the highway.

21

S OMETHING ABOUT THE MAN sitting across from her in the hotel room made Traci feel a bit uneasy. It was something very vague, so imperceptible that it was difficult to grasp, but it was there. It wasn't the hotel room. It was actually nice. She'd performed tricks in much seedier locales.

He was certainly a handsome man—tall, blonde, piercing blue eyes—so it wasn't his physical appearance that made her uncomfortable. In fact, there was a sort of glint in his eyes that only served to alleviate her discomfort. The fact that he was white didn't bother her; their money was still green no matter what color their skin was. He seemed like a nice enough man, although how nice could he be if he was out picking up hookers?

Don't judge them, honey. It takes all kinds. You've had business executives, family men, even preachers. Just do what they want and take their money.

The man hadn't been rough or rude like many of the johns; he really hadn't said much at all. Perhaps that was what bothered her. His unusual silence.

"So, what is it exactly that you do for my hard-earned forty bills?" asked the man. They were the first words he had spoken since arriving at the hotel room.

"I do any—" She stopped herself when she realized she wasn't "talking the talk".

"Well, honey," she purred, "I do whatever your sweet ass wants Traci to do." She leaned toward the man, letting her lips brush against his as she spoke, allowing him to feel the warmth of her breath. That always seemed to turn the guys on. The more they liked their encounter, the more likely they were to come back. After all, the competition on the streets was tough.

"I give you a good blow, just to get things started." She lowered her hand to his thigh, rubbing upward until she found the center of his crotch. "Then, when we get down to more serious business, I give it any way you want it. Top, bottom. Somewhere in the middle. Whatever you want. But the pay is up front."

The man cracked a faint smile. Finally, Traci thought. He shifted slightly on the bed, reaching for his wallet.

"You like this big ass, don't you?"

The man pulled out two twenties and laid them on the nightstand. "I don't mind a little dark meat now and then," he said, and laughed. It started as a small giggle, and Traci began to laugh with him. But then the man started to laugh louder, building slowly at first, then climbing to a hysterical cackle.

The laughter brought all of Traci's anxieties roaring back. Something about this guy was weird. And she couldn't be too careful these days.

Three prostitutes had already been found murdered and mutilated, Jack the Ripper style, on the dirty streets of Detroit, all in the last few months. The local authorities tried to calm the public's fears by claiming the murders were too random to suggest a serial killer. But the cops couldn't deny the similarities in each case, especially when it came to the ravaged states of the victims' bodies.

She and her friends suspected that the cops just didn't give a damn about it, since it was just prostitutes who had been killed. No one cared as long as regular citizens weren't harmed. Hell, if the guy got the hookers off the streets, he should be given a freakin' medal, not a prison sentence.

Now, as the man sat on the bed laughing, Traci realized what had been gnawing at her from the onset of her encounter with this man.

This could be him.

"Well, are you gonna earn your money or not?" Traci was thankful that the creepy laughter had ended.

"Yeah," Traci said, her lips quivering slightly. "Yeah." She reached for the money on the stand.

In her consuming notion that something was unsettling with her latest customer, and the sudden terrifying thought that she could be staring into the eyes of a cold-blooded killer, Traci forgot the first and foremost rule by which all ladies of the night should live.

The idea that this guy might be a cop never entered her mind.

The crash from the bathroom door was sudden and unexpected. Traci jumped backwards, screaming, away from the man on the bed. Her first thought was that the killer had been hiding in the bathroom, that this man whom she had picked up was his partner, and now they were going to have their way with her.

Traci stumbled against the dresser and looked up as she caught herself against the wall.

"Vice! Sit it down!"

When Traci saw the first police badge waving in her face, she was at once relieved and infuriated. She had let her guard down; she had been set up. Fears for her own safety had clouded her perception, dulled the sixth sense that prostitutes seem to develop over time. She had fallen for a police scam.

But at least she would still be alive.

"Shit," she muttered as she dropped her purse to the floor. She glanced at her would-be trick, expecting to see the handsome blue-eyed man smirking knowingly at her.

But she was met only by the piercing blue eyes. Cold, emotionless. Like a blue-eyed shark.

Traci was taken aback momentarily, but when she felt the cold steel of the handcuffs tighten against her wrists, her street savvy returned.

"You sorry mother fucker! Man, I can't believe this is happenin'!"

"Save it, babe," one of the officers said as the cuffs clicked shut.

"I get you, you son-of-a-bitch! I kill you!"

"Cool it, girl. You're gonna take a little trip downtown with us. Give you something to think about. Maybe you'll question yourself a little harder before you hit the streets next time."

"Why ya'll be doing this? Ain't you cops got nothing better to do? Ain't they no crimes you can stop?"

"What do you call this, sweet thing?"

"Bullshit, that's what I call it."

"At least you're still alive," one of the cops said. "Some of your friends can't say that anymore."

"Shit. I don't believe this," Traci stomped her foot like a little girl denied her after-school milk and cookies, breaking a heel.

After being wheeled around, she was shoved rudely toward the front door, where the unmarked police cars waited to transport her to Jackson Center. Traci shouted a few more profanities and twisted her neck to glance back into the room. She continued to protest, because that was what was expected. But when she made eye contact with the frosty orbs that belonged to the cop that had led her astray, she didn't feel like yelling any more.

She just felt cold.

•　　•　　•

The main office of Precinct 103 in downtown Detroit was unusually active for a weeknight. The new plans being conducted by the Vice Squad worked better than anyone could've imagined. It made for some busy nights.

"Six more," Sergeant Lemmon said. "Not bad for four hours work."

"Better than a run an inning," the man at the computer said.

Sergeant Lemmon patted the man on the back. "Good work, Devin. You played it perfectly. They never knew what hit them. If I didn't know any better, I'd swear you go out and pick up hookers in your spare time."

"Thanks, Sarge," said the cop with a laugh.

Devin Stoner turned away from his superior and focused his attention on the computer monitor in front of him. The file of one Traci Jean Willard graced the monochrome green screen. He busied himself with the task of updating the woman's file. This was the last of the paperwork on the six prostitutes they had busted for the night. Fortunately, this one was a repeat offender, and a quick update of her record was the only work involved.

Two and a half years and several Festerings had passed since Devin Stoner had relocated to Detroit, Michigan. The small town of Potters, Maine had worn out its usefulness. The annual and increasingly violent Festering ceremonies had slowly built a desire inside Devin's soul that he could not deny.

The lurid call of the big city beckoned. His thirst for blood had grown since the Festering of '93. He could no longer stay in the more secluded areas, could no longer take the chances that his lust was forcing him to take. As far as he knew, no one in Potters had ever learned what had really become of Jackie Coogan. The sheriff's office searched for several months, but found no leads, no clues that would solve the old man's disappearance. They finally dismissed the case, officially stating that the old drunk had just drifted on to another town. And good riddance.

But that had signaled the end of Devin Stoner's relationship with the small farming community at the foot of Saddleback Mountain.

In a town like Detroit, it was much easier to slink around the shadows, actively seeking out the homeless and the street slime so prevalent in the city. No one would miss the guy named Joe that slept under the Highway 94 bridge. No one would miss the wino that scoured the back alleys of Motor Boulevard, searching trash cans for any bottles that might still contain a drop or two of the golden juice. If anything was left, the police department would search the scene, file the case, try to scare information out of the other street people, talk about it for a week or two, and then forget it.

And that's just the way Devin Stoner liked it. Everything got caught up in the jumbled mess of a congested and tired judicial system. He could do things in a heartbeat with no thought of the aftermath, a situation he could never risk in a small, rural town.

It was like a scaled-down version of the Festering every night.

Devin ripped the sheet from the printer and filed Traci Jean Willard's information along with that of the other five girls. They would probably all be walking the streets by the time the sun set the next day, and that was just fine with Devin. In fact, it was the way he always planned it.

He perused Willard's paperwork before dropping it into the hanging folder. 101 Industrial, Unit 12B. He memorized the address and slid the drawer shut.

•   •   •

Traci stood halfway between the shadows supplied by the awning covering the entrance door to Bert's Tattoos and the light spilling down from the streetlamp at Jefferson and Beaumont. The light was both a blessing and a curse. It made her visible to her potential customers, but it also made her visible to the cops. And after the events of the previous evening, she couldn't be too careful. She didn't feel safe in her own neighborhood anymore. Not that she ever did, but it was worse now.

She didn't want to go to jail again. Her pimp wouldn't like it.

Several layers of foundation caked on her face managed to hide the bruises for the most part, but there was nothing she could do about the disfigured lip. Her pimp didn't like it when he had to bail out one of his girls. His whores were supposed to be smarter than that; they were supposed to know all the cops' tricks. Never mind that his girls were more worried about winding up in a grave than in a cell. His girls were supposed to think, goddamnit.

Traci was thinking tonight.

She had seen too many of her friends die out here in this cruel and unforgiving cityscape, and she didn't just mean from this possible prostitute killer. She'd seen them murdered at the hands of regular johns who got too rough or fall victim to the diseases and drugs of the streets.

Sometimes, Traci felt that it was only a matter of time before her number came up.

Traci saw the man in the overcoat and dark glasses approaching her at the exact moment the police cruiser turned left on Jefferson. Her instinct to avoid the cops took over so she slumped back into the shadows of the night. She might lose the potential trick hiding like this, but she couldn't let the police see her.

The cruiser rolled slowly past Traci. She heard the whine of the engine as the car accelerated and cruised on down the boulevard. She peeked around the corner, watching its taillights disappear over the horizon, and tried to find the stranger she had seen earlier.

He wasn't there. This concerned Traci. He hadn't walked past the alley—she would've seen him. She finally spotted him standing partially in the shadows about two alleys from her. Something seemed familiar about the man that she couldn't place. Perhaps he was a regular, and she didn't recognize him with the heavy overcoat on.

It had rained earlier, hence the overcoat, but that didn't explain the sunglasses. He was probably a married man, maybe even someone semi-important, and didn't want to be recognized while out whoring.

The man had evidently spotted Traci, though she couldn't see how. She was still completely in the shadows. The man gave a casual, almost unnoticeable nod of his head and motioned Traci toward him.

Somewhere deep in Traci's soul, a warning went off, another part of her sixth sense. She glanced at her watch. It was already after one in the morning. The stepped-up activities of the vice squad scared away a lot of customers; she hadn't turned a trick all night. Coupled with last night's arrest, that was two profitless nights in a row. If she came back empty-handed tonight, no amount of makeup could hide what her pimp would do to her.

Just as her instinct for survival had made Traci leery of the cop the previous night, the same need to prosper overrode her apprehension tonight.

Traci moved into the light toward the man. When she made it past Bert's Tattoos, the man motioned her onward and disappeared into the alley.

Traci stopped. There was no reason that she could think of for the man to call her into a dark alley. Everything inside of Traci screamed for her to turn back. But spurred on by what might happen if she didn't, she carried on.

"Hey, cutie," she called out to him after she stopped a few feet from the alley. She hoped her terror was not evident in her voice. "Why you hiding in the dark? You shy?"

No answer, save for his breathing.

He's just a harmless pervert, she told herself. He wants to play cat and mouse.

Traci peered around the corner. The alley was cloaked in complete darkness; she could see nothing. She waited a moment to let her eyes adjust to the lack of lighting, but it did no good.

"C'mon, honey. I don't wanna play no games. Now, do you want some action or not?"

No answer. The darkness was silent.

Fuck this, Traci thought. I'll just work a little later, maybe call up a regular, maybe even take what her mack daddy would dish out. Ain't nothing worth this shit.

Traci started to turn back to the light when a movement caught her eye. It was low to the ground, not at the height of the man who had disappeared into the alley.

"Is that you, honey?"

She was answered only by the same silence. Rats, she assumed. Just rats.

Traci reached into her purse for a cigarette to calm her nerves. She placed the smoke between her swollen lips and struck the lighter, watching it flare to life.

She registered the dog a moment before its fangs sank into her soft, meaty throat. There wasn't even time for a scream.

If there was any consolation in the attack, it was the fact that Traci Jean Willard could take solace in knowing that she would be off the streets at long last.

22

NATASHA PULLED JEREMIAH'S TRUCK into the parking lot of the general store in Caribou Park. This was the first time Natasha had brought all four of the kids into town at the same time. The thought worried Natasha a bit. She knew she couldn't keep an eye on all of them; they had already made it clear that they were going their separate ways once they reached town. She had reluctantly agreed to let them go.

As she expected, none of them chose to stay with her.

"You guys meet me back here in two hours," she told them.

Luke and Simon, always together, headed south down the main drag. David, as he always did in town, went directly across the street from the general store to the bookstore. Natasha found that interesting, as his father had been a bit of a bookworm. And Tiara went in the opposite direction, away from the buildings and the main bustle of town life. She went off alone more and more lately, spending less time with her brothers, and even less with Natasha.

Natasha sighed. She knew this wouldn't be easy once she had brought the children into their new world. There would be thousands of things they'd want to do, to learn, to experience.

That's what worried her.

•   •   •

David stepped into the brightly lit bookstore and inhaled deeply. He loved the smell that always greeted him in this magical place: the fresh print, the pastries and fresh brew from the coffee bar. It was invigorating.

David headed first to the newsstand. He grabbed the latest issue of *Time* and flipped through it. He had learned so much from this place in so little time. Names of many of the countries he longed to see, names he knew somehow, yet knew nothing about, graced the pages of magazines such as *World News Report* and *Newsweek*. The names of many famous people, wondrous machines, and fascinating sciences filled the magazines.

After half an hour, David searched for the reason for this visit to the bookstore. He turned down the aisle marked *Nature* and stopped. There it was, sitting neatly on the shelf, flanked by two much smaller, thinner books. David reached for the book as he had so many times before. But there was something different about its touch this time, something wonderful, almost spiritual. This time the book would be his.

David pulled the enormous tome, *Brazil and Its Rain Forests*, from the shelf. He resisted the urge to open and peruse its wondrous sights; he would wait until he got home. It meant more that way somehow. David checked the price once more, a hefty seventy dollars, and reassuringly patted the pockets of his jeans. Jeremiah and his mother had paid the kids for chores they did. That, added to the small allowance his mother gave him every two weeks, had finally reached the seventy-dollar mark.

David tucked the book under his arm and headed to the front of the store when a book titled *Colleges & Universities* caught his eye. David stared at the volume for a moment, then noticed that there were many other similar books surrounding it. There were also some with odd titles such as SAT, MCAT, ACT and other abbreviations.

Curious, David reached for the first he'd seen. He quickly went to the table of contents. There was a listing for schools in the United States and Canada. David thumbed through the book in search of Canadian universities. He scanned the long list until he found the name he was searching for: the University of Alberta. That's not too far from here, he thought. David briefly skimmed over the list of information: enrollment, courses offered, faculty. He stopped at tuition. The amount made the seventy dollars that he had worked so hard to obtain pale in comparison. Dejected, David slid the book back onto the shelf. He would never be able to afford that.

•   •   •

Tiara peered around the corner of the old, abandoned warehouse, making sure that the area was clear. She sprinted across the graveled road, slowing down as she approached the last building on the stretch. The building's walls were tall and constructed of badly rusted sheet metal. Rows of shattered windows towered in the gloom, scores of pigeons flapping in and out of the structure. Through those windows, Tiara could hear the music playing. She couldn't place the band, but it had a driving beat that she liked. It made Tiara want to move.

Tiara slowly approached the wide opening in the face of the building. She could hear laughter over the blare of the music. Tiara moved up next to the open doors and peeked in.

Tiara remembered the girls from a week earlier when she and Natasha ventured into town on an errand for Jeremiah. She watched them moving down the sidewalk as she and her mother passed. The thing Tiara remembered most about them was the clothes. The girls wore tight, ripped jeans, small cropped T-shirts, and loose-fitting flannel shirts tied at the waist. Tiara glanced down at her own body draped in the omnipresent old sweatshirt and faded jeans and frowned. She hated the way she looked with her straight hair and plain face and hand-me-down clothes. She longed to be like these girls, the girls in the magazines, the girls on television.

The music suddenly stopped. "Hey, who's there?" one of the girls called out.

Tiara stepped into full view of the small cluster of teenaged girls. The four girls —two blondes, one quite a bit taller than the other girls and two brunettes—congregated in the center of the huge warehouse, sitting on old barrels and empty crates smoking cigarettes. Their portable CD player, situated between them, ready to blare out more nameless tunes.

Tiara thought they were probably her age but corrected that when she remembered that she was actually only three years old, and barely that. The girls were probably sixteen or seventeen.

"Who the hell are you?" one of the blondes asked.

Tiara stood motionless just inside the doorway. This suddenly seemed like a bad idea. She wanted to meet the girls. She wanted to be around other girls her own age. Now she wished she had stayed with her brothers.

"Are you a cop?" the girl asked.

"No. No, I'm not anything," said Tiara. She stepped a little farther into the building.

The blonde, who seemed to be the leader, walked toward Tiara. The others put out their cigarettes on the grimy floor and followed.

"What's your name?" the leader asked. She sounded slightly less menacing.

"Tiara."

"Tiara what?"

Tiara shrugged. "Just Tiara."

"Tiara," one of the other girls, a petite brunette, said. "That's a pretty name."

"Thanks," Tiara said with a timid smile. "What are you doing?"

The apparent leader didn't answer, and it seemed the other girls weren't allowed to speak unless she did. She stared a moment longer, her eyes scanning Tiara from head to toe. "Nice outfit."

"I was working earlier," she lied, hoping that would explain the plain clothing. "I don't live around here."

"No shit," the tall blonde said. "I'm Jenny. This is Michelle, Stacy, and Rhonda. So, what's your story, Tiara?"

"I live out in the country," explained Tiara. "I don't have any friends in town. I saw all of you last week, and I followed you here. I was wondering if we could, you know, hang out."

The girl named Jenny took a final drag of her cigarette and flicked it away into the darkness. She shook her head. "Uh-uh. We don't need any new friends. Least of all some frumpy country bumpkin."

Tiara studied the other girls. They seemed to convey their apparent leader's feelings, except for the small girl, Rhonda. Her eyes didn't seem filled with apathy like the others.

Tiara protested. "But I could get some clothes. You could show me how to dress. I just need someone to teach me, that's all."

Jenny turned to the other girls and pulled them back away from the new girl. They talked among themselves while Tiara awaited Jenny's approval.

Finally, Jenny returned her attention to Tiara and lit another cigarette. "You smoke, Tiara?" The other girls returned to their perches to watch the confrontation, like sparrows on a wire.

"No. I've never tried it."

Jenny smiled and handed Tiara the lit cigarette. She stared at it for a second, watching the burning tip glow and drop ashes to the floor.

"Take it," Jenny ordered.

Tiara reached for the cigarette, hoping the girls wouldn't notice her fingers shaking. Jenny grinned at her. Tiara developed an immediate dislike for Jenny. Tiara placed the cigarette between her lips and breathed through her nose.

"You have to inhale."

"I know," Tiara mumbled through the cigarette. She fluttered her eyes and took a deep drag. Tiara thought she would vomit. The smoke coated her throat and burned her lungs. Tiara lurched forward and coughed hoarsely. Jenny and the other girls laughed. Tiara placed her hands on her knees and coughed again. She finally stood up straight and glared at Jenny.

"If you can't handle a simple little cigarette—" the tall blonde started to say.

"Well, maybe I haven't been smoking since I was five," Tiara said, and flicked the cigarette at Jenny. The burning smoke struck Jenny on her left breast and fell harmlessly to the floor.

Tiara's quip brought giggles and hushed "ooohs" from the other girls. They moved closer to Tiara.

"You bitch!" shouted Jenny, reaching for Tiara's throat.

Tiara's arm shot forth quicker than Jenny's mind could register. She grabbed the offending hand. Jenny struggled against the vice-like grip of the smaller blonde-headed girl. Jenny stood a good six inches taller than Tiara. But the mean glare was all but gone from the taller girl's eyes.

"Don't you ever try to touch me again, you cheap whore," Tiara whispered, her mouth just centimeters from Jenny's face.

The other girls stood idly to the side, unsure of how to react to their leader's sudden display of weakness. Jenny tried to free her wrist from Tiara.

"I just wanted to talk to you, to try to be friends," Tiara said, pulling the girl lower. Jenny bent her knees to follow Tiara's lead, certain that the bones in her wrist would snap if she didn't.

Tiara shoved the tall blonde backward, causing her to fall over one of the crates serving as make-shift chairs. She stood a moment longer, glaring first at the fallen Jenny, then casting furtive glances to the rest. The other girls made no moves toward Jenny or Tiara.

Then, Tiara turned away, her long blonde mane whipping around, and exited the building.

"Tiara!" Rhonda called.

Tiara didn't turn around to face the girl, but instead, kept walking. The shorter girl caught up to Tiara, her breath slightly ragged.

"That was pretty cool what you did to Jenny back there. I've never seen anyone talk to her that way."

"She's a bitch," Tiara stopped and glared back in the direction of the other girls.

"Hell, you think I don't know that? I've known her since third grade. She always acted like that."

Tiara could tell that Rhonda had taken an instant liking to her tenacity. "You've lived here since third grade?"

"Longer than that. All my life."

"I don't see how you can stand it," Tiara half-whispered to herself.

"It must really drive you crazy out where you live," Rhonda said.

"It's okay. Sometimes."

"Where do you go to school?"

"Don't go to school."

"You dropped out?" There was a tinge of something like envy in the girl's voice.

"Never went to school,"

"What, were you raised by wolves?"

Tiara laughed aloud. "Something like that."

"Look," Rhonda motioned to the area they had just left. "We hang out around here every weekend. Why don't you come by next Saturday? We may go to the mall in Fort Vermillion."

"What would Jenny say to that?" Tiara asked in a sarcastic tone.

"I don't know. She'd probably kill me if she even knew I was talking to you."

"No, I don't think so."

"No, I don't think so either."

The two girls strolled onward toward town, talking and laughing. Tiara smiled inward. With Rhonda already won over, she would be running the show before long.

•   •   •

Luke and Simon stood behind the other boys inside the convenience store, watching them play video games. All three of the video games were in use. The game in which two karate experts beat one another's brains out and the baseball game didn't interest either Luke or Simon. They were watching the one with the little fuzzy animal fighting off all kinds of obstacles. The game made them laugh, especially when the big lightning ball came down and struck the fuzzy animal, causing its hair to stand on end. That's probably what started the fight.

The big kid playing the game had just lost his last "man" to the dreaded lightning ball. The little animal squealed and screamed. When it was over, only a smoking, blackened husk of its former self remained. A funeral dirge played through the game's speakers, and the words "game over" rolled onto the screen.

Luke couldn't help but laugh; the little cartoon animal was so funny.

Apparently, the big kid didn't agree. "What are you laughing at, asshole?" he said, turning around to face Luke and Simon.

Luke tried to stop laughing but couldn't. Simon tried to push his brother back. "Nothing," Simon said to the kid. "He just laughs when he sees the thing get fried like that."

"Yeah, well I don't think it's so funny, you know. I lost a quarter. Do you think that's funny?" The kid moved closer to Luke.

"No," Luke said. "No, that's not funny. The game is."

"If you think it's so fucking funny, I think you oughtta pay for my next game." The big kid held his hand out palm up. "My next four games. Gimme a loonie."

The smile left Luke's face. "I'm not giving you a loonie."

The bully wasn't very old, maybe fifteen, but he was big. "I said, gimme a loonie."

"C'mon, Luke," Simon urged. "Let's get out of here."

Luke didn't move from the spot. "No, Simon. We didn't do anything wrong. He can't make us leave."

"Oh, I can't, huh?"

"No, you can't."

"Hey, you kids," a man yelled from behind the counter, sensing trouble. "If you're gonna argue, take it outside."

The kid glared past Luke and Simon toward the front of the store. "It's none of your business."

That seemed to strike a sour note with the man. He slammed the register shut and bolted around the corner toward the video games.

"Goddamned smartass kids!" he shouted. "Out of my store! All of you! Out!"

"But we weren't doing anything," Luke protested.

The owner grabbed Luke and the big kid and frog-marched them out the door. Simon darted hurriedly past the store owner to his brother. The big kid and his friends gathered.

"C'mon, we better get back to Mom."

Luke gave the big kid one last glare and turned away. "Okay."

Luke and Simon turned away toward the feed store.

The big kid knocked Luke to the ground and landed on top of him, knocking Luke's breath out of him. Simon went to grab the kid's jacket, but he was, in turn, grabbed from behind. When he tried to escape the grasp, another boy drove his fist into Simon's stomach. Simon dropped, wheezing to the ground. He saw the big kid push Luke's face into the ground.

Luke forced his head up off the ground and turned toward Simon. There was a wild gleam in Luke's eyes, and Simon thought he heard a low growl emanating from his throat.

"No!" Simon shouted. "Luke, no!"

"Stay outta this!" Another kid snarled and kicked Simon in the rear. Simon fell forward, closer to Luke.

Simon struggled to his knees and reached into his pocket, fishing for a dollar from his jeans. He tossed the bronze-colored coin at the big kid. It hit him on the nose and fell to the ground. "Here's your damned money," Simon said. "Now leave us alone."

The big kid stood up, pulled Luke up by the back of his shirt and shoved him down again. Luke meant to retaliate, but Simon stepped between them.

"Luke. No, forget it. Let's go."

"Yeah," the big kid taunted. "Go back home to Mommy."

Simon pulled Luke away.

"Why'd you do that? Why'd you give that jerk a dollar?"

"Because you were about to rip his throat out, that's why! I thought you were going to wolf out."

"I can't change by myself. You know that."

"Well, I didn't know for sure."

"We didn't do anything wrong," Luke muttered "I just laughed. I just wanted to play the game, too."

"I know," Simon said, placing his hand on his brother's shoulder. "I know."

"I don't like it in town. I don't like it here. There's too many people. People are mean."

"I know, Luke. I don't like it either."

The two boys waited at Jeremiah's pickup. They were both eager to get home.

23

THE EVENTS OF THE DAY filled Tiara's young and hungry head, swirling and dancing in a myriad of out-of-control thoughts that followed her into her dreams.

The dream was dark, surreal, discorporate. She thought she stood in the warehouse where she encountered Jenny and the other girls. Although she could see very little, she was painfully aware that she was still clad in the woefully fashion-challenged sweatshirt and jeans. She could hear voices, faint and distant, coming from the center of the warehouse.

As she made her way slowly toward the noises, she felt boxed in, as if she struggled her way through a narrow, stifling tunnel rather than a spacious warehouse. Then, the dream wavered in and out of reason for a while. Tiara seemed detached from herself, floating in a smoky cloud inside the warehouse, drifting toward the windows. And then the voices returned.

The dream resolved itself. She was back in the warehouse, now well-lit by the light of the full moon penetrating the high broken windows lining the perimeter of the building. She could hear the girls' voices more clearly and followed them.

Suddenly, the voices stopped, and the moon ceased to supply its nocturnal light. Frightened, Tiara began to inch her way further when her foot hit something on the floor. She started to kneel to inspect the obstacle when she heard something ahead of her. It sounded deep and guttural, like the warnings of the large male wolves in Jeremiah's pens.

Tiara could see only a pair of red eyes gleaming ominously in the dark at first. When Tiara's eyes adjusted to the darkness, she could make out the outline of the wolf, huge and black, against the dim background. Her first instinct had been to scream and run, but something in the wolf's crimson eyes calmed her spirit. There was a sense of familiarity in the glowing orbs. Shafts of pale, pinkish light emanated from the wolf's eyes, enough to light the area directly in front of her. When Tiara looked down, she saw glints of moonlight bouncing across exposed bone. She had almost tripped over Jenny's mangled body.

Tiara awoke with a start and sat up in bed, clutching her pillow tightly. Clammy sweat clung to her T-shirt. She clenched her eyes shut tightly, willing away the gruesome image of Jenny's ravaged body. Then, the image of the wolf with its glowing bloody eyes bore into her memory, and the fear began to subside. When Tiara again opened her eyes, the light of the moon shining through her window soothed her feelings completely.

●   ●   ●

Natasha stood outside David's room, listening momentarily at the door before rapping softly against it. David answered as if his thoughts were elsewhere. Natasha pushed the door inward. David lay on his stomach on the bed, his face between the pages of a large book. He glanced up at his mother, and once again, Natasha had to fight the shock of the similarity to his father.

"Hi, Mom," David said, returning his attention to his reading.

"Just wanted to tell you that you don't need to clean the kennels tonight." Natasha stepped into the room. "Tiara's already done them."

A mock expression of surprise crossed his face. "Tiara? Tiara, my sister? She did a chore voluntarily?"

Natasha laughed. "All right, that's enough. She doesn't always have to be reminded. Besides, she went off to a friend's house to spend the night."

"Oh? Who?"

Natasha shrugged. "Some girl she met in town. I told her she could go if she finished the pens first, and if she promised to be home by ten tomorrow morning."

"Well, good for her," David said. He turned a page in the book.

"Is that what you bought in town the other day?"

David nodded.

"Can I see?"

David closed the book, keeping a hand inside to mark his place and let Natasha read the cover. "Brazil and Its Rain Forests," she read.

"This is fascinating, Mom," David sat up. "Did you know there are over five thousand species of plant life in the Amazon? Over two hundred types of insects per square mile? The Amazonian rain forests have the most diversified biology of any spot on the globe."

"And this is all interesting to you?" Natasha asked.

"Yeah." David noticed the confusion on his mother's face. "Yeah, shouldn't it be?"

"Well, sure. There's nothing wrong with being interested in other places. I just thought your immediate area would be more interesting to you, at least for a while."

"It is interesting to me, Mom. It really is. But I've been reading a lot of magazines. There's a lot of articles on Brazil. The rain forests may not be around forever." He gazed for a moment longingly at the cover. "I'd like to see them before they're gone."

Natasha sat next to her son. She stroked David's hair. It hurt her to see David like this, trapped in a stifling environment with little hope of ever escaping. She dearly wished that the children would be happy with what they had, with what they were, but she knew all along that she expected too much. The children were extremely intelligent and would want to branch out, away from the wilds of Canada.

"So inquisitive," whispered Natasha, still patting David's hair. "So much like your father."

"What?" David started.

Natasha shook her head. "Nothing," she said. "Nothing. I was just thinking."

"Mom, who was my father, our father?"

There it was. Plain and simple. It had been coming for a long time. One of these days, one of the kids was bound to ask the dreaded question. And now, that day had arrived.

"David," Natasha began, "someday I'm going to sit you down, sit you all down, and we're going to have a long talk about things. But right now ... I don't feel this is the time, okay?" David nodded in understanding. "But I will tell you this. He was the greatest man that ever lived."

David smiled. "I understand. When you feel like it."

Natasha leaned over and kissed David on the forehead. She left him alone in his room with his books and his magazines and his dreams of faraway lands.

•   •   •

Natasha had just started dressing for bed when the knock came at her bedroom door. She hurriedly finished buttoning the old flannel shirt she slept in and opened the door to see the somber faces of Luke and Simon.

"Hey, guys," she said, startled by the sad looks on their faces. "What's up?"

The boys answered with a subdued greeting. Natasha started up the hall, pushing the two boys along in front of her. "Did you feed the dogs?"

"Not yet," Luke answered.

"Mom," added Simon, "we were wondering if we could do the chores later."

"Simon, the dogs need to be fed before anything else, you know that."

The boys sighed in unison and looked down at their toes.

"Okay, let's have it," said Natasha, sensing their unease. "What's wrong?"

"We wanted you to help us change so we could go off into the woods for a while," Luke said.

Natasha exhaled a sigh of relief. That's all it was. From the expressions on their faces, she expected something much more serious, perhaps even inquiries about their father, as David had sprung on her earlier. "You can go to the woods later, after you do the chores."

"Mom, we hate doing the chores!" Luke raised his arms and dropped them to his thighs in exasperation.

Natasha turned, stunned at the emotion in her son's voice.

"I'm sorry, Mom," said Simon, "we know you want us to fit in here, to do things like normal kids, but we're not normal. We can't fit in."

"I don't like living like this, Mother," Luke continued. "I don't like living in this world, in man's world. We tried to fit in. We tried to go into town, to be with other people, and I got beat up!"

"Wait a second," Natasha interrupted. "You got beat up? Who beat you up?"

"It doesn't matter who beat me up, Mom. What matters is that this isn't right. We can't fit in because we don't know this life. That's all we know," Luke said, pointing out the window to the tree line that started just beyond the barn. "That's the only way we know. Being animal is the only thing we know how to be."

"Okay," she said finally. "I'll feed the dogs. Let's go outside."

24

T IARA STARED INTO THE EYES of the girl glaring back at her, as if waiting for her to make a move. The girl's clear blue eyes bore into her soul; the shadow, eyeliner, and mascara expertly applied in a way which pulled one's attention directly into the sparkling azure orbs. The girl's lips, glistening crimson and moist as morning dew, encircled her gleaming white teeth, hiding discreetly what could have been either a genuine smile or a knowing smirk. The perfect amount of color in the girl's cheeks narrowed her pretty face. The long blonde mane, teased and tossed, framed the entire setting, giving this strange new girl a sense of power and sensuality that Tiara had never seen.

Tiara could hardly believe the image that stared back at her from the full-length mirror was actually her.

"Wow," Rhonda said in a hushed tone. "That's quite a difference."

Tiara turned slightly, catching her new look in a seductive profile. She let her eyes trace a path from the angelic, yet devilish, face down the length of her body, mesmerized by the manner in which the small, slinky dress clung to her body in all the right places.

"Yeah," was all Tiara could say in response.

"How come you never did this before? Your parents weird?"

"No. I didn't even know makeup existed. I mean, I knew it existed, but we never had any around the house."

"Damn, how did you survive?"

Tiara shrugged. "I never gave it much thought. At least, until recently."

"You're one of those girls who can get away with wearing just a little makeup," Rhonda said. "Your skin is so fair. Your face is pretty."

"It sucks, though," said Tiara. "I like this look. But I don't know." Tiara turned to the other side and pulled the satiny material at her thighs, stretching the dress tighter across her breasts. "Maybe this dress isn't right."

"Oh, you're suddenly a fashion expert," Rhonda teased. "What's wrong with it?"

"I don't know," Tiara repeated. "Maybe I should show a little more. What do you think?"

"More skin?"

Tiara nodded.

"I don't know. It's pretty cool out."

"I don't care." Rhonda had no way of knowing that Tiara's special abilities protected her from extreme temperatures. Tiara grabbed the dress at the hemline and slipped it over her head. The dress fell at her feet in a whispered hush. Something didn't feel right, even with the dress removed. Tiara couldn't quite place the uncertainty in her feelings until she thought of the first time she had changed into her new human form. She remembered the way she had been only mildly interested in the playful banter her brothers had instigated. She recalled sitting atop the damp rock, bathed in the pale moonlight, the smooth touch of the stone cool against her bare skin. She had been enthralled more than anything else by her new body, perfect in its complexion and sleekness.

Staring into the mirror, she was reminded that she still was entranced. Tiara reached behind her back, shoving her hair aside, and unclasped the frilly bra. She shrugged her shoulders, and the garment joined the dress on the floor. A quick bend at the knees, and the satin briefs joined the pile.

Now, the picture was complete. Tiara stared at herself, her slender frame now complimented by her newly enhanced face. It was the first time she viewed herself nude under adequate lighting. Her hair fell about her pale shoulders, across her chest and ending just at the apex of her breasts. Tiara shoved her hair aside, the silky strands brushing teasingly across her nipples, straining them slightly. She traced a line between her breasts, down her belly, circled her navel once, and continued down, stopping above the patch of golden hair between her legs. Tiara shuddered softly.

"What about this?" asked Rhonda, having moved up behind her.

Tiara met Rhonda's eyes in the reflection in the mirror. The other girl was slightly shorter than Tiara. Tiara could see the unvoiced surprise in Rhonda's eyes, and it excited her. There was an attraction there; Tiara knew it, though the girl would probably never admit it. It wasn't a sexual attraction; it was more like hero worship. Tiara smiled at Rhonda's reflection. Rhonda returned the gesture with a delayed grin.

Tiara turned away from the mirror and took the new outfit from Rhonda. There wasn't much to it.

"My dad won't let me wear this," Rhonda said. "At least, unless he doesn't know about it. He says it's too skimpy."

Tiara slipped a foot into the pair of denim shorts. The cutoff shorts were barely more than a denim strap. Daisy Dukes, Tiara had seen them called in a fashion magazine. Tiara pulled them up around her waist and buttoned them. The shorts rode low on the hips, exposing more of her midriff. Tiara slipped her arms into the lacy bra top and adjusted the straps. Loing into the mirror, she agreed with what she saw.

"You're not going to wear any underwear?" Rhonda asked. "None at all?"

"No," said Tiara casually. "It's too constricting."

Tiara again saw the admiration in Rhonda's eyes, and she smiled. Rhonda, at least, would answer to Jenny no longer. And it wouldn't be long before the rest of Jenny's former gang did the same.

"C'mon," Tiara said. "Let's go meet the gang."

•   •   •

"What the hell's she doing here?" Jenny stood beneath a shaft of sunlight beaming down from the warehouse windows. The rest of the gang cast furtive glances at her, then turned their attention to the new arrivals.

It had taken a moment for the tall blonde to say anything. Tiara thought Jenny didn't recognize her in her new guise and half-expected Jenny to go through her dominance act all over again. Jenny's voice was defiant, but her eyes showed only doubt and a trace of fear.

"She spent the night with me," said Rhonda. "I invited her."

Rhonda's voice now held an air of cockiness that the other girls picked up on. She showed no signs of concern about how Jenny would react to her new friend.

"Cool outfit," Michelle said. Jenny shot the girl a mean glare, but it bounced away harmlessly while Michelle and Stacy stood to get a closer look.

"Rhonda helped me with it last night." Tiara performed a slow pirouette for her new friends.

"Aren't you cold?"

"No, I don't get cold. It's something in my blood, I guess."

"So, what's the plan for today?" Rhonda asked.

Tiara focused her attention on the conversation at hand but also glanced occasionally at Jenny. She lingered back from the group, unsure of how to react to the apparent shift in power in the hierarchy.

"The guys are supposed to drop by," Stacy said.

"That should be interesting." Rhonda teased loose strands of Tiara's hair falling across her shoulders.

"Guys?" Tiara asked.

"Yeah, just some guys from school."

Tiara nodded her head in approval, but something inside of her was nervous. Despite her influence over the girls, despite her unknown abilities, she had never had much contact with members of the opposite sex other than her brothers, Jeremiah, and the few older men who came into the feed store. She was unsure of how to act around boys, but she would have to adapt. Any sign of weakness now could severely damage the strides she had already made.

Suddenly, there was a loud rap on the side of the old warehouse building. Tiara jumped. Rhonda laughed and grabbed her hand. "I think that's them now," she said. "They always have to make an entrance."

Four silhouetted frames filled the large overhead doorway. Tiara couldn't make out any of their features. They had to be attractive, though. All her new friends were attractive. Even Jenny, in a bitchy sort of way. She watched as the boys approached, their heavy boots stirring up tiny cyclones of dust on the old warehouse floor. Tiara heard the clinking of glass. One of the boys carried a twelve-pack of something in each hand.

"Hey, they brought some brews." Michelle gave a cheer of approval. "Nice!"

Beer, Tiara thought. Her mind started swirling in that odd fashion that came with a new experience. She had heard of beer, knew what it was. For some reason, something in the back of her mind gnawed at her, an annoying voice telling her that the thought of beer was wrong. Another part of her wanted to indulge in the new experience, to live it for all it was worth. She supposed she felt normal conflicts from the human side of her : the uneasy tug of humanistic morals versus the rebellious devil-may-care attitude of the teenager.

The girls sauntered over to greet the guys. She noticed that Jenny had moved past them and was the first to reach them. Tiara tried sneaking a peek at each boy. They were all dressed pretty much alike. Oversized jeans, flannel shirts. A few of them wore winter hats.

"Guys, this is Tiara," Rhonda said, grabbing Tiara's arm to pull her in front of them.

When she locked onto the first boy's eyes, all her inhibitions melted away. The fire in his eyes said it all, and Tiara knew. Whatever charismatic hold she had over these girls, the power would increase tenfold with the boys. She inclined her head to each one, from left to right, smiling seductively, psychologically marking each one. She stopped at the last boy.

He stared at her for a long moment, neither of the teenagers backing away. Tiara gave him a subtle smile, almost a smirk, and licked her lips to make them glisten. The boy did not shy away as the others had. This caught Tiara off guard, if only for a moment. The boy stared her down, and he was winning.

"Now I know where I saw you," he finally said.

"You've already met?" asked Rhonda. She glanced at Tiara, then back to the boy.

It was then that Tiara recalled where she'd seen him. He was the boy she had talked to at Jeremiah's, the boy whose family had been checking out the pups. "I remember now."

"Yeah, you live way out on highway 38," he said. "With the wolves." Everyone laughed. "Well, you know what I mean."

"Yeah," said Tiara. "I live with the wolves." *If he only knew.*

"My name is Craig, in case you've forgotten."

Tiara took the boy's hand. His hands were big and rough, and Tiara let her fingers slide across his palms. He likes me, she thought. He wants me. And I want him. Craig was attractive, kind of tall, but well built. His muscles were evident even through the loose-fitting clothes he wore.

That was when Jenny moved up behind Craig and slipped her hands around his waist. Her face appeared over his right shoulder, glaring at Tiara.

"Craig is my boyfriend," she said. Tiara didn't back away from Jenny. She knew the girl defined her property. It was a defensive maneuver; she had already lost her hold on the girls. When Jenny finally broke eye contact with her, Tiara glanced furtively at Craig, giving him a smoldering shot whose intention could not be missed.

One of the boys knelt and came up with a beer bottle dripping with condensation and twisted off the cap. "No sense in letting it get warm," he said. He handed another bottle to Tiara. He seemed to be the boldest of the remaining three boys. Tiara didn't know what the boyfriend/girlfriend status of any of the other kids was, but none of the girls seemed to take notice of the boy's advance.

Tiara mentally shrugged and accepted the bottle from him. She could entertain herself, practice a little on this one. The rest of the teenagers snatched the remaining beers.

Tiara twisted the top on the beer bottle. She knew that she had come too far now to show any sign of weakness. She put the chilled bottle to her lips, turned it up, and drank. She had never expected it to taste so bitter. Some of the beer went down as she swallowed; some of it went up her nose. She stood back up and wiped her mouth on her arm.

Rhonda uttered a good-mannered snicker, but Jenny laughed loudly at her. "First beer?" she asked. "Don't worry. I gagged on my first one, too. When I was eleven." She rubbed Craig's bicep as she did so.

Tiara stared at the laughing girl, then back at Craig. She looked at the bottle in her hand, and something inside of her stirred. It was a strange feeling, and it frightened her at first. It was not unlike the rumblings she felt deep inside of her body when she transformed. She found herself becoming more aware of her surroundings, her senses heightened to astonishing degrees as they did in her canine form. For all the world, she felt as if she would change.

Tiara closed her eyes for a moment, then opened them, standing tall and straight again. The feeling was gone, but her senses were still keen. She could smell the beer from each open bottle, the breath of each person. She could hear their breathing, could hear the rumbling of a train still miles away. Tiara breathed deeply, cast a mean stare at Jenny, then turned the bottle straight up, downing the beer in three gulps. It went down smoothly, effortlessly, as if it was mere water. Tiara flung the empty bottle into the far distance of the warehouse, the shattering of glass almost deafening to her sensitive ears.

"It just went down the wrong pipe," she said, then motioned for the boy to toss her another.

He handed her the bottle, coyly slipping his other hand around her waist. His beer-chilled fingers were cold on her bare flesh, but they warmed quickly. Tiara scooted closer to the boy and mindfully watched the others. The other boys would momentarily study each girl, but they would lock onto her. She did not reciprocate their glances. She paid only a little heed to the boy whose arms were wrapped around her, a boy whose name she did not know, nor did she care. Tiara watched Craig intently. He sat on one of the barrels with Jenny perched on his lap. She watched him as his face nuzzled into Jenny's warm neck, as his hands glided slowly up and down her denim-covered thighs.

But his eyes never drifted from Tiara's, and hers stayed faithful as well. *He wants me*, Tiara said to herself again. She knew it. She could feel it. She could smell it. She could taste it.

25

D EVIN STONER HAD BEEN WATCHING the woman at the far end of the bar for over an hour, studying her, waiting for the right opportunity. She wasn't like the others—he knew that from the moment he saw her. Or more correctly, from the moment he smelled her. At first glance, he thought she was a prostitute and, therefore, a good candidate for what he had set out to do. She wore a short, clingy black dress, and her hair was wild and tossed. But she wore no makeup. Although the attractive woman didn't need it, Stoner thought it odd for a prostitute to wear no makeup. After all, they were a business, and the focus was to put out their best product.

That's when the first familiar scent drifted down the length of the maple wood bar, burrowing its way determinedly through the thick haze of bar smoke, through the heavy scent of alcoholic beverages both domestic and foreign, through the cloying odor of worthless lives following the relentless drive to continue the species. The scent was obvious, almost overpowering. This was no prostitute, no little girl lost; no drunken, party-crazed sorority girl.

This was a fellow lycanthrope.

Stoner had expected to start seeing them, to begin smelling their entrance into his fair city any day now. The first frigid bite of the new season worked its way through the state, stripping trees bare of their fading autumn colors, sending wild animals into hibernation in the rural areas, and luring Stoner's kind into the dilapidated city streets.

Autumn was in full swing, and with it came the Festering.

And with the Festering came the lycanthropes.

Devin approached the woman. "Can I buy you a drink?"

She quickly downed the remainder of her beverage and let her eyes scan the full length of the tall, handsome man standing in front of her. Their eyes connected for a long moment, communicating in unspoken volumes.

"What I drink isn't served here," she said seductively.

"Oh, is that so?"

"That's right. Do you know where I can get it?"

"I know exactly where you can get it."

The girl smiled, revealing sharpened canine teeth. She stood, taking Devin's hand and leaving the bar with him.

•　　•　　•

"Where have you been?" Natasha demanded trying valiantly not to let the anger in her heart show in her voice. She stood at the front door as Tiara came straggling up the steps.

"I told you last night. I spent the night with Rhonda."

"I know you spent the night with Rhonda, but you were supposed to be home by ten o'clock this morning," Natasha said. "It's now ten o'clock at night."

Tiara tossed the leather jacket that Rhonda had loaned her on a chair near the door as she pushed her way past her mother. "I lost track of time."

"And look at what you're wearing. It's a wonder you didn't freeze to death. Where did you get those clothes?"

"They're Rhonda's."

"Does she dress like that, too?"

"Sure, she does. They all do."

"Who are 'they'?"

"The rest of the kids." Tiara strutted defiantly into the small, dimly lit kitchen.

"I'm not through talking to you." Natasha chased her daughter down.

Tiara grabbed a soda out of the fridge and popped the top. "Mom, you said I could spend the night with Rhonda, and I did. We went to another town this morning, and we had a lot of fun. I forgot all about the time, and I'm sorry."

"I said you could spend the night at a friend's house." Natasha absentmindedly grabbed a dish towel from the sink, wringing it in her hand. "I did not tell you that you could run around with a bunch of wild kids, dress like a tramp, and not come home 'til the following evening."

"C'mon, Mom. Give it a rest."

"'Give it a rest'? Is this a new way to speak that you learned, too?"

"Mom, I'm tired and I want to go to bed."

"You are not going to bed until we get a few things straight, young lady," Natasha blocked Tiara's exit from the kitchen. "You didn't come home all day. You didn't do any of your chores, which by the way, I was very lenient with last night so you could start this charade in the first place. You disobeyed me, Tiara, and I want to know where you were all day."

"I told you." Tiara groaned. "I was with some friends in Caribou Park. We went to the mall."

"All day?"

"I said I was sorry, Mother. Can we drop it now?"

"No, we cannot drop it!" Natasha said, raising her voice for the first time with her daughter. "You disobeyed me, and you're going to be punished! I don't want you going over to Rhonda's house again! I don't want you out late again! I don't want you wearing your underwear over your clothes again!"

"Oh, Mom, you can't be serious!"

"I can be and I am."

"You don't want me to have a life! You don't want me to have friends outside of this place, do you? You want to keep me here, doing all these stupid chores and shoveling shit!"

"You watch your mouth, young lady," warned Natasha.

"I'm going to bed now," Tiara pushed her way past her mother.

Natasha moved aside and watched as Tiara disappeared around the corner, stomping off toward her room. A moment later, Jeremiah appeared, leaning against the door.

"Trouble?"

Natasha sighed, ran her fingers through her hair, and leaned against the stove. "Did we wake you?"

"No, I was up."

"What's happening here, Jeremiah? What am I doing wrong? The kids are unhappy. David feels confined. Luke and Simon hate their lives. Tiara's starting to be trouble. What's happening to them?"

Jeremiah approached Natasha and put his arms around her. She reached around his broad back, buried her head on his shoulders and cried.

"Life. That's what's happening. Look, no one said it was going to be easy. It's hell raising normal teenagers with normal lives in normal households. Believe me, there's nothing normal about any of this."

"I know." Natasha sniffled. "But I didn't know it would be like this."

"Of course you didn't know," said Jeremiah. "That's why it's so difficult. You take four very different personalities and throw them into a completely new world, and they're all going to react differently. Simple as that. You'll just have to help them through it, let them adjust and adapt to their new world. In the meantime, you'll just have to go along with what they want to try."

"You mean I shouldn't forbid Tiara to see her new friends?"

"I wouldn't," Jeremiah said. "I think she should be punished, but I wouldn't forbid her to see them. That'll only push her farther away. Just let her play this new game. It's exciting for her. She's seeing and trying new things. Eventually, she'll decide what she wants to do. They all will." Jeremiah wiped a tear from her cheek.

"What if what they want doesn't include me?"

Jeremiah held his silence for a long moment, then answered, "Then you'd just have to accept that, and move on."

•   •   •

The woods were dark and menacing. A thick, congealing fog drifted low to the ground, rolling and twisting, slithering around trees like an ethereal viper. Tiara found herself in the middle of these frightening woods, naked, vulnerable. She pushed on. Something in the distance called to her, beckoning onward. A strong, powerful scent invaded her senses, pulling her toward the shrill, piercing howl of a wolf, and the scent was thick with the coppery tinge of blood.

Tiara walked on. The mist caressed her feet, danced up her legs. The moist grass was exhilaratingly cool to her bare feet.

Her mother's voice cracked the foggy darkness.

Tiara saw Natasha in a clearing just ahead of her.

I'm sorry, her mother said. *I'm sorry I shouted at you. I'm sorry I didn't like your friends.*

Tiara choked back tears and stumbled toward her mother.

I was wrong about your friends, Tiara. I said I didn't like them, but in fact ...

Tiara stopped in horror as her mother lifted Rhonda's severed head and bit deeply into what was left of the teenager's throat.

... in fact, they were delicious.

Scattered around Natasha's feet were the bloody bones of her new friends. Tiara meant to run when her foot bumped against something. She once again found the bloody remains of Jenny lying at her feet. Tiara felt something warm and sticky dribble across her bare breasts, and she saw that she now held Jenny's head in her hands.

Her heartbeat quickened as she felt the steaming liquid roll across her smooth skin.

Tiara turned back toward her mother and saw the large red eyes directly behind her. The large, black wolf stood behind Natasha, his nostrils blowing clouds of steam high into the chilly, night air.

•　　　•　　　•

Natasha dragged the heavy bale of hay into Sargent's pen and paused to stretch her back. David bent before her and snipped the metal wires. He retrieved the pitchfork leaning against the fence and spread the hay around while Sargent watched. "He's getting used to you," Natasha noted.

"Mom, what would it take for me to go to school?" The question seemed to come out of nowhere.

Natasha was taken aback. She wiped her hands on her jeans and grabbed another pitchfork.

"You want to go to school?"

"Well, I was just wondering."

Natasha joined her son in spreading the hay around Sargent's pen. "David, I'm not sure you can go to school."

"Why do you say that? Is it the money?"

Natasha sighed. "Partially. But that's only part of the problem."

"I don't understand."

"Honey, you can't go to school because technically you don't exist. There are no records that prove that you were even born."

"So?"

"So, you need records like birth certificates, citizenship cards, things like that in order to get into school. You're just about college age, and you haven't even gone to first grade."

"But I know all the things that someone my age who did go to school would know."

Natasha dropped the pitchfork into the next pen and turned back to her son. "I know, but that wouldn't matter. You'd have to take tests to get into a college, records of previous education. You don't have any of those."

David didn't answer. Instead, he seemed to stare off into the woods. The woods, Natasha thought. It seemed to be a haven, a place of refuge, an escape from their sometimes-cruel new world for all the kids. *Perhaps I should have left them as they were.* To grow up as free-spirited wolves, to grow old and die in the wilderness. Then they wouldn't have to worry about things like college or bullies or makeup.

"I could still learn all those things, couldn't I?" David still stared toward the forest. "The stuff they teach kids in school, in college. Everything's in books, right? That's how college kids learn. I could still learn it, without going to school."

"Yes, yes I suppose you could, honey."

David faced his mother.

"Is that what you want to do?" asked Natasha. "Do you want to learn from the books?"

"Books can be so expensive. The one I bought the other day was seventy dollars."

"You can get books at the library. You can borrow them; you don't have to buy them."

"Will you help me, Mom?"

Natasha reached out and hugged her son, the son that reminded her so much of his father and her lover. "Of course I will, David. I'll help you in any way I can."

26

NATASHA DRESSED FOR THE DAY in a slow and deliberate manner, as if to delay the inevitable task that she had at last decided to assign herself. As she went about the ordinary routine of making the bed, brushing her teeth, showering, she thought about her upcoming revelation, and she thought about David, of her previous life with him, of her morning walks and endless hours of ball-chasing. Those times seemed like someone else's memories now, or bits of a movie she saw long ago of which she could remember only tiny fragments. As she slipped her shoes on, Natasha pulled open the drawers and removed the papers.

They were nestled in a drawer with some of her personal belongings. A pinecone, chipped and brittle, a handful of pocket change—the remnants of the $20 bill that Coogan had given her before sending her off to Canada, a few yellowed newspaper clippings, and a photograph.

There wasn't much to the clippings. The reporters from the local newspapers had apparently thought little of the incident. "Local Man Killed by Pet Wolf". A smaller, back page article read: "Wolf Hybrid to Be Destroyed". Another: "Mauling Victim Laid to Rest in Arizona".

Natasha felt the tears well in her eyes; one spilled over and splattered on the weathered articles. Natasha picked up the photograph and gazed at David's image.

"I wish you could see your children," she choked. "Our children. They've grown into fine adults now. They're beautiful. One of them even looks like you. You'd be proud of them. And they'd be proud of you."

She pulled the picture tightly to her breast. Her gaze drifted to the open window, looking out onto the forest line that began beyond the hay barn. If the hay barn were removed from the picture, Natasha thought, the scene would resemble the view from David's back yard in Maine.

"Today's the day," Natasha said to the picture. "Today's the day I tell them about their father."

Natasha gently placed the items back into the drawer and pulled out another. It was a small leather-bound holder, used for storing checks. Natasha opened it and pulled another article from inside the case. Slowly, painfully, she unfolded the clipping and read.

It was an article that Jeremiah had brought back with him only weeks after Natasha's arrival at his dwelling. He had spotted it in the local newspaper during a trip to meet with a stateside feed distributor.

The headline on the first page read: "Popular Local Deputy to Leave Potters for The Big City". Natasha did not care to read the rest; in fact, she had never read it. Never would.

Natasha neatly folded the clipping and slid it deep into the confines of the leather case. She then placed it inside of a box, which she hid far to the back of the drawer, safe from any eyes but her own.

●　　　●　　　●

Natasha sat just beyond the banks of the little stream where she had first guided the children into their new world. It had only been a few months, but it seemed like such a long time ago. Jeremiah's words always entered her thoughts and rang true: *you have to let them decide for themselves.*

The kids sat across from her at the edge of the stream. David, attentive and somewhat concerned. Luke and Simon, apparently itching for this to be over so they could have a romp through the woods. Tiara, distracted and aloof.

"Kids," Natasha began uncertainly, "I've been meaning to have this conversation with you for a long time now. But it's always worried me. I didn't know how you would take it, and I didn't want to pile anything else on you so soon after what happened the first time we all came to this stream."

"What is it, Mom?" Luke asked.

"Is this going to take long?" asked Tiara.

Natasha took a long look at her daughter. The tension had eased somewhat since Natasha relented and told Tiara that she could still see her friends. Tiara sat atop a rock, her bare feet dangling just above the water. Tiara had taken an old pair of jeans and cut them extremely short, and she had done the same with an old T-shirt. Natasha had sworn that she would not say anything else about the way Tiara chose to dress, but she didn't have to like it.

She could tell that it sometimes made the boys a little nervous as well, especially when they got into one of their harmless little wrestling matches. Natasha found that somehow slightly comical. After all, on the night Natasha had introduced them to the human world, the children had played and wrestled in the water, each of them completely unadorned. Now, the boys seemed to be bothered by the mere showing of some of their sister's skin. Natasha smiled to herself. They were so completely natural in their new world that night. It didn't take long for the human mannerisms to surface.

"Well, I guess I'll tell you what I came here to tell you," Natasha said, showing the kids a case. From within, she pulled out a small, framed picture. She turned it so the children could see it clearly.

"Do you know who this is?"

Luke leaned forward, viewing the photo more carefully, and turned to his brother. "It's you," he said to David. He turned back to Natasha. "When did you get that done?"

"It's not me," said David.

Natasha smiled. "It's not your brother, Simon. This man was a little older."

"It's our father," David confidently offered. "Isn't it?"

Natasha wanted to weep right then and there, but she fought off the urge. "It is your father."

"Really?" Tiara suddenly seemed more interested. She scooted to the edge of the rock and leaned over between David and Simon. "Really, Mom? That's my father, our father?"

"It is," she said.

"What was his name?" asked Luke.

"It was David," Natasha answered, then looked at her son of the same name. "Just like you."

"I was named after him," David surmised.

"Who was he? Was he one of us?"

Natasha prepared herself. The questions were going to come flying at her full speed from all directions now that she had told them about their father. "No," she said in response to Simon's question. "He was human."

"We all look like him," said Luke. "David more than any of us. But we all have his features. Dark hair, brown eyes. Except for ..." Luke let his sentence trail away.

Natasha glanced at her daughter, her daughter who looked nothing like her.

"I don't look anything like him." Tiara didn't sound angry or hurt, just indifferent. "Blonde hair and blue eyes."

"Your grandmother had blue eyes," said Natasha.

"You knew her, too?" David asked.

"No, I heard of her from your grandfather."

"So, you knew our grandfather?"

Natasha nodded.

"Mom, what happened to our father?"

"I knew one of you would ask that soon enough." It's not going to be an easy thing to hear, or to tell." She reached back into the bag and retrieved the newspaper clippings. Natasha first read the articles aloud, then passed them along to each child one at a time so that they could read and observe and interpret the news in their own manner.

"What was he like?" asked David, after a long, uncomfortable silence.

"Good." Natasha allowed a tear to escape. "Kind, loyal, gentle, yet strong."

"This man—this lycanthrope—who killed him," Luke said. "Where is he now?"

Natasha thought of the hidden newspaper clipping, the only one she did not bring. She sighed and told a lie—the only one that she would ever tell the children in her life. "I don't know. Like I said, after your grandfather sent me to live with Jeremiah, I never heard from either of them again."

"Why would he do such a thing?"

"He was just ... a bad man," was all Natasha could say in response.

Natasha turned her attention to Tiara. She had remained silent since her mother read the articles. Natasha noticed that Tiara was staring blindly at her feet, as if in a daze, or in deep thought. Natasha followed Tiara's line of vision and found that her daughter was staring at the picture of her father.

"Tiara?"

Her daughter did not answer.

"Tiara?" Natasha repeated, louder.

Tiara looked up, and her bright blue eyes met Natasha's stare. "What?"

"Something wrong?"

"No." Tiara shook her head. "Just thinking."

"If you need to talk ..." Natasha began.

"I'm okay, Mom," Tiara answered. "Really." She smiled at Natasha, but Natasha could see there was not an ounce of sincerity in it.

"Mom, can you help us wolf out, now?" Luke asked.

"Yeah," Simon chimed in. "I'm bored just sitting here."

"Okay," said Natasha. She turned to David. "David, are you up for a run through the woods?"

"Well, I was going to go back to the house and hit the encyclopedias."

"Oh, c'mon," his mother urged. "You need a break from those books. Your brain's going to bust from all that information you're forcing into it."

"Okay, I guess I could use a break."

"Tiara?" Natasha turned to the rock where her daughter had been sitting, but she wasn't there.

"No, you guys go on without me," answered Tiara from up the trail leading back to the house.

"C'mon, let's make it a family thing." The boys had begun removing their clothing, though they seemed to grow more sheepish about it with each transformation.

"Mom, I said 'no thanks'," Tiara said, a hint of annoyance in her voice. "I'm supposed to call Rhonda." Natasha frowned. "Mom, you're not going to start that again, are you? You said it was okay."

"No, no," said Natasha, shrugging. "If you'd rather go off with your friends ..."

"I would," she said, then seemed to detect the disappointment in her family's eyes. "It gets old running through the woods, you know. I guess I just don't like it as much as you guys do."

"It's cool, Sis," David said. "Go on and have fun."

"Thanks, David," Tiara gave her brother a warm smile. "Bye."

Natasha watched as her daughter bounded back up the trail, eager to communicate with her new friends. Flashes of sunlight broke through the foliage of the trees and bounced brightly off Tiara's legs. Natasha watched Tiara disappear over the horizon, until David nudged her and brought her attention back to the boys.

27

TIARA FOUND HERSELF ALONE in the mist-shrouded forest once again. This time, there was no lonely cry of a distant wolf, nor the heavy scent of blood riding the nocturnal wind patterns. Yet, something seemed to be guiding her feet, driving her onward through the leaf-laden path. The late autumn winds and chill had stripped the multi-colored leaves from their mother branches. The dew-moistened leaves made only a dull crunch under her feet.

Then she heard the first cry, the same wolf howl that she heard before. Tiara cocked her head and shoved her blonde hair away from her ear. She strained to hear the wolf's song. It was still faint, distant. But there seemed to be something else in the eerie howl. Something Tiara couldn't quite determine.

Was it the wind whipping around the trees? The sound of water cascading down a distant mountain stream? Insects singing in the bushes? Owls hooting from the trees?

No. It was none of these.

It was a voice.

Low and distant. Indecipherable.

Tiara followed the sounds of the howl and the unseen voice. Her feet carried her to the base of a steep hill, devoid of trees or other plant life. Her bare toes sank into the soft, loose soil that comprised the terrain. Tiara climbed the hill. The higher she climbed, the brighter her surroundings grew. She saw the outer edges of a great corona of light peering just above the horizon. Tiara crested the hill and scanned the night sky.

She saw lights. Rows and rows of bright, glowing lights of all colors and sizes. The lights stretched to the stars, so brilliant in their intensity that they overpowered all but the brightest stars in the night sky.

And the howl continued to ring out, and beneath it, the words. Low and rumbling. Soft, yet demanding. Subconscious, yet clear as day.

Come to me, child. Come be with me, my child. Come join me.

Tiara followed the other side of the hill and found herself under a tall pole that flashed colors of red, green, and yellow. Damp concrete chafed her bare feet. An odor permeated her surroundings, the smell of rotten things and ruined lives. She moved naked down the sidewalk, passing dark, faceless shadows that seemed to take no notice of her nudity. And Tiara paid them no heed. She concerned herself only with finding the owner of the voice.

Come to me, child. It is time.

Tiara navigated through the dark streets. Gradually, the coppery scent of blood overpowered the foul smell of the streets. The scent beckoned her, enticed her. She felt her nipples harden with the lick of the stiff wind howling around the corners. Her belly ached with an unknown desire that reeked of power, of blood. She thought of the girls in her group, of Jenny, of the boys who wanted her. Her legs rubbed against that certain spot as Tiara walked, and the voice continued to call.

She stopped at the entrance to an alley. There was no light here, but Tiara didn't need it. She could see well into the dark recesses of each corner.

A man stood, shaded and mysterious, at the alley's back wall. Without hesitation, Tiara moved, catlike in her grace, toward the man. She stopped just before him. He stood tall, much taller than her, and his eyes glowed a familiar red.

Join me, my precious child. Be one with me at our time of gathering.

The man reached forward, clenching Tiara's buttocks and pulling her forward. His mouth moved forcefully to hers, and his strong, steely hands glided up and down her nude body, squeezing her breasts. Tiara could feel a heat growing in her belly, and it slowly spread to her lower regions. Tiara felt the man move up behind her, felt something rigid brush her backside, and she gasped as she moved to accommodate him.

The wolf howled, its shrill cry echoing around every bend and street corner of the brightly lit, deeply shadowed city.

•   •   •

Tiara awoke the next morning with a pleasurable feeling of satisfaction. The sheets were wet with sweat, and her thighs had a sticky feeling to them. She rolled out of bed, pausing to throw on her robe, and headed for the shower.

Tiara had wondered several times before if the wolf in her reoccurring dream was supposed to be her father. She didn't know why this thought had crept into her head. Perhaps the uncertainty of her father's identity had found its way into her subconscious mind and invaded her dreams.

Tiara stepped from the shower and donned her bathrobe, eager to get herself made up for the day. The picture of her mother's former lover, of Tiara's own father, had done nothing for her. No tears of sadness from seeing the image of a father she would never know. No pangs of sorrow for the tragic loss of the man responsible for bringing her into the world. There was nothing there.

Tiara remembered looking at purses and wallets at the mall she and her friends had visited. She recalled seeing the nameless faces that graced the insides of the various accessories.

Her father's picture was just like that. A nameless nobody in someone's brand new wallet, an image destined to be torn from its confines and tossed into the trash, waiting to be replaced by the images of loved ones.

Tiara stood before the mirror, examining the makeup she had so quickly learned to apply. It was perfect. Her face was perfect. Her outfit—another sexy look provided by Rhonda—was perfect.

It was time to make a phone call.

•   •   •

Tiara watched her mother heading back up the road to the house. She waited until Natasha had disappeared over the horizon. When she heard the screen door slam shut, Tiara pulled up a bale of hay and sat down.

"You coming?" David asked, turning back to her from the trail.

"No," answered Tiara. "I'm going to stay out here a while."

"In the barn?"

Tiara peered into the thick line of trees that began about twenty paces from the hay barn. Her keen vision picked up a hint of movement here and there in the thick underbrush. Luke and Simon. Natasha had just helped them through the transformation. They preferred to spend their Friday nights drifting through the forest in wolf form, but they still needed their mother's help to do so.

"Yeah," Tiara finally replied.

"Hey, Tiara," David said, concerned. "What gives?"

"Nothing."

"Something's up. It's not like you to just hang out in the barn."

"I'm meeting some friends here tonight, okay?" she admitted. "Don't make a big deal out of it."

"Does Mom know?" Tiara shrugged. "She's not going to like it. You're in enough trouble with her as it is."

"Mom took back what she said about seeing my friends."

"She meant you going to them. You know Jeremiah doesn't like having strangers here. It's not a good idea. Anything could happen."

"Don't worry about it, David."

"I do worry about it, Tiara. I worry about you. About how you defy Mom's rules, how you forget to do your chores, how you talk about Luke and Simon and the whole transformation thing."

"David, c'mon. Be cool about this, will you? Don't say anything to Mom. I mean, we're just going to hang out back here for a while. It's away from the house. There won't be any noise. Please, for me?"

Something in David's demeanor softened, and Tiara picked up on it. She jumped off the bale of hay and reached for her brother, kissing him on the cheek. "Thanks. You know, you're welcome to stay and join us."

"No, I'm going back to the house to read."

"You're always reading, David. Why don't you have some fun for a change?"

"I don't want any part of this, Tiara."

Tiara put her hands on her hips. "Well, just go on back to your books and your little picture of our dearly departed father."

David stared at his sister with anger and hurt in his eyes. "What's gotten into you, Tiara? I don't think I even know you anymore."

"Maybe you don't." Tiara twirled in a circle atop a hay bale. "May I don't even know myself."

David stared into Tiara's eyes, which suddenly seemed to grow a frostier, colder shade of sinister blue. He hoped for a sign of weakness, of sincerity, but it wasn't there.

•   •   •

"This is pretty cool," Michelle said. "We're at least a mile from the house. No one can hear anything from this far away."

"You know it," said Tiara. "That's why I picked it."

"Let's put on some tunes," Rhonda suggested. She moved over to the stack of hay where the CDs and the portable player sat. "What are you in the mood for, Tiara? Nirvana, Pearl Jam, Toadies?"

"How about some Chili Peppers? Did you bring any of their stuff?"

Rhonda placed a round disk inside the unit and closed the drawer. She programmed the player to go directly to the song "Love Rollercoaster". She knew it was Tiara's favorite. They had danced to it nearly all night when Tiara stayed over.

Tiara moved and swayed her hips to the beat as she lit a fire inside one of the fifty-five-gallon drums that littered the grounds. The dry hay and sticks caught quickly, and soon, the girls had a roaring fire to dance around.

"Turn it up," Stacy said.

"When's Jenny getting here with the guys?"

Tiara turned quickly to face the girl. "Jenny?"

"Yeah, Jenny's coming," she said. "Did you not want her to?"

"No." Tiara allowed a coy smile to slide across her face. "No, that's cool."

"They're bringing beer."

That bitch, thought Tiara. Michelle knew that Tiara wouldn't have wanted Jenny at her impromptu party, but she invited herself anyway, apparently. And Jenny was bringing guys and beer. The guys Tiara didn't mind. She didn't mind the beer either really. But there would be a lot of explaining to do if her mother were to find out.

Suddenly, a chorus of vicious barking and growling drifted down the hill from the kennels. Tiara's heart raced. Maybe it was just a raccoon or a skunk that had wandered through the yard. But in her heart, she knew better.

"That stupid bitch," Tiara mumbled. "Don't tell me they're walking straight through the yard."

"Yeah," said Michelle. "I thought it was okay."

Tiara moaned and raced out of the barn and up the hill. The others followed behind her.

They met Jenny and the boys halfway up the road. The hybrids were still barking fiercely. Tiara expected to see the house lights come on any minute.

"Hey, guys," Jenny called out. "What's happening?"

"Keep it down, Jenny," Rhonda whispered, trying to help Tiara.

"What's with the dogs, man?" one of the guys said.

"They're not dogs, dumbass," Tiara snapped. "They're wolf hybrids."

The others laughed aloud, and the dogs broke into another fit of barking. Tiara motioned for Rhonda to lead the others back toward the barn. Tiara approached the fence. She looked back, making sure the others had moved away from the kennels, and dropped to one knee. She peered into the eyes of Kula, the leader of the pack. He barked ferociously twice more, then his ears pricked high, his head tilted, and he fell silent. The other wolves ceased their antics as well. Kula whimpered once and dropped his tail between his legs. Tiara reached through the gate and stroked the fur on his head, then turned and raced toward the gang.

"See," said Craig. "They stopped barking as soon as we all left."

"Yeah, and I don't think it woke anyone up."

"Put something else on," Stacy said. "I'm tired of this shit."

"Soul Asylum," one of the boys said.

"You belong in a soul asylum," Michelle laughed

"So, where's the beer?" asked Tiara. She met Jenny's eyes, read the dismay in her adversary's eyes.

"Right here," Craig said, opening the cheap Styrofoam case.

Numerous hands reached into the chilly melting ice. Glass clanked, and caps whooshed from bottle tops.

The music rang loud and clear into the night.

•   •   •

Tiara sat close to Andy, the boy who had showed her the most attention upon her first meeting with the males of this group, the boy whose name she did not know until later. She raised the bottle to her lips, took another swallow of the bitter liquid. She was getting used to the taste now, but the alcohol did not affect Tiara at all. The group made short work of the case of Ice, and most of the members were feeling the effects of it. This Andy character certainly was.

"Everybody's paired off, it looks like," he said, leaning awkwardly against Tiara's shoulder. The words "looks" and "like" slurred together drunkenly.

From their vantage in the first loft, Tiara could see Rhonda and her boyfriend. As far as she could tell, they had not progressed past the kissing stage yet. Somewhere to the right, she could hear Michelle moaning, and surmised they had. Stacy had gone up into the second loft with Kevin.

Tiara did not care about any of these, nor did she care about the drunken fool that was currently drooling on her bare shoulder.

She wanted to find Jenny and Craig. She had watched them exit the barn, heard Jenny say it was too crowded in the hay lofts.

"Oooh, listen to Michelle, baby," Andy whispered into Tiara's ear. "He must be sticking it to her good."

"Must be," Tiara said absentmindedly.

Andy turned up the last of his beer and slung the empty across the barn. It landed somewhere in the hay with a soft thump. He burped softly, and Tiara smirked.

"You know what?" You sure are pretty." He scooted a little closer to Tiara.

Tiara could feel his breath on her neck as he leaned against her hair. She could smell the alcohol on his breath, could smell the dinner he had eaten earlier. Hamburger. Under cooked. Raw and bloody.

Tiara felt Andy's beer bottle-cooled fingers slide deftly under her bra and brush her nipple. The guy moved quickly for a drunk, but Tiara moved quicker.

Andy didn't seem to realize for a moment that his throat was being squeezed tightly shut. Tiara held her grip firmly on the kid's neck. "Don't you ever touch me again, you son of a bitch. Do you hear me?" she said through gritted teeth. "I'll kill you."

Before Tiara realized it was happening, she felt her teeth elongate, felt her nails shooting forth slowly, digging into the soft flesh of Andy's neck. Tiara could smell the warm scent of blood as it dribbled down his neck. She closed her eyes tightly, willing it to stop.

She opened her eyes to stare into Andy's terrified face. She could tell by the sudden odor that he had pissed himself. Tiara gave him a coy smile, just enough for Andy to see the tiny fangs just beyond her crimson lips. Tiara released the inebriated fool and shoved him backward. He toppled off the bale of hay and landed on the hard flooring of the loft.

Tiara stood over the boy's limp, terrified body. "Maybe you should just try kissing a girl to start with next time," she said, and turned away, exiting the barn.

•　　•　　•

Tiara heard heavy breathing coming from the smaller barn where Jeremiah kept the larger bags of various types of feed. It wasn't very big, but plenty big enough to accommodate what Tiara was hearing. She leaned her ear to the sides of the weathered building and listened to Jenny and Craig.

Tiara moved along the perimeter of the barn, searching for a wide enough gap in the boards through which she could peek inside. She stopped at a missing board.

Jenny was on top of her boyfriend, sliding her head down the length of his body. Tiara watched in fascination the act about which she had heard so much but had never actually seen committed. Jenny's head moved across Craig's chest, her lips softly kissing his chest, his stomach. When Jenny's head moved past Craig's waist, Tiara could see the boy's penis, erect and reaching for the barn's dilapidated old ceiling. Tiara's eyes widened at the sight. She had seen her brothers' genitals whenever the boys changed, but their members were always hanging flaccid. Craig's didn't appear to be too large, but it still seemed impressive in its current state.

Tiara heard Craig mumble something, and Jenny placed her lips to his straining penis. Tiara watched as Jenny's head bobbed up and down, along Craig's length. Jenny's head turned slowly to the right, and her eyes trained directly toward the gap in the thin walls. Her eyes connected with Tiara's, and Tiara thought she could detect a faint smile on Jenny's lips form around the circumference of Craig's organ. Tiara did not turn away from the girl's gaze. She then saw that familiar tinge of uncertainty and worry in Jenny's eyes, and Craig's girlfriend looked away.

The act excited her in a way that she had never known. She always felt odd stirrings in her belly when she saw herself naked in front of a mirror, or mornings after a pleasurable dream. She felt her nipples pressing against the tight material that held her breasts to her chest. She felt a growing tingle in the pit of her stomach, spreading outward from her navel in ever widening patterns, until the burning sensation reached the area between her legs.

Slowly, her body moved against her will. Tiara's hand moved under her shirt. Her fingers found the hardened buds that topped her small breasts and squeezed them gently. Tiara's heartbeat quickened, her pulse throbbed in her wrists, her neck, her temples. Her other hand drifted down to her thighs, grabbing at the clingy material and pulling it upward, then sneaking back up the thighs to a warm, moist spot. Tiara's knees weakened with the touch. She threatened to buckle, and she closed her eyes.

Tiara inhaled deeply the night scents: decaying leaves, the distant musk of animals, rain-softened earth combining with the human scent of sweat and sexual arousal. Tiara turned her head to the skies, and with her eyes still closed, could see the glorious moon shining in its full glory, though only a sliver of it shone in the night above her. She felt a sharp pain between her legs, and her arm moved away involuntarily. Tiara heard the sound of ripping fabric and guttural snarls.

She stared back into the barn, her view now from a lower perspective than when she had first peered into the building. Craig was now moaning softly, and Jenny kissed at what remained of his shrinking penis. Tiara stepped back away from the barn, shaking off the remnants of torn clothing that stuck to her paws, and trotted at a quick gait to the tree line beyond the barn.

•   •   •

The two male wolves shifted playfully through the brush, picking up the possible scent of an opossum. Their heavy snouts rooted through seasons of decayed leaves and plant life, searching for a stronger hint of the underlying odor.

Suddenly, the lead wolf looked up from the forest floor, his ears erect and pointing to the treetops. His companion saw it too.

It was a she-wolf, standing between two large trees about twenty feet ahead of them. The two wolves glanced at each other, as if communicating their next move in some unknown animal tongue. The other male snarled softly, and the two wolves headed toward the female in large circling patterns.

This she-wolf's scent was familiar. She was from the same pack. The light silvery colored female stood motionless as the two males moved forward to investigate. The males exchanged another confused glance. Was this a member of their pack? Had she gotten separated?

The males suddenly stopped and lifted their muzzles to the air. There was a scent about this female. A strong, different scent. The bitch was in heat.

She took a few steps toward them, and they stopped quickly, growling a warning. The bitch barked sharply, commanding.

The bitch moved up to the males, pressing her muzzle to the heads of each. Her tongue flickered out, licking at the blackened lips along their gum lines. The female moved along the sides of the males, sniffing at each until she reached their backsides.

The males growled savagely, but another shrill bark from the female silenced them. She turned and backed up toward the largest of the two males. He whimpered and backed away, but the female continued to direct a rear advance. She grabbed the other male by the back of his neck and pushed back against the one behind her. He lifted his front legs off the ground and prepared to mount the she-wolf.

He could hear the soft growl of the female beneath him, and the male wolf's excitement grew. The female's growl turned strange, different in pitch, and he felt her backside shift and move. An odd sensation began to well deep within his own body, and a searing pain overtook him.

•　　•　　•

Luke opened his eyes to see his swollen penis resting across his sister's bare behind, her long blonde mane cascading across her smooth, creamy back. His eyes moved in shock to the eyes of his brother Simon, who sat on his knees directly in front of his sister. It took the boys a long moment to clear the cobwebs from their minds and fully grasp the scope of the situation.

They were in a sexual position with their sister.

"Jesus Christ, Tiara," Luke cried, backing away from his sister. "What the hell are you doing?"

Simon jumped to his feet. He felt as if he would be sick.

Tiara rolled over in the soft dirt and crossed her legs, wiping her hands clean. She allowed her gaze to go from Luke to Simon, then her eyes dropped to their waists. Luke quickly attempted to hide his still erect penis with his hands.

"What the hell happened?" Simon shouted. "How did we get like this?"

Tiara laughed. "What's wrong? We didn't do anything."

"How do you know?"

"Because I remember," she answered.

"How do you remember? I don't remember anything."

"I remember what happens when I'm a wolf," Tiara said. "You guys don't yet, I guess."

"I don't remember anything," said Luke.

"Well, don't worry about it. Like I said, nothing happened."

"If you remember what you did when you were wolfing out, then why did you do it?" Simon asked.

"I was just kidding around, you guys." She stood up, bending over for a moment to wipe the dirt from her knees. "I found you guys out here, and I decided to see what you would do if I ... offered myself to you." She gave her brothers a big toothy smile.

"You scare me, Tiara," said Luke. "You're not like us, not like us at all. You're not like David; you're not like Mom."

"No shit."

"You don't act like us, you don't think like us. Human or wolf," Simon said. "You're just different ... that's all."

"Guys, it was just a joke," said Tiara. "I didn't mean anything by it."

Luke began to back away from his sister, and Simon joined him. "Stay away from me, Tiara. Just stay away."

The two boys ran through the forest and back up the trail. Tiara watched them run, two pale bottoms bouncing up the path, and she laughed long and hard in the pale moonlight.

28

NATASHA KNEW SHE HAD TROUBLE on her hands from the moment she connected with her daughter's eyes. There was ice in those frosty blue eyes. Ice. Distance. And something else. *Apathy?* God, but she didn't want to think that.

"So, I suppose you're automatically assuming that I'm responsible for this?" Tiara said, her arms folded in defiance across her breasts.

"Tiara," Natasha said, no hint of backing down in her voice, "cut the crap. Who else could it be?" She set the empty beer bottle down, the stagnant vapors still drifting from the small amount of stale liquid remaining at the bottom.

"Well, heaven forbid it could be 'wolf-boy #1 or wolf-boy #2'. No, it just couldn't be them. They just wouldn't do anything like that now, would they? They'd rather just run and run and run through the woods. And, no, it couldn't be 'Mr. Savior of Our Planet'. It just couldn't be the bookworm. He hasn't taken his nose out of his books in three weeks. So, who does that leave? Why, it must be Tiara. Tiara, that crazy bitch who dresses like a cheap whore. That insane slut who stays out all night drinking beer and getting laid."

Natasha's open hand found the soft flesh of Tiara's cheek before she even realized what she had done. Regret appeared a second later. "Oh, Tiara." Natasha rubbed her stinging palm. "I'm sorry. I'm so sorry."

The icy glaze that shielded her daughter's eyes faltered not a bit. In fact, she even smiled.

"Isn't that why you blame me, Mother?"

"Tiara, I'm just worried about you is all, honey. If you had people over last night, drinking and doing God knows what, we need to talk about it. This is not our property, Tiara. Jeremiah has done so much for us. What if a spark had gotten out of the barrel and found the hay? Then what?"

"The barn is still standing." Tiara pointed mockingly out the window toward the venerable structure.

"I know the barn is still standing. But when I said you could still see your friends, I didn't mean you could have them over here, especially without Jeremiah's permission. What if one of them saw something? Something they shouldn't have seen?"

Tiara thought back to her act of voyeurism between Jenny and Craig. Jenny was aware that Tiara was watching their sexual act. Had Jenny witnessed Tiara's transformation?

"No one saw anything, Mother, and I'm tired of having to get permission for everything I do. No one else around here has to have your blessings every time they want to do something."

"That's not true and you know it! The boys have to have my permission just as much as you."

"Oh, get off the power trip, Mother!" Tiara shouted back. "Do you know what your problem is? You want us to all be one happy family. You want us to be a bunch of sugar-sweet kids coming home from school to the loving mother and housewife and wait for Daddy to come home from work." Natasha thought the frosty blue in Tiara's eyes turned to sadness. "You want us to be normal, Mother. But we can't. You want me to be normal, but I can't. Don't you see, there's nothing normal about us, and there never can be."

Natasha waited, the fierce gaze between mother and daughter unwavering. Was Tiara right? Was she trying to do the impossible? Deep down, didn't Natasha dream every night of living a normal life with David the breadwinner, still alive, coming home to a house full of adoring children? Isn't that what she really wanted?

Tears welled in Natasha's eyes. Tiara was right. They could never be normal. There wasn't a chance.

"Maybe we can't be normal. But I still expect you to do as I say."

"You know what? I'm tired of your shit."

The words caught Natasha with full force, knocking more wind out of her than a kick to the stomach. Stunned, she could only watch as Tiara fled out the back door. Tiara was halfway to the woods before Natasha's mind could function enough to guide her feet to move. She pushed open the screen door that had slammed so forcefully upon Tiara's exit.

"Tiara!" Natasha shouted. "Come back here!"

She was at the far end of the kennels. The hybrids bounded up to their gates, expecting to be played with, but the girl sprinted past them.

"Tiara!"

Tiara turned at the end of the kennels, moving past the feed storage building to the woods beyond. Natasha started after her, knowing she could never catch the speedy younger girl. As she chased after her daughter, Natasha saw Tiara's blouse fly up into the air behind her. Tiara stopped for a moment, long enough to slide her jeans from her body, and she was gone again. Her long blonde mane whipped in the wind; her legs moved across the land with a grace that Natasha couldn't help but find beautiful. She didn't understand why Tiara would be removing her clothing. The only time the kids did that was when they wanted to ...

Natasha couldn't believe what she was seeing. Her daughter's back began to visibly arch as she scrambled for the woods, stretching and lengthening, dipping closer to the ground. A fine line of silvery hair began to cover her smooth human skin. Her legs shortened and altered their shapes.

Natasha stopped, her breath coming in ragged gasps, and stood in stunned silence as she watched the wolf disappear into the forest beyond the hay barn.

That's impossible, Natasha thought to herself. She shouldn't be able to do that. The kids have always needed my help to undergo the transformation. All of them.

Natasha scanned the distant tree line, but Tiara was gone. Natasha couldn't fathom what she had witnessed. It was a long time before she could master the transformations without the assistance of another lycanthrope, and even when she began to do it, it was a slow, excruciatingly painful process. Tiara had just pulled it off effortlessly.

"My God," Natasha mumbled through a steady stream of tears. "What is she? What has my daughter become?"

She collapsed to her knees on the gravel road and broke into ragged, fitful tears.

•   •   •

Jeremiah found Natasha not long after Tiara disappeared into the forest. He said nothing as he helped Natasha back up the road to the house, but he had a fairly good idea of what had transpired. He noticed how much older she appeared. Not in actual years; that was impossible. But the stress of raising a family in this unusual environment was getting to her, just as it had her father hundreds of years before.

"I've lost her, haven't I?" Natasha said, her voice quivering. She continually stirred her coffee without taking a drink. "She's not coming back, is she?"

"She'll be back, honey," Jeremiah reassured her. "She doesn't want to leave you. She just got upset. Too much has happened to her in too short a time. She can't cope with it."

"Was I too hard on her? Should I have let it go?"

Jeremiah spread his hands across the table in a pseudo-shrug. "What's the answer to that? You can't let them get away with everything, and you can't drive them away."

"If you could have just seen the look in her eyes, Jeremiah," said Natasha, shuddering. "I've never seen such a hateful stare before Almost like ..."

Jeremiah took a sip of the scalding coffee. He hadn't witnessed what Natasha had described, but he knew it all too well.

"And she changed. She did the transformation with no problem at all. So easily. No pain, no sweat. My God, Jeremiah, how did she do that?"

"She's powerful, Natasha. I think she's got more of it in her blood than her brothers, maybe even more than you."

"But how?" How is that even possible?"

"I don't know. I've never seen it in a mixed breed before. You're fifty percent lycanthrope, the kids twenty-five. Not like me or your father. We're both full-blooded. It takes a while for a mix to fully master the powers. I can't explain it any better than that."

"Do you think it's possible that ..." Natasha changed her mind. "Never mind." She leaned back in the chair. "Oh, Jeremiah. What have I done? I don't want to lose my daughter."

Jeremiah mulled over Tiara's abilities. He had an idea that Natasha thought the same thing. "You know, when I told you about my kids all going their separate ways years ago?" Natasha nodded, reaching for her coffee cup. "Well, I had a big blow-up with one of them. Just like you and Tiara."

"What happened?"

Jeremiah shook his head, as if to chase away an old, powerful memory. "We never saw eye to eye. Always at each other's throats. He ran off one day, just like Tiara did today."

"Did you ever see him again?" asked Natasha. "Do you know where he is today?"

Jeremiah stared at his reflection in the black liquid for a long moment. "Never saw him again," was all he said.

Natasha began to weep. She let her head drop to the table as she sobbed into the coffee-stained table spread. Jeremiah stood and massaged her shoulders.

"She'll be back," he said, hoping to reassure the troubled young mother. "She'll be back."

Jeremiah lifted his head and gazed long and hard out the kitchen window. The top of the hay barn was just visible over the horizon, and beyond that, the woods where Natasha had last seen her daughter. Jeremiah thought of his son, his less than amiable departure, and a tear—a rare thing for this man—fell from his own eye.

"She'll be back," he forced out, though he couldn't convince himself that he really meant it.

·   ·   ·

The first quarter moon high in the sky brought a minimum of light through the window. Natasha lay sleeping in her bed, her breathing short and fitful in her restless, troubled slumber.

Tiara moved stealthily alongside the bed, her soft footsteps not making a sound. She stopped in front of the nightstand. Her mother lay silent to her right. Tiara reached for the top drawer, pulling it open quietly on its rollers.

The face of the man whom Natasha claimed was Tiara's father stared back at her. Tiara moved the other items on top of the picture. She reached her hand deeper into the drawer, further back, until she felt the cool touch of a metal box. Grasping it, she removed it from the drawer. Tiara found a single, leather-covered booklet inside the box. She opened it, felt between the numerous pages until she heard the crinkle of dry, brittle paper.

Tiara unfolded the clipping and silently read. And she knew. The truth was in her hands. The blonde hair. The blue eyes. The icy glint in his chilling orbs.

"Tiara?" Natasha said sleepily as she turned over in bed.

Tiara stared down at her awakening mother. Natasha sat up. her face brightening. "Tiara!" she exclaimed. "You came back! I knew you would!"

Natasha threw the sheets from her body and reached for her daughter. Tiara drew back, slapping away Natasha's advancing hands.

"What's wrong?"

"You lied to me," Tiara said, her voice barely a whisper. "You lied to all of us."

"What do you mean? What are you talking about?"

Tiara shoved the yellowed clipping into Natasha's face. "This," she said with a hateful sneer.

"Oh my God," Natasha said. "You found it."

Tiara reached back into the nightstand drawer and retrieved the photograph of David Wagner. Before Natasha could react, Tiara had twisted the framed photo, shattering the glass. "This isn't my father," she said, letting the ruined frame drop from her fingers. She held up the small color newsprint of Devin Stoner. "This," she said. "This is my father."

Natasha was too shocked to speak.

"Isn't it?" Tiara shouted.

"I don't know, Tiara." Natasha stooped to retrieve the photograph of David. "I really couldn't tell you truthfully. If he is, I never knew. I would've never lied to you, honey. I was just trying to protect you and the boys."

"Bullshit!"

"No, it's true. Devin Stoner is an evil man. A lycanthrope of the worst kind. He killed David. I'm sure he killed your grandfather, too. He killed your grandmother, my mother hundreds of years ago when he was William Booth. He's not your father, Tiara. He can't be."

"The blonde hair," said Tiara, her voice cool and calculated. "The blue eyes. Doesn't take a genius to figure it out. You fucked this David Wagner, but you fucked Devin Stoner too, didn't you?"

"Tiara, no. He raped me. Don't you understand? He raped me!"

"Then he could be my father," Tiara mercilessly added, "He could be the boys' father, too."

"No, he's not your father. He can't be."

"Mother, I don't fit in here. I don't act like the rest of you. I don't like it here. Don't you see it, Mother? There are just too many differences."

"But even if Devin Stoner is your father," argued Natasha, "I'm still your mother. Shouldn't that mean something?"

Tiara turned away, and it was then that Natasha noticed the suitcase. "It should," said Tiara. "But it doesn't."

"No, Tiara," Natasha pleaded. "You can't leave. Please, no. No!"

Tiara stormed out the doorway with Natasha close behind. Tiara carried the heavy suitcase deftly down the hall toward the front door.

"No, Tiara! Where will you go? What will you do?"

The disturbance began to wake the rest of the household. David appeared in the doorway of his bedroom, his hair disheveled.

"Tiara," he said. "Where are you going?"

Tiara stopped in front of David. "He's your father. Not mine," she said. "I have to find him."

"What are you talking about?"

Tiara turned the knob and pulled open the door without answering her brother. Jeremiah appeared down the hall and stopped behind Natasha.

Luke and Simon moved up beside David but lingered in the background when they saw their sister.

Tiara pushed the screen door open, and with a clang, she was gone in the night.

"NO! NO! Tiara, please don't leave me!" Natasha shouted. "I need you. We all need you!"

Natasha started for the front door, but Jeremiah grabbed her shoulders from behind. He buried his head in her hair, saying, "No, Natasha. No." He wrapped his arms around Natasha for comfort. "Let her go, baby. It's all you can do now. You have to let her go."

Jeremiah felt Natasha's form turn to putty in his arms as she broke down and sobbed uncontrollably.

Outside, the wolf-hybrids cried and howled to the night skies.

•   •   •

"You," Craig leaned against a pick-up parked in the driveway, one of his father's stolen beers in his hand. He was quite surprised to see Tiara slinking seductively up to his parents' house, especially at such a late hour.

Tiara saw that he was pleasantly surprised to see her. She knew he would be.

"When Rhonda called and told me to be waiting out here, I expected Jenny."

"Disappointed?" she asked. Tiara shifted her hips to one side, casually placing her hands on them. She moved closer to the light so that Craig could get a full view of what he had in store.

"Hell, no."

He moved closer to Tiara. She had stopped by Rhonda's after leaving home, changing into something that she thought—no, she knew—Craig would appreciate. Craig slipped his hands around Tiara's waist and, smiling, moved his face closer to hers.

"You know," said Tiara. "I saw you last night. With Jenny."

"I know. I wasn't that wasted."

"No, I mean in the grain barn."

Craig's eyes widened, and Tiara noticed the flush of color that suddenly came over his cheeks. Tiara pointed her index finger to Craig's stomach and let it trail down to his crotch. "Pretty impressive."

"Holy shit," he muttered.

Tiara moved her lips to Craig's mouth, barely brushing his lips. "Is there somewhere we can go?"

"Yeah," Craig said. "Yeah, my parents are out of town."

"How convenient," Tiara whispered.

Craig clasped Tiara by the hand, leading her nervously back up the porch and inside the house.

•   •   •

Tiara waited in the familiar old warehouse building where she had first encountered Rhonda, Michelle, Stacy and Jenny on that fateful day not so long ago. The weak moonlight filtered through the shattered windows high on the aluminum walls, casting faint shadows across the length of the concrete floor.

It hadn't taken much to convince Craig to make the phone call, once Tiara had got him going. A fevered, excited voice with a request to meet him at the warehouse was sure to work, and it did. Now, Tiara had only to wait.

Tiara stood naked in the pale moonlight, the soft illumination creating highlights across her alabaster skin. The memory of her encounter with Craig was still fresh on her mind, as were the remnants and scent of their lovemaking. Tiara smiled and chuckled aloud. If she had just lost her virginity, as it would seem, it had certainly been anticlimactic. The girls had talked about how badly their first few times had hurt, about how it felt like their guts were being stabbed with a baseball bat. But Craig was just a human, a mere mortal. There would be others who would satisfy her better.

Tiara let her fingers work into the folds of her womanhood, where Craig's penis had been only hours earlier. She drew her hand upward, across her soft belly to her breasts where his lips had touched.

"Craig?" The voice echoed in the cavernous warehouse.

Tiara waited. She could see the girl's body silhouetted against the structure's opening. Tiara moved on soft bare feet toward the girl.

"Craig?" she said again. "Stop fucking around. You're scaring me."

"Craig's not here," Tiara moved into Jenny's view.

Jenny stepped backward in fright when she saw Tiara's naked body.

"What ... w-what are you doing here?" Jenny stammered, obviously caught off guard by her adversary's nudity. "Where's Craig?"

"You got shit in your ears? I told you Craig's not here." Tiara stuck her fingers in her mouth and let them slowly slide down her body, working their way through her pubic hair and rubbing the fleshy mound underneath. "But he was here," Tiara said, then dragged her hand up her stomach. "And here." She cupped her breasts in her small hands. "And here. He was everywhere."

"You're crazy," Jenny said, her voice quivering. All thought of resistance toward the girl who had entered her life months ago and turned her world upside down fled from her mind. "You're crazy. What do you want from me?"

"What do I want from you?" asked Tiara. "That shouldn't be too hard to figure out, even for you, Jennifer. You know, it didn't have to be like this. We could've been friends, but you had to play the bitchy, domineering type to impress all your friends. But you know what, babe? You pissed me off. I could just let it go, but my kind doesn't like to be pissed off, especially by tramps like you."

"Your kind? What are you talking about?"

Tiara moved closer to the terrified girl, inch by excruciatingly slow inch. Jenny backed away, tears of fright streaming down her face, colored purple by the smearing mascara. "Get away from me, you bitch," she pleaded through her tears. "You're insane."

"Insane? You think I'm insane? No, I'm not insane, but I'll tell you this, I'm not normal." She pressed against the taller girl, looking up into Jenny's fear-racked eyes. "I'm not normal at all, and I wanted you to be the first one to see why."

Tiara threw her head back and shrieked loudly into the air, the shrill howl echoing maddeningly inside the huge warehouse. She reached out, grabbing Jenny's throat, and lifted the girl with one hand. Tiara cried to the moon again, inhaled the faint scent of dried blood that remained around her vagina, and she closed her eyes. She felt the hair breaking from the skin on her arms, felt her nails growing, curling, turning into claws.

Jenny released a haggard scream through the pressure that cut off her air. The act itself ruined her vocal cords for the rest of her life, which would be all of forty-five seconds.

The large, silvery wolf stood over the girl's blood-drenched body, one of her arms cracking to powder in the beast's powerful jaws.

Tiara smiled and sang to the powerful night.

•　　　•　　　•

The blonde girl, appearing to be no more than seventeen years old, boarded the bus and moved through the sea of mundane lives to the rear of the vehicle. To unknowing eyes, she could be anyone. A teenaged girl running away from home, destined to wind up with needles in her veins and diseases in her blood as gifts from life on the cruel city streets. An unwed mother, fifteen and pregnant, three children to feed and care for at nineteen, working two jobs to put food on the table. An attractive young hopeful, Hollywood bound, all gung-ho to tackle show business and beat down doors, only to return home months later, beaten and defeated.

Of course, this young attractive blonde-haired, blue-eyed girl was none of these.

Tiara smiled as she heard the hiss of the brakes releasing, saw the steam rise into the air, felt the bus begin to roll. The taste of blood and sex and defiance and power was still fresh in her being, swimming around the senses like a school of savage piranhas, devouring to bone any remaining hint of the girl that a woman named Natasha called daughter.

29

D EVIN STONER STOOD at the window of the vice department headquarters on the sixth floor of Precinct 103, staring out across the expanse of light and steel and concrete that was downtown Detroit.

They're out there, he thought to himself. One by one they arrive. A few here. A few there. But arrive they do.

He had already encountered several, including the blonde with whom he had shared a most fulfilling evening, some as nothing more than a knowing nod to one another. But they were here, and more arrived daily.

Detroit. The perfect place for the party. A town of random and indifferent violence. The nocturnal activities that were soon to beseech the Motor City would be passed off in the following weeks as just an unusually violent period. The victims—the homeless, drifters, whores, junkies—would have their names filed away, their manilla files shoved into some final steel drawer resting place like a corpse in a morgue and forgotten. If any innocent victims were had, the cases would be studied for a month or two. With no leads to follow, like so many other cases, they would simply grow cold and drift away, memories only to loved ones.

Stoner allowed his eyes to scan the massive downtown structures, and he felt the vibrations of life in the city streets. The Festering never failed to bring his blood to a boil. Friends from decades, even centuries before teemed on those city streets, waiting to rejoin him in their annual salute to the violent and bloody ways of the lycanthrope.

But there was something different about this year. It was not an altogether unpleasant feeling. It was more a feeling of impatience, for lack of any better way to explain it. He had only felt something close to this strange sensation once. The Festering of 1994. The last year he called the little hamlet of Potters, Maine home. The year he lost his mate.

Something in the moon was calling Devin. Something was out there, stalking, watching, sniffing. Hunting him down. Was it her? Had she at last decided not to shun the moon? Would she come for him, to join him in this bloodbath as he dreamed?

Devin closed the window blinds and stepped away from the night view. Blocking out the night did nothing to shake this undeniable feeling of longing, this sensation of lust and desire for something intangible, something unknown and unforeseen, an entity that rode the night waves, seeking out his heat.

Whatever it was, Devin Stoner/William Booth welcomed it. And waited.

•　　　•　　　•

Natasha moved effortlessly and quietly through the dense underbrush. A wolfen tromp through the woods always helped to clear her mind. Years of shapeshifting had allowed her to master the ability and think with a human mind while in the form of the wolf. But it had taken a long time. Tiara, Natasha thought, was capable of that now.

Natasha stopped and sat on her haunches atop the high mountain plateau. From this vantage, she could see across the northern Alberta wilderness. The United States lay far beyond the distant tree line.

Tiara was out there somewhere, Natasha thought, off in search of Devin Stoner. Natasha sighed and admitted the fact. Stoner was Tiara's father. Was he the boys' father as well? She didn't think so.

David resembled David Wagner too much to not be his child, and Luke and Simon had some of his features as well.

But Tiara had none of them. Looking back, Natasha figured she must've known all along, but just didn't want to admit it. Other than the obvious physical differences, Tiara had always struck Natasha as being … just different. Even in the kennels as pups.

She often stayed away from her brothers, choosing not to engage in their childish acts of play. After being separated from her brothers, Tiara had grown even more distant and aloof. And finally, once the transformations had begun, it had become obvious to Natasha. Tiara thought differently, she moved differently, carried herself differently. The painful truth was that Tiara had always reminded her of Devin Stoner. That was a frightening, tragic memory to bring up, and Natasha had refused to make a connection between her daughter and the cold-blooded killer named Stoner.

Natasha pondered how Stoner could've fathered Tiara. It had been Stoner who first mated with her. Jeremiah had explained to Natasha that many animals can have offspring from separate fathers in the same litter. The same applied to lycanthropes.

And if Stoner was truly Tiara's father, then she had every right to search for him. Natasha could only pray that Tiara would not like what she found and would return to her rightful family.

•   •   •

Natasha entered the breakfast area sleepily, her mind still trying to shake away the morning cobwebs. David and Jeremiah sat at the kitchen table, the remnants of eggs and waffles on their plates.

"Good morning," Natasha said.

Neither man answered. Natasha turned to face them, and it was then that she noticed the grim visages of their faces.

"What?"

"David, you'd better let me talk to your mother alone," Jeremiah said.

David scooted the chair back and started for the door.

Natasha grabbed his arm as he moved past her. "David, what is it?"

David looked back at Jeremiah and let his eyes drop.

"Natasha, let him go," said Jeremiah.

"I'm sorry, Mom."

Natasha watched her son shamble down the hall. She turned back to Jeremiah, panic rising in her throat. "Jeremiah, what's wrong?"

Jeremiah positioned the morning paper where Natasha could read it. The first headline read in large, bold print: "Local Teen Found Dead".

"I don't understand," Natasha said.

"Read it."

Natasha glanced from Jeremiah back to the paper, skimming the article for details. "Jennifer. Jenny. Wasn't that one of ..." Jeremiah nodded. "But I still don't see—"

Jeremiah grabbed the paper. "The police thought she was murdered at first," he said. "Now they think it was an animal attack." Natasha felt her knees buckle, and she groped for the nearest chair. "A large dog."

"Tiara," Natasha whispered, her voice barely audible. "Dear God."

"She's not coming back, Natasha," Jeremiah said, his voice soft but firm. "I tried to comfort you all this time, but I think we have to face the facts, especially after this."

"But there's no proof. No one knows Tiara did this."

"You're right. No one knows she did it, no one will ever know. Officially, Tiara doesn't even exist."

"She couldn't have done this, Jeremiah," Natasha said, the tears and frustration of the last few days finally coming to a boil. "She's just a baby. She's my baby."

"She's a bad seed, Natasha. I hate to say it, but you need to face the truth now. Deep down, you know it as well as I do. We've both known all along." Jeremiah stood behind Natasha, his large, weathered hands gently massaging her shoulders. "Let her go, baby. She was never yours to begin with. She's gone to be with her kind. And she's not coming back."

"She's not coming back," Natasha repeated, as if to confirm within herself the words.

"It's hard to let go, Natasha. Believe me, I know. But they're a different breed. It was in her all along. There's nothing you or I, or anyone, could've done to prevent it. The Festering was drawing her. That's the way it had to be."

Natasha sniffed back a few lingering tears. "I know you're right, Jeremiah. But I just can't think of my baby as a killer. I just can't." Natasha pushed the chair back and stood up. She turned and stared into Jeremiah's eyes.

"And I can't believe that she's never coming back. I can't and I won't."

•　　•　　•

Natasha stood on the back steps, staring out toward the kennels and the forest beyond.

"Mom, are you okay?" asked David.

"I did what I thought was best, you know," Natasha said without looking at her son. "I had to let you kids decide."

"I know, Mom," David placed his arm around her.

"If I could just go back and change it, change everything, I would."

"It would've happened anyway. Jeremiah said so. If Tiara is that bad, she would've been pulled away regardless of anything you tried to do to prevent it."

Natasha placed a hand on David's cheek. "You're so much like your father. He'd be proud of you, of all of you. You're so bright and intelligent, so eager to learn. You know more about the Amazon and ecology and everything than any college student. And you did it all on your own. Just you and the library. Luke and Simon, so innocent, so natural, so unchanging.

"Do you really believe your sister is bad?"

David gazed into his mother's eyes. Her face was young, soft, radiant. But her eyes did not match. There were years in those eyes, years of loneliness and confusion and pain.

"I don't know what to believe any more," David said, brushing a strand of hair from Natasha's eyes. "You don't believe she is."

"I can't believe anything that came from mine and your father's love could be bad," answered Natasha. She let her fingers glide along David's face, through his hair. She looked up into his (David's?) eyes. He was taller than his father, she thought (it was so hard to remember these days). Natasha closed her eyes, and she was there, in Potters, Maine, a scared and confused child, bathed in the warmth of a roaring fire and the genuine love of a gentle man. Natasha pressed her lips softly to David's—her son David—and it did not feel wrong. Neither participant pulled back. It was innocent, so innocent.

The soft kiss ended, and Natasha opened her eyes and met David's (David's?) gaze. The back door of Jeremiah Reed's house stood in the background, but Natasha was in David Wagner's living room.

Natasha burst into tears, clenching her son tightly.

David held his grieving mother in his young, sturdy arms. He cursed himself, for what reason he didn't know. He cursed Tiara, a child as innocent as he, a young girl doing only what was in her soul. He cursed his mother, his dear mother, for caring so.

As David held Natasha, his eyes focused on the kennels, the barns, the woods beyond, and he made up his mind.

•   •   •

Late that night, when the house was quiet and all were asleep, David slipped out the front door and headed on foot toward town with some belongings stuffed into an olive-green duffel bag: a few articles of clothing, some food, thirty dollars, and a picture of an attractive, blonde-haired, blue-eyed girl.

He had no idea where he was going, just that he was going.

•   •   •

Tiara sat at the counter at the truck stop, finishing off the burger and fries she had ordered. The bus would be leaving in fifteen minutes; she had time to order more. She had thought she was hungry, but the meal did little to quell the uneasiness she felt in her body. Feeling uncomfortable, she shifted in the spinning bar stool, gripping the sides of the seat with her hand. When she brought her hands back up, her finger raked across an exposed screw.

"Shit!"

A small drop of blood oozed from the tiny wound. She put her finger to her lips and sucked. Instantly, the anxiety in her body melted somewhat as she tasted the coppery warm blood.

Tiara's gaze happened upon a trucker seated eight stools down. His eyes explored her body, slithering up and down her slender form. Tiara smiled at the man, and he winked at her in return.

Tiara's tongue caressed her bleeding fingertip, winding around and around the wound, and she suddenly realized what she was hungry for.

30

D AVID STOOD AT THE COUNTER of the bus station, waiting patiently for the line to dwindle. There were only two late night travelers awaiting tickets: a lone young man about David's age and a middle-aged woman with two small children in tow.

David left Jeremiah's about an hour earlier; he wanted to be out of town as soon as possible. Jeremiah and Natasha would be looking for him as soon as they noticed he was missing. David knew they would try to make him come home, he couldn't do that. The look on his mother's face and the hurt in her heart had driven him to action. She wanted so desperately for their family to work. And it would work. Tiara had just gone off the path a little, and David was sure that, if he found his sister, he could steer her back where she belonged.

"Next," the man behind the ticket window called, jarring David from his thoughts.

The lady and the sleepy children had moved on to the farthest terminal. David stepped up to the window.

"Where to?"

"I ..." David began. "I'm not sure."

The man rolled his eyes and smirked. "Well, I can't tell you where to go," he said, then laughed at his little joke. "Well, I guess I could."

David dug in his wallet and retrieved Tiara's picture. He held it up to the window, and the man leaned forward, his eyes growing wider.

"Je-sus," he said.

"Have you seen this girl?" asked David. "She would've been here last night."

"I saw her in my wet dream, buddy."

David frowned, trying to ignore the lewd remark. "She might've come here last night."

"I wish I could come here tonight." The ticket man laughed.

His laughter was quickly silenced when David reached through the circular cut in the window and clenched the man's wrist, jerking him forward. The ticket taker gurgled something unintelligible. David pressed the picture against the window. "Take a good look and nod 'yes' or 'no'," David said. "Did you see this girl in here last night, and if you did, where did she go?"

The man stuttered and shook his head slowly. David released his grip. "N-n-no," the ticket man stuttered. "I didn't work the window last night. I ... I didn't see her."

"Can I see that?"

David had just turned away from the window, almost stepping into the young man who had been standing in line earlier. David stared longer than comfortably into the young man's deep brown eyes, trying to get a read on him. David did not have much experience with strangers.

The man's eyes glanced downward, and he motioned with his head. "The picture," he said.

"Oh, yeah." David handed him the photograph of Tiara.

"I was here last night," the man said. "Didn't have no buses headed my way last night."

David nodded and watched the man hold the photo up to the light. "Pretty girl," he said. "Girlfriend?"

"Sister," answered David. "She ... she ran away last night."

"That's too bad. Yeah, yeah, she was here last night. I saw her for sure."

"You saw her?" David said, his voice suddenly filled with excitement.

"Yeah, she was in line ahead of me."

"Do you remember where she went? Please say you remember."

"Detroit," the man said without hesitation.

David threw his head back in relief. "Oh, thanks. Thanks a lot …"

"Reginald. Reginald Finch. Call me Reggie."

"Reggie," said David, returning his handshake. "Thank you so much. Are you sure it was Detroit?"

"Positive," Reggie said. "Because I could remember thinking to myself, 'Why is a pretty young girl like that going to Detroit?' Detroit's a mean place, man."

"I know," David said. "I know."

"She runnin' away from something?"

"Yeah, I guess you could say that."

"Well, Detroit's no place to be runnin' to. I'd thought she'd be running away from Detroit."

The hiss of air brakes filled the still night air, and Reggie rose to his feet. "That's me, brother," he said. "I hope you find your sister. Bring her home."

"Thanks, Reggie. Thanks for everything."

Reginald turned before heading out the door and gave a thumbs up.

David watched the door close and the young stranger climb aboard a bus destined for Anywhere, USA. He waved, but Reggie didn't see.

David had suspected Detroit since reading the newspaper clipping hidden in his mother's bedroom. David went to the ticket window and bought a round-trip ticket to Detroit, Michigan, United States of America.

•   •   •

Tiara stepped off the bus in downtown Detroit onto the city's steamy streets. She had boarded a connecting bus to Detroit in Winnipeg, after hitchhiking some twenty miles into town once she had taken care of the overly eager truck driver. The delicious smell of his blood and flesh had lingered pleasantly in her nostrils for many miles, but as Tiara stepped off the bus, the vigorous aroma and aura assaulted her full force.

The smell was exciting, invigorating. It was blood. It was thrills. It was life.

The smell of anxiety, of lost souls, of perspiration and desperation, and most of all, blood, drifted on the winds of the night.

But there was another feeling to the chilly night air. A sense not so much of excitement, but of belonging. The scent was new and refreshing, yet oddly familiar.

In another life, in another body, Tiara might describe the aroma as grandmother's homemade apple pie cooling on the windowsill, as honeysuckle and hyacinth floating on the wind patterns of a warm summer breeze, of mustard and relish on a ballpark hot dog, of the fresh, earthy scent of a distant spring shower.

But this wasn't another life; it wasn't another body. This was Tiara. This was blood. This was Detroit. This was the Festering.

It sure smelled like home.

THE GIRL STANDING at Devin Stoner's door could've been any of the countless number of prostitutes he had encountered since joining the Detroit vice squad. She had the dress; she had the look. She could've been any of his past arrests, or any of his nameless rabble of victims. But something in her eyes—shocking blue, just like his—and her scent told him differently. This girl was one of them.

"Who are you?" he finally asked, after his gaze had followed the length of her smooth, pale legs to her blonde head.

"Devin Stoner?"

Stoner looked her over once again, then returned his gaze to the stranger's eyes. "Yeah," he answered. "Do I know you?"

The girl sauntered into the apartment, brushing against Stoner provocatively. Normally, he would've been highly defensive about a stranger entering his dwelling, but he was too stunned by the girl's boldness and presence to intervene.

He shut the door behind him and watched the girl as she stood in the center of the living room, her back to him. Once again, he found his eyes tracing a path up the back of her legs, pausing to appreciate the round, firm buttocks that lay hidden beneath the black, clingy fabric of her skirt, then higher, drinking in her long, blonde mane as it cascaded across her shoulders, covering her bare back.

"Nice place," she said.

"Who are you?" Stoner asked again.

"Not that it matters at the moment, but since you're so determined to know ..." The girl turned around to face Devin Stoner. "My name is Tiara."

"You're a lycanthrope."

"Of course I am," answered Tiara. "You knew that before you asked."

"Do I know you?" Perhaps they had met at last year's Festering. There were so many faces, so few names.

"We've never met."

"How did you know my name? How did you find me?"

"I was drawn here," she said. "To Detroit. Finding you was easy. I just followed your scent."

"There are many scents out there tonight. How did you know which to follow?"

The girl stared into Devin's eyes for a long moment, blue on blue, ice on ice, then a thin, mocking smile crossed her red lips. "Let's just say I picked the best one."

"Did I see you last year?"

"No. This is the first time I've come to this gathering."

"The Festering," Stoner corrected.

"Yes."

"Why is it your first?"

"Because ... because I didn't know what I was before."

"You didn't know?"

"I knew, but I didn't know."

"How did you know of me?"

"I heard you were the best," Tiara said, smiling seductively.

"And who told you that?"

"Can we cut out all these questions?"

"No, not until you explain some things a little better," he said. "I don't trust anyone."

"Not even your own kind?"

"That's not the point," Stoner argued.

"Not even your own daughter?" She eyed Stoner up and down, a trace of the cunning smile still on her lips.

"My ... my what?" he said, his eyes wide.

"Now, do you understand, 'why you?'"

"I don't believe you," said Stoner, though the tone of his voice was not quite convincing.

"Believe me, Bill," Tiara said, moving closer to her father. "Or should I say, William. As in, William Booth."

That sent Stoner's reeling mind into high gear. Three hundred years of nocturnal activities and bloodlust spun past his eyes. New York. 1761. Jonathan Lucas. Sarah Lucas. Coogan. Jackie Coogan. Potters, Maine. David Wagner . . .

"Natasha," Stoner whispered, the words barely audible on his lips.

"Mommy." Tiara's lips moved softly against the nape of the cop's neck. "My dear mother."

Stoner's eyes closed; his head fell back. Tiara's lips nibbled and sucked at his gruff neck. The feeling was intoxicating for the cop. "Natasha," he mumbled. "Natasha."

"Natasha," Tiara whispered into his ear.

His hands suddenly clenched Tiara's shoulders tightly, and he shook the girl who claimed to be his daughter. "Natasha! Where is she?"

Tiara gazed up into the tall man's eyes, but the steely look of cunning and determination did not falter under Stoner's manly display of aggression. "That doesn't matter."

"The hell it doesn't," said Stoner, squeezing Tiara tighter. "If you're really my daughter, then you know where she is. Tell me!"

"I didn't come here to find you just so I could talk about my mother. She's the reason I left." Tiara's hands moved to find Stoner's, and she fondled his powerful fingers until he released his grip.

"Left where?"

Tiara drew back from Stoner and crossed her arms. "Alberta," she said in an annoyed huff. "She's in Canada."

"We must go," Stoner paced about the room, seemingly agitated.

"No," said Tiara.

"What did you say?"

"I said, 'no'."

"If I'm your father then you'll do as I say."

"Don't play that paternal crap with me, William," Tiara said, her voice raw with edginess. "I left Canada to get away from all that family bullshit, and I don't intend to go back."

"Oh, you don't, do you?" Stoner liked the fire in this girl's eyes. No woman stood up to him like this ever before, not even fellow lycanthropes. He found it exciting, and most sexually arousing.

"No, I don't," said Tiara. Her hands moved up behind her back, unclasping her bra. The filmy garment slid smoothly across her breasts, exposing them. "At least, not until I've seen how the other half lives."

Stoner's gaze lowered from the girl's face to her breasts, round and pale, then down to the small strip of black fabric that covered her waistline. Tiara's hands slid slowly over her breasts, paused to tweak the nipples, then slid down her white belly. She grasped the bottom edge of her skirt and pulled it upward. Stoner's eyes fell on the light-colored patch of hair there.

"You've been a bad girl," he said.

Stoner felt Tiara's tiny fingers tug on his belt, and in a moment, his jeans were falling past his erection. He tilted his head back and moaned as he felt the warm wetness on his penis.

This girl was wild. She was uninhibited. She was a lycanthrope.

This girl was his own flesh and blood.

•   •   •

David stood at the steps of Precinct 103 in downtown Detroit. The wide concrete steps were foreboding in their ascent to the double doors of the police station. A steady stream of uniformed officers made their way into the building, the most frightening, offensive-looking human beings David could've ever imagined dragging behind them. Prisoners, he assumed.

David had never seen a building taller than three stories. Now, above his head, skyscrapers reached infinitely for the sky until their peaks disappeared into the clouds. The cops continued to parade the offenders of society into the grimy building. Homeless people drifted by, glaring at David, begging for money, smokes, liquor. Sirens cut the dense air in all directions.

David was out of his element. He was frightened beyond belief; he wanted to cry.

But the thought of Tiara, alone …

… or with her father …

… alone in this seething place of inhumanity drove David on. He must find his sister.

But where to look? He knew the answer.

Find Devin Stoner, and more than likely, he would find Tiara.

David sighed deeply and ascended the steps.

•   •   •

The inside of the police station was even more frightening than the outside. Various outcasts lined the benches in front of the counter, hands cuffed behind their backs. Detectives in suits, their sleeves rolled up and ties loosened sloppily, paced the halls behind the counter, barking commands and orders. The odors of perspiration, stale cigar smoke and coffee hung in the air, creating a visible barrier. The works of amateur artists graced the filthy walls in the shape of overly endowed females and grossly disfigured phalluses.

"Say, man," a man said from the bench. "I was framed, man. Tell them that. Tell them I was framed. You know that." He was talking to David.

David stepped back. "I … I don't know you."

Suddenly, the man kicked out at David, though he was restrained by a pair of cuffs connected to the bench. An officer swiftly pushed the prisoner back, shoving his head back against the wall.

"You here to report something?" the officer said, sounding as if David's presence annoyed him.

"No," said David. "No, I'm looking for someone."

"Pay the cashier," the cop said, pointing down the hall. "She'll tell you what the bail is set at."

"No," David said. "I'm not here to pick anyone up. I'm looking for a policeman. A particular policeman."

"Oh, yeah?" the cop said. For the first time, he turned and really studied David, apparently sizing him up. "Who?"

"Stoner," answered David. "Officer Devin Stoner."

The cop shook his head. "He ain't here. Vacation."

"Vacation?"

"Yeah, vacation. Stoner's a good man. He deserved a vacation. He took one. He always takes one about this time of year." The officer grabbed a stack of files and hurriedly scampered back down the hall.

"Wait," David called to him. "Can you tell me where he lives?"

The cop turned around. "Kid, I can't tell you that."

"Please, I must know. Please."

"I can't give out an officer's home address. It's against regulations. Not only that, but it's also dangerous." The cop must've finally picked up on David's emotions. "You a friend?"

"Sort of. I need to find him. It's extremely important."

"Sorry, kid. I can't help you."

The cop left David alone in the heavy atmosphere, no closer to finding his sister than when he left home.

•   •   •

"Jeremiah, we have to go after them," Natasha pleaded. "We simply must. They're alone—God knows where—all by themselves in a world they know nothing about."

It was obvious that David had gone off in search of his sister. He had left no note, no clues as to his whereabouts. But his duffel bag was missing, his cash box empty, and the determination that Natasha knew existed in David—a steely resolve that had come from his father—surely had moved him to action.

Jeremiah leaned back in the chair and sighed. "That's the key thing you just said, Natasha. 'God knows where'. We have no idea where they went."

"We didn't even hear him leaving," Simon stood at the counter slapping together peanut butter and jelly sandwiches for his brother and himself.

"Nope, not a sound," Luke agreed.

"But David must've figured out where Tiara went," Natasha differed. "He wouldn't have gone off blind trying to find her. What about Detroit? That's where Stoner is."

"Natasha," the big man said. "Think about what you're saying. Sit down, catch your breath, and rationalize. Tiara has gone off in search of Stoner, her father. The Festering drew her there, though she wasn't aware of that. Tiara is going to wherever the Festering is being held this year, and that doesn't necessarily mean Detroit. Now, how David found out where she went—if he even did—I don't know. But Natasha, there's no way we could find them. I know it's hard for you, but we're just going to have to wait it out. David will come back, regardless of what he finds. Hopefully, he'll bring Tiara back with him."

Natasha let her face fall into Jeremiah's chest. "I can't wait, Jeremiah. I just can't."

"You have to," he said. "It would do absolutely no good to have us all running around searching for Tiara."

"Because you don't think she's coming back, right?" Natasha looked up into Jeremiah's blue eyes. "Do you?"

"I don't think she is," Luke said, biting into his sandwich. Simon nodded his agreement. "She wanted nothing to do with this life."

"I'm sorry, Natasha, but if the Festering was drawing Tiara away from us, then no, I don't think she'll be back, either."

"I can't believe that," said Natasha. "I won't believe that. No matter what that bastard Stoner has to do with anything, Tiara is still my daughter. She's still fifty-fifty good and evil. I won't believe what you say. I won't."

•   •   •

Jeremiah Reed stood on the front porch, gazing down the length of the highway, as if waiting for someone to arrive. And perhaps he was.

He knew in his heart that David would return. He doubted very seriously that David would find what he was looking for. In fact, Jeremiah prayed deep in his soul that David wouldn't find it.

If David managed to catch up with Tiara in whatever unholy spot the Festering was taking place, he would be in dire trouble.

One innocent lycanthrope in a vast sea of the likes of Devin Stoner. He wouldn't stand a chance.

But that wasn't what was troubling Jeremiah. He really didn't think David would have any luck in his search for Tiara.

But he knew, absolutely knew, that Tiara would find Stoner. There was no doubt about that. It was written.

Tiara was drawn to her father. She was drawn to the dark side, and the annual bloodletting called the Festering. Like a bug finds a light from ten streets away, like a shark finds a wounded fish from a distance of fifty miles, Tiara would find him.

She would tell him everything. Stoner would know where Natasha was. Lycanthropes mate for life. Even the evil ones.

And much as Natasha may refuse to admit what Jeremiah knew for fact, Tiara would never be Natasha's daughter again. This he knew from experience.

And if she did come back, she wouldn't be the Tiara that Natasha once knew.

Not after Stoner. Not after the Festering.

And if she did come back, she wouldn't be alone.

Jeremiah Reed stood on the front porch, gazing down the length of the highway, as if waiting for someone to arrive.

32

T HE WHORE CAME WILLINGLY. She may have thought it a bit odd that the man and woman wanted to conduct their threesome in a wooded area in a Detroit suburb, but the man had money. A nice wad of it, too. And he was handsome. Tall, blond, blue-eyed. And the young girl was attractive, too. The prostitute hadn't done many lesbian acts in her day, but she wasn't totally alien to the idea. It didn't matter anyway. Whatever paid the rent.

•   •   •

David wandered down the streets of Detroit, drifting farther and farther away from the police station that had failed to supply him with any clues in his search for Tiara. As he walked, the sounds of the inner city faded. The night became more still, more silent, the streets darker.

David had no idea where he was going, nor what his next move would be. His perusal through a Detroit phone book had proved fruitless, as had a call to the operator. The thought of abandoning his search for Tiara and heading home crossed his mind a few times already. If he couldn't find Stoner's home, he had no hope of finding his sister.

David continued to walk through the dimly lit streets. Perhaps he would think of something else, another angle he had not yet explored.

David heard a sound behind him, glass being kicked along the sidewalk. He glanced over his shoulder but saw nothing. He stopped and turned around, gazing down at the long expanse of street. The sidewalks were empty.

He turned and hadn't gone two steps when the blow came from behind.

The weight of the impact knocked David to the ground and sent his face sliding across the rough cement. He rolled over swiftly to see two boys not much younger than himself, standing over him. Before David could speak, a foot slammed into his rib cage. David grabbed at his side and cried out from the pain. Another foot smashed into his face as he felt a warm gush of blood from his nose.

David crawled forward along the sidewalk, his mind racing, his heart pounding. A hand grabbed the back of his collar, lifting him up. David was jerked around to face his attacker.

"Way to go, dumbfuck!" one of the boys shouted. "You let him see your face."

The boy's fist drove into David's stomach; David doubled over as the air rushed from his lungs. He grabbed at his injured ribs, and he felt a hand rummaging through his coat pockets.

No, David thought. I can't let them take my wallet. They'll get my money. My return ticket. I'll be stuck here.

David fought to push the attacker's hand away.

"Stupid fucker's still got some fight left in him!"

David felt a heavy boot against the base of his shin, and he fell to the ground. He grabbed at his leg, simultaneously rolling away from the offenders.

"C'mon, man," a voice said. "Quit jackin' around and take his damn wallet."

The blood continued to pour from the wound on David's face. He tried valiantly to scramble away from the muggers, but they were on him again, once more clawing for his belongings. The pain in David's ribs and shin was excruciating. Some ribs were definitely broken, and possibly his ankle. The hurt throbbed in his stricken leg, and the blood pounded in his temples. David felt the boy's hand pull away from his body.

"Got it!" the boy shouted with glee.

Another blow landed on David's already throbbing leg, and it felt as if the bone had splintered. Blood leaked into David's eyes; his vision blurred. The bone shifted in his leg, moved, reshaped …

Oh my God, David thought with sudden realization. Oh, dear God, I'm changing.

The boys stood over David's crumpled form, dropping whatever didn't interest them from his wallet.

"Hey, check this out," one said.

"Nice looking' lady."

Got to fight it, thought David. I can't change. Not now. I can't control it. I'm not experienced enough.

But the bones reshaped and lengthened, his muscles expanded, his innards shifted. David tried to shout at the boys, to frighten them away, but the only sound that emanated from his throat was an unearthly howl.

One boy dropped the wallet seconds before fangs tore into his throat.

•   •   •

This girl is powerful, Devin Stoner thought. To do what she does, and to have known what she is for so short a time, she is incredible.

He watched the she-wolf licking at the remains of the slaughtered prostitute. The quarter-moon hung high beyond the outstretched arms of the leafless trees. Steam rose from her snout and the still warm open wounds of their victim.

He circled the wolf, once, twice, then faced her. His cold blue eyes stared into hers.

You know who I am, he said into the she-wolf's mind. *You know what I'm saying.*

Yes, Father, the she-wolf answered.

She is powerful. She controls the wolfen mind. But she is still unaware of her capabilities. If his other children were as wonderful as this, there was no limit to what he might accomplish.

Let me show you, he said to the she-wolf.

He stood before her and shifted his appearance. The long snout shortened, appearing more human-like. His front legs drew back into his body, his rear legs lengthened until he stood on two legs. His body became humanoid, yet the wolfen features remained.

"You can do the same," he said. "Take my hand."

The she-wolf approached him on command. She sat on her haunches before him. Stoner took Tiara's head in his hands. He caressed her long, soft snout, rubbed her ears.

"Watch me," he said.

Stoner's head blurred and shifted, becoming completely human. The rest of his body, though humanoid shaped, remained covered with the wolf's hair.

"You can do the same."

Stoner watched his daughter. Looking down at her, he could see the bone structure under her face move and ripple beneath her fur. Her backbone began to reshape itself, and her haunches began to rise closer to him.

"No, just the head. Concentrate on the head."

The she-wolf whimpered, but her rear legs lowered back into their wolfen form. Her icy blue eyes looked up at him. Lashes sprouted from them; the fine silky hairs retreated. Flowing locks of blonde hair began to spill from between her ears, even as her ears shortened, then widened, growing pink and hairless.

Stoner gazed down at his daughter, a she-wolf with the head of a beautiful human girl. She was indeed quite powerful for one so inexperienced. He would teach her. She would grow with him.

Tiara smiled at her father, and the rest of her body made the transformation.

"I didn't even know I could do that," she said.

"There's a lot you don't know yet about our ways," said Stoner. "But you are very powerful. I am proud to call you my own.

"But it's time now," he said. "We must return to Canada. Your mother is rightly mine, and I will have her. And I will have the rest of my children."

"Yes, father," Tiara said. "You will have them all."

•   •   •

The wolf moved through the back streets and alleys of the suburban city streets, limping on its wounded leg. Somewhere in the back of its mind, thoughts of its attackers played. If given a chance to flee, the wolf would've done so. But it had been cornered, frightened, and wounded, and its only means of escape was through aggression.

Dogs barked ferociously as the wolf hobbled down the alley. Many scents filled its blood-encrusted nostrils: the odor of dogs and other animals, the ungainly scent of smoke, distant food.

It smelled something familiar ahead. The hunger pangs rumbling in its stomach drew it to the scent. Food, it thought. The smell reminded it of good things.

The wolf stopped when the alley ended. The smell was stronger, more familiar. But it didn't smell like food. It was something different.

It put its muzzle to the ground and followed. Somehow, the wolf felt it must go to this strange, yet somehow pleasurable scent. The odor continued to pull it onward.

The wolf stopped. The scent ended at a door in a large building. The wolf sat on his haunches panting, tired and hungry. There were no people around. It was late.

The beast turned. It would hide and wait. Perhaps the door would open, and it could find the scent that it so desperately followed.

The wolf trotted down the sidewalk and slipped into an abandoned shed.

•   •   •

David awoke to find himself nude and lying atop a pile of dirty, oily rags. The shell of an older model car sat in the center of the small garage. Several missing boards allowed a draft to filter into the garage, chilling his naked body.

"What happened?"

He started to stand up when a bolt of pain shot through his leg, and he remembered. Instinctively, his hand reached for the area where his wallet should've been.

"Oh no," he muttered.

I must've changed into the wolf, David thought. He felt his mouth and chin. There was dried blood there. Maybe it's mine, he thought. But he wondered. The ferocious attack had triggered the transformation in him, and his wolfen body and mind had taken over. A wounded, frightened wolf would've surely attacked in that situation. David didn't want to think about it.

He surveyed his surroundings. Luckily, there was a pair of old, greasy coveralls hanging on a nail, and David slipped them on.

A pair of combat boots lay scattered nearby. Not the nicest of clothes, but they would have to do.

David stepped out of the shed into the chilly, bright day. He seemed to be in a suburb, probably not far from Detroit. There was no telling how far the wolf had travelled the previous night.

David knew he needed to go to the nearest store or gas station and find out where he was. The garage where he had spent the night wasn't far from a large apartment complex.

The tall three-story buildings loomed high above the sidewalk, nice compact units with balconies facing out over the street.

David stopped suddenly. A familiar smell drifted into his nostrils, faint but obvious. He had no idea what it was, or why it would be so familiar to him.

He was about to shrug it off when he noticed the car. Tiara, he thought. He connected the car with Stoner, and that's why he was picking up on the familiar smell. Perhaps this was Stoner's car, an unmarked detective's car, and Tiara was with him.

David peered into the window of the car. He scanned the interior of the vehicle, uncertain as to what he was hoping to find. His gaze moved downward across the seat, where lay a notebook and a manual of some sort.

David peered down to the floorboard. A receipt lay crumpled against the worn carpet, but David could make out the signature.

Devin Stoner.

David had found his sister.

33

TIARA COULDN'T BELIEVE HER EYES. When she heard the doorbell ring in Devin Stoner's apartment, she didn't think anything of it. It could be a maintenance man, here to repair a leaky faucet. Or the newspaper boy, here to collect for the week's papers. Or a lost pizza delivery driver with two sixteen-inch pepperonis with extra cheese.

She never expected to see her brother.

Yet he stood in the doorway, wearing a pair of dirty coveralls. His eyes glanced furtively at Tiara before swiftly meeting Stoner's steely glare.

Oh shit, David, Tiara thought. How the hell did you ever find me?

The thought of David following her for several thousand miles infuriated Tiara, yet it also touched her in a way. He must've risked a lot coming all this way, spent a lot of time and effort and money. Just to come looking for her? His sister who had left him and his brothers and her mother in search of a different life?

"Yeah?" Stoner said, facing the kid at the door.

"Are you a policeman?" asked David. "The one that drives the car parked out there?"

"How did you know it was a cop's car?" Stoner eyed the boy suspiciously.

"There's a couple of guys out there snooping around it. I heard one of them say it was a vice squad car." "

Stoner turned to Tiara. "Stay here," he said, then headed out the door to ward off the intruders.

Tiara watched as her father disappeared around the corner of the apartment building, then turned to face her brother. "David, are you crazy? What the hell are you doing here?"

"I'm glad to see you too," David reached to hug his sister.

Tiara pushed him away. "David, what the hell do you want?"

He seemed taken aback by Tiara's response. "What do I want? I came to take you back home. Mom's worried sick about you. She keeps—"

"David, what do I look like to you?" Tiara seemed disgusted. "I'm not some teenaged runaway that's lost in the streets of some slimy city. I left for a reason, David. For a purpose. I'm not like you or Mom or Jeremiah. I came to find a new life, one with my father."

David took Tiara's shoulders in his hands. "Tiara, if you'd just listen."

Tiara pushed her brother away. "David, you can't come in here like this. If he sees you hugging me or touching me, if he knows who you are, he'll kill you."

Devin Stoner entered the doorway. "There's no one there now. What did they look—," His words trailed off when he saw the young stranger and his daughter standing so close.

"What the hell are you doing with my daughter? Who are you, kid?"

"I'm Tiara's—," he began.

"Boyfriend," Tiara interrupted. "He's an old boyfriend from back home. He followed me here." Tiara glared into her brother's eyes, imploring him to remain silent.

"Boyfriend, huh? How did you find this place?"

David paused, trying desperately to think up a story. "I ... I knew you were a cop. Tiara told me before she left. They told me where you live at the station."

"Bullshit," said Stoner. "They wouldn't give out my address." He moved in close to David, staring into the younger man's eyes.

"Well, they did," David answered, not backing down. "Must've been a rookie. You should tell them to be more cautious."

Stoner smiled at the kid, then glanced at Tiara. "So, you're my daughter's boyfriend, huh?"

David smiled at Tiara, then turned his attention back to the cop. "That's right."

"Well, I guess you know it's over between you and her. I don't care what you or she says about it, I say it's over. Got that?"

David said nothing. He didn't know how to react.

"Get your bags," Stoner said to Tiara. "Get them in the truck. We're going."

"Where are you going?" David asked Tiara.

"Away," Stoner answered for her. "Not that it's any of your business. We're going away, and you're just going ... away."

"Where are you going?"

"David," warned Tiara.

"David?" Stoner said, turning back around to face the two siblings. "Is your name David?" David nodded.

"David, you'd better leave now, okay?" Tiara pleaded. "Just go."

"No, no, no," said Stoner, holding his hand out. "Don't leave." He moved closer to the younger man. "You look familiar. Have I seen you before somewhere?"

"No, no you haven't."

"I could swear I've seen you before. Do I know you?"

David grabbed Tiara's hand. "Come on, Tiara. Let's go."

"David!" Tiara protested.

Stoner laughed. "Well, son, whatever you and Tiara had going in your little play land, it's evidently past history now. So why don't you go on home now like a good little boy?"

"I'm not leaving without you," said David.

"David, don't you understand? I don't want to go home!"

"You're coming back to us whether you like it or not!"

Stoner stopped laughing. "Us?" he asked.

Tiara pulled her hand away from David and looked at the floor.

"Who's 'us'?" Stoner asked.

"Dammit, David!"

"I think I know why you seem so familiar to me now. 'Us' means you and Mom, doesn't it?" Stoner looked from Tiara to David. "You're not Tiara's boyfriend. You're her brother. David. You're Wagner's kid."

David stared into Tiara's eyes, but he didn't see the cooperation and compassion that he wanted to see. Stoner placed his massive hands on David's shoulders and pulled him closer. David smelled something rotten on Stoner's breath.

"Yeah, you're Wagner's kid." Natasha's child. But you know something, kid? I fucked your momma before Wagner did." He laughed. "You could even be my kid. Wouldn't that be something?"

Tiara moved the suitcases to the front door as Stoner held her brother.

"But I know you're not my kid. You're nothing like your sister. You're dead inside. You don't know what life is about." David's heart raced. "You're just like that waste Wagner. And I bet your neck would snap just as easily as his did."

"Daddy, please don't," Tiara pleaded.

"You bastard," whispered David.

"Bastard? Yeah, I'm a bastard all right, you could say," Stoner said. "My father died a long, long time ago. Just like yours died."

"Daddy, don't hurt him," Tiara said.

"Hurt him?" said Stoner, looking at his daughter. "Hurt him?"

David felt Stoner's vice-like fingers tighten around his neck, the tips pinching into the cord-like veins that bulged in his throat. To his horror, David could see tiny hair sprouting on Stoner's exposed forearms, growing in thickness to a dirty brown/black patch of fur. He could feel Stoner's fingernails turning into sharp, deadly claws that bit into his neck. Tears began to run down David's face, mixing with beads of sweat. His eyes met Stoner's, so blue, like a Canadian lake in summer, like the cloudless wilderness skies.

All thought left David's mind as he felt the transformation begin.

•　　•　　•

The Ford Explorer pulled off the rural road to climb its way through the hilly region, dodging trees and boulders before coming to a stop somewhere in the wilds across the United States/Canada border near Ontario. Doors opened on both sides. Tiara and Devin Stoner stepped out into the countryside.

"Thanks for not hurting him," said Tiara, placing her arms around her father.

Stoner snapped his fingers, and the wolfen David jumped from the vehicle's front seat. The wolf stood silently, staring straight ahead as if drugged into a stupor.

"I wouldn't have hurt him, Tiara," Stoner said. "After all, he is your brother. And my stepson, I suppose."

Stoner snapped his fingers once more, and the wolf trotted down the mountainside in no particular direction. "He won't bother us out here, and he'll be free."

"You made it so he'll never change back?" asked Tiara.

"Yep."

"How did you do that?"

"A little trade secret," Stoner answered. "Maybe I'll show you someday."

Tiara leaned her head on Stoner's strong shoulders. "Well, thanks again for letting him go."

Stoner watched the wolf disappear into the misty horizon, and a smile crossed his thin lips, a glint shone in his icy blue eyes. "Like I said, I wouldn't hurt any of them."

34

DEVIN STONER AND TIARA stood outside the barn where Tiara had seen Jenny and Craig making love on that night not so long ago. The drive to Jermiah's place had taken several days. The need to quench their lycanthrophobic thirst had demanded a few side excursions along the way. They parked the Explorer a few miles down the road, safely hidden from view. The full moon adequately lit the path that led up the hill toward the dog kennels and the house where Tiara had grown up.

"There's a light on in the kitchen," Tiara said. "Mom's probably up."

"That's good," said Stoner. "We don't want to wake the others. We just want to get Natasha and get her away from here."

"You still think that's the only way?"

Stoner turned and grasped his daughter's hands in his. He stared into her eyes so proudly. His daughter was beautiful; she was certainly the product of his lineage. "Tiara, I never stopped loving your mother. But she couldn't understand the true ways of the lycanthrope. We mate for life, and she was mine. She insisted on being with David Wagner. I'm certain she still feels a lot of resentment towards me. We must get her away from here, talk to her alone, just you and me and your mother. We can convince her to join us. I know we can, but I need you to understand."

Tiara returned the smile he offered her. "Okay, let me go up to the kennels first. The wolves know me."

Tiara walked up the gravel path. Stoner's keen eyes followed her. Most of what he had said was true. Lycanthropes do mate for life. He did still love Natasha, had never stopped. But there would be no talking, so discussing the matter. Natasha and Tiara would join him; they would experience the first of many Festerings. They would both bear him children who would grow to be strong, powerful lycanthropes.

Stoner followed his daughter. He could hear some of the wolves growling defensively, a few of them uttering low warning barks. They may have forgotten his daughter's scent. Stoner couldn't take the chance of the wolves making a ruckus and warning the inhabitants of the household.

He came up behind Tiara. "They must've forgotten me," she said. "I think there's a few new ones, too."

"Here, let me—" Stoner started to say.

Tiara knelt before the wolf in the first cage. The wolf stared back with deep brown eyes filled with fear and mistrust. Tiara reached out her fingers, her steely gaze never wavering from the wolf's eyes, and touched the forehead of the beast. The wolf stood still and silent.

"Incredible," Stoner said. "You truly are a marvelous lycanthrope."

"I used to hypnotize them all the time when I was sneaking into the house at night," Tiara smiled.

One by one, Stoner and Tiara moved down the length of the kennels, hypnotizing and silencing all the inhabitants of the cages. When the grounds were quiet but for the sound of chirping crickets, they moved closer to the back door that led into the kitchen.

·   ·   ·

"Mother," said Tiara, looking at her mother's long brown hair that fell across her shoulders.

Natasha stood swiftly, defensively, wheeling about at the sound of the voice. Upon seeing her daughter, Natasha's eyes brightened, a wide smile crossed her lips. "Tiara?" she said in wonderment. "Tiara, oh my baby! I knew you'd come back!"

Natasha threw her arms around her daughter and hugged her fiercely, fighting back tears. Tiara hugged Natasha back, and for a moment, she too felt the tears of reunion that her mother felt.

"Jeremiah!" Natasha called out.

"No, no, no," Tiara whispered forcefully. She put her fingers to her lips to quiet Natasha. "Don't tell anyone yet."

"But they've all been so worried about you, darling."

"I know. But I want to talk to you for a while, just you and me." Natasha smiled. "Okay, Tiara. If that's what you want."

"It is," said Tiara. "And there's someone outside that wants to talk to you, too."

Again, Natasha's eyes lit up. "David," she said. "David found you and brought you home."

The door swung open, the screen door tapping softly against the wall. "Not quite."

Natasha's knees buckled underneath her when she saw Devin Stoner's tall, powerful frame filling the doorway. She wanted to scream, to say something, anything, but nothing would come out of her throat. All at once, all the memories of her life in Potters, Maine came flooding back. Mud-soaked doghouses. Pinecones. Roaring fires. Plush couches. David. Coogan. Everything.

"Tiara," Natasha finally said, glaring at her daughter with accusation in her eyes.

But Natasha could not pull herself away from Tiara's blue eyes. Something in those eyes—the color of early morning skies and crystal-clear streams—calmed her, soothed her panic. It made her feel safe, wanted, needed.

Stoner moved up behind Natasha and placed his hands on her shoulders, pushing her forward gently.

"Excellent," he said to Tiara. "Well done."

●　　　●　　　●

Thoughts filled the wolf's troubled sleeps, thoughts that it shouldn't have, thoughts that it didn't understand. It could see trees and mountains and streams, grasses and boulders and animals. The wolf whimpered in its sleep and rolled further into the crevice in which it had lain.

The odd images continued to assault the wolf's confused brain. Objects fell from the blue skies and crashed into the mountain streams, only to rise again in swirling patterns above the water. The objects were pinecones.

Something solid and tangible formed in the mists stirred up by the falling pinecones. It was an elderly man, his face weather-beaten, his appearance unshaven and disheveled. He wore dirty denim overalls and worn hiking boots. Gripped in each gnarled hand was a plastic garbage bag. The pinecones flew from one bag and swirled around in the air before dropping into the stream.

The wolf cried out in its sleep, disturbed by the frightening dream. The old man in the dream reached into the other bag and retrieved a book. The cover read: *Brazil and Its Rain Forests.*

Don't forget who you are, Sonny, the old man said, his voice distant and discorporate. *Don't forget what you are, what you were born, what you will always be.*

Your mother needs you now. Your sister needs you. They are in dire trouble, and you can help save them. But you must remember, Sonny. You must remember.

When the wolf awoke from the incredible dream, it was hairless and stood on two legs.

•　　　•　　　•

In a stolen sweatsuit he pulled from a clothesline, David stood on the outskirts of some town. He didn't know whether he was in Canada or the States. He was still barefoot.

The closest place of business David could see was a gas station. He trotted across the road on his bare feet. He needed money badly. He had to get back to his mother before Stoner and his renegade daughter could reach her, and he would never beat them there on foot.

David crossed in front of the gas pumps and glanced inside the store. He couldn't see anyone, but the door was open. David had never considered stealing from anyone in his life. Desperate times made for desperate men.

"Kind of cold to be running around barefoot, ain't it?" the station attendant asked.

David jumped at the sound of the man's voice. In his deep thought, he had not heard the man approaching. "I like to jog barefooted," he said. "It's more natural."

"You buying anything?" the man asked suspiciously.

"No," said David. "No, just resting." He feigned being short of breath, bending over and resting his hands on his knees.

"Well, don't loiter too long," the man said, then disappeared into the building.

David leaned against the Coke machine and frowned. He was stuck. He needed money for a ride home, but where was he going to get it? He had pretty much resigned himself to the fact that he was going to have to obtain it dishonestly. David turned and banged his head a few times against the Coke machine in frustration, and the old man from his dream spoke again.

Don't forget who you are, Sonny. Don't forget what you are.

Who I am, David thought. I know who I am. I know what I can do.

David closed his eyes and remembered what he was.

A few hours later when the gas attendant came out to fill the Coke machine, he would wonder how the front of the door had been ripped down the center in three distinct jagged lines.

35

JEREMIAH REED WAS WORRIED. He often awoke in the mornings to find Natasha nowhere around. She was an early riser, much more so than himself or the kids. She would often take walks through the woods or do a few early morning chores. But there was always some evidence that she'd already been up and about. Last night's dishes cleaned and drying on the counter, a half pot of lukewarm coffee. Jeremiah could see none of these things on this morning. He could only smell her scent.

But that wasn't the only powerful scent lingering amid dwindling odors of fried bacon and pipe tobacco. Tiara's scent was undeniably present as well. And another male's scent that he couldn't place. But he thought he could guess who it belonged to. Jeremiah had to assume the worst.

Jackie Coogan had hidden Natasha well. If William Booth ever found out where Natasha was, he would come for her. It wasn't a question of loyalty. Evil lycanthropes care little about that virtue. It's just the way of the lycanthrope, the pull of the moon's powers. He would come for his mate.

Jeremiah went back to his bedroom and retrieved his 30/30 deer rifle. He seldom used the old shooting iron anymore; never had the need to. That may change today, Jeremiah thought.

He was alone in the house. Luke and Simon had stayed out as wolves the entire night, as they so often did. The boys had a wild and free spirit, wanting nothing of the human side of their lives.

Jeremiah spilled a box of bullets onto the kitchen table and loaded them into the rifle's magazine. He placed the remaining bullets in the deep pocket of his overalls.

He paused at the back door. The three scents mixed overwhelmingly here, and the odor drifted down the steps before disappearing in the cool morning air.

•   •   •

David ascended quickly and deliberately up the mountain road, hobbling only slightly on his injured leg. He was close to home; he could sense it. God had smiled on him with the fortune of a ride with a trucker who was hell bent on making a deadline delivery to the outskirts of Alberta. He had even refused the change David had managed to collect from the gutted Coke machine, thankful for the company and the help staying awake on the long haul.

The smell of the dogs that he had grown so accustomed to was powerful to his senses. He could smell the pellets of animal food, the particles of hay that danced in the air, the diesel of the delivery trucks that passed by on the mountain road. Reed's Feed and Grain Store had to be nearby. David quickened his pace.

The climb through the high roads was grueling. He figured he was at least a day behind Stoner and Tiara. The truck driver had carried him as close as Manitoba, a smaller town that David figured to be about fifty miles from Caribou Park. He had to make up the time. He hoped Stoner had not gone straight to Jeremiah's place. David had to warn Jeremiah and Natasha.

The familiar smells were so powerful now. David continuously glanced past the trees on both sides of the road. Perhaps he had become disoriented during his rigorous climb up the mountains. For all he knew, he could be approaching home from the opposite direction. He searched for the familiar house and barns in all directions.

But nothing looked familiar. The trees were different; the landscape perhaps slightly steeper. David thought he must be too high in the mountains. Or perhaps still climbing.

But the scents were so strong. He was certain that his mother was close.

Don't forget what you are, Sonny, the voice said in David's head.

The dream came back to him again. Who was this old guy that was constantly jumping into his head? Where did he come from?

You're not that close to home. It just smells like you are.

David stopped and knelt to the ground, squinting and rubbing his eyes. Sweat dripped from his brow. The climb got to him. The sheer exhaustion of travelling thousands of miles in such a short time had taken its toll.

Remember your beginnings, boy. Remember the moon. Remember its powers.

David caught a hint of another scent high in the air. This was very familiar and obvious.

Natasha.

•　　•　　•

The Explorer rolled and climbed up the hilly region with rugged ease, climbing higher into the Caribou Mountains. Tiara looked at her mother sitting next to her in the back seat, still in a dazed stupor. Tiara thought that Stoner must've done something to Natasha for her to be so docile. She hadn't said a word since they had taken her from the kitchen that morning.

Tiara watched the scraggly trees roll by. "Where are we taking her?" she asked.

"We have to get far away," said Stoner. "Up into the mountains."

"But why so far?" Tiara questioned. "Just to talk?"

Stoner glared fiercely into the back seat. "Do you want us to be together? Do you want us to be a family like we should've been all along? Then don't question what I say!"

Stoner glanced into the rear-view mirror. His voice softened. "They'll come looking for us. They may be able to follow her scent. We can't take that chance. Not until we've had a chance to talk to her."

"Okay," said Tiara, satisfied with her father's answer.

"I can smell old wood, residual smoke somewhere up here," Stoner continued. "I think there may be an abandoned cabin up here. We can go inside, get warm, and talk this thing out. Feel better?" His eyes met Tiara's in the mirror. She smiled at him and nodded.

Stoner looked ahead. Yeah, they would talk all right. But it didn't matter what Natasha had to say. He had her now. And there was no way he was letting go of her this time. No way in hell.

•　　•　　•

Natasha's scent was strong, a straight line slicing a trail through the woods and into the mountains. The twin paths cutting through the fallen leaves indicated a vehicle had travelled through only a short time before. Jeremiah gripped the deer rifle tightly in his hands and followed the trail into the hilly region.

•　　•　　•

His mother's scent carried David off the main road and into the woods. The smell of car exhaust fumes mingled with the scent of Natasha. There were ruts in the mud just off the shoulder of the road, and several small trees had been crushed. He seemed to remember the vehicle that he had ridden in before Stoner had dropped him off back in the States.

Good boy, the voice in David's head said. *Now you're startin' to think like you should.*

36

"TIARA, YOU SHOULD NEVER have brought him here," Natasha told her daughter upon waking up from the hypnosis.

"But I wanted us to be a family," Tiara persisted. "Like we should."

"I can't be with him, Tiara. He killed the only man I ever loved. David Wagner died in my arms."

"You were mine before you were his," Stoner interceded. "It's you who broke the boundary. Our kind mates for life."

"Humans are supposed to mate for life, too. But it doesn't always work out that way."

Tiara stood back and folded her arms across her chest. Natasha sat in a small wooden chair inside the abandoned cabin while Stoner paced before her.

"You were gone from me for a long time because of what that fool Coogan did. But now, thanks to our beautiful daughter, I've found you again. And I don't intend to let you go."

"Mom, can't you see he loves you?" said Tiara.

Natasha stood and held Tiara's face in her hands. "Honey, you're confused. He doesn't love me. He doesn't love any of us. He only used you to take him to me. Can't you see that?"

"No, no, he wants us to start a new life together."

"Does he? Is that what he wants?" Natasha turned back to Stoner. "What about David? Luke and Simon? Are they included in this new family ideal of yours?"

"They are not my children," Stoner said. "Besides, you needn't worry about David anymore. He's where he belongs."

Natasha felt her pulse quicken, her heart pound in her chest. "David. He found you." She gazed at the blue-eyed monstrosity that had ruined her life so long ago, and now threatened to do so again. "What did you do to him?"

"I didn't want you to find out," said Tiara.

"What?" Natasha said sternly. "Find out what?"

"He did something to David. Turned him into a wolf. Permanently, I think."

"I took away his mind," Stoner said, smiling. "He's completely and irreversibly animal now."

"No," Natasha whispered, sitting back down in the chair. "No, you couldn't have. Not David. He's so bright."

"But he's okay, Mom," Tiara said, placing her hand on Natasha's shoulder. "He's free and he's safe now."

Stoner peered out the cabin window toward the Explorer. "C'mon, we need to be going soon."

"Where are we going?" asked Tiara, still comforting her mother.

"Back to Detroit," Stoner said. "The Festering isn't over yet."

Natasha looked up with tears on her face. "You expect me to go with you after what you've done? To my love, to my son? How dare you even think that I would stay with you." Natasha stood up and approached Stoner. "I despise you, William Booth, Devin Stoner, whatever the hell your name is. You ripped my one true love away from me. You took my son away from me. You've taken my daughter away from me."

"Your daughter is one with the Festering," said Stoner. "Nothing I did swayed her."

"I hate you," Natasha said. "I wish I could kill you this very instant, but then I'd be resorting to your tactics. That's how you handle things, isn't it? If something doesn't agree with you, you just do away with it. Where will it end, Stoner? How many more? My mother. My father. My lover. My son. My daughter. Just how old are you? Are you Satan himself? How many lives have you taken; how many people have you destroyed for your own selfish reasons? Where will it end?"

"Get off your grandstand and get in the car," Stoner ordered.

"And what about you, Tiara? I know you hate me now."

"Mother, I don't hate you," Tiara said, pain in her voice.

"But where will it end for you? Will you be just like this? Will you go on for thousands of years destroying existences for your own pleasure? I know you've already killed one. And why? Because you didn't like her? Because you liked her boyfriend? Was she the only one? Have you killed more since you've been gone?"

Tiara stood still, stunned into silence by her mother's harsh words. She could feel a tear form in her eye, dribble warmly down her cheek.

"Get in the car," Stoner repeated.

"Hypnotize her like you did me," said Natasha. "That's how you operate. Yes, you're powerful. I'll give you that. But is it always like that? Give people a choice, but if their decision doesn't suit you, just brainwash them, suck their will right from their minds?"

"Get. In. The car."

Tiara moved past her mother and gripped the handle of the door of the cabin. She pulled it open to find David standing in the doorway.

•　　　•　　　•

Jeremiah could see the cabin through the trees. He couldn't see any shapes through the shade-covered windows, but he could tell by her scent that Natasha was in there. He started up the hill slowly, walking carefully on padded wolfen feet to make as little noise as possible. His large human hands gripped the cold barrel of the rifle, his finger resting lightly, but firmly, on the trigger.

When he was less than fifty yards from the cabin, Jeremiah Reed threw his head back and released a long, shrill howl into the cool mountain air.

•　　　•　　　•

"Get in here," Stoner said fiercely, grabbing David's arm and pulling him into the cabin.

"David," cried Natasha, grabbing her son and hugging him. "I was so scared for you. You should never have gone off alone like that."

"I had to, Mom. I had to find Tiara."

"How the hell did you get back here?" Stoner snarled. "How did you find the moon again?"

"It doesn't matter how I got here," said David. "All that matters is that I'm here, and I'm leaving with my mother … and my sister."

"David," Tiara said, exasperated. "I told you, I don't want to leave my father."

Stoner stomped about the cabin, growing impatient. "No one's leaving anything. Look, kid. I don't know how you managed to make it back, but you're not leaving here."

"What do you mean?" asked Natasha, her voice shaking.

Stoner reached into his coat pocket and retrieved his police service revolver. He flipped open the magazine, checking to see if it was loaded, then snapped it shut again.

"Dad, you can't be serious," Tiara said.

"Only if I have to, baby," said Stoner. "I want you and your mother in the car right now."

Just then, a shrill cry split the air outside the cabin, echoing and wrapping around the mountainside, bouncing off stones and trees and returning again and again. But it wasn't just one howl. It was many.

All through the mountains, dozens of wolves answered the initial call. The hills were alive with the sounds of wolves.

"It's Jeremiah," said David. "Jeremiah found us."

"Who the hell's Jeremiah?" Stoner asked, glancing out the window.

"He's your worst nightmare, buddy," David said cockily.

"All right," said Stoner. "I'm tired of playing these stupid games." He turned and aimed the pistol directly at David's chest.

"NO!" Natasha cried, leaping for Stoner's arm. The sudden weight of her body brought Stoner's hand down. He quickly recovered and shoved Natasha backward, knocking her into the cabin wall.

"You can kill me," David said. "But it won't help you any. They're still coming for you. Face it, man. You're not going anywhere."

Stoner cursed and slammed the butt of the revolver against the top of David's head. David stood wavering unsteadily for a millisecond, then his eyes rolled into his head, and he fell to the floor.

"David!" Natasha cried, leaping to her feet, running to her fallen son. She cradled David's bleeding head in her hands, and a swarm of powerful emotions whirled threw her mind in hurricane-like proportions. She was back in the woods in Potters, Maine, holding a dying David Wagner in her arms and crying herself to sleep. "How could you?" Natasha cried.

Tiara looked down at Natasha. Tiara thought Natasha was talking to Stoner, but Natasha stared up at her daughter with tear-stained eyes. "How could you let him do this to your brother?"

"Come on," said Stoner, running out of patience. He lifted Natasha by the arm and put the gun to her head.

"He's not my brother," Tiara said.

•　　　•　　　•

Devin Stoner could see the dozens of wolves loping through the trees just beyond the secluded mountain cabin. They were normal wolves as far as he could tell. He could certainly control a few at a time, but there were far too many for he and Tiara to handle.

He moved out into the open, one arm firmly pinning Natasha's arms to her body, the other holding the gun to her head. "All right, Jeremiah!" he shouted into the air. "Whoever you are! Call the wolves off!"

He must be a damned lycanthrope, Stoner thought, to have gathered this many wolves so quickly. I knew it.

"You let her go!" a voice drifted in from the trees.

"Can't do that!" Stoner yelled back. "Call them off or you'll be feeding her brains to them!"

"Don't do it, Jeremiah!" screamed Natasha. "Don't listen to him! He's already hurt David! He's inside the cabin!"

"Shut up, bitch!"

Stoner heard the man howl, and the wolves started to close in. He fired a warning shot into the air, but the wolves did not cease their advance. He leveled the gun at one of the wolves and fired. The wolf yelped and fell, but the others kept coming.

Stoner angrily shoved Natasha away, knocking her to the ground. She rolled over and stood. "You're not so brave when you're outnumbered, are you?"

"But I'm not stupid," he said, grinning. "You can go on, Natasha. Go on back to your safe, human life with your good friends and family. Leave me again like you did before. Break the ways of the lycanthrope. Shun the moon all you want. But you won't have your daughter anymore."

Suddenly, Stoner reached out and grabbed Tiara, pulling his arm forcefully under her neck, choking her. He put the still-hot tip of the revolver to Tiara's head, nuzzling it into her hair.

"D-d-daddy." Tiara struggled to speak. "What ... what are you doing?"

"Now," said Stoner, "I'm giving you one final choice, Natasha. Come with me, and we all live together as one big, happy fucking family. Leave ... and Tiara dies."

"You can't mean that," Natasha said. But she knew he did.

"Daddy ... don't."

"Shut up," he spat. "Oh, you know I mean it. You have one final decision to make. The choice is yours."

Natasha gazed into Tiara's eyes filled with absolute fear and shock.

Natasha turned to the tree line. "Call them off, Jeremiah!"

There was a rustling from behind. Stoner wheeled about, still gripping Tiara tightly. Jeremiah stood near the corner of the cabin, a groggy and bleeding David standing at his side. The deer rifle trained on Devin Stoner.

"Hello, son," said Jeremiah.

"You," Stoner said through gritted teeth. "It's you."

"Yeah, it's me." The rifle did not waver.

Stoner smiled. "I always wondered where you'd gone off to."

"Now you know," said Jeremiah. "You know it all. Coogan brought Natasha here after you killed David Wagner. He hid her well. You'd never find her up here, Coogan said. But I always knew you'd be back some day, even after you left. You're like a disease, boy. You may go into remission, but there's always a relapse. I knew what Tiara was from the day she was born. And I knew someday that she would be pulled away from us, that she'd find you, and that you'd be back for Natasha.

"I was prepared, son," Jeremiah said. "Believe me, I was prepared."

The wolves were less than twenty yards away now, moving slowly and methodically, their unison growling sounding like a minor earthquake rattling through the Canadian mountains.

"You're powerful, William," Jeremiah said. "But you can't beat us all."

Stoner pressed the pistol harder into Tiara's head. "You shoot me, old man, and I pull the trigger. Is it worth it?"

"You tell me," Jeremiah said calmly. "Is it worth it?"

"Daddy. Please." Tiara squirmed restlessly against Stoner's grip.

Stoner glared at Natasha. "I know you don't love me, but you love your daughter. Do you want her to die? Do you want her head splattered all over these hills?"

"Don't," Natasha begged.

"Get in the car, then. Now!"

"Jeremiah, I can't risk losing Tiara again," Natasha said. "Please call the wolves off."

Jeremiah stared into his long-lost son's icy blue eyes. Finally, he began to lower the rifle. A smile began to cross Stoner's lips. Jeremiah made a loud growling noise, and the wolves headed back for the trees.

"Drop the rifle now," said Stoner. Jeremiah let the butt of the rifle touch the ground, then released it. The gun toppled over onto the crunchy leaves.

Natasha pulled the latch on the rear door of the Explorer and opened it. She expected Stoner to lead Tiara over to the open door. He did not.

She watched in horror as he placed the gun at the back of her daughter's head. Everything happened in slow motion in Natasha's mind. The gun pressing against Tiara's head. The muscles in Stoner's hand tensing as he prepared to pull the trigger. Jeremiah stooping to retrieve the rifle. Natasha leaping from the car and lunging for her daughter.

The large silvery wolf hurling its body through the air toward the tall, blond man.

Tiara jerked free and fell toward Natasha, her mother's arms bracing her fall. Stoner stumbled backward, raised the revolver defensively and fired. Blood splattered from the wolf's shoulders as the bullet found its mark, but it did not impede the animal's progress. It came crashing down on top of Stoner, knocking him backward and into the cabin wall. Almost simultaneously, an identical wolf burrowed into Stoner from the other side, sending the revolver flying.

Leaves and dust flew into the air as the wolves bit into Devin Stoner's flesh. The wounded wolf rolled away from the skirmish. As blood poured from its wound, its shape altered and shifted, until a teenaged boy lay bleeding on the ground.

"Luke!" Natasha screamed. She tore herself away from Tiara, grabbing the bleeding boy to pull him away from the battle. Tiara joined Natasha at her brother's side.

Stoner pushed with all his might against the wolf. His free hand clawed frantically at the ground, searching desperately for the fallen pistol. It was not there. Stoner could not fend off the wolf this way. He began to change.

Soon, there were two large wolves rolling about in the leaves, one silver and one black. The silver one began to weaken under the black wolf's superior strength and agility. It had the silver wolf on its back, and just as the black wolf's jaws locked onto the other's throat, a shot rang through the mountain air.

•   •   •

William Booth felt the bullet pierce his hide and tear through his black heart. He shuddered at the pain and fell away from the silver wolf. He rolled over on his back and felt his bones move and shift for the last time.

So many years. So many lives. So many Festerings.

He gazed up at the blue skies, at the bright sun. Off in one corner of his rapidly blurring vision, just above the line of coniferous trees on the horizon, barely visible in the glare and radiance of the sun, was a faint, silvery sliver of the moon. William Booth cried out to it, calling on its unbridled glory, but to no avail. The sun was more powerful, at least for this moment in time. In his dying breath, it had failed him.

The moon had at long last shunned William Booth.

Epilogue

Three months later

TIARA AND HER MOTHER said their goodbyes. A lot had transpired between everyone involved. Luke and David had recovered from their injuries. Jeremiah accepted the fact that he had been forced to take his estranged son's life. Luke and Simon completely shunned human ways and disappeared into the woods for the last time. David prepared to head to the west coast of the United States with a group of college kids from the University of Alberta to protest the cutting down of thousands of acres of temperate rain forests—a belief in which he had always felt strongly.

As Natasha stood on the front porch watching her daughter prepare to leave her for the second time, a million thoughts swarmed inside her congested mind. Was it fair to lose her anyway after everything had been more or less straightened out? Perhaps Natasha should consider herself lucky that they were even on speaking terms. Tiara had been forced to witness her father's death, in addition to discovering his true concern for his own daughter only moments earlier. Perhaps an amiable parting was the best Natasha could hope for in this situation.

"Do you have everything?" Natasha asked.

Dressed in her familiar old worn jeans and gray sweatshirt, Tiara gazed up at her mother with her crystal blue eyes, eyes that seemed more relaxed and less cruel than before. Natasha suddenly recalled the times when she would watch Tiara as she sat on the hill gazing at the cars and trucks rolling along the country highway. She was a grown woman now, but she was still just a child to Natasha.

Tiara patted the suitcase she held in her hand and nudged the other with her foot. "Got it all."

"Hug?" Natasha asked, holding out her open arms. Tiara held her mother in her arms and squeezed.

"I love you," Natasha said.

"I love you, too, Mom. I really do. But I can't change what I am. This is all so confusing. I thought my father loved me, wanted to be with me. You were right. He just used me to find you. He was going to kill me all along, I think. But despite everything he did, there's still a part of him, a part of that whole lifestyle, inside of me."

"William Booth was vile and evil. Jeremiah, your brothers, me, we're all good. Maybe a lycanthrope doesn't have to be one way or the other. Humans don't; you see good people do bad things, you see bad people do good things. Maybe there's a balance somewhere in the middle."

"Maybe you're right," said Tiara. "I'm not all good. I know that. I never have been. But maybe I'm not all bad either."

"Right," Natasha smiled.

Tiara smiled in return and pushed a few strands of windblown hair from Natasha's face. A trace of concern crossed her face at the subtle wrinkles in her mother's face, the emotional weight that showed in her eyes. "Are you feeling okay, Mom? You're looking a little ... older."

Natasha shrugged. "I'm fine. I just haven't ... you know, done the wolf thing in a while."

Tiara nodded. "I'll write," she said. "Tell you how everything's going in LA. The photographer's got a place set up for me. Don't worry about me. I'll be fine."

A taxi pulled up to the shoulder of the highway and honked. "That's my ride to the airport. It's a long trip just to the plane."

"Yeah," said Natasha, wiping a tear away.

"Mom. We said we weren't gonna do that."

"I know," Natasha sniffed. "But I can't help it."

The taxi driver honked again. "Well," Tiara said. "I'd better go."

"Yeah," Natasha said, pulling away. "Get going. Call when you get there."

"I will." Tiara bounded toward the taxi with the suitcases in tow. "Good-bye. I love you!" she shouted, turning around and waving.

"I love you, too!"

Natasha watched as the taxi disappeared over the horizon.

"I love you," Natasha whispered.

She stood in the cool dewy air of the early spring morning. Natasha knew that spring was a time for rebirth, a season for new beginnings. But she also knew that was not to be the case on this day. Natasha's eyes lingered on the spot in the road where the taxi had disappeared.

It was a long time before she went back into the house.

•   •   •

"I really do think that I've lost her, Jeremiah."

Jeremiah turned his coffee cup to his lips and drank. "She said she'd write."

"And she will," said Natasha. "For a while. Jeremiah, I have no doubt in my mind now that she loves me, especially after all we went through. But let's face it. She's going to California with a very good chance of becoming a successful model. She'll write a few times, she'll get a few more fashion shoots, make a few trips overseas. She'll write once every other month or so, and before you know it, the letters will stop coming. I'll never hear from her again."

"You really believe that?" asked Jeremiah.

"Yeah, yeah I do. You know, you said before that Tiara would never come back, but you knew that she would."

"I knew William would bring her back," Jeremiah corrected.

"Do you think she would've come back if not for him?" Jeremiah shrugged. "Do you think she'll ever come back this time?"

"Natasha," Jeremiah began, sighing deeply, "you know now that all that advice I gave you about losing kids came from experience. Because of what I went through with William. I was wrong about

Tiara; she wasn't a bad kid, like I thought. But William was. I don't really know what to tell you."

Natasha nodded and stared out the window at the distant tree line. The trees always made her think of the countless hours and days spent tied to a chain in David Wagner's backyard, and how she had always longed for freedom. In those days, she had no choice. Now, she did.

"I've been thinking," said Natasha. "The kids are all gone. I've lived this life for a long time now. As a human, I mean." She looked up into Jeremiah's eyes. "Do you think you could handle things around here without me?"

"I did before you came here." He smiled. "You want to leave, don't you?"

Natasha's gaze did not waver from the window. "Luke and Simon are out there. They're the only family I have left, not counting you. Tiara is gone. David's leaving soon. Looking back, although I can't really remember it all, I think I was happiest when I was just a wolf. There're too many things to worry about when we're like this, Jeremiah. I don't want to worry anymore. I've worried enough. I want to be free."

"I could find you when David or Tiara come to visit," Jeremiah said.

Natasha smiled. "Yes, I'm sure you could."

•   •   •

David and Natasha stood at the end of the path, next to the barn, looking out through the trees.

"You'll be out there with Luke and Simon, then?" asked David.

"Yes, I want to run free for a while," Natasha said. "Is that all right with you?"

"It's fine, Mom."

"You save those trees for me, you hear?" Natasha said, hugging her son. "If they get those, they'll want more. They may eventually work their way up here. I don't want them to take our trees."

"Not if I can help it," said David.

Natasha buried her head in David's chest and fought to control the tears. "I guess you're leaving today."

"As soon as the guys get here," David said. "I'll be all right, Mom. Don't worry about me."

"I won't," Natasha agreed. "And you don't worry about me."

"No," said David. "But I do kind of worry about Tiara. Out there in Los Angeles with all those sharks. All alone."

"Don't worry about your sister. She can take care of herself."

David laughed. "Yeah, I suppose she can."

"Yeah," Natasha said, running her fingers through David's hair. She placed the softest of kisses on her son's lips. A kiss for David, a kiss for her other David, for Tiara, for Luke and Simon, for Jackie Coogan, for Jeremiah Reed.

•　　　•　　　•

David wiped from his brow the sweat that the hot South American sun had beaten out of his body. The tiny oscillating fan in the thatch roof hut did little to comfort him, and at only ten in the morning, it wasn't going to get any better.

But David loved it. He had finally made it to Brazil after five years of tailing ecologists and environmentalists alike, nosing in on all their doings, waiting for the right opportunity to move in. And that had come two years ago when a company based in Oregon had allowed him to join them in Brazil as a laborer. The company had gone to set up a communications system for the Yanomami Indian tribe in the deep wilds of the Brazilian rain forest. David worked his way into the brains of the organization, and he now found himself heading a group assigned to protect one hundred acres of rare and valuable mahogany trees. If the rain forests of Brazil were going to be destroyed in David's lifetime (and that could be a very long time indeed), it wouldn't be for lack of trying on his part.

Paiakan, a local tribe member and David's right-hand man, stepped into the temporary office. He stood before David, sweat pouring down his bare chest, and pulled off his baseball cap.

"Just got word from Redenacao," Paiakan said. "The Kayapos cut a deal with some loggers. Seventy-five American dollars per foot."

"Where?" asked David.

"About fifty miles east of here. Too damn close for my taste."

"Mine too," David agreed. "We'd better check it out. The four-wheelers gassed up?" Paiakan nodded. "Call Marty and get him to bring some weapons. We want to be safe."

"Si, amigo," David's partner said. He turned and headed out the door with David close behind. David watched as the native put a pair of headphones on and slid a CD into a portable player. David glanced over his friend's shoulder.

"What are you listening to?"

Paiakan held the CD cover up and pulled the headphones off until they rested around his neck. A beautiful, sultry woman, dressed in a tight black dress and straddling a microphone, her blonde mane cascading to the floor, graced the CD's cover. "Tiara, man. She's hot."

David smiled. "What would you say if I told you that was my sister?"

"I'd say I want to fuck your sister."

David slapped him playfully across the shoulder with his baseball cap. "Hey, that's my sister you're talking about!"

Paiakan looked back at David and stopped. "Your sister? I mean, for real, your sister?" His eyes showed disbelief. David nodded. "Are you shitting me?"

"No."

"Big famous model, singer, actress. This is your sister?" he asked, holding up the cover. "Why didn't you ever tell me?"

"Two reasons," said David. "One, I didn't know you were into her stuff. You know being from Brazil and all—"

"There you go talking that ethnocentric bullshit again, man," Paiakan interrupted.

David laughed. "Sorry. And two, I don't tell many people. You know, it just causes a lot of commotion."

"And this is really your sister?" David nodded again. "Man, how did you ever get a sister like this?"

"Just lucky I guess."

David and Paiakan climbed atop their respective all-terrain vehicles. "You know, she likes to shock people," David said, in reference to some Hollywood reporter's comment about Tiara and her obvious joy of controversy.

Paiakan started his four-wheeler and began to creep forward. He laughed and turned back to David saying, "I've seen a lot in my nineteen years. Nothing she could do would shock me, amigo." He accelerated and sped off into the woods.

David kicked the starter, turned the ignition and took off in pursuit of his partner. He shook his head and laughed at his friend's innocent statement. Yeah, David thought. Maybe, maybe not. But there is one thing Tiara can do that might just surprise you a tad.

David steered the all-terrain vehicle between a pair of tall, majestic mahogany trees. The sun beat down relentlessly in the humid air. Birds and howler monkeys screamed in the distance. Thousands of insects flew past him, and David disappeared into the thick Brazilian rain forest.

•   •   •

The old she-wolf stood on shaky legs atop the cliff, staring out across the domain that she had for so long called home. Friends and companions roamed the hills and valleys below, but her tired mind found it harder and harder to remember them. Bits of memories would drift in and out of her conscious mind like summer rain clouds. Faces would appear and disappear. Names would come and go, but nothing that she could fathom anymore.

Sometimes the she-wolf would sit back, and her animal intelligence would recall places and things—a small house near a row of trees, a shiny silver chain, a fireplace, a man—but they would drift away before she could put any logic to them at all. They had begun to come with less and less frequency, until the old she-wolf didn't remember at all anymore.

Her weak knees buckled slightly, and the she-wolf looked up to the sky. The sun was just beginning to disappear over the distant mountains, and the sky was turning a soft purple across the horizon. She turned her head skyward to howl into the approaching night, but she was just too weak.

Then she saw it. Soft and pale in the twilight sky. The moon, round and yellow and full. In all its wondrous glory. At one time, the moon had meant so much more to her, but exactly what she didn't know anymore. As the darkness continued to fall, the moon became rounder, clearer, brighter, and in its full and awesome power, the she-wolf found the strength to issue one last cry into the darkening sky.

Weakened by the effort, her breath coming in erratic gasps, the old she-wolf backed down the ridge until she felt the rough bark of a pine tree on her hindquarters. She dropped gingerly to her belly, stretched out her forelimbs and rested her head across them. She closed her weary eyes, and for a moment—just a fleeting instant—the faces returned, wavering for a brief moment in time before they were gone again. Somewhere deep in her soul, the old she-wolf remembered, and she smiled at distant but pleasant memories.

The she-wolf shuddered and exhaled a ragged breath. Her body relaxed, her spirit loosened, and somewhere on the mountaintops in the wilds of northern Alberta, amid the sweet aromas of rain-soaked earth, the decaying pine needles scattered across the forest floor, and smoke from a distant chimney, the she-wolf closed her eyes and slept.

ACKNOWLEDGMENTS

I WOULD LIKE TO THANK everyone at Water Dragon Publishing for believing in this book, particularly Steven Radecki and Lisa Jacob for all their hard work and answering my many questions. Also, big thanks to Kelley and Hannah at Graveside Press for forwarding the manuscript to Water Dragon when it wasn't right for them.

Many thanks to Scott Brents and Evelyn Adkins for all the reads and edits of the original manuscript way back in the 90s. It's been a long road, but if you keep everything tuned properly and the tank always full, every road eventually leads somewhere worthwhile.

ABOUT THE AUTHOR

Terry Campbell wrote extensively during the 1990s, appearing in numerous anthologies (*Horrors! 365 Scary Stories*, *Blood Muse*, *Kiss and Kill: the Hot Blood Series*) and small press magazines (*Terminal Fright*, *After Hours*, *Into the Darkness*). But sometime during the 2000s, he drifted away from the keyboard. Then, in 2023, spurred on by an odd dream he thought would make a good story, his wife surprised him with a new laptop. And the bug was back. He started writing again and hasn't stopped, with appearances in anthologies such as *What Lurks?: A Cryptid Anthology*, *Hellbound Book's Horror Anthology*, *After Dark: A Horror and Thriller Anthology*, and many more. Visit him on his website at *alittlewestofweird.com*.